DOUBT

A CAROLINE AUDEN LEGAL THRILLER

DOUBT

C.E. TOBISMAN

Text copyright © 2016 Cynthia Tobisman
All rights reserved.

Published by Thomas & Mercer, Seattle

www.apub.com

Amazon, the Amazon logo, and Thomas & Mercer are trademarks of Amazon.com, Inc., or its affiliates.

ISBN-13: 9781503936829
ISBN-10: 1503936821

Cover design by David Drummond

Printed in the United States of America

For Nicole, in gratitude for all of her support and patience. Richard Ford once said: "Marry somebody you love and who thinks you being a writer's a good idea." He was right.

CHAPTER 1

The doctor's steps were light as he jogged down the tree-lined path. When he reached the hill that paralleled the coastline, he increased his pace, attacking the incline just like *Runner's World* said to do. Even as he labored, a warm glow of satisfaction rose in his chest. All his sacrifices had been worth it. His professional life had been fraught with hard decisions, trade-offs, and difficult calls. But now he could justify every one of them.

He let himself revel in his triumph. An unseemly emotion to indulge around others, he could still enjoy it alone. How many people could say their life's work mattered? That their time on Earth counted for something? Today, the doctor knew with certainty that his did.

Pushing hard toward the top of the hill, he squinted into the sun, trying to make out the shape of the Bon Air Beach Club. The gray structure squatted on the shore a mile around the broad curve of the bay. By this hour, his friends would be hunched over the club's mahogany bar, regaling one another with Hollywood war stories and boring each other with laments about wives and lovers. But he had no use for any of it. Not anymore.

When the trail plateaued, he eased off his pace. His legs burned with the expended effort of the climb that now lay behind him. Life always seemed to be like that. It wasn't until he'd slowed down that he felt the pain. But by then he'd achieved his goal. He'd arrived at the peak. Victorious.

The doctor's musings were cut short by the sight of two men on the path ahead.

One lay on the ground. The other leaned over his fallen comrade. Their bikes were parked side by side under a grove of palm trees thirty steps away.

"Are you guys all right?" the doctor called out to the lanky, pale man who was still standing. He had a red birthmark the shape of a lima bean on his cheek and wore one of those hipster ski caps that seemed impossibly hot in the California sun.

"I'm fine," the pale man answered, "but my buddy needs some help. We were racing up that hill back there, and he just wiped out after we got to the top."

"Let me take a look," the doctor said.

He crouched beside the injured man. Shorter and heavier than the first but just as pale, the man clutched his ankle and groaned.

Giving him a cursory assessment, the doctor noted that—oddly enough, given his accident—the man had no dirt on his biking pants. Lucky break for the wardrobe.

"I haven't practiced for a while," the doctor said, "but I haven't forgotten how to evaluate a fracture." He gently grasped the injured man's leg, palpating the soft tissue of the ankle while monitoring the man's face for a wince. There was none.

Instead, a look passed between the men.

Suddenly everything became horribly clear. The bikes parked too neatly, too far from the path. No sweat on the fallen man's brow. No dirt on his clothes.

The doctor's heart began to hammer in his chest.

"Probably just a sprain." He straightened up to standing. "I've got an Ace wrap in my car. It's just down the hill. I'll go grab it."

He took two slow steps away before breaking into a sprint back the way he'd come. He hoped he'd misconstrued an innocent scene. He considered how strange his behavior would appear to the two men if he had.

But then he heard a muffled thud, and two blazing points of heat seared into his thigh.

A Taser gun!

The doctor stumbled, his muscle spasming with electricity.

Swinging a hand blindly for the cause of the pain, he snagged one of the leads, breaking the connection and stopping the current. Still, his leg screamed in agony.

But the pain paled in comparison with the shattering recognition that his fears had been founded. Fears he'd dismissed as late-night paranoia. Fears now horrifically realized as he staggered down the deserted path. They'd come for him! My God, they'd really come for him.

He shouted for help. But there was no one around. Just an empty plumber's truck parked on the side of the road bordering the running path.

The path! The doctor's eyes raked the edge of it. Beyond it, a chaparral-dotted embankment dipped sharply down toward the beach a hundred feet below.

Digging deep, he threw himself over the lip.

His shoulder hit the ground hard, scraping the skin exposed by his tank top.

He rolled down the hill, scraping and jolting his way through the rocks and scrub brush until he came to rest on the beach.

Groaning in pain, he propped himself up on one arm to look around for help.

His eyes met nothing but empty sand and indifferent sea. He was alone.

The doctor had no illusions about what his pursuers intended to do when they reached him. He was going to die. Right now. Right here on this beach.

The knowledge hit him with such force that he almost crumbled under the weight of it. But then he remembered. There was one last thing he needed to do. One final task to complete before the curtain closed.

He fumbled with the zipper of his waist pouch, forcing himself to concentrate.

Once he'd pulled out his phone, he tried to type his password. But his hands, slick with arterial blood from a deep gash on his wrist, slid across the touch screen.

A cascade of pebbles rained from above. His attackers were side-slipping down the hillside, approaching rapidly. They'd be on him in seconds.

The doctor wiped his hand on his shirt and tried again. He had to get critical information free from his mind before it died with him.

Forcing his trembling hand to steady, he entered his password. Then he moved on to writing the text message. The letters and numbers came more quickly. He'd planned for this. With adrenaline coursing through his body, the doctor no longer felt his injuries. His entire existence boiled down to the glowing screen he held.

He couldn't fail. Not now.

He hit "Send" just as the crunching of footsteps stopped behind him.

His eyes blurred. His head swam. The clinical part of his mind told him he'd lost at least a pint of blood. He'd lose consciousness soon.

But he was still conscious when he turned to face the killers.

He was still conscious when he met their cold eyes and begged, "Please, no."

And he was still conscious when the tall, pale man stepped behind him, gripped his neck, and twisted it hard, bringing down the final darkness.

• • •

The man in the ski cap crouched beside the corpse. Middle-aged. African American. Nonpracticing doctor. Definitely his target.

He pried the phone loose from the dead man's hand and looked at the screen.

Then he met the eyes of his compatriot and shrugged.

He wiped the phone of fingerprints and dropped it in the sand.

CHAPTER 2

Caroline Auden hunched over her laptop, her shoulders constricting in her woolen business suit. Her hair fell across her eyes as she studied the chessboard. The computer was playing the Sicilian defense. That meant she needed to play the Perenyi attack. She hated to sacrifice so much material, but if she wanted to win, she'd have to do it.

Caroline let the game's complexity distract her from the churning in her gut. In ten minutes, she'd report to her first day of work at Hale Stern, LLP, one of the most dynamic law firms in Los Angeles. Until then, she was hiding out in one of the tiny cafés that serviced the buttoned-down set. With its graffiti-art murals and its staff that smelled faintly of dope, Black Dog Café stood in stark contrast to its conservatively dressed patrons.

"It will be. I promise it will," floated a voice from across the café.

Something raw and desperate in the sound made Caroline look up.

She found the barista leaning on the counter, talking on the phone. His tattooed forearms and blue Mohawk were incongruent with the forlorn, almost childlike fear in his eyes.

"I know, but I swear I—" he began, but then his shoulders slumped. "I understand."

Hanging up, he turned to clean the counter. The haphazard sweeps of his towel bespoke the tumult in his mind.

Her chess game forgotten, Caroline watched the barista, trying to imagine what had caused his discontent. If his choice of personal styling was any indication, this was a man usually unbothered by anyone's opinion. A generally confident soul whose confidence had forsaken him on this cold, clear morning.

Caroline felt a sudden kinship with him.

"What was that about?" she called across the café.

The barista paused before answering. "My boss thinks I've been overcharging customers and pocketing the money," he said before continuing his assault on the innocent countertop, the strokes of his rag hard and angry and ineffective.

"Did you?" Caroline asked.

"No. But the register dumped a bunch of charges. I can't find them anywhere." He shot the offending machine a scornful glare. "Stupid fucking computer."

Caroline nodded. She'd seen people crumple in the face of technology, laid low by a password-protected banking site or an application that wouldn't launch properly. She knew the problem was almost always user error.

"Can I see it?" she asked, rising from her table. Even if she couldn't stop the worries that circled her own mind like hungry crows, she could stop his.

The barista eyed her.

She knew what he saw. A petite woman with mahogany hair, messy despite her best efforts to tame it. But smart eyes, quick and alert. She didn't fit the stereotype of a tech geek.

She could feel him judging.

After another moment's hesitation, he moved aside.

"I'm dead if I can't find those charges," he muttered.

7

Caroline took stock of the interface. Unix platform. Antiquated point-of-sale software.

She glanced at the barista, who now stood beside the espresso machine, drying coffee mugs. He held the rag in his right hand. Okay, so he was right-handed. That meant he handled the register with his left hand while serving hot beverages with his right.

Scanning the left side of the register's interface, Caroline noted the inventory keys.

"Did you recently restock?" she asked.

"Yes," the barista answered.

Caroline's fingers flew across the screen.

"It's not supposed to look like that," the barista said, his voice rising in alarm.

"I'm just isolating the recently modified records." She changed the filter and hit "Enter." "You must've hit the menu key when you were restocking. The charges got saved as an inventory file. It's all fixed now. Everything's back where it belongs."

Caroline retreated to her table to gather her things. She'd stalled long enough. It was time to go.

As she shut down her laptop, she regarded her discolored leather bag. Passable in the tech world, it struck her as too coarse for the legal world. She'd have to get a new one when she got her first paycheck. Or not. Saving up to move out of her mom's house was more important than a laptop bag without stains. Sanity first. Accessories later.

"I don't know how you did that," the barista called from the register, "but you saved my ass."

"It was nothing." Caroline shrugged. It was nice to be able to fix something. The tech emergency was far more fixable than the carnage she'd left at home. Her uncle snoring on the couch, still wearing last night's clothes, reeking of Grey Goose and Drum. Her mom listening to that same damn Jason Mraz song on Spotify all day long until Caroline wanted to blow her brains out.

Before heading out the door, she'd tossed her uncle's car keys in the bread drawer. That would keep him from driving until he was sober.

"Can I get you a cup of coffee?" the barista asked.

"I'm good with hot chocolate." Caroline didn't want to explain that coffee left her vibrating like a whirligig in a hurricane. With a natural disposition like a tuning fork, she was having a hard enough time keeping her mind steady.

"Next time, it's on me," the barista insisted. "You work around here?"

"I'm starting a new job today." Caroline's stomach torqued, even without the coffee.

"Let me guess—computers," the barista said, grinning at her.

"No. Law."

The barista's eyebrows climbed up his forehead. "Really? Why not computers?" he asked. "You're good with computers."

Caroline stayed silent. It was a good question.

• • •

Caroline rested her head against the window of her new office. She exhaled a long breath, leaving a blurry white continent on the glass, moist and fleeting, dissolving around the edges. Her pulse throbbed in her ears, drowning out the sounds of lawyers and assistants and staff in the halls ramping up for another day's work.

An hour earlier, she'd learned the document-management program. She'd enrolled in the firm's health plan. She'd even given her address to the health club downstairs so she could start her week of free membership.

Now she waited for her career to begin.

When the office administrator left, he'd promised her that no one waited long for their first assignment. But the last hour had passed slowly in a Chinese water torture of worried moments, conjuring the same prickling agony Caroline had experienced before boarding her first roller coaster. Trepidation mixed with hope. Mostly trepidation.

She reached into her pocket for her worry beads. Her fingertips brushed empty fabric.

Damn. What a day to forget them.

It didn't matter, she told herself. She deserved to be standing on the thirty-fifth floor of a skyscraper. Louis had chosen her. Of all the students the master litigator had taught in his clinical course at UCLA School of Law, he'd plucked her out of the lecture hall and offered her a job.

But Caroline couldn't forget the statistics. The hiring trends. The attrition rates. The fact that only 15 percent of female associates survived to become partners and that unless they had a strong mentor at their law firms, their chances were closer to zero.

Doubts circled like flies attracted to the stench of self-pity. Why had she left the tech world? Mother's milk and coding. She'd been raised on both. But the latter had never really sustained her, she reminded herself. Even worse, tech brought out aspects of her personality that were . . . problematic. She had good reasons for becoming a lawyer. She just needed to learn her new trade. At warp speed if possible.

Caroline's phone lit up with an incoming page.

Her assistant's voice crackled onto the line.

"Louis wants to see you," said Silvia.

"Please tell him I'll be right there," Caroline said.

Louis Stern. The man she'd come to work with and the smartest person in the firm.

She took a deep breath and brushed her hands down her suit.

It was game time.

• • •

Caroline stood at the threshold of Louis's office. If practicing law was like learning tennis, her first lesson wouldn't be with the kindly old instructor at the local park. No, she'd signed up to learn from the King of Clay, Rafael Nadal. She waited, gripping her racket, preparing for him to serve at 150 miles per hour.

She tapped on the open door to announce her presence.

Louis Stern looked up from the papers on his desk.

"Ah, Ms. Auden. Welcome. I do hope Silvia's taking good care of you." He raised his white eyebrows above the top curves of his wire-rimmed glasses, creating the impression of two fuzzy caterpillars resting atop them.

"She is," Caroline answered, matching her boss's breezy tone. She was glad her voice betrayed none of her nerves.

"Thanks for sharing her with me," she added. Louis's decision to assign his assistant to her desk was either a mark of favoritism or a way to keep an eye on her. Or both.

"Silvia's quite good. She knows all about computers and whatnot." The white-haired partner waved a hand around, vaguely encompassing his own computer, which remained asleep, its monitor a black mirror reflecting the deepening light of the day.

Caroline suppressed a smile. Louis's distaste for technology was legendary. Not only was his computer dark, so was the office lighting system. The only illumination came from an antique floor lamp, its green shade casting a glow on pictures of Massachusetts in the 1800s.

Louis himself evoked a bygone era. In his glen-checked bow tie and herringbone blazer, he looked like he'd stepped out of one of the pictures on his wall. He wore a gold ring on his right hand, adorned with the pig's head crest of Harvard's elite, old-money Porcellian Club.

"Have a seat." Louis gestured to the guest chair positioned in front of his heavy walnut desk.

Sitting down, Caroline clasped her hands in her lap. Her fingers itched for her laptop, but Silvia had warned her that Louis "found it distasteful" to look over a screen to speak to someone.

"Where's your legal pad?" Louis asked.

Caroline just grimaced and shook her head.

"Always bring paper and a pen to meetings." Louis offered her a Montblanc from his penholder, then handed her a yellow-lined legal pad from the top drawer of his desk. "It signals you've come for more than just idle conversation."

Louis spoke with the broad *A*s and clipped endings of the eastern elite, a species rarely seen west of the Mississippi. Caroline knew his story. He'd moved to Los Angeles fifteen years earlier when Thompson Hale had offered him the helm of his respected firm. Since then, Louis had regularly topped the legal papers' lists of bet-the-company litigators. Meanwhile, Thompson had taken emeritus status, collecting a share of the firm's profits while practicing his golf game.

Now Caroline waited for Louis to make the next move. These early salvos of this first conversation were important. Even though Louis knew her from class, he'd no longer be comparing her to other law students. He'd be comparing her to the talented attorneys at his firm. Although his offer of employment was a vote of confidence, she still needed to earn a spot in their ranks. Even these early niceties were a way of probing her worth. So far, she'd done nothing to impress him.

She silently vowed to do better.

"Now that we've finished the idle-conversation part of our meeting," Louis said, a hint of amusement playing across his patrician features, "I'd like to give you your first assignment."

"I'm ready." Caroline waited, borrowed pen poised over borrowed legal pad.

"I'm putting you on the *SuperSoy* case. I'm sure you've seen it in the news." He raised his eyebrows again, his expression hopeful.

Caroline shook her head. She hadn't heard about the case, and she didn't want to lie.

With a pang in her stomach, she noted the flicker of disappointment in Louis's eyes.

"*SuperSoy* is a major milestone in mass tort litigation," Louis explained. "It's the first major case brought against a biotechnology company for injuries caused by a genetically modified organism."

Caroline dutifully wrote down the information.

"The financial stakes are huge. Last year, biotech companies grossed twenty billion from genetically modified seeds. One of the most profitable seeds on the market today is SuperSoy."

"So people are suing the manufacturer?" Caroline asked. The issue wasn't obvious.

Louis nodded. "The problems first showed up among athletes. Extraordinarily fit people suddenly went into renal failure. Doctors soon began seeing the same phenomenon among babies. Athletes and children. These two populations with nothing in common except general good health were stricken with rapid-onset kidney disease. It didn't make sense. But then someone realized the common ingredient: soy." Louis punctuated the conclusion with a jab of his index finger.

"Let me guess," Caroline said, "the athletes were drinking soy-based protein shakes, and the kids were drinking soy-based baby formula."

"Correct." Louis nodded. "Many products contain Med-Gen Biotechnology Company's high-protein SuperSoy. Have you heard of Rapid Burn?"

"Yes," Caroline said, relieved to have a chance to appear well informed. Not that it was difficult when it came to Rapid Burn. After its flashy rollout, Rapid Burn had become the protein of choice for athletes and health junkies. The name alone conjured images of glistening bodies pumping iron on billboards and late-night infomercials.

"How about Nature's Comfort? Soy Gentle? Soy Satin?"

"Yes." Caroline had seen those baby formulas and soy milk products in the aisles of her local grocery store.

"They're all still on the shelves," Louis said. His tone was matter-of-fact.

"Really?" Caroline's eyebrows rose. Having been sued on the theory that its products were killing people, Med-Gen's decision to keep them in stores seemed inexcusable.

"Unless and until we win this motion, these products will remain on the market. Med-Gen's subsidiaries will keep selling them. People will keep buying them and getting sick."

Louis paused to let the gravity of that moral offense sink in.

"My friend Dale Anderson is the clever lawyer who discovered the common ingredient," Louis continued. "He's also the reason we're involved in this case. He brought us in about a month ago. He represents hundreds of *SuperSoy* plaintiffs down in Texas."

"Texas?" Caroline stopped scribbling notes. "This is a multidistrict litigation?"

"Yes. There are about fifty thousand *SuperSoy* cases all over the country." Louis held Caroline's gaze. "I do hope you recall what we studied in class about multidistrict litigations."

Caroline fought the same unease she'd always felt when Louis had used her as his interlocutor during the Complex Litigation Strategy course he'd taught as a visiting instructor during her third year of law school. His penchant for putting students in the hot seat had driven some students to avoid his class. But Caroline had always been either masochistic or tough enough to enjoy a challenge. Especially when it was the price for learning indispensable knowledge.

"Has a steering committee been selected?" Caroline asked, refusing to blink. Even though they hadn't spent much time on mass torts, she recalled the lesson about multidistrict litigation. Airplane crashes. Dangerous drugs. Defective cars. These were unusual situations where many courts in many states could face many almost identical cases. To streamline the judicial process, all of the common issues were funneled to a single judge, whose decision would bind every court in the country.

Caroline also knew that a committee would steer the multidistrict litigation for all of the plaintiffs. Comprised of the top lawyers representing the largest number of plaintiffs, the powerful steering committee would decide all matters of nationwide strategy.

"Yes, there's a SuperSoy Plaintiffs' Steering Committee, or SPSC, as some call it." Louis sneered out the letters in a way that suggested he didn't approve of the shorthand and wouldn't be using it. "Dale's the president, poor fellow. Leading the *SuperSoy* attorneys is rather like herding cats, yet far less gratifying. At least when the cats are wrangled, you can get some rest."

"How'd Dale end up becoming president?" Caroline asked. She noted with relief that her new boss's tone had become more familiar. Apparently she'd passed whatever initial test he'd erected for her regarding her knowledge of multidistrict litigation.

"Dale's a prominent personal injury attorney. He's also a rather likable fellow. Apparently, he was the only member of the Committee that no one loathed." Louis smiled slightly. "Regrettably, he's more of a politician than a strategist."

As Louis finished speaking, his eyes traveled to a table by the western window of his office. With brass fittings holding its ancient joints together, the small pedestal table had only one chair positioned in front of it. Atop it sat an antique bone chess set. The pieces were positioned midgame, some of the black-and-white figurines beside the board, already forced from the battle.

Caroline didn't recall the chess set from her last visit to Louis's office, but she wasn't surprised to see he played. While he exuded an old-world grace, Louis's reputation as a master tactician spoke of a street fighter beneath the cultured exterior. Chess was a gentleman's game—every bit as nasty as a bar brawl, only infinitely more deliberate.

"Dale wants your advice on strategy, doesn't he?" Caroline surmised, her nerves now almost forgotten as she probed the role this prominent litigator had taken in this high-stakes case.

"Among other things." Louis nodded. "I told Dale to coordinate the *SuperSoy* litigation before Judge Samuels here in Los Angeles."

"Why Judge Samuels?" Caroline asked. Louis never did anything without careful thought and a sound rationale.

"Judge Samuels has been on the bench for three decades. He's a talented jurist with experience handling multidistrict litigations."

Caroline nodded. Those were good, sensible reasons.

"Also, his wife is on dialysis." Louis's eyes twinkled with the secret knowledge. "As a result, I expect that Judge Samuels knows something about kidney disease and the terrible toll it takes on its victims . . . and their families."

Caroline opened her mouth to ask her boss how he'd learned about the judge's personal life, but Louis held up a hand.

"Information is power," he said simply.

Caroline had heard the litigation platitude before. It was one of many that Louis had shared with his classroom of rapt students, each future lawyer scribbling down the golden nuggets of wisdom he cast in his wake. She'd felt an immediate affinity with her professor upon learning that he, like she, was an information hound. She preferred the phrase to the less savory term *stalker*.

"In addition to advising on strategy and monitoring the proceedings here in Los Angeles," Louis continued, "we'll be assisting the Committee with the preparation of our side's opposition to Med-Gen's *Daubert* motion."

"The other side's challenging the science," Caroline stated rather than asked.

"Yes. Judge Samuels will get to decide whether it is scientifically possible for SuperSoy to cause a kidney to fail. If he isn't convinced that the scientific literature demonstrates such a link, he'll dismiss the entire litigation."

Caroline silently absorbed the significance of Med-Gen's motion. A single fallible individual would be acting as the gatekeeper for every *SuperSoy* case in the entire country.

"A *Daubert* motion is to be expected in a case of this magnitude," Louis continued. "It's Med-Gen's best chance to drown this litigation in the bathtub." He exhaled softly. "Sadly, they have a rather good chance of doing exactly that."

Caroline's eyes widened. The Louis she'd known from class had always exuded confidence. A supreme mastery of all pieces in the game. This unvarnished skepticism about their chances of beating Med-Gen's *Daubert* motion seemed out of character. And unsettling.

"You must understand the obstacles we face," Louis said. "The biotech industry has always painted the public's fears about GMOs as alarmist. As ungrounded in any actual science. To win, we must prove that the public's fears have now come to terrifying fruition. And to do that, we must prove something no one has ever proved before—that GMOs have the capacity to kill people."

The frown on Caroline's mouth mirrored her boss's. The task ahead was going to be hard. Creating new precedent always was. But this was especially true when an entire industry would be affected by a court's decision. Especially a lucrative, powerful industry.

"The good news is that to obtain relief for our clients, we needn't try all fifty thousand cases," Louis said. "We only need to beat this motion. If we can do that, if we can convince Judge Samuels that SuperSoy has the capacity to damage kidneys, Med-Gen will settle."

"How do you know?" Caroline asked. She silently lamented the lack of practical education at law school. She'd spent three months studying the dormant Commerce Clause, but not three seconds learning how to evaluate a case for settlement. It was one of the reasons she'd loved Louis's class. His lessons on procedural maneuvering were akin to learning how to sneak past the velvet rope at an exclusive club. Useful. And fun.

"If Judge Samuels denies Med-Gen's *Daubert* motion, the *SuperSoy* cases will go to trial. Juries are unpredictable. Med-Gen could get hit with huge verdicts. Many of them. All over the country. The company won't tolerate that kind of risk. Instead, it'll cap its exposure by setting aside enough money in a settlement fund to pay for treatment for all of the plaintiffs, plus a little something extra to encourage them to opt in."

While Caroline enjoyed Louis's description of what would happen if they defeated the motion, she knew what would happen if they failed. There'd be no settlement. There'd be no gigantic fund to pay for treatment. Instead, every *SuperSoy* plaintiff in the country would be shut out of court. Forever.

"Everything points to a swift settlement," Louis said. "Most of the victims are responding to a combination of dialysis and medication. But the medication is quite expensive."

Caroline imagined the sacrifices the victims' families were making to pay for treatment. How much would a family sacrifice to save a baby? A spouse? What would they give up? A house? A college fund? Their sacrifices would be as necessary as they would be heartbreaking.

"When's our opposition due?" she asked.

"One week from today. The hearing will be three days after that."

Caroline looked at the dates she'd scrawled on her legal pad. A week was no time at all.

"Unfortunately, the current draft of our opposition has some rather significant . . . issues." Louis pressed his lips together. "Lawyers from a number of the firms on the Steering Committee have written various sections of our side's brief. The procedural sections. The description of governing law. But everyone knows the real meat is the science. That's where we'll win or lose. As a result, every firm on the Committee has reviewed the scientific literature to look for proof of a clear link between SuperSoy and kidney injury."

DOUBT

Louis shook his head, his light eyes mournful. "So far, no one has had much luck."

"Doesn't the proximity in time between the plaintiffs' injuries and their ingestion of SuperSoy products prove a link?" Caroline asked.

"Certainly," Louis allowed, "and Dale's shop has already written up that argument. But it may not be enough. Without some support from the published science, convincing a judge to let hundreds of millions of dollars of litigation go forward will be difficult. I suspect some members of the Steering Committee are quietly panicking."

"Quietly?"

"These high-rolling plaintiffs' lawyers are cowboys," Louis said in his blue-blooded accent. "They're brash and confident. They never admit any weakness. But they're also smart people. They know they're vulnerable. That's why Dale wants us to see if we can find anything in the scientific journals. I figured you could take a look. Lawyers with science and technology backgrounds are quite unusual, after all."

Louis smiled. "You're a rare bird."

The compliment made Caroline feel like a freak, but she returned his smile anyway. Receiving an assignment where she could both work directly with Louis and add real value to a case was more than she'd hoped for in her first month, let alone her first day. Even if her assignment sounded only slightly easier than defeating the Nemean lion . . .

Louis studied Caroline's face, as if scouring its surface for signs of misgiving.

Schooling her features into submission, Caroline refused to show him any.

"You really are a bit junior for this project," Louis said, halfway to himself.

Caroline started to bristle, but he was right. She could hardly be more junior.

"And yet," he continued, "I know your work from class. You're always quite thorough. And your background is perfect. I believe you'll come at the science from another angle. You may well find something everyone else missed."

A reflexive surge of determination blossomed in Caroline's chest. Even though Louis didn't resemble her father in affect or in manner, both men shared a similar exactitude. On the rare occasions when Caroline's father had overseen her homework, he'd made her redo it if she'd made a single typographical error. And when she'd missed even a single legal issue on a test, Louis had made her stay after class to discuss it. While Caroline couldn't decide whether she liked or loathed the high expectations both men placed on her, one thing was clear: she wanted to meet them.

"Just tell me what to do," she said, leaning forward.

"The articles are in the war room. Please set up shop there." Louis's voice strengthened, like a general ordering his troops to battle, infusing them with confidence to get the job done. "Review the science. Find me a link between SuperSoy and kidney damage. Give us something we can argue beyond Dale's pet argument about proximity in time to injury."

Caroline's fingers ached with the effort of scribbling notes. She'd known that in leaving tech, she'd be leaving the twenty-first century. But the reality of it still surprised her. And hurt her hand.

As if reading her thoughts, Louis gestured with his chin toward her legal pad. "Please take your notes on the scientific literature in longhand. It's an old discipline but one that I find quite useful. Something about forming words on a page creates links in the mind."

He paused for any objections.

Resisting the urge to wince, Caroline gave him none.

"Dale, too, is going to want to see everything in hard copy," Louis said.

"Understood," she said, still battling her dismay. Just because the Magna Carta had been written on sheepskin parchment didn't mean it wouldn't be way more searchable if loaded onto an iPad. But she held her peace. She knew that lawyers loved their paper.

"Depending on how you do with your review of the science, I might let you take on additional responsibilities," Louis said. "Otherwise, I can pull in one of the partners working on the *Telemetry Systems* matter. That case goes to trial in two months, and we still have much to do, so I'd prefer to leave things as they are . . . but if I need to . . ."

"I can handle it," Caroline said quickly. She didn't like hearing her boss making contingency plans in case she failed.

"Good. We don't have much time."

"How about I come by your office by five to tell you what I find?" Caroline offered, not knowing whether what she'd promised was actually possible, but determined to make it so.

"Perfect," Louis said.

• • •

"Hey, Silvia," Caroline greeted her assistant, who had a pierced nose and hair a shade of red only seen on fire trucks. "Can you tell me where the war room is?" The term felt ridiculous in Caroline's mouth. As if they were soldiers heading into battle instead of paper pushers ensconced in an office building.

Silvia nodded, looking serious. "It's in the basement. Load the doomsday machine down there with lots of Diet Coke and paper, then set it off. No one will live, but we should win this war."

Caroline smiled. She liked her assistant. She could tell they'd work well together. Just as soon as she figured out what to do with an assistant.

"It's on the thirty-third floor, across from the kitchen," Silvia said. "It's just a conference room. No weapons in there. Just a bunch of boxes full of scary-looking text and diagrams."

Thanking Silvia, Caroline hurried toward the elevators.

As she speed-walked toward the war room, her eyes skated across the scene before her. Dark-wood credenzas separated the assistants' workstations from the outer ring of attorney offices. Assistants sat in cubicles formatting documents or playing Solitaire. Attorneys paced their offices, talking on phones with clients or friends. In every respect, Hale Stern presented just another mundane law firm tableau. Same as every other office. Same as every other building.

Except for the walls.

There, hanging on tension wires spaced ten to fifteen feet apart, were canvases. Farmers laboring in fields. Salisbury Cathedral at dusk. Renaissance portraits of old men in floppy hats. The placards beneath the images read like a who's who of old masters. Rembrandt. Cézanne. Goya. These weren't the artists' top-shelf paintings. These were the sketches and studies the masters had used to produce their great works. Still, Caroline knew that any one of them was worth more than she'd earn in a lifetime.

She came to a stop before a small canvas depicting men wielding swords. In the foreground, a woman in a billowing ivory dress held her hands up to the heavens, beseeching the watching angels for help. The lighting seemed especially designed for the image, the red blood on the soldier's silver swords vibrating against the dirt-brown tones of the battlefield. The placard beneath it read: MASSACRE OF THE INNOCENTS, PETER PAUL RUBENS, 1611 (STUDY FOR 1613 CANVAS AT LOUVRE, INVENTORY NO. 22344).

Out of the corner of her eye, Caroline saw someone stop beside her. Silvia.

"They're Louis's," the assistant said, answering Caroline's unspoken question.

"Where does he get them?" Caroline asked.

"Auctions, mostly. Sometimes from his clients' private collections. He'll take art in trade instead of fees. It isn't like he needs the money," Silvia added with a sideways glance.

Caroline nodded. She, like everyone else at Hale Stern, knew Louis's aristocratic persona. His white-shoe summer parties at his San Marino mansion. His annual trip to the Beaufort Hunt in Gloucestershire. His charity work for the Huntington Library.

"Louis's curator handles the purchases because the auctions can get stressful. Some people like them, but Louis 'doesn't go in for that sort of thing.'" Silvia mimicked Louis's upper-crusty tone. "He only cares about the art."

Caroline studied the logo embossed on the small card mounted beneath the Rubens: FLEMING CURATORIAL SERVICES. The curator, presumably. Halfway down the hall, she noted an open spot on the wall with a blank placard mounted beneath it.

"He's got a new one coming in," Silvia said. "It's a Picasso. He's had his eye on it for ages. It finally went up for auction at Sotheby's about a month ago. When he won it, he tried to keep up that dignified demeanor he's got going, but you could tell that inside he was jumping up and down and clapping."

Caroline smiled at the mental image of Louis losing his composure.

"Oh, I have some good news for you," said Silvia, turning toward Caroline. "There's a bigger office coming open soon. It's on the north side of the building. You know, the side with the good views. I can put in a request for it if you'd like."

Caroline took a mental inventory of the north side of the floor. All the offices were full. She didn't recall seeing any e-mails about any imminent departures.

"Who's leaving?" she asked.

"Greg Portos. One of the associates working on the *Telemetry Systems* case."

Caroline hadn't met Greg, but she considered his terrible timing. The whole firm seemed abuzz with preparations for the *Telemetry Systems* trial. Losing a member of the team couldn't be helping those efforts.

"Greg messed up pretty bad yesterday." Silvia lowered her voice to a conspiratorial whisper. "He won't be here much longer . . ."

"I'm okay where I am," Caroline said quickly.

"Suit yourself." Silvia shrugged. "You get lost on the way to the war room?"

"Guess I got distracted by the pretty pictures," Caroline said, smiling. But then her grin faded.

"I think I'm procrastinating," Caroline said. Despite her determination to climb the mountain that Louis had pointed her toward, she was balking at the foot of it, daunted by the obvious height of the cloud-ringed peaks. Not a good sign.

Silvia gave Caroline a knowing look. "Louis gave you some crazy-impossible task with some absurd deadline, right?"

Caroline resisted the urge to nod.

"Louis takes a keen interest in associate development," Silvia said, mimicking Louis's accent again.

The assistant held Caroline's eyes. "In other words, he'll kick your ass, and you'll learn a ton . . . if you can handle it."

At the unspoken challenge, Caroline squared her shoulders.

"I'd better get going. I've got a lot to do."

CHAPTER 3

Caroline found the war room across from the clatter of dishes and the murmur of voices in the firm's kitchen. The smell of fresh popcorn beckoned, but she kept her eyes trained on the door of the war room. As it was, she'd be skipping lunch. She had no time for popcorn.

But just as she reached out a hand to grasp the door handle, a woman emerged from the war room, stopping her progress. The woman wore a sky-blue suit with an eggplant-colored silk flower pinned on the lapel. The string of pearls around her neck served as an homage to the traditional, but the rest of the ensemble screamed couture. Her eyebrows had been plucked within a micron of their lives.

"Excuse me," Caroline said, trying to step around the woman, who now blocked her way.

"Wait," the woman said.

Caroline stopped.

The woman raised a pencil-thin eyebrow. "You're the new girl."

"Yes—" Caroline began to excuse herself, but the woman continued.

"I'm Deena Pensky. From New York. Stuck here for the conceivable future on the bloody *SuperSoy* case. Though at the moment, I'm trying to figure out where to get a decent meal around here." Deena spoke in a tommy-gun staccato of words that blazed from her mouth at a velocity suggesting she had no time to let the words in her sentences breathe just a little.

"New York?" Caroline didn't recall Hale Stern having a New York office.

"I work at Wainwright, Callisto, and Phillips," Deena said. "My boss is Anton Callisto. He's on the Steering Committee. He sent me out to assist Louis with whatever the court orders. Basically, my boss is loaning me to your boss. Not that your boss is having me do much, unless you count giving me time to surf the Internet for shoes."

Deena cocked her head at Caroline's suit. "Secondhand? I've gotten some wicked pieces at secondhand stores. But just accessories, not the suit. Never the suit." She shook her head and made a tutting sound as if such a thing were too outrageous to contemplate.

Heat rose to Caroline's cheeks. She'd bought the navy suit on sale at an outlet. She thought it worked, that she came off as polished. But seeing herself reflected in Deena's eyes, she felt like a child playing dress-up in her mother's mildewed closet of dowdy old looks.

"You're old for a first-year, aren't you?" Deena asked. She paused long enough to suggest her torrent of words might have come to an end. Or at least have taken a short break.

"I worked for a few years as a software engineer," said Caroline.

"Computers? That's interesting," Deena said in a tone that made clear it really wasn't. "Why'd you change to law?"

"To help people," Caroline said.

Deena crossed her arms and smirked.

"Really," Caroline insisted. "The law is a great tool for helping people avoid having . . . bad things happen to them. I had an experience once with it . . . once."

Caroline closed her mouth to stem the flow of information. Deena didn't need to know about her family's legal troubles. Or her unforgivable part in causing them.

"What, you get picked up for prostitution or something?" Deena bark-laughed and then made an exaggerated show of looking over Caroline's suit again.

Caroline stayed silent. The guilt that coiled next to her heart like a constant companion stirred, but she refused to give it voice. This wasn't the time or the place or the person to spill her story about the sordid reasons she'd left the tech industry.

"Come on. You can tell me. Why'd you go into the law?" Deena asked, her eyebrows arched in prurient curiosity that promised repetition far and wide of whatever Caroline answered.

"To help people," Caroline repeated. It wasn't the whole truth, and they both knew it.

After a beat, Deena waved off the nonanswer. "Well, I'm a lawyer because I didn't want to be a doctor like my mom. She's head of neurology at St. Luke's Hospital in New York, but she's spending the month here at Northridge Hospital because my family's thinking of moving out west, Lord knows why. We've already established you people have never heard of a cronut."

Deena glanced at Caroline, then to the door of the war room, then back to Caroline. She pursed her lips and shook her head.

"Oh my God, don't tell me Louis stuck you with reading those articles for *SuperSoy*." Deena began tutting again.

"Yes," Caroline said, "he wants me to find a link between—"

"SuperSoy and kidney damage," Deena finished for her. "There's nothing to find. I've looked. Everyone has."

Deena regarded Caroline with a raised eyebrow. "I suppose it's a good assignment for the new kid, since you can't mess up looking for something that isn't there."

Caroline weighed her responses. She wanted to tell Deena to go screw herself, but that hardly seemed polite on the first day of work.

"Maybe he wants to make sure you didn't miss something," Caroline said finally.

Deena's face flushed. "Trust me, you'll find nothing. But if you need some help or whatever, my door's always open," she said before walking down the hall to her office and closing her door.

Caroline looked in the direction Deena had disappeared. She found she didn't care whether Deena or Dale or anyone else had already read the articles. She rarely trusted anyone else's judgment. In this way, she and Louis were similar, she decided.

She needed to earn Louis's faith.

The articles inside the war room were her path to doing just that.

• • •

Caroline's plan to fly off to the rescue of *SuperSoy* plaintiffs everywhere deflated at the sight before her. Six bankers boxes sat atop a Carrara marble table that filled most of the conference room's square footage. A quick look revealed that each box held two large binders of articles. And each binder held up to five articles.

Caroline did the math. Six hours to read sixty articles. It was a dauntingly large elephant for a very small snake to digest in woefully little time.

Her chest tightened. Panic threatened to rise like a thunderstorm in the distance, just below the horizon. It didn't matter that no one else expected her to find anything in the many volumes on the table before her. Louis did, and his was the only expectation that mattered.

Taking a calming breath, Caroline forced the panic away. She needed to stay focused. Organization was one of her strengths. Reducing tasks into their tiny component parts had helped her conquer law school. It also helped her conquer her nerves.

Now she made a plan. Word searches would limit the universe of articles to those containing certain key phrases applicable to the *Daubert* issues. If she could avoid wading through reams of paper, her review of the science could be fast. It had to be. Evaluating the science in only one day was ambitious, if not "crazy impossible," as Silvia had called it.

Caroline picked up the phone on the credenza beside the window and dialed.

"Where can I find the links to the articles in the war room?" she asked when her assistant answered.

Caroline got a chuckle in response.

"I have no idea," Silvia answered. "Louis just uses paper. He's a dinosaur. A dinosaur with an expensive fountain pen."

Hanging up the phone, Caroline narrowed her eyes at the boxes.

She'd just have to figure something else out. Fast.

Caroline knew that in all fields, a new hire's mystique began early or not at all. A shimmer of supernatural speed. A glimmer of super-competence. Some hint that in hiring you, the company had captured a golden butterfly. Or else you showed yourself to travel down at street level. Land bound and plodding. Just another merely mortal pedestrian.

And Caroline knew that Louis was worse than most bosses in making quick yet indelible judgments about new associates. During her callback interview, junior partners had cautioned her in hushed tones that Louis decided quickly whether someone was worth the effort to train and the expense to pay. He didn't hesitate to fire people with stellar credentials, great recommendations, and distinguished clerkships.

Caroline had heard the tale of one unfortunate associate who'd mis-read a case, mistaking dictum for the holding. That had been the end of the poor woman. She'd limped along for another few months before leaving without so much as a good-bye coffee in her honor. Her office had remained empty while Hale Stern searched for the right person to take her place. Louis had insisted on picking the next hire himself.

He'd picked Caroline.

Now she needed to prove he hadn't made a mistake.

• • •

"You read all of them?" Louis asked. Behind him, the late-afternoon sun ignited the particulate matter in the Los Angeles sky a polluted shade of gold. The glow washed across the black-and-white photographs on Louis's walls, turning them to sepia.

"I only read the abstracts," Caroline admitted. "But then I circled back and read the complete texts of the most promising articles. I kept notes." She held up her scribble-covered legal pad to prove it but put it down when she realized it looked like a chicken had stumbled through a puddle of ink before strutting around the paper.

"Did you find anything we can use?" Louis asked, holding her eyes.

"I didn't find a direct link between SuperSoy and kidney injury," she said, hating that her initial conclusion echoed Deena's. "But we might still establish an inferential link."

Unlike Deena, she hadn't stopped at the absence of any direct link. In her desperation, she'd gotten . . . creative. She only hoped that Louis would appreciate her conclusions.

"Explain," he ordered.

Caroline took a breath. Just as in class, Louis would expect a compelling delivery of her pitch. He'd be rating her not only on content but on how clearly and confidently she spoke. That meant pushing past her nerves. Steadying her voice. Staying on point.

"The concept behind genetic engineering is that you insert a new gene into a plant's DNA to force the plant to do something it doesn't usually do. For instance, scientists inserted a gene from an anglerfish into the DNA of a potato plant to make potatoes that glow in the dark when they need to be watered. Cool but creepy, right?"

When Louis gave no reaction, Caroline hurried onward. "The problem is that inserting a new gene into a plant can have unintended consequences. One company tried to engineer cotton plants that would resist pesticides, but the new gene made all the cotton bolls fall off the plant. The Hahn article reports on it. Dr. Hahn concludes by expressing concern that a new gene could change a cell's metabolic processes in ways that would cause an otherwise harmless plant to start producing toxins that hurt people."

"And that's what we think happened here." Louis nodded.

"Yes. That's the theory. Med-Gen created SuperSoy by inserting a jellyfish gene into soy DNA to increase protein content. But maybe increasing protein isn't all that the new gene did. Maybe it also prompted the soy cells to create a kidney toxin."

"We need proof, Ms. Auden, not theories," Louis said. "What do we have to work with?"

Caroline winced at his tone.

She tap-danced a little faster. "We've got an article by a scientist named Dr. Feinberg, who says SuperSoy can thin the membranes of kidney cells in rats. Then we have another article by Dr. Tercero that says the thinning of cell membranes is a precursor to spontaneous cell death. And we've got yet another article by Ambrose that tells us that if enough cells die, a kidney will fail. We can put those three articles together to argue that SuperSoy can cause a kidney to fail."

Caroline studied Louis's face to gauge his reaction.

Louis shook his head in disappointment. "Others on the Steering Committee have already suggested that sort of inferential reasoning. It isn't enough. Without a direct link, this is going to be a tough sell. Judges like proof that if you take thalidomide, you'll get a deformed baby. Cause and effect. Simple and direct."

"I didn't see anything like that." Caroline made her voice strong even though she knew she was delivering bad news. She braced herself for Louis's displeasure.

But instead of anger, Louis met the news with quiet contemplation. He tipped his head back, studying the ceiling where his antique lamp cast green circles of light. When he met Caroline's eyes again, his gray eyes held a hint of vulnerability, a look that said Louis Stern, who usually won his cases, might lose this time around.

"Are you sure we can't do better than an inferential link?" he asked quietly.

Caroline didn't know what to say. She'd already explained her best idea for using the materials in the war room to fashion a coherent argument.

In the silence, a frown formed on Louis's lips.

Caroline's face flushed. She could feel the assignment slipping away.

"Actually, I did find one last thing," she blurted.

Louis raised an eyebrow in silent invitation for her to continue.

"I found a . . . a lead." She didn't know how else to describe it. "While I was reading those articles, I did some research. Online."

Though Louis had forced her to take longhand notes, he hadn't expected her to completely forgo technology. On her laptop, she'd run dozens of queries. She'd found links to digital versions of the articles. She'd used word searches to skip through the data quickly, sifting studies like a prospector panning for gold. She'd also googled the names of the scientists. She'd read their laboratories' websites. In other words, she'd done everything possible to broaden the field of information. To find something more than the meager pickings the war room had offered up.

"Feinberg's study comes closest to saying what we needed it to say," Caroline continued, "so I looked around to see if he'd ever said anything else about SuperSoy."

"Had he?" Louis asked.

"Sort of. Dr. Feinberg attended the Pan-Pacific Innovations Conference in Hawaii six months ago. He posted a message just last week on the conference's chat board about one of the presentations he'd seen. Apparently, some guy named Dr. Franklin Heller gave a talk on flu vaccines. At the end of his talk, Dr. Heller gave the audience a little teaser about a new article he was writing on SuperSoy. Feinberg brought it up on the chat board to see if anyone had heard anything more about that article Heller teased."

Louis tilted his white-haired head to one side, his lips pursed.

Caroline swallowed. She realized how desperate her efforts sounded.

"And did anyone know anything about this Heller article?" Louis asked finally.

"No, not really. Dr. Heller never published it. But it's pretty clear he planned to. The *Fielding Journal of Molecular Cell Biology* was going to publish it for him."

"And you learned all of this from a . . . a chat board?" Louis asked.

Caroline couldn't tell if his tone held admiration or disbelief.

"Some of it," she answered. "The rest I got out of Dr. Feinberg himself."

"He spoke to you?" Louis's eyebrows rose. "Scientists tend to be fairly closemouthed in my experience."

"I pretended like I was doing follow-up for the conference's organizers. I said I was gathering reviews, feedback about the speakers. That sort of thing."

Louis's eyes narrowed at her subterfuge.

Concern lanced Caroline's chest. She couldn't retract her words. She could only hope that Louis saw merit in her results. If not her social-engineering methods.

"Once Feinberg began talking, it was easy to get more information out of him. He told me that after the presentation, he overheard Dr. Heller talking with the editor of the *Fielding Journal* about publishing his new article. Feinberg said Heller sounded excited about it. So did the editor."

"This is all very speculative," Louis said, leaning back in his leather chair.

"I know," Caroline said, looking down.

"And yet . . . I believe it deserves some further inquiry," Louis said.

Caroline met her boss's bright eyes.

"Please make some calls," he said. "See if anyone has a copy of that article. Don't waste a lot of time on this, though. I don't want you spinning your wheels if there's nothing to find."

"I could call the *Fielding Journal*," Caroline offered.

"Good plan."

"I'll get right on it," she said, her tone the equivalent of a sharp salute.

But then she paused.

"Other than trying to track down that article, is there anything else you want me to do?" Caroline fished. Louis had mentioned putting a more senior lawyer on the *SuperSoy* team to take over after she'd finished her initial review of the science. Maybe now he'd do that and she'd sink to third chair. Or fourth.

"Please go ahead and take a shot at drafting the section of our *Daubert* brief discussing the scientific literature. The inferences we can draw from the Feinberg, Ambrose, and Tercero studies aren't as strong as I'd like, but they give us something to say beyond 'people who ate SuperSoy got sick soon afterward.'" His tone left no doubt that he put little faith in Dale's pet argument. "If we find that missing article, it may become the centerpiece of our arguments. But for now, I want you to organize what we have."

Caroline resisted the urge to cheer. Louis was expanding her involvement in the case.

"I want an outline of your argument on my desk in two days," Louis finished.

Two days? Caroline blanched, her nascent celebration rained out.

Louis lifted an envelope from his in-box.

Caroline easily read his body language. The meeting was over. That was fine. She had much to do and little time to do it.

But at the door of Louis's office, she stopped. She had one more question. A proposal, really. Much as she hated to make it, the tight deadline compelled her to.

"There was this associate, Deena," Caroline began. "She said she was here to help us—"

"I'd prefer that she not be involved." Louis's voice was hard as a mallet on ice.

Caroline's eyebrows knit. Why was Louis looking at her like she'd just suggested letting a team of baboons into the office to help out?

Louis placed his envelope aside. "Deena's boss, Anton Callisto, isn't just a member of the Steering Committee, he's an ex-marine. Everything's a war to the man. Make no mistake, his lending of Deena to us isn't a favor. It's espionage."

Caroline stayed silent. She'd assumed that in litigation, the fight would be with the other side. Apparently that was wrong.

"It isn't just Anton." Louis folded his hands atop his ink blotter. "The members of the Committee don't trust anyone. They don't trust us. They don't trust each other. They want their own people out here in Los Angeles, where the action is. They want to keep an eye on what we do. I agreed to host these associates because Dale asked me to. But I don't like it."

Louis turned his attention back to his mail. "You may use the loaned associates for assistance on minor tasks, spot research projects and the like. But I want one of my own people taking the lead on tracking down that article. And writing up the science."

"You mean me," Caroline said. She didn't need to see Louis's nod to know the burden remained on her slender shoulders.

Hurrying out of Louis's office, she formulated a plan. A timetable for completing all tasks necessary to finish the assignment in time. It was Monday evening. She had until the end of Wednesday. Forty-eight hours to corral the science into an outline. She could meet that deadline. Forty-eight hours was a lot of time, she told herself . . . if she didn't sleep. Or eat. And possibly limited her trips to the bathroom.

But first things first: call that editor and find that article.

Without realizing it, she'd hurried her step until she was jogging toward her office.

• • •

"Dead?" Caroline asked into the receiver, even though she'd heard perfectly well.

"Yes," the *Fielding Journal's* editor said. "He fell off a cliff in Malibu. The ground gave way under his feet. He broke his neck."

"That's horrible." Caroline pondered the capriciousness of the Fates. You just never knew when a meteor was going to fall out of the sky and pulverize you. She took solace in the fact that a lawyer's only serious occupational hazard was getting a paper cut.

"Yeah, it was terrible news," the editor agreed.

"Do you know anything more about what Dr. Heller was working on?" Caroline asked.

"No. When I talked to him in Hawaii, he told me his new paper would blow the walls off SuperSoy. He said we'd save lives when we published. But he didn't give me a lot of details. He didn't want to get scooped. That's the way these scientists are. Until they circulate their papers, they never say much about them."

"But he never circulated it."

"Sadly, no. We were really looking forward to shaking things up with that piece."

"What do you mean?" Caroline asked.

"These big biotech companies make sure the favorable studies get published. No one champions the unfavorable ones," the editor said. "We try to fight that trend."

Caroline knew it was true. She recalled that the Hahn and Ambrose articles had both been published in earlier issues of the *Fielding Journal*.

"After Dr. Heller died, we tried to get his paper from his lab, but we couldn't." The editor huffed audibly. "Not even from his coauthor."

"Coauthor?" Caroline's ears tingled with the news.

"Dr. Anne Wong. She's kind of a rock star in the world of research science. Her father is a respected biochem professor at Berkeley, but her work has eclipsed his. She's done some really cutting-edge stuff since she joined Heller's lab."

"But she wouldn't give you the article?" Caroline asked.

"It wasn't like that. I couldn't even find her to ask for it," the editor said. "The lab said she took a leave of absence after Heller died."

"You mean like bereavement leave?"

"Family emergency is all they'd say. They couldn't tell me where she'd gone or when she'd be back or anything else, so I gave up on trying to get the article," the editor said, his voice tinged with resignation.

Caroline thanked him and hung up.

In the silence of her office, the peril of her situation settled around her. Telling Louis about the Heller article had been an act of desperation. The plane had been going down, so she'd tried one last thing to avoid cratering. And it had worked. Louis's excitement about finding the article had saved what would've been a disappointing performance. Failing to find it now might be worse than never mentioning it. In Louis's mind, she'd become that morally ambiguous associate who'd duped Dr. Feinberg. She needed results to obliterate the memory of her transgressions.

She needed Dr. Wong.

Caroline pivoted toward her laptop. She ran a search for a "Dr. Wong" on the faculty of UC Berkeley's biochemistry department.

There was only one: Dr. Chao Wong, professor of the Graduate School Division of Biochemistry, Biophysics, and Structural Biology. Specialization: macromolecular complexes.

Caroline dialed Dr. Wong's office number.

"This is Dr. Wong," a man's voice answered in heavily accented English.

"My name's Caroline Auden. I'm a lawyer working on an important case that involves your daughter's research. I was hoping you had a phone number where I could reach her," Caroline began.

Now there was only silence on the other end. Strange.

Caroline checked to make sure the connection hadn't been dropped. It hadn't.

She cleared her throat and tried again. "Your daughter's lab said she took a leave for a family emergency—"

"I do not know any of this," Dr. Wong's voice said in Caroline's ear.

Caroline chilled at his dismissive tone.

"I do not talk to my daughter in three years," the elder Dr. Wong clarified, "so I cannot help you with this. I have to go."

Without waiting for a response, he hung up, leaving Caroline holding a phone full of dead air.

Caroline looked at the receiver, dumbfounded. If the editor of the *Fielding Journal* was correct, Anne Wong was a superstar scientist who'd done her father proud. So then, what could have driven such a wedge between father and daughter that they hadn't spoken in years?

Caroline turned back to her laptop and ran a search for "Heller Laboratory Dr. Anne Wong."

The search retrieved nothing illuminating the strained relationship between the older and younger Dr. Wongs. Instead, Caroline discovered hundreds of sites describing Anne Wong's research achievements. What she found was impressive. Dr. Wong's innovative methods had led to breakthroughs in cancer research when she'd been a mere research fellow. Most recently, she'd studied the therapeutic effects of cannabinoids on epilepsy.

Caroline considered the information. Science proving that marijuana could treat illness was an area struggling for legitimacy. Perhaps that was why Dr. Wong's dad had stopped talking to his daughter? It seemed an unduly harsh response to an unorthodox choice of research topics.

Caroline shook her head. Her own relationship with her father wasn't exactly close. Perhaps Dr. Wong's father had left his emotionally unstable wife and moved across the country, leaving his daughter to cope with the smoldering wreckage. That could do it. Caroline knew firsthand.

Pushing her own family history from her mind, Caroline skimmed websites, hunting for some hint about Dr. Wong's family emergency. Her travel plans. The names of her family members. Her friends. Anything suggesting a destination for the missing scientist.

At the bottom of the page, something caught Caroline's eye.

Dr. Wong had been scheduled to present her cannabinoids research at the Hughes Medical Symposium a month earlier, but she'd pulled out. The symposium's organizers had posted a revised schedule of presenters online and an asterisked notice that in lieu of Dr. Wong there would be a breakout session to discuss current advances in ADHD research.

Caroline cocked her head at the screen.

The Hughes Medical Symposium was one of the most prestigious venues for research scientists. Dr. Wong had missed a chance to bring credibility to her research on cannabinoids. For someone who had devoted her life to research, missing that symposium was a big sacrifice. Whatever had happened to Dr. Wong, whatever had driven her to take a leave of absence from her laboratory and miss the symposium, must have been really serious. Perhaps an illness or surgery? Or a close friend or relative's illness?

Google offered no answers.

Caroline frowned at the laptop. The Internet really should contain the answers to everything. To all secrets, to all questions. She knew it didn't, but the volume of content available online created the illusion of omnipotence. She hated when that illusion failed.

Especially when her job depended on it.

Trepidation tugged at Caroline's mind like a riptide, and a wave of worry crested before her, towering and dark.

She had no article. No author. No direct link between SuperSoy and kidney damage. All she had were fragments of inferential reasoning. Rags she was tasked with sewing into a wedding dress. In two short days.

Her phone rang in her bag.

Yanking it out, she checked the screen. Her mother.

"Sorry to bother you," Joanne Auden began when her daughter answered, "but I need a favor."

"Sure," Caroline said, grateful for the distraction.

"I'm thinking of taking Elaine up on her invitation. She just e-mailed me a ticket to fly up today. Morning or evening, my choice."

"You want me to keep an eye on Uncle Hitch while you're gone," Caroline surmised.

"If it wouldn't be too much trouble . . ."

"I'm happy to." Caroline knew her mom's best friend had been trying to lure her mother up to Portland to go camping. She also knew why her mother hesitated.

"How's Uncle Hitch doing?" Caroline asked. Ever since her uncle had lost his job with the police, he'd been staying at her mom's house. But unlike Caroline's laudable goal of saving up enough money to move out, her uncle's stay represented a way station on a steep slide into the bottom of a bottle.

"Hungover like usual, but alive," Joanne said.

"Good, so then go to Oregon. We'll be fine while you're gone." She imagined the household without her mother's organizing presence. Vodka bottles and law books. Grim.

"But Elaine's going to try to set me up with some guy while I'm up there," Joanne said.

"Let her," Caroline verbally shrugged. It had been a long time since her father had left her mother, and even longer since he'd moved to Connecticut with his second wife. It was time for her mom to move on. Or to begin to, anyway. A date with a geographically impractical man handpicked by her mother's best friend seemed like a perfect step.

Silence, as Joanne tried to figure out how her daughter was wrong.

"If you don't go this morning, I'll help you pack when I get home," Caroline said, silently wishing she'd be packing herself up instead.

"You're a good kid," Joanne said.

"Not really," Caroline answered. While she had good moments, she wasn't good. Not entirely. No one could be if they'd done the things she'd done . . .

"What's wrong, honey?"

"Just a rough first day," Caroline said, attempting to redirect the conversation. But at her admission, her temples began to throb. Louis had a reputation for success. His clients banked on it. Now he was going to lose, and fairly or not, he might see it as her fault.

"Honey, you can do this," Joanne Auden said, interrupting her daughter's spiral of self-doubt. "You're my special girl. You're the kid who dressed up like Thor with a pasta strainer for a helmet and a red towel for a cape."

Caroline remembered. In her mind's eye, she'd been seven feet tall, muscular, and immortal. Simple things like chores and sleep and the need to pee didn't concern Thor. He had more important things to do. It had been a good feeling.

"You do know I'm not eight years old anymore, right?" Caroline asked.

"Fine," said Joanne. "You're the young woman who got a science grant to go to Harvard and who graduated second in her law school class from UCLA."

Now it was Caroline's turn to be silent.

"Everyone has a first day," Joanne said. "Even superheroes."

"You mean wannabe superheroes."

"That's all anyone is," Joanne said softly. "No one expects you to have all the answers. Not yet, anyway," she added with a smile that Caroline could hear on the line.

"Thanks, Mom," Caroline said, and she meant it. Even when her mother had grappled with her own sometimes formidable demons, she'd supported her daughter. As much as she could, anyway, with brain chemistry that made stability an occasionally visited province, seen only fleetingly on Joanne's swing from emotional pole to emotional pole. Meds had helped. Fortunately.

The thumping in Caroline's chest began to slow to a tolerable cadence.

Soon, rational thought reasserted itself. She still had many avenues to research before she wrote her professional obituary. It wasn't time to panic. Not yet, anyway.

"I promise I'll take care of Uncle Hitch while you're gone," Caroline said to her mother. "But right now I've got to get back to work."

Hanging up, Caroline took a long, slow breath.

Then she turned back to her laptop. Someone in the dead scientist's life had seen that article. She just needed to figure out who that person was.

Caroline ran another search, this time for "Dr. Franklin Heller."

Hundreds of search results spilled onto her screen, blaring headlines:

Scientist Found Dead on Beach

Jogger Falls from Popular Running Path

Tribute to Dr. Heller, Scientist, Doctor, Visionary

Other headlines described the dedicated scientist's stunning achievements on a shoestring budget and speculated about what would happen to his lab now that he was dead.

Caroline opened the first obituary.

Dr. Heller had been running alone on August 21 when he'd fallen from a scenic overlook in Malibu and broken his neck. Friends and family expressed shock and dismay that someone so worthy could die so ignominious a death. He'd been survived by his wife, Yvonne Heller, who requested that all donations in her husband's memory be made to Children's Hospital.

Caroline checked the scientist's age. Fifty-four. He'd been younger than she'd imagined.

For some reason, she'd envisioned an old guy standing on the cliffs admiring the view. She hadn't considered that he might be a fit middle-aged man out for a run. That he'd been about the same age as her own father made Dr. Heller's death feel . . . personal.

A tap at her office door startled Caroline from her research reverie.

She found Silvia standing in her doorway, holding a thick file in her arms. The assistant's red hair stood out in jagged angles, as though she'd just jogged down the hall.

"Louis asked me to give you this." Silvia handed the file to Caroline. "There's a status conference tomorrow. He'd planned to attend, but he's got a scheduling conflict, so he wants you to cover it for him."

Caroline's mind reeled, trying to catch up.

"He said you did a competent job evaluating the science," Silvia said, mimicking Louis's eastern accent in a way that let Caroline know that the words were his. "He's quite confident you can handle this hearing for him. He asked me to apologize for the short notice, but today's been a total clusterfuck. My words, not his." Silvia smiled and used one fire truck–red fingernail to push an errant strand of her hair behind her ear.

"What happened?" Caroline asked.

"Greg Portos let Alexei Harod sneak out of a deposition yesterday," Silvia said.

Caroline recalled hearing something about Greg. Something bad.

"Who's that?" Caroline asked with morbid fascination.

"Harod is the president of Telemetry Systems," Silvia said. "Greg saw him duck out of a bathroom during a break, but he didn't realize what was happening. By the time he told Louis about it, Harod was gone."

"Wow. Louis must be furious."

"He hasn't had time to be. Harod had a ticket to fly back home to Greece this morning. We had to file a bunch of emergency motions to stop him."

"This all happened today?" Caroline asked, amazed that in all of her conversations with Louis, he'd never revealed any hint of the inner turmoil the emergency must have caused him.

"Yep, Louis moved for a contempt order, an order to compel attendance, and an injunction enjoining Harod from boarding the plane." Silvia released a puff of air and shook her head. "It wasn't pretty, but we got it done."

"What happened with the motions?"

"Oh, the usual," Silvia said. "Louis got everything he wanted. He convinced the court to order Harod to stay at the airport for twelve hours so he could depose him in one of those little conference rooms."

The pride in Silvia's voice echoed Caroline's admiration. This was the Louis at whose feet she'd come to learn. The creative litigator who found solutions to impossible problems.

But then Caroline thought of Greg Portos. The failed associate whose tenure at Hale Stern had come to an abrupt end. That, too, was the Louis for whom Caroline had come to work.

The thought sobered her.

"Just tell me where to be," Caroline said.

"North Hill Street at the Central Justice Building. Department C-23. Louis says to make sure you're there by nine."

Caroline scribbled the information on her legal pad. At least it was a morning hearing. That would leave the rest of the afternoon and the whole next day to locate the missing article and finish the outline.

Silvia pointed at the file on Caroline's desk. "You've got the docket there, plus all of the complaints and answers that have been filed by everyone in the case so far. Those should help you in case the judge has any questions."

Caroline eased the ream of papers from the file folder. The docket alone was over fifty pages long. Single spaced.

"You said this is just a status conference, right?" Caroline asked. She knew the Federal Rules of Civil Procedure required periodic meetings between the judge and the attorneys, but she didn't know what exactly they met about.

"Yeah, should be short. The judge probably just wants to discuss the procedure for the *Daubert* motion or something." Silvia shrugged. "I doubt he wants to talk about discovery issues or settlement negotiations, but you never know."

Caroline's eyes traveled back to the thick pile of paper. "Will anyone else from the Steering Committee be there?"

"No one's told me, but I'm guessing not. None of the members of the Committee are from California. I'm sure everyone will show up for the *Daubert* hearing, but for this little status conference? Probably not. Then again, you never know . . ." The assistant turned to go. "Remember to report to Louis when you get back from court."

"Will do," Caroline called to Silvia's departing back.

Caroline looked at the clock. It was already 6:13 p.m.

The day was ending too soon. Everything was happening too fast.

She needed to find Dr. Wong. She needed to draft the outline. And now she needed to learn the procedural posture of the case and get familiar with all of the key players and theories of relief. The flurry of assignments reeled in her mind like a blizzard, piling up and weighing her down.

But Caroline forced her attention to the near path ahead.

She had no time for fear. She had no time for dead scientists or missing research partners.

She had a case to master. She had a hearing to attend.

She settled in to study deep into the night.

CHAPTER 4

Caroline didn't know what she'd expected from her first trip to court, but this wasn't it.

Sickly white-green lighting.

Chipped floor tiles.

The occasional child running down the corridor, oblivious to the strained formality around him.

A knot of people at one end of the hall attested to the location of the *SuperSoy* hearing. Their voices echoed, humming like a hushed note of anticipation, an orchestra tuning up for a concert.

Caroline wove through the dense throng.

She found an empty spot on the stone bench outside the locked doors of the courtroom. With the close proximity of so many people, she could almost feel the pulsing of thoughts and sound through the soles of her feet.

Trying to ignore the oppressive sensation, Caroline sat down and placed her brown accordion folder beside her laptop bag at her feet. Across the top Silvia had pasted a big "*SuperSoy* Litigation" label, as if Caroline had some other case with which she might have confused the folder. Caroline took the label as a sign of Silvia's optimism about her future at Hale Stern.

But first she needed to make it through the hearing. Without fanfare, she was about to become a true lawyer, allowed to appear in court because she'd passed the licensing exam.

Hooray for me, Caroline thought, wondering how much longer she had to wait before she lost her courtroom virginity.

She pivoted her body so she could read the calendar tacked beside the doors.

There was only one case listed: *In re SuperSoy* Litigation, 9:30 a.m.

Caroline's eyes widened. The judge had reserved the entire morning for *SuperSoy*?

Silvia had said this was just supposed to be a short little status conference. Quick and easy. Nothing major. Blocking out a full three hours of court time suggested the judge had something more substantive in mind.

Caroline's stomach clenched.

If the hearing lasted long enough, the judge was bound to ask her something she didn't know. Even after studying, she had only a thimbleful of knowledge about an ocean of a case. She knew only a few of the procedural twists. She knew even less about the individual plaintiffs and their claims. Or the discovery motions. Or the potential settlement overtures.

This was insanity. Other than appearing for jury duty, Caroline had never been to court, much less as the sole representative of thousands of people gravely injured by a multi-billion-dollar biotech company . . . and after practicing law for exactly a day.

A fearful rhythm struck up in Caroline's chest.

No, she told herself, don't think about it.

Caroline pulled her laptop from her bag. Action often bound her anxiety. Distraction might help now.

She resolved to use the time before the hearing to find the missing article. But how?

Running a hand across her forehead, Caroline bent her mind to finding potential avenues of research. Perhaps Dr. Heller had teased his article at other conferences? Or maybe someone at his lab, perhaps a lab tech, had some fragment of it? Or a lead on where to find the whole paper?

Caroline focused on the screen, waiting for the laptop to connect to the Internet.

Instead an image of a dinosaur appeared beneath a message: *You are offline.*

She tried again.

But still, she couldn't connect.

Sitting back, Caroline looked around at the jaundiced cinder-block walls of the courthouse. Built with a 1960s nuclear apocalyptic sensibility, the thick concrete walls were preventing any signal from reaching her laptop.

She exhaled in frustration. She needed to give Louis her outline in thirty-six hours. She didn't have time for technical difficulties.

She snapped her laptop shut. She couldn't worry about it now.

She moved down to the next worry on her list. The outline.

Opening her bag again, she pulled out the legal pad where she'd written her notes from her initial evaluation of the scientific literature. She found a blank page and resolved to write as much of the outline as she could before the hearing began.

But as she stared down at the vast expanse of empty lines, a pang of dread ricocheted around her chest before finally settling in the deepest part of her gut. She still had nothing beyond her initial theories. Her underwhelming plan to use Feinberg, Ambrose, and Tercero to draw inferences about SuperSoy. She had no new insight. No spark of inspiration. Just three weak, tangentially relevant scientific articles. Three rotting pieces of timber with which to try to keep the case afloat.

A wave of dizziness roiled through her.

Caroline reminded herself that no one on the Plaintiffs' Steering Committee had found any direct link between SuperSoy and kidney injury. If the case sank, it wouldn't be her fault.

But that wasn't how Louis would see it. He'd given her the assignment to find exceptionality. She needed to show him some.

Except . . . she couldn't.

Unbidden, she recalled Greg Portos. His fatal offense had been failing to notice a deponent sneaking out of a bathroom. Just a simple mistake. Not even a failure of legal analysis. An error of observation, not a disappointing performance on an assignment.

And yet here she was, sitting at this stupid courthouse instead of looking for the Heller article or making another pass through the war room for material she could use to avert disaster. Trapped in the courthouse, she could only wait until the hearing happened.

The hearing. Her first hearing. Of any sort. Ever.

It occurred to Caroline that the hearing would be transcribed. A court reporter would type every word spoken by the attorneys. Louis would read the transcript. He'd see how well—or how poorly—she'd conducted herself.

Caroline's heart hammered out a timbale beat of worry.

What if the judge had set aside the entire morning for the *SuperSoy* case because he intended to pressure the Plaintiffs' Steering Committee to settle? What if he'd noticed the absence of any direct link between SuperSoy and kidney damage? Maybe he planned to call the lawyers into his chambers to browbeat the plaintiffs' representative into coming to terms with the unavoidable need to give up the fight. If so, this first court appearance would be a nightmare of the darkest degree.

Taking a calming breath, Caroline reached into her pocket and withdrew a strand of beads. Azure blue and silky smooth, she'd bought them on a trip to Greece after law school when she'd maxed out her credit card to keep up with her best friend, Joey, who didn't want to stay at youth hostels. In a shaded storefront on an island in the Western Cyclades, a leather-skinned man had shown her how to flip the beads around in a circle, like a janitor twirling his keys over a finger. He'd called the beads *komboloi*, which meant, "each breath a prayer." A good motto. Except when the breaths came hard and shallow.

Like now.

The scene before Caroline flickered and fragmented, her vision blotched with patches of darkness.

Gripping the edges of her legal pad, she braced her elbows on her knees.

She knew what was happening. She'd had an anxiety attack once before, after moving home to go to law school. Back in her mom's house after years of living on her own, she'd witnessed her mother's disintegration. Her father's absence. And her own shattering uncertainty about her path. She'd always known how to conduct herself in the tech world. When people hit, she'd hit back. Hard, if necessary. On Quora and Slashdot, she'd defended the little guy, stood up to frat-boy brogrammers, and answered questions about everything from how to mitigate bad code to how to get a good seat at the next Women Who Kick Ass panel at Comic-Con.

In leaving tech, she'd left those moorings. Moving home hadn't helped. With her dad gone and her mom sinking into a quicksand of meds and booze, the seams of her life had strained until one day, she'd found herself short of breath in Contracts. Dizzy and terrified, she'd fled to the health center, where she'd been offered pills. She'd refused. She couldn't risk it. Not with her family history of addiction. Instead, she'd turned to other means to calm her mind. Breathing exercises. Meditation. These tools had worked.

Until now.

Caroline's heart beat faster and faster, thundering in her ears until it drowned out all other sounds. Some part of her mind wondered how much harder it could hammer without stopping.

This is not a heart attack, she told herself, imposing the words like a doctor talking to a small child about a minor cut. But even as she knew the fear wasn't real, she couldn't escape it.

Her legs flexed, ready to run.

Sweat beaded on her forehead and palms.

She clamped her eyes shut and bore down.

She could not leave. She had a hearing to attend. She. Could. Not. Leave.

Unable to break free of the terror, Caroline rode the updrafts of the hurricane that tore around inside her chest until gradually, slowly, the attack began to pass.

Her pulse slowed.

The vise around her chest loosened, leaving her hollowed out and exhausted and . . . depressed.

She'd been lying to herself. The realization settled over her soul like a funeral shroud.

She'd always thought that she could manage her demons. That she could tame them, if not into docile house cats, then into declawed tigers safely ensconced in the basement. But maybe that wasn't true. Maybe she was just like her mother and her uncle. She shared their biochemical tendency to shatter. Their unsure footing on the slopes of sanity.

No amount of will or good intentions could change what she was. Or who she was.

And if that was true, then maybe she'd been lying to herself about reinventing herself. About remaking herself with the better raw materials of her nature into someone she could respect. Into a lawyer who helped people instead of a tech geek with a seriously shady side.

Perhaps she should stop running from the tech world? Even if she couldn't practice the dark arts that kept calling to her like a Siren's song, maybe she should've remained a software engineer.

But what about all of her efforts to change careers? All of her studies? Maybe those were all folly . . .

Caroline exhaled shakily.

What she needed was some sign, some reassurance that she'd made the right choice.

Like a flare launched out into space, she sent a silent question to the universe:

Why was she doing this?

She waited with her eyes pressed shut. But no answer was forthcoming.

Instead, she felt the prickling sensation of someone watching her.

She opened her eyes.

A man wearing a blue-checkered flannel shirt and Wrangler jeans stood before her. His oval brass belt buckle was at eye level.

When he didn't move, Caroline looked up at his face.

Jowls curved low on the man's cheeks, hangdog and droopy. His closely set eyes were surrounded by crow's-feet that had formed from years of squinting in distrust.

His gaze flickered down to the folder at her feet.

"You one of them *SuperSoy* lawyers?" he grunted, his lips held tightly.

"Yes." Caroline didn't tell him that this statement had been true for only a little over twenty-four hours.

"You represent the sick folks?" he asked.

"Yes," she said again, glad that her voice sounded normal in her ears.

"Good. I need to talk to you."

"Okay," Caroline said, the word rising at the end in question.

"I'm Jasper. That's my brother over there. Tom." Jasper jutted his chin toward another man in a flannel shirt, sitting on a bench across the hall. Taller and broader than Jasper, and with hair graying at the temples, the man was surrounded by a group of twentysomething men and women who seemed to be tending to him.

"He's on dialysis because of that damn SuperSoy stuff," Jasper continued.

"I'm sorry to hear that," Caroline offered. She eyed Jasper's brother, looking for indications of infirmity. She found it. Tom's manner was slow and deliberate. Like someone who'd been surprised to see a teacup shatter at his feet and who now didn't trust his weakened grip on simple objects.

"Yeah, we're all sorry to hear that," Jasper said. His tone was hollow rather than mocking.

"Who are those people with him?" Caroline asked. She watched a woman beside Tom smile at something the frail man had said. The woman didn't look old enough to be Tom's wife. Nor did she look young enough to be his daughter.

"They're his kids," Jasper said. "He teaches ninth grade."

"Those aren't ninth graders," Caroline said, stating the obvious. Some of the "kids" had full beards.

"They're his old students. Tom coached volleyball. He'd stayed late to mentor those kids. They didn't forget. When they heard he was sick, they signed up for alerts from that Listserv the Plaintiffs' Steering Committee set up."

At Caroline's blank look, Jasper said, "You know, the Listserv they set up for SuperSoy victims—the idea's to get people to show up at hearings so we can show the judge the real stakes here. The real people hurt by that damn company. There's also a Facebook page."

Caroline was impressed by the Committee's coordinated efforts to use the victims to manipulate the judiciary's sympathies. Judges were supposed to be impartial. But judges were also human. Forcing Judge Samuels to see the faces of the people affected by his adjudication couldn't hurt the *SuperSoy* plaintiffs' cause. Not one bit.

"You see that guy bringing my brother water?" Jasper asked.

Caroline noted the earnest-looking man in a sport jacket and blue jeans extending a paper cup toward Tom with two hands, waiting patiently for the older man to take it.

"That's Andre. Both of his parents are in jail," Jasper said. "Tom gave that kid a place to stay during his senior year so he could graduate. Set him up in the guest room. Treated him like a member of the family. He's a teacher now himself. He teaches fourth grade out in Arcadia."

"It's nice they came to support your brother," Caroline said.

"They'd all tell you it's the least they can do. He's done so much for everyone . . . including me." Jasper's voice broke. "Seeing him with a tube in his arm because his own kidneys can't do the job . . . It's killing me to see that. You've got to do something to help."

At the obvious agony in the stranger's eyes, a sense of desperate emotion welled in Caroline's chest. An intensity of feeling that had nothing to do with herself or her own worries. Here was someone with real problems, not insecurities or chimerical fears.

She focused her attention on erasing the bereft expression on Jasper's weathered face.

"He looks like he's hanging in there," Caroline offered.

"The treatments help, but he needs a kidney. Tom's on a list for one, but he's got to stay healthy or they'll take him off. Problem is, those meds are too damn expensive. I've raided my retirement. I've sold my bass boat on eBay. Unless we get a settlement from that biotech company, we can't keep going. We're running out of money."

Caroline looked at the gruff retiree with compassion.

"We were going to travel together, my brother and I," Jasper said, "you know, to make some good memories before . . . in case he doesn't get a kidney in time . . ." He trailed off and looked away, his eyes filling with unshed tears.

Shaking his head to gather himself, Jasper met Caroline's eyes again and set his jaw.

In his tight-lipped expression, Caroline saw the toughness of a man who had survived hard combat but who knew he might still lose the long war.

"Our lawyer says if we win this motion, Med-Gen will settle," Jasper said. "Tom ran marathons. Benched 270 pounds. Right after he switched over to that new protein powder, *bam!*—total renal failure. They know they'll lose in front of a jury. They'll pay us out instead. Unless they win this motion, of course. Then we won't see a dime."

"I understand," Caroline said.

"Do you?" Jasper met her eyes and searched them. "You need to win this thing."

"We're going to do our best." Caroline winced at the *we*. As if she spoke for anyone other than herself.

"You need to do better than that." His expression was tense and flushed. Then he looked down at his feet and kicked the linoleum.

"Please," he said softly.

"We'll win," Caroline said with a certainty she didn't feel and an authority she didn't have. She instantly wished she could take the words back because she doubted it was true, but she knew he needed to hear it, and she was the only person around to say it.

"Good," Jasper grunted and turned away, back toward his brother.

Watching him go, Caroline realized she'd just made a promise she had to keep.

• • •

Caroline sat alone at the wooden table at the front of the courtroom. A pink plastic pitcher of water with a short stack of white paper cups beside it occupied one corner of the sticky surface. A meager but much-appreciated offering from the court to nervous litigants and their lawyers. Caroline considered pouring herself a cup but rejected the idea.

She feared her hand would tremble. So instead she sat frozen. Waiting for the hearing to begin.

Behind her, people jammed the benches like churchgoers who had been promised cupcakes after services. The only empty seats were in the jury box, where the heads of sleeping jurors had left stains on the ancient wood.

The bailiff entered the courtroom and walked to the front, swinging around to face the gallery.

The murmur of voices stilled.

"All rise," the bailiff called out.

With a rustle like falling rain, the assembled crowd stood up as one.

"Court for the Southern District of California is now in session. The Honorable Judge Edmund Samuels presiding."

When the bailiff finished speaking, the door of the chambers clicked opened.

The judge emerged, hunched and slight. His black robe hung loose on his body. His thin white hair stood up like a rooster's comb. He moved slowly across the front of the courtroom, then climbed the stairs to the tall, black, leather chair.

Gesturing with age-spotted hands, he silently asked for the audience to be seated.

"Good morning, everyone," he began in a voice no louder than if he'd been talking to a friend across a dinner table.

A polite murmur of hellos rippled through the courtroom in response.

"Please state your appearance," the judge ordered. "Who's here for the plaintiffs?" He scanned the sea of faces.

Caroline stood up. This was it. The rite of passage.

"Caroline Auden. Here on behalf of the SuperSoy Plaintiffs' Steering Committee." Her voice sounded strong and clear in her ears. Good.

"Thank you, Ms. Auden," the judge said.

Caroline released the breath she'd been holding. She had pulled off her first statement of appearance without passing out or vomiting on her shoes. Her future was looking bright.

She waited for the judge to call for an appearance from Med-Gen.

But instead she heard a man's voice announce, "I'm Eddie Diaz of Tiller, Brenner, and Hidalgo. I'm also here for the Plaintiffs' Steering Committee."

Caroline turned around to find the voice's owner.

A man with tousled black hair stood behind her, just beyond the low wall that divided the counsel tables from the gallery. He wore a gunmetal-gray suit and a tomato-colored tie that was loud enough to be assertive yet quiet enough to be credible.

"Thank you, Mr. Diaz," the judge said. "Who's here for the defense?"

A woman rose from defense counsels' table. "Annette Fujimoto for Med-Gen. I'm from Sakai, Anderson, and Day."

Caroline studied the petite defense attorney. She recalled seeing the woman's name and bar number on the caption page of Med-Gen's *Daubert* motion. At the bottom, where the most junior associate's name went. Caroline took solace in the fact that the defense, too, had entrusted the low girl on the totem pole to handle the hearing.

"Thank you, Ms. Fujimoto," Judge Samuels said.

He turned back to the entire audience seated in the courtroom.

"I scheduled this status conference to make an announcement," the judge said. "Because my wife has been placed on hospice, I'm taking a leave to care for her. I'm transferring this case to New York, Southern District. Judge Todd Jacobsen will be your new judge. He'll be taking over the *SuperSoy* litigation. I am sorry to miss such an interesting case, but real life has unfortunately demanded my attention."

A ripple of murmurs shot through the crowd like a shock wave.

"All pending deadlines remain on calendar," Judge Samuels continued. "Plaintiffs' opposition to Med-Gen's *Daubert* motion remains due on October 5. The hearing on the motion will still be October 8. All scientific evidence must be filed by October 6."

His announcement completed, the judge stepped down from the bench.

Everyone in the gallery rose, standing silently, their hands clasped respectfully before them as he began his slow walk back toward his chambers. But just outside the door, the judge paused and turned once more to face the lawyers.

"Please remember to file your applications to appear pro hac vice in New York," he said.

Caroline jotted the Latin phrase on her legal pad, then waited, hoping he'd illuminate its meaning. But instead, the judge turned and finished his departure from the courtroom.

The instant that the chambers door clicked shut, voices rose all around as the crowd digested the news that the rest of the *SuperSoy* multidistrict litigation would be taking place all the way across the country.

Caroline knew she needed to figure out the implications of the move, too, but at the moment, she had a more burning curiosity. She spun around, her eyes sweeping the courtroom for the other attorney who'd purported to represent the Plaintiffs' Steering Committee.

She spotted him walking toward the door, holding his phone to his ear.

Weaving through the crowd, Caroline jogged down the aisle to catch up with him.

• • •

Caroline needn't have rushed. The attorney she'd chased was waiting outside the courtroom.

He smiled when he saw her, his obsidian eyes full of welcome, and Caroline found herself smiling back. His manner felt so familiar that it seemed as if he already knew her. And maybe he did. In Caroline's experience, some people just . . . shined. Who knew why? Past lives intertwined, perhaps? Some glow of necessity, of meaning in this life-time. Some hint of some role to play. Whatever the reason for the shine, this man had it.

"I'm Eddie Diaz," he said with a slight drawl. "I work with Paul Tiller out in Atlanta. He's on the SuperSoy Plaintiffs' Steering Committee."

He extended his right hand. Caroline noted his fingernails looked recently manicured. At his wrists, square gold cuff links glittered in the institutional lighting.

"You're a long way from home," she said, shaking his hand and finding it warm.

"It's a long field trip; that's for sure." He chuckled. "When this hearing was put on calendar, my boss, Paul, sent me to help y'all out on whatever briefing got ordered. I'll be working down the hall from you for the next couple of weeks. You're Caroline Auden, right? That new hire at Hale Stern?"

"Right." Caroline's eyes narrowed at the man.

"When my boss said you'd be covering this hearing for Louis, I checked out your bio on your firm's website so I'd know what you looked like," Eddie said.

"I guess I'm at a disadvantage," Caroline said. Now she had another explanation for why this man had looked at her as if he already knew her: he'd Internet-stalked her.

Eddie smiled again, and the corners of his eyes crinkled into well-worn folds. Caroline's mother had always said you could trust people who smiled with their eyes. Caroline wondered if that rule applied to stalkers.

"Sorry to rattle you," Eddie said.

Caroline studied his face, trying to discern if his words held a dou-ble meaning. Had he seen her before the hearing, struggling to pull herself back together in time for court? She consoled herself that it was unlikely he'd have noticed one small woman tucked onto a bench amid the dense crowd outside the courtroom.

"I'm not rattled," she said. "I just need to get back to the office."

She began walking toward the elevator.

Eddie kept pace beside her, his footsteps almost silent.

Caroline stole a glance at him. Full lips graced a generous mouth. High cheekbones attested to some Native American ancestor. He was handsome. But even more than that, he had a natural grace. He moved with the subtle confidence of someone who knew he belonged in every room where he found himself.

"So, you're on the Hale Stern team giving a final look at the science?" he asked.

"I *am* the Hale Stern team," Caroline said. "There's no one else. Except for Louis."

Even without looking over at Eddie, Caroline could feel his eyebrows rising in surprise.

"Well, then, how's the science looking?" His voice held a hint of mirth.

"Hard to say," Caroline said, hedging. "Louis put me on this case yesterday and then sent me to court today. So I haven't had much time."

"That's just Louis's way, I hear," Eddie said. "He throws y'all in the deep end to see if you float."

"Or drown," Caroline muttered under her breath.

"Let me help," Eddie said. "It's what I'm here for, after all."

When Caroline didn't answer, Eddie stopped walking.

Caroline stopped, too. Turning to face him, she watched him scowl, his handsome features darkening as if clouds had moved cross the sun.

"Louis told you I'm Paul Tiller's spy, didn't he?" Eddie asked. "That he only let me come out here because he was being—"

"—diplomatic," Caroline finished for him.

Eddie's black eyes flashed. "Diplomacy is saying, 'Nice doggy,' while you look for a rock. I promise I'm no pit bull. We're fighting on the same team here." The urgency in his voice suggested he had something to prove to someone. Probably to his boss, Caroline realized. She knew the feeling.

"If I need any help, I'll come find you," she finally acquiesced. Even as she recognized that Eddie was another of the loaned associates, she found it difficult to maintain her wariness. Unlike Deena, whose abrasive manner sparked hostility, Eddie's soft drawl and easy manner exuded likability. If Deena was like a car sideswiping her way through the tunnel of life, Eddie glided, leaving no marks from his passage.

"Good," Eddie said, gracing her with a luminous smile.

A phone buzzed in Eddie's pocket.

He withdrew it and glanced at the caller.

"My boss. Calling me back," he said, looking at Caroline with an apologetic expression. "This'll just take a second."

Caroline stepped back to give Eddie symbolic privacy, but she watched him while he talked. With his well-styled hair and well-tailored suit, he looked the part of a confident young lawyer. But on his neck, just above his perfectly pressed collar, there was a small burn scar, perhaps the size of a cigarette tip. She wondered how he'd gotten it.

Eddie hung up and turned back to Caroline.

"Sounds like this new judge is trouble for us," he said.

"Why?"

"Paul didn't say much, but he didn't sound too happy about the shift to New York. He just said Jacobsen's a god-awful draw for us."

"Maybe Louis knows something," Caroline said, already hurrying toward the elevator.

• • •

Caroline sat in Louis's guest chair with a legal pad balanced on her lap and a pen in her hand, waiting for her boss to say something.

Louis stood silently by the window, his glasses perched atop his head, his neck craned down at the file's contents. In his gray suit, he looked as monolithic and formidable as the gray buildings behind him. Upon learning the name of the new judge, he'd called Silvia, who'd appeared in his office seconds later holding the file folder with the judge's name typed across the top. Now he studied the pages. One by one. Deliberate but fast.

When he'd finished the last page, Louis scowled. "Paul Tiller's right. Judge Jacobsen is a dreadful draw for us. He defended companies against asbestos litigation for decades before being appointed to the bench. He also did some graduate work in molecular cell biology prior to going to law school. By nature and by training, he's going to be skeptical of the science."

"Can we get a new judge?" Caroline asked.

"No. Jacobsen's involvement in asbestos litigation isn't enough to require him to recuse himself. We'd have to move to disqualify him, and I'm not comfortable with our chances of success. If we fail, we'll have poisoned the well. If you shoot at a king—don't miss." Louis shook his white-haired head. "I'm afraid we're stuck with him."

"So what do we do?" Caroline asked.

"We write a singularly compelling brief. We make it impossible for Judge Jacobsen to deny the existence of a link between SuperSoy and kidney damage."

Caroline nodded. It was a good speech. A great set of aspirations. Unfortunately, reality wasn't being so cooperative.

"I'd feel better about our chances if we had some science showing a direct link," she said.

"Agreed," Louis said, letting the mask slip enough for Caroline to see his concerns. When she'd told him about Dr. Heller's death and Dr. Wong's apparent disappearance, he'd taken the news with the grim determination of a cavalry lieutenant facing a wall of cannons.

Now he exhaled softly.

"All we can do is to play the hand that's been dealt to us," he said.

"But what if it's a bad hand?" Caroline asked.

"Then unless you play very well or you are very lucky, you lose."

Louis's eyes flickered over to the chess game on the small table by his window. Caroline noted that neither side had moved since her last visit to the senior partner's antiquated domain. It was a slow, deliberate game that Louis played. But while he might win his chess match, Caroline couldn't see how he'd win the *SuperSoy* case.

Litigation wasn't chess. A game of chess always began the same way. The pieces lined up, identical on both sides. Who won and who lost depended on each player's skill. Litigation was different. Sometimes the evidence just didn't fall into place. Sometimes you couldn't win.

The thought depressed Caroline. Still, she waited for Louis to say something inspirational. Something hopeful.

But the only sound she heard was the ambient hum of activity in the firm's halls. A hum that had nothing to do with SuperSoy.

Caroline studied Louis's face. She worried she'd started to see traces of disappointment. In the faint tightening of his mouth, in the soft sigh of his breath when she'd told him that she hadn't managed to locate the Heller article, she feared she saw his interest in her waning like a balloon with a slow leak, its bright sheen growing limp before crumpling into a rumpled heap.

"The transfer of this case to New York is going to create some issues for us," Louis said finally. "I need you to prepare a pro hac vice application for me so I can appear before the district court there."

"Will do." Caroline had googled *pro hac vice* at a stoplight on her way back to the office from the hearing. Wikipedia had provided a superficial description of what the Latin phrase meant. Translated as "for this one occasion," pro hac vice was a lawyer's request for permission to appear in a court where he was not licensed.

"New York allows appearances by out-of-state attorneys so long as they're sponsored by a local attorney and they provide a Certificate of

Good Standing from the state bar," Louis said. "Silvia has my Certificate of Good Standing on file. Please arrange to have Anton Callisto sponsor my application."

"I'll get right on it," Caroline said. She kept her face neutral even as she noted that Louis only planned to request permission for himself to appear. She wondered if he'd even ask her to attend the hearing in New York. Or whether she'd be staying home.

Louis removed his wire-rimmed glasses and placed them gently on his ink blotter. Without his glasses framing his light eyes, his gaze held a pale vulnerability. He looked out the window, his aristocratic features distracted.

"I suppose it might be time to give up on finding that article," he mused aloud. Unsaid was *since you failed abysmally at finding it.*

Unsure what else she could say, Caroline nodded her understanding and left his office.

• • •

As she walked away from Louis's office, Caroline didn't notice the staff at the workstations in the halls. She didn't notice the box of doughnuts laid out on the credenza, a gift from some grateful client. Instead, she chewed the inside of her lip and considered her dilemma.

Hale Stern didn't hire the usual way, sorting through hundreds of applicants during the on-campus interviews hosted by the law schools, holding back-to-back conversations with candidates in cramped hotel rooms across the street from campuses. No, Hale Stern handpicked its candidates from clinical courses taught by the firm's partners at the top law schools in the country. It invested substantial time in selecting its new attorneys. And when those attorneys arrived, they were expected to perform. Immediately.

And she wasn't performing. Not yet, anyway.

Caroline felt like an Olympic diver attempting a trick with a high degree of difficulty. If she pulled it off, she'd stand on the victors' podium for sure. But if she failed, she risked braining herself on the diving board. At this point, a belly flop seemed likely. Even inevitable.

She consoled herself that she could go to another firm if things didn't work out at Hale Stern. But the consolation fell flat. If she left too soon, she'd be seen as damaged goods. Her short stint at Hale Stern—or her gap in employment if she left the firm off her résumé—would be an indictment. She'd be lucky to find another position. And that meant she'd be stuck at home longer. In that house full of ghosts. Full of her uncle . . . She didn't know if she could stand it.

All of which brought her back to her problem. The Heller article. Because of her inability to find anything else of use in the war room, her success or failure at Hale Stern had telescoped down to a single question: whether she could find Dr. Heller's missing article. She'd pushed all her chips into the center of the table, gambling on finding it.

But she'd already tried the easy pathways to information about the article. To find it, she might need to try some . . . harder ones.

Her chest grew cold, as if a ghost had passed through her.

She knew the price of information. There were always ways to find things out. Some of those ways were legal. Some were not. She knew the lines of demarcation. After her father had been arrested for hacking, those lines were tattooed indelibly on her soul. Yes, Caroline knew the toll of information. The human toll. To herself. To those she'd loved . . .

She was fairly sure she could find the article through legal means, but the slope was a slippery one. She knew how addicting the hunt for information could become. How difficult it was to stop once she'd started . . . Even when prudence dictated caution, she'd shown herself heedless of the imperative to retreat from the hunt.

Caroline slowed her steps.

Glass windows beside office doors provided glimpses of the Hale Stern lawyers inside. As she passed each one, she studied their faces.

Old faces and young. Male and female. Of myriad ethnicities. But all of them practiced at the pinnacle of the legal world. All of them had made a professional home at one of the most well-respected firms in the country.

Their offices reflected their success. Some, like Louis's, were decorated with antiques. Brass fittings and carved walnut furniture. Persian rugs and elegant lamps. Others had opted for more modern trappings. Caroline idly wondered whether the partners received a decorating stipend or whether they paid for their furnishings themselves. They could certainly afford it.

Caroline stopped before an empty office. A small one. An associate's office that contained only an oak desk and metal bookshelf holding the ubiquitous Code of Civil Procedure issued to all first-year associates. Beyond the sparse furnishings, a panoramic view of the San Gabriel Mountains rose up in the north.

She read the nameplate on the door: **GREG PORTOS.**

Pulling back as if touched by electricity, Caroline turned and hurried to her own office.

• • •

Before she began, Caroline shut her door. What she was about to do wasn't forbidden. Subterfuge might be morally reprehensible, but no law barred it. Still, she didn't want to explain her methods to anyone. People might judge. Even she herself could not escape the pang of conscience that settled in the pit of her stomach, a reminder of the dread she'd experienced the last time she'd dug too far for information . . .

Bringing her fingers to her laptop, she ran a search for Dr. Franklin Heller.

As before, dozens of obituaries appeared on the screen. But this time, she wasn't interested in the details of the scientist's death. Instead, she scrolled down until she found the information she sought: Dr. Heller was survived by his wife, Yvonne Heller.

Perhaps the dead scientist's wife knew something about the article.

There was only one way to find out: she needed a phone number.

She hoped that finding it would be relatively simple.

As expected, she found nothing in the publicly available telephone databases. A general search for "Yvonne Heller" failed, too. It retrieved hundreds of pages. Too many to be useful.

Caroline knew she needed to limit the universe of results.

She restricted her results to Yvonne Hellers who lived in Los Angeles County.

Still, a dozen hits marched down the page.

Navigating back to the obituaries, Caroline skimmed until she found the piece of information she needed: Yvonne's middle name. It was Ophelia.

Caroline breathed an internal sigh of relief. The letter *O* was unusual enough to limit her results to probable hits.

Sure enough, a search for "Yvonne O. Heller" retrieved two dozen results, most of which discussed Dr. Heller's death and all of which presumably related to the correct Yvonne Heller.

Caroline digested information as fast as her fingers could probe the corners of each hit. Yvonne had been born in Pasadena. She'd attended high school in Glendale. Her volunteer work at Children's Hospital garnered the praise of the mayor and other civil leaders.

On the third page of search results, something caught Caroline's eye: Yvonne O. Heller was a member of the American Institute of CPAs.

Accountants had offices. With phones.

Caroline's fingers tingled. She was closing in on her prey.

She ran searches for "Yvonne O. Heller, CPA," "Yvonne Heller, CPA," and "Yvonne Heller, accountant."

But she retrieved no hits. Instead, the only reference to "Yvonne O. Heller, CPA," outside of the AICPA directory itself, was a mention of a seminar a year ago at Claremont McKenna College's economics and accounting department. Yvonne had sat as a panelist discussing the usefulness of accounting degrees in running small businesses. Yvonne didn't have an accounting practice anymore. If she ever had.

Caroline sat back and considered how to find another point of entry into Yvonne's life. Where did Yvonne live? Dine? Play? Who were her friends?

Caroline knew how to find out all of those things: Facebook.

She began with the obvious avenue of attack: Yvonne's user profile.

As expected, Yvonne had set her privacy settings so that only her friends could view her personal information.

It was time to get creative.

Caroline navigated to Facebook's home page.

The social networking site asked if she wanted to log in to an existing account or create a new one. She opted for the latter. Then she contemplated what to name her alias. She decided on Taylor Albert. A good gender-ambiguous name that would broaden the pool of potential faces to whom Yvonne might attach the name.

Now Caroline just needed to set up a false e-mail address and fill in the details on the profile, constructing a false identity, the plausibility of which Yvonne would justify for herself.

What kind of stranger would Yvonne accept as a friend? The wife of another research scientist? A neighbor?

Suddenly, a better idea occurred to Caroline.

With rapid keystrokes, she filled in the profile. Taylor Albert would be twenty-one, have graduated from Claremont McKenna College, and be pursuing a career in accounting. He'd like a half dozen accounting pages and organizations, including the Seminars and Speakers Series on the college's Facebook page.

Now the last step: Taylor Albert needed some friends. Caroline didn't have time to write her own code, so she navigated to blackhat-bots.com to grab the latest Facebook account-creator bot. She loaded

Facebook Flooder and set its parameters, and in moments, she had three dozen false Facebook identities with which to populate Taylor Albert's friends page. Now Taylor would look like a real person instead of a hastily constructed tool designed for phishing.

It was time to bait the hook.

Taylor Albert sent a friend request to Yvonne. If Yvonne probed to see who this stranger was who wanted to Internet-befriend her, she'd assume that he was just an earnest student who'd attended her seminar. Flattery would lead her to accept this stranger's friend request.

Fifteen minutes later, Caroline's efforts were rewarded when Yvonne accepted the request. Now Caroline had access to Yvonne's pictures, timelines, favorite websites, and, most importantly, her personal information, including her mobile phone number.

Grabbing her phone before her nerves could prevent her, Caroline dialed.

A woman's round, rich alto answered.

Having used subterfuge to find Yvonne's number, Caroline opted for honesty in her approach to the widow.

"Please pardon the intrusion," she began. "My name's Caroline Auden. I'm an attorney working on the *SuperSoy* case—"

"How did you get this number?" Yvonne asked, her tone so quick that Caroline winced, waiting for the click.

When Caroline didn't hear one, she hurried onward. "I'm one of the lawyers representing the plaintiffs." At the silence on the line, she kept going. "Our case depends on something your husband wrote. I know that sounds a little dramatic, but it's the truth."

Heartened that Yvonne still hadn't hung up, she got to the point of her call.

"We hoped you might know where we could find your husband's article on SuperSoy," she finished.

"I'm sorry, but I really can't help you," Yvonne said slowly. The venom had left her voice. Instead, her tone sounded almost . . . regretful.

An instinct tugged at Caroline, a shadow of an idea forming in the far corner of her mind.

"I would prefer that you not call me," Yvonne said.

The silence hung between them, pregnant and potent.

"I'm sorry for your loss," Caroline said finally. "I won't call again."

Hanging up, Caroline pondered the strange conversation. Either Yvonne Heller was a complete freak or . . . or what?

The buzz of a cell phone startled Caroline.

She looked down at the caller. Daniel Hitchings. Her uncle.

Caroline groaned. She didn't have time for his antics. But she'd promised her mother she'd look after him . . .

"Hey, Uncle Hitch," she answered.

"I hate to bug you," her uncle began, his voice gravelly and slurring.

Caroline resisted the urge to disagree.

"I just need you to lend me some money," he said. "Your mom was supposed to leave me some cash, but she only left me five and I need another twenty dollars, plus fifty-three cents."

"I'm not helping you buy vodka," Caroline said.

"Who said anything about vodka, kiddo?"

"Grey Goose costs $25.53." She'd seen the labels on his bottles. She knew the price.

"No, but I—"

"I'll see you later," Caroline said, hanging up.

She flushed with annoyance. She'd been to meetings. She knew alcoholism was an illness, blah, blah, blah. She knew she was supposed to let go of trying to fix her uncle's disease. But she hated witnessing it. She just needed to move out of that house, with its echoes of her mother's madness and her uncle's death spiral into the alcoholic unknown.

The phone on the desk rang.

Gritting her teeth, Caroline answered, "I can't believe you're calling me on my work line—"

"Excuse me?" Silvia's voice asked on the receiver.

"I'm so sorry," Caroline backpedaled. "I thought you were someone else."

"Apparently so." Silvia chuckled.

Caroline thanked the law gods that she hadn't yelled at Louis. She doubted he'd be as forgiving as her assistant.

"Louis is on the line. I'll join the calls together now," Silvia said. Without waiting for Caroline's assent, the line clicked over, and Louis's patrician voice came onto the line.

"I'd like for you to come with me to Las Vegas tomorrow morning," he announced.

Caroline mentally replayed his words. What could possibly be in Las Vegas?

"The Plaintiffs' Steering Committee is meeting there," Louis said.

"Are there a lot of plaintiffs in Las Vegas?"

"No, there's a lot of food. The attorneys on the Committee are all over the country. They meet in Las Vegas every few months to strategize. Their regular meeting was scheduled for this week. Now that our firm is helping out on the *Daubert* motion, they want me to attend. I'd like you to be there, too."

Caroline warmed at the invitation. Perhaps she'd been wrong about Louis's waning interest in her career. But then she eyed the pile of articles. How could she travel to Las Vegas and track down the Heller article and finish the outline? She had time for one task, maybe two. But not all three.

"I know I've given you quite a lot to do," Louis continued, "so it's your choice. This isn't a command performance."

"I'm happy to come," Caroline said.

"Excellent," Louis said, his tone leaving no doubt that she'd given the right answer. "Dale is curious to meet you. He'll be interested to hear your view on the scientific evidence."

Caroline made a mental note to reread all of her notes before she met Dale.

"Please have Silvia get you a ticket for the nine a.m. flight out of LAX on Southwest," Louis said. "We'll fly together so I can bring you up to speed on the dynamics with the Steering Committee."

"Dynamics?"

"We must be sensitive to our position in this case. We aren't members of the Committee. Instead, we're rather like Dale's subcontractors. We mustn't forget that fact. We're here to help the Committee, yes, but we're also here to make Dale look good." Louis paused and cleared his throat. "To that end, I've spoken with the Committee about our efforts to synthesize the existing scientific literature."

"You mean my inferential reasoning argument?" Caroline asked, wondering why she hadn't been invited to attend that call.

"Yes. Some members of the Committee see some merit in the argument. Others think we can beat Med-Gen's motion by simply showing the proximity in time between ingestion of SuperSoy and kidney failure."

"You mean Dale's pet argument."

"Correct," Louis said. "Those who believe most strongly in that proximity-in-time argument are concerned that our inferential argument about the Feinberg, Ambrose, and Tercero articles will weaken our presentation."

"But it's better than nothing," Caroline blurted.

"Yes, yes, I agree," Louis said, his tone mollifying. "But I must say, I'm worried. I agree with the Committee that it isn't very strong."

"I'm still looking for that Heller article," Caroline said. "If it's out there, I will find it."

"Fine, fine," Louis said, and Caroline could imagine him waving an aristocratic hand around dismissively. "In the meanwhile, I've put together the rest of our *Daubert* brief using the various pieces that the Committee provided to me. Dale has asked that our shop handle the filing. That means I'll need permission from the New York District Court. So please make getting my pro hac vice application filed a top priority."

"Will do."

"See you at the airport tomorrow morning," Louis added, clicking off.

Caroline turned to her laptop.

She'd get Louis's pro hac vice application filed.

She'd get her bags packed.

And then she'd find that article.

Since without it, nothing else on her schedule had much point at all.

CHAPTER 5

Two conversations had kept Caroline up, staring at her ceiling deep into the night.

The first was her conversation with Louis. She'd replayed it in her mind a dozen times, mining the words for hidden meaning. Every time, she came to the same conclusion: if she didn't find the Heller article, Louis wouldn't invite her to come to New York. He'd invited her to Las Vegas, yes, but that was a far cry from including her at the *Daubert* hearing. To solidify her place, she needed to produce something more than she'd produced so far.

The second worrisome conversation was the one she'd had with Yvonne Heller. Again, she heard it in her mind. The pauses. The subtext. The whole tone and tenor of the interaction carried some hidden meaning just beyond the edge of her comprehension. Like a splinter worrying its way up to the surface of her mind.

Unable to sleep, Caroline had arrived at the airport far earlier than she'd planned.

She found a spot near the tall windows fronting the runways, where she could watch the planes take off and land. Beside her, a group of travelers dragged matching rolling bags past the bank of orange plastic seats next to the gate where she'd board in an hour.

She saw no sign of Louis. Good.

Opening her laptop, Caroline resolved that when she saw Louis, she would have made progress on locating the article. Now she just needed to figure out how to make that resolution a reality.

She began with general searches, the equivalent of sinking dozens of lobster traps into the ocean in the hope of catching some unfortunate crustacean that wandered into her clutches. SuperSoy. Franklin Heller. Anne Wong. She searched them all, alone and together.

Each query retrieved gazillions of hits. None of them useful. Most she'd already read before.

She changed her strategy. She tried chronology. Perhaps someone had said something new about Dr. Heller.

She opened the most recent newspaper article, an investigative piece in a local Malibu paper on the failure of the city to stabilize the land along the bluffs. The intrepid journalist had examined the dangers of eroding cliffs to tourists, joggers, and other unsuspecting souls out to enjoy vista views. Caroline read a litany of it's-not-our-fault quotes from the members of the Malibu City Council. "Hillside stabilization is a waste of city money," one councilmember had told reporters. "The scrub brush prevents crumbling." He went on to insist, "Dr. Heller's death wasn't caused by erosion or by the city's failure to install guard railings."

Caroline paused at the picture accompanying the article. When she'd first heard about Dr. Heller's death, she'd imagined a cliff. But the hillside where the scientist had perished wasn't steep. It was really more of an embankment than a precipice.

The police had investigated Dr. Heller's death. The Malibu City Council had made sure of it. But there were no witnesses to Dr. Heller's demise. Because there was no evidence of foul play, it was ruled "an unfortunate accident." Just the sad sort of tragedy that strikes the seemingly safe.

An unfortunate accident. Caroline tried on the explanation for size.

In her experience, the stories people told were often convenient ways of avoiding dealing with hard truths. That bruise on Uncle Hitch's cheek wasn't caused by the cat darting in front of him when he'd come home late at night. That argument between her parents hadn't really been about her father's busy work schedule. People tended not to look beneath the surface, but in Caroline's world, there was always something beneath the surface.

Unbidden, she thought of Yvonne Heller. A woman whose husband would never again come home. Would never again enter the kitchen holding a bag of groceries. Would never again tell his wife about his day. What a strange way to lose him . . . a tumble down a hillside. A broken neck. The whole thing was so . . . so strange.

Even Yvonne Heller was strange. Again, Caroline could hear the odd cadence of the widow's rich alto. Her flare of fury. Her sudden softening when she'd learned which side Caroline represented. Stilted and deliberate, Yvonne's diction had felt . . . constipated.

Shaking her head, Caroline delved deeper into the results. She knew that search engines prioritized mainstream news outlets and paid sites. To thwart the search engine's bias, she added specific terms to her search: "death," "fell," "investigation," "GMOs." Perhaps someone somewhere had said something about Heller's research and who had picked up the baton to continue it . . .

Now her query retrieved more obscure articles about Heller's death.

Caroline's finger scrolled down through the pages, farther and farther away from the mainstream results.

She stopped at the web page of an organization called GMO Global Action Network. Between screeds lambasting biotech companies for compromising ecological diversity and killing bees, the Network's director lauded the brave scientists who resisted the biotech companies' efforts to discredit anti-GMO studies. At the very end of the home page, the director lamented the "suspicious timing of the death of Dr. Franklin Heller, coming so close on the heels of the filing of key motions in the *SuperSoy* litigation."

In the back of Caroline's mind, a worry began to stir.

She opened her bag and rummaged around until she found Hale Stern's security token. The code on it changed every fifteen minutes to protect the firm's server.

Caroline keyed in the password and remotely accessed the firm's document management program. Then she quickly navigated to the *SuperSoy* matter.

She pulled up Med-Gen's *Daubert* motion.

The stamp on the upper right-hand corner of the caption page read: AUGUST 24.

Now Caroline flipped back to the Malibu article about hillside erosion.

She scrolled to the second paragraph and stopped. Dr. Heller had died on August 21.

Just three days before Med-Gen filed its motion.

She glanced back at the picture accompanying the Malibu newspaper article. The incongruence between the official cause of death and the innocuous hillside bothered Caroline. While it wasn't completely outside the realm of possibility that a healthy fiftysomething scientist had tumbled down the slope and broken his neck, it seemed . . . unlikely.

She reread the introduction to Med-Gen's *Daubert* motion. It boldly proclaimed that no published science anywhere on the planet linked SuperSoy to kidney damage.

Well, that was certainly true; Caroline huffed in exasperation. She'd researched every scientist who'd ever penned anything remotely connected to SuperSoy, and she'd found no one who'd ever drawn a direct link between the genetically modified soybean and renal failure. She'd spent hours on symposium chat boards and conference Facebook pages.

Not that Louis would care. He only cared about results. And she still didn't have any to show him.

She reminded herself that no one else on the Plaintiffs' Steering Committee had managed to find a direct link. But Louis's disappointment aside, the unavoidable fact remained that they'd likely lose if they couldn't find a direct link in the scientific literature.

Slowly, a horrible possibility dawned in Caroline's mind like a perverse sunrise.

There was no science showing a direct link between SuperSoy and kidney injury . . . because the scientist who'd written what looked to be the key article establishing that link . . . had died in a freak accident . . . right before he could publish it . . .

A flock of goose bumps landed on Caroline's back and fled down her arms.

How had Dr. Heller died?

Was it really an accident?

Perhaps the defense had bided their time, waiting to file the motion after they knew there'd be no evidence to refute it. The fact that they'd had a huge motion ready for filing so soon after Dr. Heller died certainly didn't negate the possibility.

She considered what else she knew. Dr. Anne Wong had disappeared shortly after her research partner had died. She'd pulled out of that conference, sacrificing the opportunity to present her latest research on cannabinoids. That had been a big sacrifice.

Too big.

Maybe Dr. Anne Wong hadn't taken a leave.

Maybe she'd run.

The possibility set Caroline's gut to churning, low and menacing, and an itch began behind her ears, a tingle faintly felt the way a gazelle on the African savanna first perceives the presence of a predator lurking in the tall grass. Something was wrong here. Very wrong.

Caroline considered what to do with her nascent conspiracy theory. Perhaps there had been a police investigation that the newspapers hadn't covered? Perhaps someone could tell her conclusively that Dr. Heller's death really had been an accident, that in her desperation to win, she was letting her mind spiral down a whirlpool of paranoia?

Before she could decide, she spotted Louis strolling across the terminal. His white-haired head was visible over those around him, as if he moved at a different altitude than the mere mortals in his midst. He wore khaki pants, a red polo shirt, and Top-Siders. He had a small duffel bag slung casually over his shoulder.

Looking down at the navy business suit she wore, Caroline cringed. She'd guessed wrong about the uniform she was supposed to wear for the trip. While it wasn't a vacation, they were apparently supposed to have dressed as if it were.

"Sorry I'm late," Louis said, sitting down beside Caroline. "Things were quite hectic at home this morning." He leaned back, stretching his long legs in front of him. "My wife insists I take the dogs for their morning walks. Today, they woke me up before dawn. They must have eaten something last night that didn't agree with them, because they . . ." He trailed off, but it was too late. Caroline smiled at the mental image of the dignified litigator cleaning up dog poop.

Louis ran his hands through his white hair, and Caroline noted he wasn't wearing the Porcellian Club ring he always wore. She took it as a sign of the kind of morning he'd had.

Louis assumed a philosophical tone. "In life, you can set a person up for success or failure. Sending me on a walk with two overly pedigreed dogs in dire intestinal distress on a day when I need to catch a flight was most definitely setting me up for failure."

"What kind of dogs do you have?" Caroline asked, trying to draw out the conversation. She liked this Louis, talking about normal things. He seemed less remote. More approachable. Plus it distracted her from the cloud of doom that had settled over her.

"Pembroke Welsh corgis. I know a top-notch breeder. There's always a long wait for puppies, but if you're interested, I could arrange something." His eyes glittered with delight at his ability to make something happen where others could not. "Pedigree is everything, after all," he added with the ghost of a wink.

Caroline wasn't sure if he was talking about himself or his dog.

Louis cleared his throat, the patrician mask back in place.

"So, will I have my outline tomorrow, Ms. Auden?" he asked.

It sounded like a dare.

"Definitely," Caroline promised. But then her stomach knotted.

She needed to tell Louis about her conspiracy theory, but her position was precarious. And whatever she said would sound paranoid. That couldn't be good for her long-term prospects at the firm. And yet, she couldn't *not* mention her concerns . . . if only so Louis could put a stop to the fear that now coursed through her veins like antifreeze.

She took a breath to steady her nerves.

"In the course of looking around for that missing article, I found out some other . . . stuff. There are some . . . circumstances . . . around Dr. Heller's death that are just weird. The timing, for one thing. And I took a look at the place where he broke his neck. The hill isn't that steep . . ."

"What are you driving at?" Louis's eyes narrowed. "Are you suggesting Heller was murdered?"

Caroline stayed silent.

Louis chuckled. "You've seen too many movies, Ms. Auden."

Caroline flushed. She hated sounding foolish to her boss.

"Witness intimidation and perhaps even the occasional murder may occur among criminals," Louis said, his tone conciliatory, "but it is not something that happens in fights over money. Not business disputes or personal injury cases, anyway. There's a reason why we're civil attorneys."

Caroline appreciated his effort to smooth over her paranoia. She hoped he'd forget she'd ever said anything. Quickly.

"We do have some real-life worries, however," Louis said. "I assume you've read this morning's decision in the *Scziewizcs* case? Putting aside for a moment that it is unpronounceable, that decision is going to be a problem for us."

"I haven't seen it," Caroline admitted. She chastised herself for missing the decision. She'd been so wrapped up in hatching insane biotech murder scenarios that she'd forgotten to check the advance sheets.

She braced herself for a teachable moment.

But instead, Louis reached into his duffel bag and withdrew a short stack of papers stapled in the upper left-hand corner.

"Please give it a read," he said, handing the papers to Caroline. "It's a case involving a multidistrict litigation over a diabetes medication that the plaintiffs allege causes liver damage. A federal district judge in Nevada found that proximity in time between ingestion and injury is insufficient to defeat a *Daubert* motion. She dismissed the case."

Caroline's face flushed. This was bad. Really bad.

"But it's just another district court in a different circuit, so it doesn't bind Judge Jacobsen in our case, right?" she asked.

"Correct, but it's still persuasive authority. Judge Jacobsen may choose to adopt *Scziewizcs*'s reasoning, even though it isn't binding."

"We need Heller," Caroline said, articulating Louis's unspoken conclusion.

Louis nodded grimly.

"Did Dale ever say anything about that article?" Caroline asked. It occurred to her that she'd been so focused on finding an Internet solution to her research quest that she'd failed to run down all possible avenues for obtaining human intelligence on it.

"No, but that doesn't mean you shouldn't ask him about it," Louis said. "One lesson every lawyer learns is that you never get the whole truth. There's always something that someone hasn't told you. Your client. Your key witness. The other side. Even your co-counsel. There's always some fact of critical importance that you simply don't know."

Caroline considered his words. "Because they're trying to hide something or because they don't know it's important?"

"Sometimes one. Sometimes the other. This is why a good lawyer must know everything he can possibly know about his case. Hard work wins cases far more often than courtroom eloquence . . . which is why I need you to work hard."

"I'll grill Dale," Caroline vowed. "I'll find out whether he has some lead for us on the Heller article."

"Good. You'll get your chance to talk to Dale at the luncheon when we arrive."

• • •

During the airplane's descent, Las Vegas had struck Caroline as an improbable metropolis that had sprung from the cracked earth fully grown, like an overfertilized version of Jack's beanstalk. A speed freak's dream, colored in neon and hopped up on drugs.

Now she stood at the threshold of a gaudy anomaly within a gaudy anomaly. Safe House. The restaurant had made the list of top ten restaurants not just for its food but for its dramatic decor. Across the vaulted ceiling, long chains of fabric were washed with gold light, creating the illusion that the dining room sat inside a woven sack of money. The carpet, too, played on the theme, with images of international currency scattered among diners' feet.

But the pièce de résistance was the floor-to-ceiling wine cellar rising up from the center of the vaulted space. A pulley system lifted a scantily clad waitress up the glass chamber to retrieve a bottle every time someone ordered. A burly man dressed in a guard uniform made a great show of punching the combination into a lock on the front of the tower each time the wine wench needed to retrieve a bottle.

It was a silly gimmick. And yet Caroline couldn't stop looking at it. The spectacle distracted her from her imminent meeting with the Steering Committee. If Louis's description was accurate, these were the men who fashioned, manipulated, and profited from the largest litigation in the country, cultivating cash cows of monumental proportions, milking their herds so they could feast on the fruits of their labors in places like this. And they wanted to meet her.

Caroline steeled herself for the meeting. These were just people, she reminded herself. Just a bunch of stuffed suits. Richer, certainly, but no better than her.

And yet, after her anxiety attack at court, each sound and scent and sight risked tripping the tenuous balance she'd only recently regained. She hated that was so. She wanted to feel as badass as she once had. As capable. As competent.

The hostess gestured for Caroline to follow her into the restaurant.

Sound rose up like a wall. Voices and silverware. And in the gaps between those, the clangs and sirens of the hotel's casino, all hitting Caroline's ears in jangling waves.

Finally, they arrived at the epicenter of the sound: a big table filled with middle-aged men talking so loudly the rest of the restaurant had to raise its collective voice to be heard.

No one had to tell Caroline that this was the Plaintiffs' Steering Committee.

At one end of the table, Louis sat ramrod straight, looking formal even without a tie under his sports jacket. Next to him sat a broad-shouldered man with dyed-blond hair and a mouth that seemed too large for his face.

On the other side of the table, Caroline spotted Deena. The New York associate wore what had to be a designer dress. Blood-red and cut to show plenty of cleavage, the dress clung to Deena like a wet bathing suit. Caroline's little black cocktail dress, which had seemed like a safe bet, now just seemed timid.

As Caroline approached the table, the blond man beside Louis rose to his feet.

"I'm Dale," he said, holding out a meaty hand. "It's a pleasure to meet you, Miss Caroline." He smiled a boyish smile, the dimple in his right cheek deepening. His manner reminded Caroline of the family friend who's come to the door with a plate of cookies, apologizing for not being a better cook. The wolfish gleam in his eyes as he glanced at the low neckline of her dress, however, made her think perhaps he wasn't so much the family friend as he was the mischievous postman who'd fathered kids all over the neighborhood.

Caroline sat down in the empty chair between Dale and Louis.

"When Louis called to see if I needed any help on this here case, I was happier than a tornado in a trailer park. There's no one better than this guy right here at putting a case together." As he sat back down, he moved to slap Louis's shoulder but stopped. Louis wasn't the backslapping type.

"To tell you the truth," Dale continued, "I'd have reached out to Louis myself if I'd thought he'd be interested in taking a contingency-fee case. He doesn't put up those pretty pictures in his office by taking cases on the come. So when he offered his services at a cut rate—I sure as heck counted my blessings that day."

"Some cases are worthy of a special arrangement," Louis said simply.

"How do you two know each other?" Caroline asked, looking back and forth between the two men, trying to imagine where the austere northeasterner and the avuncular Texan could have crossed paths.

Dale flashed another one of his winning smiles. "I went to school with this guy. He was a senior at the fraternity when I was just a lowlife freshman pledge. He's been looking out for me ever since."

Caroline's brow knit. Harvard had both fraternities and final clubs. The Porcellian Club was a final club, not a fraternity. Maybe Dale had used the more common term for her benefit? With his Texas accent and cowboy boots, Dale didn't convey the old-money credentials the Porc usually required of its membership. Perhaps he had a New England steel magnate or robber baron somewhere in his family tree? It wouldn't be the first time a privileged New Englander had passed himself off as a down-home southerner.

Glancing at Dale's hand, Caroline looked to see if he wore the same ring that Louis usually wore. He didn't. But he did wear a wedding ring.

"Louis got me into Columbia Law School," Dale said. "I know he'll deny it, but he made it happen. I had far too much fun in college to get the grades I needed to get into Columbia. But when you've got Louis on your side, all things are possible."

Louis smiled an enigmatic smile but said nothing.

Dale turned back to Caroline and put his thick hand on the back of Caroline's chair.

"So what's your story, Miss Caroline? Tell me all about yourself." As he held her eyes, the thumb of the hand behind her touched the bare skin on her back exposed by her dress.

"I'm working on the science for our *Daubert* brief," Caroline said, being deliberately obtuse.

She leaned forward to take a sip of water, breaking contact with Dale's thumb, which she knew remained perched on the chair behind her, just waiting for another chance to pounce.

Dale deflated slightly. It wasn't the response he'd sought.

"Oh. Right," Dale said. "I hear you've been reading all those articles we sent y'all."

"Yes. I also found something interesting on a chat board—"

"You know what's interesting?" Dale asked. "That wine tower over there." He gestured with his chin toward the spectacle, inviting Caroline to join him in his admiration.

"Yeah, I saw it. It's amazing," Caroline said. "But I wanted to ask if you knew something about this scientist who—"

"You know what else is amazing?" Dale leaned toward Caroline so that his shoulder grazed hers, touching tentatively in another silent overture.

Caroline pulled away, drinking yet more water. Dale would either think she was superthirsty or he'd get a clue.

After a moment, she tried again. "There's a missing article, and I was hoping . . ."

She trailed off as Dale took his hand off her chair and turned to watch a waitress walking across the dining room. With breasts the size of small grapefruits and legs that went on for yards, the reason for Dale's distraction was obvious.

He pivoted his body until he faced away from Caroline.

The blatant nature of his disregard struck Caroline like a slap. His interest in her had lasted exactly as long as he'd thought there might be a chance of seducing her. He wasn't interested in her views. He didn't care about her efforts to win.

A wave of annoyance rose in her chest.

She'd encountered guys like Dale in tech, where bro culture reigned supreme. She'd rebuffed the approaches of overgrown teenage boys who had enthusiastically suggested launching an app to share pictures of women's breasts and asked to see hers . . . for research.

Louis leaned toward Caroline's ear. "Dale can be a bit of a boor when he's had too much to drink. Par for the course, I'm afraid."

Caroline turned to her boss with surprise. He'd apparently noticed Dale's behavior. Even worse, he'd expected it.

"I apologize for not warning you about him," Louis added. His tone held remorse.

"I'm fine," Caroline said quickly. "I can take care of myself." As in the tech world, she would show no sign of weakness. Weakness was like catnip for assholes.

"Good," Louis said. "In law, just as in life, one must be able to handle oneself."

"I agree," Caroline said. She'd heard Louis's sermons on self-reliance. She knew his philosophy. Still, some advance warning about Dale would've been nice.

She eyed the rest of the people on the Plaintiffs' Steering Committee. People who hadn't greeted her or even acknowledged her when she'd arrived at the table.

A familiar gloom settled over her.

In leaving tech for the law, she'd assumed she'd find a world where gender wasn't so much of a . . . thing. She hadn't left tech because she'd been fleeing the puerile brogrammers who were as much a part of the industry as late-night pizza. She'd been good at her job, and the other engineers had shown her respect. Enough of them, anyway. Never one to shrink, she'd spoken up during code reviews, pointing out problems she'd seen in other engineers' code. But sometimes it seemed as if she spoke into an abyss . . .

"Once you get to know Dale, you'll find he isn't so bad," Louis said. "When he's away from home, he drinks too much, but he's a good lawyer and a good man. His ability to connect with juries is unparalleled. He's done some real good. Many of these fellows have."

Louis turned to regard the other faces around the table.

"Those guys over there are the lawyers from Chicago, Philadelphia, and New York." Louis gestured with his chin toward a cadre of men in subdued suits. Dark blue, black, and gray. Apparently the only three colors suitable for lawyers from east of the Mississippi.

Deena, in her red dress and long gold earrings, was a splash of color against the drab background. She listened attentively to something the thick man beside her said. Anton Callisto, Caroline guessed. Built like a linebacker, Anton exuded a sense of coiled menace. His bulbous nose gave him a vaguely pugilistic affect. His crew cut aligned with the ex-marine Louis had described, and he didn't look like he smiled very often.

"And that's Paul Tiller," Louis said, nodding his chin toward a short, bald man with a cherubic smile sitting across the table. "He's the self-proclaimed hottest plaintiff's lawyer in Atlanta, and I have to admit he's quite good. He's got the biggest piece of the *SuperSoy* litigation in the South. He narrowly lost out to Dale to be president of the Steering Committee. And you already know Eddie."

The Atlanta associate sat directly across the table. He wore black trousers and a white Oxford shirt tailored to accentuate his broad shoulders.

He caught Caroline's eye and smiled his crooked grin.

Caroline smiled back, finding sanctuary in Eddie's warmth. Reminding herself to be grateful that Dale wasn't her boss, she refocused on her mission: discovering whether Dale had any leads that might lead her to Heller's missing article.

When the waitress disappeared from view, Caroline cleared her throat.

Dale turned his attention back to her.

"Pardon my manners, darling," he said. "Now, what were you saying to me?" He replaced his hand on the back of her chair and leaned in but avoided making contact with her shoulder. They had reached some kind of unspoken détente.

"I'm piecing together the science for our *Daubert* brief, but there's one article that we don't have that might help us show a direct link," Caroline said.

"Louis mentioned your work. I appreciate it, but I think we'll win regardless. This judge is going to see that when these people ate SuperSoy, they got sick real soon afterward."

"But what about the *Sczuewizcs* decision this morning?" Caroline asked, wincing at her massacre of the case's name.

"It isn't binding on our court. I know *Daubert* requires us to put on some science, but we've got some science. We've got differential diagnoses. If a person went to a doctor with kidney failure, that doctor would put SuperSoy on his differential diagnosis. That's science."

Caroline wasn't so sure. Neither was the judge who'd decided that case she couldn't pronounce.

"Look, I'm glad y'all are looking through those articles, but anything we find in the scientific literature is just gravy." Dale gave Caroline a toothy smile. "I've been through this whole *Daubert* rigmarole before. The judge just wants to make sure we haven't come up with some cockamamie theory of injury. We'll easily pass muster."

Caroline remained silent. She'd already voiced her concerns.

"Judges aren't more sophisticated about science than any other educated laymen," Dale continued. "We just need to put on a good show for Judge Jacobsen. When I argue, I always use a PowerPoint presentation. Big ole screen up there to *show* the judge what we mean."

He held his hands up to show just how big a screen he meant.

"There's nothin' you can't do with a PowerPoint. Judges just love 'em." He grinned.

"I could send you materials for your PowerPoint," Caroline offered, "so you can work in the inferential reasoning part that we're writing up for you guys."

"Sure thing. Why don't you just write a memo about it for me, darlin'?" Dale said. "Now excuse me just a moment. I feel a speech coming on." He winked and rose to his feet.

Using his spoon, Dale clinked the side of his wineglass.

When the conversation around the table had stilled, he began. "As the Committee's president, I just want to say a few words. I want to welcome Louis and his associate, the lovely Caroline Auden. They've already done some good work for us reviewing those scientific articles. I wanted to offer them our sincere thanks for their efforts."

A smattering of applause rippled around the table. Meanwhile, Dale graced Caroline with such a warm smile that she almost forgot he'd just blown her off.

"When I was young, my granddaddy gave me some advice," Dale continued. "He said, 'Son, if you stand in the shadow of someone smarter than you, they will lift you up.'"

Dale's eyes again came to rest on Louis and Caroline. "Well, you have lifted me up. You've lifted us all up. We're grateful. We're glad you're on our team. We look forward to winning this thing for the thousands of folks out there who are praying for us. For the people who are depending on us to do the job right."

Dale paused to regard each of the lawyers at the table. "Like most of y'all, I've met the plaintiffs. I've sat with them and their loved ones. In hospitals. In their living rooms. I've heard their stories. That's what keeps me going." He patted his heart. "Their stories."

Studying the spellbound expressions on the faces around her, Caroline understood why Dale had so much success with juries. Calm and smooth, with enough pregnant pauses to build drama, each sentence he spoke wove emotion and meaning into a potent concoction. Even the most seasoned litigators at the luncheon showed genuine interest, not just polite attentiveness.

"We may be advocates, but we have a calling to do more than just advocate a legal position," Dale said. "We have a calling to be messengers for people too sick to speak for themselves. We are blessed to be witnesses to their suffering and, God willing, the guardians of their future health. I'm honored to work with each and every one of you. Thank you for all of your good work. You all lift me up."

When Dale finished, applause erupted at the table. Even Caroline found herself clapping.

Dale nodded abashed thanks for the generous reception. He held up his hands as though the applause was really more than he deserved, which only made everyone applaud harder.

But then Dale caught sight of the waitress again, walking with her head down, avoiding eye contact with him.

As she passed, Dale gently grasped her bicep. "I ordered some champagne, and it still hasn't arrived. I've been watchin' for it." He jutted his chin toward the wine tower, where the wine girl gracefully descended with a magnum cradled in her arms.

"Hey, I've got me a good idea," he said. "Why don't I help you go get it?"

Caroline admired the waitress's display of self-control in not rolling her eyes.

"Fine," the waitress said. She walked away with Dale trailing along in her wake.

"Hey, there," said a voice from beside her.

She turned to find Eddie leaning on Dale's vacant chair. His jet-black eyes twinkled with amusement.

"What's wrong?" he asked, taking Dale's vacant chair, his expression growing serious. "You look annoyed."

"For some reason I thought people would be talking more about the case. The details, I mean." Caroline looked in the direction Dale had disappeared. "Not just the emotional stuff."

Eddie chuckled. "Don't worry, it'll happen. On the morning before we leave, everyone'll talk shop a few minutes while they nurse their hangovers. Nothing'll get done, but we'll all plan to return in a month to do it again. It's all part of living the life. You'll get used to it. We'll wine and dine and pray like hell that one of our cases hits big so we can wine and dine again."

"You guys hardly live on a budget," she said, eyeing his expensive watch.

"True." He looked around the men remaining at the table. "Half of these guys have private jets. The other half have two. They need 'em for their depositions all over the country. It's like a gold rush. They speculate in litigation. High-rolling."

The cowboy culture of plaintiffs' attorneys wasn't so different from the bro culture of the tech world, Caroline realized. Other than Deena, there were no other women at the table . . .

Eddie smiled a disarming grin. "Now tell me what's really bothering you. You looked like you wanted to drive a salad fork into Dale's back when he was walking after that waitress."

Caroline told Eddie about the hole in the evidence and the dead scientist and her quest for the missing article and Dale's indifference and her strange conversation with Yvonne Heller.

When she finished, she exhaled softly. "Without that missing article, I'm afraid we're going to lose. I know Dale thinks the proximity in time between when the plaintiffs consumed SuperSoy and got sick is going to be enough to beat Med-Gen's motion, but what if it's not? What if we're about to lose unless we find that missing article?"

Caroline eyed the lawyers around the table, flushed with alcohol and mirth. Though she couldn't hear their conversations, she was pretty sure none of them had anything to do with SuperSoy.

"Then you've gotta find it," Eddie said. "I'm happy to help if there's anything I can do."

"Thanks," Caroline said. "I'll let you know if I have any bright ideas." She decided not to tell him the one idea she'd had since arriving in Las Vegas. An idea she knew she'd pursue as soon as she got back to her room. An idea she feared pursuing . . .

Eddie smiled at her. "Perhaps we'd do some better thinking at the bar?"

Instead of answering his invitation, Caroline looked around the table. Some of the Steering Committee members were so deep into their drinks that she wasn't sure they'd make it through lunch. Other seats were already empty, their occupants having roamed off to the casinos. And yet, Louis still sat at the table. So did Paul Tiller. And Anton Callisto. All the heavy hitters.

"I can't. Not yet," she decided aloud.

"Well, then, I guess I'm staying, too," Eddie said.

He leaned back and placed a booted foot against the strut of the table.

"I'll admit I wasn't too happy when they shipped me off to Los Angeles for this assignment, but recent developments have led me to change that opinion." He smiled, and the edges of his eyes crinkled up in well-worn smile lines. Even as the smile faded from his face, he maintained eye contact.

Caroline felt heat rise in her cheeks.

Sudden laughter drew her eyes away from the handsome associate.

She found Louis standing at the far side of the table, talking to Paul Tiller. With his short stature and bald head, Eddie's boss contrasted with Louis's towering elegance. Paul guffawed while Louis smiled, his features amused but controlled. It occurred to Caroline that she'd never seen Louis laugh. Not outright. The closest he ever came was a sardonic twinkle in his eye, coupled with a dignified grin.

"What do you think they're talking about?" Caroline asked. "Yachting?"

"More like fan boats," Eddie said. "Paul grew up on the bayou down in Louisiana. His dad was a crawdad fisher or something."

As Caroline watched the two men, Louis stopped talking. The smile he'd worn faded from his face as his eyes focused on something across the room.

Caroline tracked his gaze.

A man with a long nose that hooked over at the tip stood at the door of the restaurant. His bony countenance reminded Caroline of a scarecrow. He raised his hand to touch his forehead in Louis's direction, as if he were tipping a hat, then he turned and walked away.

Caroline turned back toward Louis, who stared at the now-empty doorway to the restaurant. His face wore an expression she'd never seen before. An expression startling in its intensity. And its passion. It took her a moment to place it.

Hatred.

"What was that about?" Caroline asked, her eyes still trained on Louis, trying to imagine the cause of his hatred. Even after he turned his attention back to Paul Tiller, Louis's preoccupation was written in his eyes, which kept flicking toward the doorway of the restaurant where the stranger had disappeared.

Eddie slowly shook his head. "I have no idea."

The hairs at the back of Caroline's neck rose. With sudden certainty, she needed to know the reason for the strange man's appearance.

She rose from her chair to make her way to Louis.

But her phone rang in her purse.

Distracted, she answered without looking at the caller.

"Hey, kiddo." Uncle Hitch's voice came on the line.

Caroline cringed, wishing she'd screened the call. But it was too late now.

"Excuse me, Eddie," she said. "I'll be right back."

She jogged out of the restaurant's doors and ducked into an alcove where she could hear well enough to have a phone conversation.

"I can't talk now, Uncle Hitch," she said into the receiver. "I've got some things I need to do here." Like figuring out what the heck just happened back at the table, she added silently.

"Your mom decided to go camping with Elaine," Uncle Hitch said. "She told me to check in with you once a day. I think she's worried about me."

Caroline stayed silent. Her uncle already knew she was worried about him, too.

"I just wanted you to know I've only had six drinks today," he said. "That's already one less than at this time yesterday . . . I'm getting sober."

"Have you gone to a meeting?" Caroline asked.

"You know I hate AA."

"It's going to kill you someday, Uncle Hitch," Caroline said quietly. Not that it would matter. Not that the former police officer and soldier cared what she said.

"Now wait a sec—"

"We can talk later. I've got to go," she finished and hung up before he could reply. She didn't want to hear his lame excuse for why he needed a drink.

Standing in the alcove, Caroline waited for her foul mood to dissipate. Her uncle's drinking frustrated her. But even more than that, his unwillingness to do anything about it disappointed her. He'd always been so strong. When her father had left, Uncle Hitch had stepped into the vacant spaces. He'd attended events for her. Competitions. Graduations. He'd helped her learn to drive. But now he was a foundering ship, and there was nothing she or her mom or anyone else could seem to do about it.

When the mood didn't pass, Caroline headed back to the table.

Maybe she'd take Eddie up on that drink after all, she thought darkly.

• • •

But when Caroline arrived at the Committee's table, she didn't see Eddie.

Louis, too, seemed to have disappeared.

So instead of sitting back down at the table, Caroline skirted the edges of the restaurant, scanning the vast space. She passed tables of laughing friends, couples long married or newly met, a tableau that played out like colorful fish in a tank that she, separated by glass and oxygen, could not be a part of.

Seeing no familiar faces in the restaurant, she stepped into the lounge.

Unlike the cavernous restaurant, the bar area was long and narrow. Golden light played on the ceiling, shining up through a long slab of quartzite. A row of well-dressed patrons stood against it, sipping drinks from elegant glassware.

As she wove between bar tables, she looked for Eddie or Louis. She saw neither man.

At the far end of the bar, a corridor bordered by velvet curtains opened onto a row of private booths.

Curious, Caroline passed into it, scanning the low tables with diners reclining on Moroccan cushions. When she reached the end of the private booths, she turned around to retrace her steps.

That's when she saw Eddie. He sat in a nook hung with cobalt curtains that obscured all but his face.

She took a half step toward him, then froze.

He wasn't alone.

Across from him sat a platinum blonde wearing a burgundy dress with a plunging neckline. The look on Eddie's face made clear that he wouldn't be interested in anyone but Ms. Platinum Blonde tonight.

Caroline retreated back through the curtained entrance to the bar with a wave of annoyance. This trip to Vegas pretty much sucked, she concluded. She could think of no reason she should have come.

"What can I get you?" asked the bartender.

"Just some water," Caroline said, giving the only answer she ever gave.

She knew why her uncle drank. She shared his sensitivity. A sensitivity so acute that she noticed subtle shifts in people's moods. She startled at faint sounds. She felt the displacement of air in a room. It was a sensitivity that had made her uncle a good cop and that made Caroline good at seeing what others missed. But while that sensitivity could be a gift, it could also spawn worries so profound it threatened to cripple her.

Yes, she understood the attraction of alcohol. She wanted to shut off the sensitivity, too, sometimes. To build a protective barrier between herself and the world . . .

"Are you sure you wouldn't prefer something with a little more to it?" came a voice from beside her.

Caroline turned to see the scarecrow man with the hooked nose leaning up against the bar. Up close, his most prominent feature was a high forehead. Without a hairline, a flock of wrinkles marched up his scalp in jagged furrows.

"No, thanks," she answered, the hairs standing up on the back of her neck.

"You're the newest member of the *SuperSoy* plaintiffs' team, aren't you?"

Caroline just looked at him. How did he know who she was?

"Please excuse my manners. I'm Ian Kennedy. Opposing counsel." He held out a hand.

Hesitating, Caroline took it.

"I'm Caroline—"

"—Auden," he finished.

At her surprised look, he said, "I make it my business to know my adversaries."

He smiled, revealing a tiny gap between his two front teeth.

"I'm new to the *SuperSoy* case, too," he said. "I'll be arguing the *Daubert* motion on behalf of Med-Gen."

Caroline stayed silent. This man had yet to explain why he was standing next to her at a bar in Las Vegas instead of working on his client's *Daubert* briefing wherever it was that he worked when he wasn't stalking opposing counsel in high-end restaurants.

"I just happened to be in town," Kennedy said, smiling innocuously. "When I heard the Plaintiffs' Steering Committee's meeting was, quite coincidentally, here at the same time, I thought I'd come see the competition for myself. Up close, as it were."

Wrinkling her nose at the smell of bullshit, Caroline prepared to deflect questions about the case. Why else would he have followed her into the bar if not to pump her for information?

"I won't ask you to compromise your case," Kennedy said, reading her perfectly. "But I think we can both agree that food manufacturers aren't inherently evil."

Finding nothing wrong with the statement, Caroline nodded.

"These biotech companies are in the business of fixing problems that plague our cash crops—pests, frost, et cetera," he continued, laying out each piece of his argument for her scrutiny. "Biotech companies design plants to thrive. There's nothing wrong with that."

Caroline sat quietly, watching the defense attorney play with his arguments like a cat played with a ball of yarn. But to what end?

"Plants have been hybridized for years," Kennedy said. "Your grandma's roses are probably crossbreeds. Those grandifloras and albas growing in your grandma's garden aren't scandalous. They're just combinations of preexisting genetics. There's nothing new under the sun, really."

"But not like this," Caroline said, deciding to play along. There was no harm in it. And if the conversation gave her a preview of Med-Gen's arguments, that would be useful information for the associate drafting some of the plaintiffs' opposition to those arguments.

"What do you mean?" Kennedy asked, his eyebrows raised in mock surprise.

"You've seen what some of these companies are doing. Taking a gene from a fish and sticking it in a tomato. Inserting human genes into corn. Jamming a spider gene into goats to make Kevlar out of their fur."

Kennedy clucked his tongue. "Those are extreme examples. You can't dispute that some genetically engineered traits are beneficial."

"Maybe so, but you can't mess with Nature and not expect it to bite you back sometimes. Just look what happened to the plaintiffs in this case."

"Oh, we can't be certain of causation. Many of these plaintiffs had preexisting renal conditions. But that's enough debate," Kennedy said, waving a hand as if to dispel the tension.

Caroline silently castigated herself for failing to stop the conversation before he had.

"Congratulations on the job," Kennedy said. "Hale Stern has an excellent reputation. I knew Thompson Hale. He was a very fine lawyer, though he never did pay his associates at the top of the pay scale."

Caroline didn't respond to what might or might not have been a veiled attempt to see if she was susceptible to bribery.

"You really could get a job anywhere," Kennedy said. "Your grades and clerkship were both tops."

Caroline's eyes widened.

"Becoming the editor in chief of the *Journal of Law and Technology* as only a second-year law student was an impressive achievement, too," he continued. "I can see why Louis wanted you."

Caroline felt her face flush. Someone had performed research on her. Deep research.

"I apologize for prying," Kennedy said. "As I said, I like to know my adversaries. You just never know when those adversaries will become . . . friends."

He smiled his gapped smile again and withdrew a business card from his pocket.

"If you ever decide you need a change, that you don't like doing the sorts of things you're doing at Hale Stern, I'd like the opportunity to talk with you. I recognize that young plaintiffs' lawyers like yourself can be idealistic, but I'd like the chance to persuade you that those of us on the defense side aren't all evil . . ."

Kennedy trailed off, his gaze traveling over Caroline's left shoulder toward the entrance of the bar.

Even before she turned, Caroline knew what she'd see.

Louis stood at the entrance. The light of the restaurant behind him ignited his white hair like the halo of an avenging angel.

"It's been a pleasure to meet you," Kennedy said, forcing Caroline to turn back toward him. Pressing the business card into her hand, he bowed slightly before turning and walking away.

Caroline swung back toward where Louis had been standing. But he was gone.

• • •

Caroline found Louis waiting outside the bar, cleaning his glasses. As she approached, he looked up. He regarded her quietly with his colorless eyes before replacing the glasses on his face.

"What did he say to you?" Louis asked.

"He said he's opposing counsel. But he knew all about me. He knew my grades and even some . . . other stuff." She shivered with a combination of revulsion and paranoia.

"Not surprising," Louis said.

"What do you mean? Who is he?"

"Remember what I said about it being highly unlikely that Dr. Heller's death was a hit?" Louis's voice was so quiet that Caroline almost couldn't hear him over the background din.

Caroline nodded.

"Ian Kennedy's presence increases the odds I was wrong," Louis finished.

Caroline's stomach twisted.

"What do you mean?" she asked.

"Kennedy is a rare and dangerous animal. He has a well-earned reputation for making his clients' problems disappear . . . by any means necessary. He knows no rules. He has no scruples." Louis paused, and his gaze darkened. "He's a fixer."

Caroline waited in silence for her boss to elaborate.

"Those of us in the legal profession are generally honorable, if not always decorous," Louis said. "But Kennedy is quite the opposite. He may be decorous, but he is the very opposite of honorable."

"You've had experience with him," Caroline surmised. That much was obvious.

"I lost a huge case because of him. My key witness disappeared on the eve of trial. I'd heard of Kennedy's reputation, of course. I knew the stories. But it wasn't until my witness came to see me, a year after that case was dismissed for lack of evidence, and told me what had happened to him, that I realized all of the rumors about Kennedy are true."

"What did Kennedy do?" Caroline asked.

Louis paused, as if weighing how much to tell her.

"My witness told me he'd come home to find a man with a gun sitting in his living room. He promised my witness that he would never see him again, but that he'd be watching. All the time. Every time this witness dropped his children off at school. Every time he tucked them in at night, this man said he would be watching. He threatened to come for my witness's family if he dared to set foot in the courthouse."

Caroline swallowed hard. While she'd seen witness intimidation in movies, she'd never heard of it happening in real life.

"These tales follow Kennedy around like ghost stories that lawyers tell to younger lawyers to keep them up at night, wondering if they should have gone into another profession," Louis said.

"You're saying he had something to do with Dr. Heller's death," Caroline said, wanting to disbelieve the words even as she uttered them.

"I'm saying it's . . . possible," Louis allowed. "Kennedy will stop at nothing to win—wiretaps, bribes, witness intimidation. Possibly even murder if the price is high enough."

"So, what do we do?" Caroline asked.

"What do we do?" Louis repeated the words slowly. "People like Kennedy never act directly. They never leave any tracks, and they never get caught."

Caroline's stomach twisted as she considered his words. Words that made it sound like she'd stepped into one of those nightmarish movies she preferred not to watch. Let alone live.

"Personally, I'd like to continue," Louis said finally. "I'd like to continue looking for that missing article. But I recognize that Kennedy's presence is worrisome."

Worrisome. It seemed like an almost criminal understatement.

"Kennedy doesn't have a reputation for targeting lawyers," Louis went on. "After all, that sort of thing would leave fingerprints, and it wouldn't help his client's cause since there's always another lawyer there to take over. So I believe we're safe continuing our work. Quiet inquiries into the location of the article shouldn't attract anyone's notice, either."

Caroline heard the truth in Louis's words. Her boss certainly believed what he was saying, but did she? How much did she trust her mentor's evaluation of the potential risks in this arena that bore no resemblance to courtroom proceedings?

"I don't want you to do anything you're uncomfortable doing," Louis continued, anticipating her misgivings. "I could put you on another matter, if you prefer."

Caroline weighed the invitation. Louis was the best litigator in the city, if not the West Coast. His name commanded respect. She'd been lucky that he'd taken a chance on a tech nerd who'd decided to change careers . . .

"I'm okay," she said.

"Good," Louis said with a curt nod and a hint of a smile. "With Kennedy involved, we have no margin for error. Our brief must sing. Dale will get a chance to hammer home our arguments at the hearing, but by the time he takes the podium, the judge will have most likely made up his mind based on the briefs. I want to see an outline tomorrow morning."

"I'll get it done," Caroline said, though finishing the outline had become the least of her worries.

• • •

The lamp cast a circle of light around the hotel room desk.

The outline glowed on Caroline's laptop.

Binders of scientific articles sat before her. Arrows filled the margins of the articles. So much information. So many concepts. Some relevant. Some irrelevant. She needed to extract what mattered. Fast. She could not digest and ponder at her leisure. She needed this to happen. Now.

But she couldn't banish her thoughts of Kennedy. He'd seemed mild, almost harmless. Yet if Louis was right, his surface affability hid a sociopathic personality. She shuddered at the possibility that she'd spoken with the man who'd engineered Dr. Heller's "accident." And she balked at visiting the dead scientist's widow.

Caroline's eyes settled on the words she'd scrawled across her legal pad: Yvonne Heller's address. The one idea she'd had since arriving in Las Vegas had been almost alarmingly easy to pursue. Reverse phone lookups weren't hard. With Yvonne's cell number, finding her physical address had taken Caroline mere seconds. But now the thought of getting into her car, driving to the widow's house, and knocking on her door seemed insane . . . but necessary.

Caroline had relegated the dog-eared and marked-up *Scziewizcs* decision to a distant corner of the hotel room's desk. But she couldn't avoid its implications. Without some scientific literature establishing a direct link, the judge might very well throw the case out, leaving tens of thousands of people dead or destitute.

Again, her gaze settled on Yvonne's address, and again, she recalled her conversation with the widow. The stilted, lurching speech pattern. Guarded and awkward, moving in fits and starts from hostility to regret. As if Yvonne had been . . . scared.

A visceral wave of nausea rippled down Caroline's esophagus.

She mentally cursed Louis. His description of Kennedy's misdeeds had fed her paranoia until it felt real. But it might not be real, Caroline reminded herself. Indeed, it was far more likely that she'd built a castle of worry in the sky. And then furnished it and moved in.

Turning back to her laptop, Caroline took a calming breath.

The outline was real. Ambrose was real, as were Feinberg and Tercero. And she needed to pull them together into a coherent outline. Now.

Hunting for gems of information she could string together as if on a necklace, her fingers flew across the keyboard and her mind whirred, revving to top speed. A wired and antsy vibration, amped up and electric, hummed through her body and her mind and the pieces came into focus. Bright and useful, each shone with necessity and carried inside it the question that would lead her to the next piece of information. One puzzle piece, then the next. Methodically but quickly she fit one in and moved on to the next. The need to create coherence out of chaos drove her forward. Until time dropped away, and she flew.

When Caroline looked up again, three hours had passed.

She sat back in her chair and gave her work a frank appraisal. The outline was good. As far as it went, anyway. She'd done a lot with a little. And yet it wasn't the irrefutable piece of logic that she needed it to be. It couldn't be. Not without a direct link.

Pushing back from the desk, Caroline walked over to the window that overlooked the frenetic, blinking neon landscape below. Dancing fountains and pyrotechnics lit the evening sky.

The display of frivolity and color contrasted with Caroline's pensive mood.

Maybe Kennedy was right. Maybe the pieces just weren't there. In all the published science, no researcher had drawn a direct connection between SuperSoy and kidney damage.

Sure, Franklin Heller might have drawn that direct connection, but he'd never published anything. He'd never even submitted his article for peer review. That meant no one had vetted it. For all anyone knew, his methods might have been shoddy. His reasoning might have been weak. It might not even be worth finding. And that meant the plaintiffs' case might never get any stronger than it was right now . . . which wasn't very strong.

No, Caroline thought. Just . . . no. She would not go gentle into that good night. The words from the Dylan Thomas poem came to her like a soothing whisper. Her mother had played a recording of it daily in the months after Caroline's dad had left. Maybe Joanne had harbored hopes of luring her husband back. Caroline, for her part, had fought to keep her father in her own life. She'd done what she could to thwart his painful absence. And he'd even started reaching out to her. In recent months, there'd been invitations to come visit him in Connecticut. Finally. Maybe too late. After so much awkwardness for so long.

The point was, she was a fighter. The death of one scientist didn't have to mean the death of the case. They could still win. With even one article showing a direct link—even an unpublished, non-peer-reviewed article—she could write a persuasive argument. She knew she could. She could take a stained piece of newsprint and fold it into origami.

Caroline returned to the desk and lifted the komboloi beads from where they lay beside the laptop. She ran the beads over her hands. Cool and smooth, they grounded her.

What next?

What of Kennedy?

If he'd really killed Heller, then her assignment had become something far more dangerous than hunting for a missing article. Safety dictated stepping aside. Even if they might lose.

And yet, if Med-Gen had killed Dr. Heller, he must have written something incendiary. His article must have been devastating to SuperSoy. That meant it was a piece of evidence well worth finding. Even if it hadn't been published or peer reviewed, it might be good. Really good. She just needed to find it.

But that meant visiting Yvonne Heller.

That meant stepping out from behind the laptop, leaving the safety of her ivory tower, and walking into the storm.

Watching the play of lights across the darkness of her room, Caroline made up her mind.

She'd visit Yvonne when she got home.

CHAPTER 6

Yvonne Heller sat in a rouge silk armchair. She wore linen trousers pressed with a confident crease. With unblemished skin the color of milk chocolate, she seemed of indeterminate age, though Caroline guessed she was in her early fifties.

"I don't have the article," Yvonne said in her refined alto. "I couldn't find it anywhere after Franklin's . . . accident."

Yvonne's eyes traveled to the window of the sitting room. Caroline tracked her gaze to the front drive. There was no one there.

"But you're not sure it was an accident?" Caroline asked slowly.

"The physical evidence at the scene was next to nil. Franklin's body wasn't found until the next morning. After the tide had come up and gone back down again . . ." Yvonne winced and Caroline imagined the widow's residual trauma at having identified Franklin's hill-battered and sea-scoured corpse for the coroner.

"The medical examiner said the injuries were consistent with a fall down the steep hillside," Yvonne continued.

"Except . . ." Caroline prompted.

Yvonne shifted in her chair. "Except these biotech companies spend a fortune developing these organisms. And Med-Gen was so . . . aggressive."

"Aggressive?" Caroline echoed.

"We began getting phone calls from Med-Gen's affiliated nonprofit entities around the time Franklin began working on that article. And then, when the editor of the *Fielding Journal* signaled to Franklin that he wanted to publish it . . . that's when we started receiving those calls almost daily."

"What were those calls?" Caroline asked. "Were they bribes? Threats?"

"Oh, it wasn't as blatant as all that. They were always unsolicited offers of grant money. They were always couched as interest in my husband's *scholarly research.*"

"But you knew it was more than that," Caroline surmised.

"We both did," Yvonne said. "Franklin always rejected money from the biotech and drug companies to fund his research. He raised his own money from independent private sources. Clean sources. He feared his impartiality would be tainted otherwise."

"He doubted his own integrity?"

"It's just human nature," Yvonne said. "A scientist who takes money wants to avoid conflicts with his patron. You begin to see what you want to see. You don't do the experiments that will show you the things you don't want to know. That's why Franklin always insisted on his own funding."

Caroline eyed the elegant sitting room. Hand-dyed wool rugs. Roman blinds fashioned of raw silk. It was clear the Hellers liked nice things. Maybe Franklin had been the one doing the decorating. But Yvonne's appearance suggested that it was far more likely that it was her taste that drove the Hellers' decor.

"That couldn't have been easy for you," Caroline said.

"It wasn't." The bitterness in Yvonne's tone held an echo of past arguments. "Did you know my husband used to be a successful plastic surgeon? His practice was very lucrative. I should know. I did the books. But he gave it all up for research."

The corners of Yvonne's mouth curved downward.

"I take it that research was less lucrative?" Caroline prompted.

"Much less. We had to sell Franklin's medical group's office building to fund his first research project."

"That sounds hard." Caroline inclined her head in sympathy. Even though she'd never lived as lavishly as Yvonne did, she could see the widow's struggle written on her face.

"I didn't like the change," Yvonne admitted. "For years, I resisted it. I only recently came to accept that this was our life together now."

Caroline lifted her eyebrows, encouraging the widow to elaborate.

"About six months ago, I started winding up the medical group," Yvonne continued, "closing the old bank accounts, auditing the group's remaining assets, going through old paperwork. That sort of thing. It's been an interesting process because my husband stashed assets all over the place."

"What do you mean?" Caroline asked.

"The medical group held all sorts of property, including several accounts at various banks," Yvonne said. "Nothing of any significant value." Caroline could almost hear Yvonne's unspoken *unfortunately* at the end of the sentence.

"Is it possible your husband stashed the article somewhere, too?" Caroline asked. "Maybe in a safe deposit box at one of those banks?"

Yvonne shook her head. "He didn't have a safe deposit box. But that article was his proudest achievement. I have to believe he planned for the possibility of . . . of this." A flash of pain flickered across Yvonne's strong features. "My husband was always the smartest guy in the room. If he did hide the article, it would be somewhere clever. His text message might have something to do with it."

"Text message?" Caroline's hands prickled.

"Franklin and I always did puzzles together. Anagrams. Number games. Decoding messages. We're both math people. Or he . . . was." Yvonne paused, her forehead wrinkling, as if in dismay at the past tense that had thrust itself into her diction against her will.

"Anyway, his final text message was just a bunch of gibberish," Yvonne finished.

"Do you still have it?" Caroline asked.

Yvonne leaned down and lifted up the Gucci handbag beside her armchair. Withdrawing the phone, she scrolled with an elegant finger.

Caroline noted that Yvonne's nails were well manicured but very short.

"Ah, here it is. 'B-a-b-c-6-20-16.5-14-9-7-13-1,'" Yvonne said.

"Just a second," Caroline said, pulling a legal pad from her bag. Louis had asked that she keep track of her research in longhand. She'd comply with that request. Even though it was stupid. Even though it yielded notes that weren't searchable or otherwise useful in any of the ways digital information could be.

As the ink dried, Caroline eyed the cryptic text. The characters glowed with significance, though she could not yet tell what that significance might be.

"I haven't figured out that puzzle," Yvonne said. "Neither have the police."

"They investigated?" Caroline asked.

"Yes, but they didn't get very far. The disappearance of first the article and then Annie Wong certainly suggested some kind of wrongdoing. And those phone calls . . . But the police couldn't find anything. No leads." Yvonne shook her head. "The coroner ended up ruling it an accident."

"But what about the text message?" Caroline asked. "Weren't they suspicious about it?"

Yvonne grimaced. "Franklin's body wasn't discovered immediately, so it's impossible to pinpoint when he died in relation to when he sent his text. In light of our past games with numbers, that text might not mean anything beyond him telling me what he was picking up for dinner that night. Also, the phone had been badly compromised by the ocean. The police couldn't even fingerprint it."

Caroline studied her legal pad. Her eyes traced the strange text. Perhaps it meant nothing. Or perhaps Dr. Heller hadn't been dead when he'd hit the beach. Perhaps he'd told his wife where he'd hidden the article that his wife described as his proudest achievement.

Yvonne opened her purse and withdrew a card emblazoned with a badge.

"The police are looking for any leads," she said, handing the card to Caroline.

Caroline wrote down the number on the card. As she handed it back to Yvonne, the door of the sitting room swung open to reveal a lithe middle-aged woman with honey-colored skin and close-cropped black hair speckled with gray. The woman pushed through the door with the easy familiarity of one who had passed that way many times before. She held a wine bottle in one hand and the stems of two Bordeaux glasses in the other hand.

"I know it's early, but I thought we could—" The woman stopped midsentence when she saw Caroline. "Oh, I'm so sorry. I didn't know—"

"Can I offer you something to drink?" Yvonne said to Caroline with a gracious smile. "This is my dear friend Trina Astin, from the club. She's been helping me since Franklin died."

"Nothing for me," Caroline said, eyeing the wineglass that she knew had not been intended for her. Suddenly the image of a scantily clad barmaid soaring up the wine tower at Safe House appeared in her mind. And the big man standing at the base of the tower in front of a combination lock . . .

"Did Dr. Heller have a safe?" Caroline asked.

"Not here at home," Yvonne answered, "but he might have had one installed at his office. I wouldn't know. I never spent much time there."

"Do you mind if I take a look?" Caroline asked.

"Of course. I could take you there now, if you'd like."

• • •

Stepping into Dr. Heller's office, Caroline's first impression was of calm, quiet order. Framed pictures hung on the walls of ships on high seas, placid ports at sunset, playing on the ocean view that Caroline could see through the window. In the center of the room, two chairs sat before a low coffee table covered by a chess set.

Caroline considered possible locations for a safe. There was no rug, and the long-plank wood floors gave no indication of any safe beneath it. Maybe the walls?

She approached the picture of the ship struggling to clear a cresting wave. She lifted the bottom and peeked behind it.

She found nothing.

She moved on to the picture of the sunset-streaked port.

Still nothing.

Stepping back to the center of the office, Caroline put her hands on her hips. She turned in a slow circle, her eyes skating across the room.

Everything was in its place. The books lined up in neat rows on the shelves. The white lab coat hanging on a hook beside the door. A heavy coating of dust lay across the floor and all the furniture, visible in the slanting sunlight.

Something wasn't right. Something was wrong with the scene.

The answer hit Caroline: the undisturbed space. If Franklin's death had been a hit, intended to keep him from publishing that article, his laboratory office should have been ransacked. Someone should have scoured it for all copies of the article. At the very least, someone should have stolen his computer . . . or hacked it.

"Do you mind if I take a look at your husband's computer?" Caroline asked.

Yvonne's eyes narrowed in distrust.

"I used to be a software engineer," Caroline explained. "My dad's a cybersecurity consultant. I might be able to figure out what happened to that article."

After another second of consideration, Yvonne nodded her assent.

"The password is 'Turing,'" she said.

"Like the British cryptographer?" Caroline asked.

"Yes. My husband loved all things World War II."

Caroline sat down in the faded leather armchair and fired up the dead scientist's computer. His desktop held links to research apps and spreadsheets. No sign of the article.

She checked his documents folder. Still nothing.

Everyone knew the article had once been on Franklin's computer. The question was: Where did it go? With quick keystrokes, she began probing the possibilities.

"What are you doing?" Yvonne's voice floated from over Caroline's left shoulder.

Caroline startled at the sound. She'd forgotten that Yvonne was there.

"When you delete something, it isn't really gone," Caroline explained. "It just goes to the unallocated space on the hard drive."

Yvonne fell silent.

Caroline was glad the widow hadn't pried into how she had learned to search places most people wouldn't—or couldn't—touch. Or why she was so good at it.

Using the GREP utility, Caroline scanned the unallocated space for bits containing three words: *SuperSoy*, *kidney*, and *injury*. So long as those words appeared somewhere on the bits of the hard drive, she'd find them.

When the utility finished running, Caroline sat back, her brow wrinkling. "There's nothing in Franklin's unallocated space." Not only had GREP failed to retrieve anything, but all of the bits were zeroed out.

Eyeing the overwritten bits, Caroline shuddered. No one had yet been able to say for certain that Dr. Heller had been murdered. And yet here, in the zeroed-out bits, was proof that someone had destroyed data on the dead scientist's computer. It was an ominous sign.

"What's wrong?" Yvonne asked.

"Someone ran a tool to overwrite the unallocated space. They were very thorough. Whatever was once on this computer is now gone."

"Did someone hack it?" Yvonne asked.

"Maybe," Caroline said, moving quickly to check the computer's event logs. Hackers avoided leaving tracks. They wiped event logs, router logs, and IDS logs to remove all records of remote connections. Empty event logs would bolster the conclusion that someone had accessed Dr. Heller's computer remotely.

But to Caroline's surprise, none of the logs on Franklin's computer had been cleared.

She stared at the intact logs in dismay. If the computer hadn't been hacked, that meant that someone had sat down in the same chair where she now sat and had deleted the articles, right here on this computer.

"Who had access to this office?" Caroline asked.

"Almost no one," Yvonne answered. "Franklin. Me. Franklin's research partner, Dr. Wong. You can't get in here without going through security."

Caroline remembered the guards they'd passed. Franklin had taken security seriously. Far more seriously than most research scientists. Not that it had helped him in the end.

"What about lab techs?" Caroline asked. "How did they share research with Dr. Heller?"

"They shared links."

Caroline pivoted around to make eye contact with Yvonne. "Would those links contain data used in the article?"

"Yes. They're over here," Yvonne said, pointing to a folder on the monitor.

Caroline quickly navigated to the list of links. Her fingers tingled with the possibility of retrieving some part of the lost article. Even without the article itself, perhaps the data would allow her to show a direct connection between SuperSoy and kidney failure . . .

She opened the first link.

A message flashed onto the screen: *Error 404—page not found. The page you are trying to reach does not exist.*

"Damn it," she muttered, opening the next link and getting another 404 error.

By the third link, Caroline knew she'd find nothing.

"These links are all dead," she said, turning back to Yvonne. "Someone took them down."

In response, Yvonne just shook her head.

Caroline sat back in the chair and let out a long breath. Her eyes wandered across the objects on Franklin's desk. A hardbound copy of the *Physicians' Desk Reference* lay on one corner. A bust of Winston Churchill sat next to it. On the other side of the desk were two framed pictures covered in a thin coating of dust. Untouched. Undisturbed. Just like the rest of the room.

The office had given up its secrets, the article, without a fight. But why? How?

Leaning forward, Caroline lifted a framed picture of Franklin standing with a small woman in a lab coat. The woman was birdlike, with jet-black hair, crescent eyes, and refined, tiny features. Franklin had close-cropped hair, graying at the temples. The woman only came up to Franklin's chest, giving her an almost childlike scale.

Caroline looked over at Yvonne with a question in her eyes.

"Dr. Wong," Yvonne said. "She worked with my husband for the last ten years."

"Was your husband tall?" Caroline asked.

"Yes, but Annie's small. Just a wisp of a thing. But a heck of a scientist. That's what Franklin always said about her."

"Would she have a copy of the article?" Caroline asked.

"Maybe. But I haven't seen her since Franklin died. She didn't even come to the funeral."

Caroline could hear the chagrin tingeing Yvonne's voice.

"Annie's boyfriend came, but not her," Yvonne added, wrinkling her nose slightly as if she'd smelled something unpleasant. Caroline got the impression the elegant socialite didn't like Dr. Wong's boyfriend very much.

"Maybe Dr. Wong got scared when Dr. Heller died," Caroline offered. She paused. "Maybe she . . . ran."

Yvonne met and held Caroline's eyes. In Yvonne's gaze, Caroline saw a reflection of the maelstrom of unspoken worries in her own.

"Wherever she is, I hope she's okay," Yvonne said. Her brow knit with concern. "Annie doesn't have a lot of family to lean on . . ."

Caroline recalled her frosty conversation with Annie's father and the evident rift between the elder and younger Dr. Wongs.

Replacing the picture, Caroline cast a final glance back at the faces of the people who'd written the missing article. Two people who knew what SuperSoy did. Both were gone now. One to the grave. The other to Lord knew where . . .

Caroline studied the only other picture on the desk. In the image, Franklin wore compression shorts, a tank top, and a racing bib with his runner number printed on it in big block numbers. He had draped a long arm around Yvonne, who squinted into the sun. Behind them, an archway of balloons anchored between two palm trees announced the finish line for a race.

Something familiar on the runner's bib caught Caroline's eye.

"What does *BABC* stand for?" she asked, pointing at the cursive letters printed above Franklin's runner number. It was the same string of letters that appeared at the beginning of Franklin's final text message.

"Bon Air Beach Club," said Yvonne. "That picture was taken at the end of the club's annual charity run."

Caroline had heard of the Bon Air Beach Club. Restricted to the wealthiest, most well-connected souls in the city, it rarely admitted new members, preferring to fill its membership rolls with the scions of prior generations.

"Are you members?" Caroline asked. The subject was delicate. Many of the clubs that dotted the shores of Los Angeles still had restrictive policies against admitting people of color. If not in their official bylaws, then in their admission practices they'd maintained the same level of homogeneity for over a century.

"Yes," Yvonne said. "Franklin's father was Terrence Heller. The congressman. He was the club's first African-American member. The club still hasn't come around on admitting gay members, but it was far ahead of the curve on race. Bon Air was always a part of Franklin's life, and so it became a part of mine after we married."

Caroline considered the location of Franklin's death, just a mile or so south of the Bon Air Beach Club.

"Do you think that BABC in Franklin's text message refers to the club? The letters are the same," Caroline pointed out, even though it was obvious.

"I hadn't noticed that," Yvonne said, breaking eye contact.

Caroline's eyes narrowed. Could it really have been an oversight?

"Maybe Franklin hid a copy of his article somewhere at the club?" Caroline suggested. She watched Yvonne carefully for her reaction.

Yvonne shrugged. "I wouldn't know."

"Can you get me into the club?" Caroline asked.

Yvonne sighed. "I suppose, but I'd need to make special arrangements. Some of our celebrity members have had some trouble with the paparazzi. I might need to get board approval to allow a nonmember to wander around the facility."

Caroline held her eyes.

"I guess I could see what I could do," Yvonne said in a flat tone.

Yvonne's lukewarm commitment gave Caroline no confidence.

"The sooner the better," Caroline said, even as her mind raced for other ways to locate the missing article in case Yvonne's efforts to arrange for her to search the club were as anemic as her enthusiasm for the idea.

"What about Annie Wong's boyfriend?" Caroline asked. "Perhaps he knows where Annie went. Do you have a number for him?"

"I don't know it, but I could probably find his address. We've gone to art shows at his loft from time to time. I'm sure I have his address around somewhere."

"Please," Caroline implored.

"I'll find it for you. But I should warn you. Henrik can be a bit . . . much."

Caroline cocked her head at the vague warning.

"Let's put it this way," Yvonne said. "He's not the most refined soul."

• • •

"What the fuck do you want?"

That's how Henrik Stengaard had answered the door when Caroline knocked.

Shouting to be heard through the rusted metal door, she'd explained her business. When the door had creaked, groaned, and grated its way open, one word had come to Caroline's mind: *Viking*. Thick as a standing stone at Stonehenge and as blond as a poster child for the Aryan Youth, Henrik exuded a physical presence that Caroline could equate only to Nordic marauders. Or football players. Swallowing a thick lump of trepidation, Caroline had entered the loft.

Now she stood in the center of the live/work space, surrounded by canvases mounted on easels. Some shimmered, still wet in the afternoon sun. Unlike the behemoth who had created them, the images were soft and subtle, plays on light and shadow exhibiting a sensitivity incongruent with the artist's brute appearance. Admiring Henrik's abstract canvases, Caroline reflected that Henrik's art was not the sort of thing that Louis would ever collect. No, her boss's taste tended toward only the most expensive old masters.

"My life's a goddamn disaster," Henrik said, pacing his home like a neurotic leopard in a too-small zoo enclosure. "I've got a gallery show starting downtown in a week. I need to finish these canvases."

The artist's big hands gestured around the space, sweeping the accumulated chaos within their reach. "But I can't focus. Ever since Annie disappeared—" He ran a hand through his shaggy mane of blond hair. "Look, I get why you're here, but I'm not sure there's anything I can tell you that'll help you find her."

Caroline watched him pacing back and forth across the vaulted workspace, from the cluttered kitchen area that reeked of old food to the sleeping area demarked by a spray-painted shoji screen. The artist looked like he walked a razor's edge. She feared what would happen if he fell off. But she'd come for a reason. She had to ask her questions. Even if they pushed him off the edge.

"Did Annie leave any hint where she went?" she asked.

Henrik stopped pacing and just shook his head no. He swallowed heavily, as if jamming his emotions, his words back down his throat.

Caroline looked with sympathy at the artist. He looked like he didn't get out much. She wondered if he had any friends to whom he'd been able to vent his pent-up emotions.

"That must be hard," she offered.

"Hard?" Henrik put his paint-spattered hands on his hips and glared at Caroline. "This whole thing's totally fucked. One second Annie's saying she wants us to move slowly—she doesn't want to move in with me too fast. Fine, I get it. She loves her house in Santa Monica. But then the next second, she's moving in. She's sold her place. Great. We're moving ahead as a couple. Just like I wanted. But then, a half a second after that, she's leaving town. It's a fucking smorgasbord of mixed messages."

"How was she doing before she left? Was she . . . preoccupied or anything?" Caroline asked. She sensed that with the slightest prodding, the sluice gates would open . . . and hopefully bring a flood of information, not rage.

"If by preoccupied you mean, was she totally shutting down on me, then yes, she was preoccupied," Henrik said. "I tried to find out what the hell was going on with her, but she wouldn't say anything."

"That must have been frustrating."

"Frustrating? It was fucking terrifying." Henrik glowered.

The artist took a breath and tried to compose himself. "You got to understand, Annie doesn't trust people easily. But she trusts me. Or she used to," Henrik said, his voice thick with emotion. "I wanted to be there for her. God, I tried to be. Even after she left town, I kept on trying. I called her a dozen times. I told her I'd go wherever she was. Screw my gallery show."

"But she wouldn't tell you where she was?"

"Worse. She left me a fucking video message breaking up with me." The artist's voice rose, his anger covering his pain.

"She broke up with you?" Caroline's eyebrows shot up her forehead.

"Yeah." Henrik's square jaw tightened, jutting slightly. "She didn't even give me the courtesy of calling me. She just sent a damn video message."

"Can I see it?" Caroline asked. She knew the message could be an upsetting, intensely personal reminder of love and loss for the artist, but it could also hold some clue about Annie's whereabouts. She had to see it. If Annie Wong could be found, perhaps the article could be, too.

In answer, Henrik reached into his pocket and withdrew his phone. He tilted it toward Caroline, his large hand dwarfing the device.

"This was from about a week after she left," he said, hitting "Play."

The screen ignited with a shaky video of a woman with long black hair. Although Annie's hair was pulled back, loose wisps caught the wind and whipped across her face. The lighting was dim and the angle was close up—the camera held only arm's length away. Caroline couldn't make out anything in the background.

"I'm sorry, Henrik," Annie began, "but you've got to stop calling me. I don't blame you for not understanding. I barely do myself." The words were spoken quickly, as if she'd been afraid to stop her momentum. But then she paused. "Even if it doesn't seem like it right now, please know that I really do love you." Her eyes softened. "I hope you can move on." Behind her, a passing light flashed by, like a car driving on a road in the distance, and then the video message ended.

When Caroline looked back at Henrik, his eyes shimmered with unshed tears.

"That's it," he choked out, pocketing the phone. "That's all she fucking said. Over a year together, and that's how she ends it." He opened and closed his hands in impotent frustration.

"Can you send that to me?" Caroline asked, her compassion coloring her voice. "Maybe something in it will give me some clue where she went."

Henrik didn't answer. Caroline waited. She knew intense people needed to find their own level. Saying anything to them in the midst of a rant was like stepping into the firing line. She had the bullet holes to prove it.

"On one condition," Henrik finally said, his mouth tense as he pulled out the phone again. "If you find her, you tell her I'd really like to talk to her. I need some closure."

"Of course," Caroline agreed and then gave him her e-mail address.

Henrik keyed in Caroline's e-mail, stabbed a button on his phone, then jammed it back into his pocket. He ran two paint-spattered hands through his hair.

"I hope you find her. Because Lord knows, I can't get any fucking closure now." To prove his point, the artist stalked over to an armoire standing in the corner of the vaulted space. He threw open its door, revealing women's clothes on hangers, shirts folded on shelves, and, on the floor, a neat row of women's shoes.

"It's like someone died around here," he ground out, "but not really, because I don't know where she went and I can't be sure she isn't coming back. I can't get rid of her stuff. I can't move on. I can't do anything."

Even as she thought of how to soothe the raging tornado in front of her, Caroline scanned the contents of the armoire beside him. Tucked among the shoes, she noticed a striped tube with marks on it. She squatted down and lifted up the object, holding it up to the light. The tube was clear.

"What is this?" she asked.

"A flowmeter," Henrik said, the request for information grounding his swirling discord. "It's one of Nolan's. That's Annie's five-year-old son. He's a really special kid."

"Five years . . . that's before you began going out. He's not yours?"

"No, but I love him like he's my own. I can't believe he's fucking gone, too." Henrik's pale eyes flickered up toward the ceiling of the loft, as if begging indifferent angels to help him out.

"And he's got asthma?"

Henrik nodded his large head. "When he'd get asthma attacks, we'd use a flowmeter to check how much oxygen he was getting. It was pretty scary. It got a lot better when Annie got Nolan into that drug trial last year."

"Drug trial?"

"A clinical trial," Henrik said. "For a new asthma medicine. It's called Telexo. It might get approved by the FDA next year, but for now, it's only available to people in the drug trials. We spent some scary nights in emergency rooms before that drug came along. It was a godsend."

Caroline considered Annie's disappearance in light of this new information. Leaving town was one thing. Leaving town with an asthmatic five-year-old dependent on an experimental drug protocol was something entirely different. If Annie had fled, she must have really believed her life was in danger. She would have weighed the stress on a child of leaving school, his neighborhood, and everyone he knew against . . . survival.

"When did Annie disappear?" Caroline asked.

"Right after her boss died last month. Like two days later. She packed up some stuff for her and Nolan, and just . . . left." Henrik's eyes began to tear. He wiped the offending moisture away with the back of his hand. "If you find her, just remember to tell her that I'd like to talk."

The big artist sat down at the dining room table and buried his face in his hands.

"I can't believe this fucking happened to me," he said, his big frame shaking with pent-up emotion, though he still would not allow himself to cry.

Caroline took a step toward him, her hand reaching for his shoulder. "I'm sorry—"

"Please leave," Henrik growled, jabbing one long finger at the door.

Without another word, Caroline slipped quietly out of the loft.

• • •

Frustration welled in Caroline's chest.

Louis handed Caroline a ream of hand-marked pages. "As soon as my edits are in, I want our brief out the door. If it isn't filed by four o'clock New York time today, the district court will bounce it. That gives you an hour."

Caroline frowned. Of course she knew the deadline. The last few days had been laser focused on getting the brief filed. Ever since she'd gotten back from her unfruitful visit to Henrik's loft, she'd been pushing hard to write the inferential reasoning section and get the *Daubert* brief filed. Louis's last-minute rounds of edits to her argument had made her scramble, but she still had time to make the filing deadline.

"I'll get it done," she said, controlling her annoyance. She knew her reaction to her boss's tone had more to do with her own failures than anything he'd said.

"I'm going to go to the club first thing tomorrow morning to look around. I'm not giving up on finding the article. The court will still accept scientific evidence until tomorrow afternoon," she said.

"Fine," Louis said, waving one hand. "It's just a shame you failed to arrange to search that social club any sooner."

Caroline's face flushed. "I've done everything I could to get in there." And she had. Leery of calling Yvonne, she had sent her a letter by overnight messenger, begging Yvonne to arrange for her to come to the club. She had just about given up hope of receiving a response when a short note had arrived at the office via snail mail. On a milky-white embossed card, the note stated only:

All set for BABC Oct. 6, 8:30 a.m.

She forced herself to take a breath. "We still have time. It isn't too late."

"Indeed," Louis acquiesced. "And I do appreciate your commitment to this case."

"Thanks, but my commitment to the case means nothing if I can't find that article," Caroline said quietly. She expected more of herself. So did Louis.

She stepped up to Louis's desk, extending a piece of paper toward her boss. "This is the signature page for the brief. You can sign it now. Then, once I get your other edits in, Silvia's standing by to scan the whole thing and upload it onto the district court's e-filing system."

But Louis didn't take the page from her.

"You should do the honors," he said instead.

Caroline's chest warmed at the unexpected compliment, especially coming so soon on the heels of Louis's disappointment in her inability to locate the missing article. She'd hoped to get her name on the *Daubert* brief as one of the lawyers working on the case. Being asked to sign, signifying that she was the author, was an honor.

"I appreciate the offer, but I can't sign it," she said. "You're the only one with pro hac vice status, so you have to sign. The New York court won't let anyone else appear without permission."

"Very well," Louis said, pulling a Montblanc pen from his penholder and twisting off the cap. He positioned the page on his ink blotter and scrawled his name in big looping letters, finished with a flourish.

He blew on the page to dry the ink before handing it back to Caroline.

Caroline looked thoughtfully down at the executed signature page.

"You know, since you have pro hac vice status, you could also argue the *Daubert* motion. The court would let you." She chose her words carefully.

"I have no intention of arguing. It isn't our role. This is Dale's show." Louis searched her face. "What's going on, Ms. Auden?"

Caroline paused before stepping out into the potential minefield. In her sprint to find the article, to locate Annie Wong, and to pull together the brief, she hadn't had much time to worry about the next big problem looming on the horizon. But it was time to deal with it.

"Dale's supposed to be preparing to argue this *Daubert* motion in a few days, right?"

Louis nodded.

"To help him out, we sent him a binder of all of the key articles—so he could study up, so he'd be ready to answer any questions the judge had about the science." Caroline paused. "I don't think he's read any of them."

"None?" Louis asked.

"None," Caroline said. "I've tried talking with him about them, but he keeps blowing me off. He isn't responding to my e-mails or calls. I think he's avoiding me."

Louis rose from his desk and walked to the window. He looked down on his metropolitan kingdom, lord of the honking cars and motorcycles far below on the streets of Los Angeles. Long white clouds streaked the cobalt-blue sky of midday.

"This is . . . concerning," he muttered. Though his back was still to her, Caroline could feel the tension rolling off his hunched shoulders. "But we need to be sensitive to the politics . . ."

He turned toward Caroline, his pale eyes flashing with sudden intensity.

"Prepare summaries of the articles. Just the five most important ones. No more than a paragraph on each. Top-level information. Fourteen-point font. Boldfaced headings. No paragraph should be more than two inches long on the page. Get it to Dale now. I'm going to follow up with him personally. We'll make sure he's ready."

Caroline scribbled down his instructions, then looked back up, waiting for the next barrage of orders.

But instead, her boss's gaze shifted over to the chessboard beside his window.

In the bright sun, each of the pieces cast a sharp shadow on the playing field.

"And please, see what you can find at that club tomorrow," he finished softly without looking away from the chessboard.

CHAPTER 7

At the early hour, the club's breezeway was quiet except for the rush of cars on the Pacific Coast Highway, the broad road carved into the base of the crumbling cliffs that rose up behind the club's grand driveway. Sunshine lit the droplets of dew still clinging to the club's gray shingles, igniting them like a scattering of diamonds.

Despite the calm of her surroundings, Caroline's head throbbed. She tried not to think about the fact that if her errand failed, they'd likely lose. But in trying not to think of it, she felt the stakes of the case in her bones. Her breath came short and shallow, as if her lungs didn't have enough room for a full inhalation.

She closed her eyes and forced herself to breathe slowly. She hated that she had to fight with her own nervous system. It was a major impediment to being a badass.

"Excuse me," came a muffled voice from beside her.

Caroline opened her eyes.

She found a Filipino valet in a starched white uniform standing at the passenger-side window of her car.

"Here for breakfast?" the valet asked. His mirrored sunglasses reflected Caroline's face back at her. She noted the dark shadows under her eyes. She'd stayed up late preparing materials for Dale. If he would read them, then the bludgeoned sensation in her head would be worth it. And if he didn't? She had no answer.

"Yvonne Heller arranged for me to have a look around," Caroline said, hoping that Yvonne had, in fact, arranged for her to have a look around.

"Ah, yes. You must be Caroline Auden. We've been told to expect you."

Caroline sent a silent thanks to Yvonne Heller.

"Nice car. It's a classic, isn't it?" the valet said.

Caroline quirked a half smile. The Ford Mustang GT was old. But classic? Fast cars had been her father's single extravagance. A strange incongruence in the usually reserved man. Caroline had inherited the car when he'd moved back east. It had been the only good thing about his departure. Held together with bumper stickers and duct tape, it probably didn't qualify as a classic. But she loved it anyway.

"It's classic, all right." She smiled back.

"Can I park it for you?"

Glancing in her rearview mirror at the pile of clothes and books in the backseat, Caroline shook her head. The valet didn't need to see her mobile closet up close.

"I'll park it myself," she said.

When Caroline returned to the doors of the club, the valet waved her through with another radiant smile and a promise to help her in any way he could.

Inside the club, Caroline found similar offers of assistance from everyone she encountered, from the cleaning crew to the tennis pros. In their navy-blue polo shirts with the club's logo embossed in gold thread, the staff exuded professionalism and courtesy. So much courtesy, in fact, that Caroline was glad when she finally found a quiet corridor where she could think, uninterrupted.

Walking slowly down the carpeted hallway, Caroline tried to imagine where a man she'd never met would've hidden something she wasn't sure existed.

If it did exist, that article had been Dr. Heller's crowning achievement. He'd braved threats because of it. He'd forgone a more lucrative career for it. He'd have wanted someone to find it.

So then, his last act might've been to tell his wife where he'd hidden a copy of the article.

The *babc* in the text message had to mean the Bon Air Beach Club. The rest of the text—the numbers strung together with dashes—looked very much like a combination.

Now, she just needed to find the lock.

Stopping in front of the club's directory, Caroline studied the floor plan until she found what she sought: the locker room.

• • •

"I can't help you," said the desk attendant. The twentysomething man wore the same blue shirt with the club's crest embroidered over his pocket, except on him, the dark blue picked up the color of his eyes, making him look like he'd just stepped out of a surf wear catalog. Behind him, rows of towels sat rolled in cubbyholes beside terry-cloth bathrobes up on hooks.

Caroline opened her mouth to speak, but the desk attendant cut her off.

"Dr. Heller's locker was cleaned out the week after he died. It's already been reassigned to someone else."

Caroline grimaced. Another dead end.

"That sure was fast," she grumbled.

"The board's always on top of stuff like that," the attendant said. "They run this place like a tight ship. They're even more aggro since they had that gnarly plumbing accident."

"What do you mean?"

A conspiratorial glint entered the attendant's eyes. He looked around to make sure no one else was within earshot.

"Six months ago, a major pipe burst in the sewage system. The smell was totally rank. It wasn't so good for attracting new members." He quirked an amused grin.

Caroline smiled back.

"The smell of raw sewage wasn't too popular with our membership, either. Everyone went nutso. There were review committees to figure out what happened. There were petitions to fire all of the board members. But then the board bankrolled a major overhaul and saved their asses."

"In other words, they fixed the plumbing?" Caroline translated.

"Yep," said the desk attendant. "Ever since they repiped the whole club, it's been perfect. The membership is stoked. Everyone's totally copacetic."

"Except me," Caroline murmured.

The surfer-boy attendant smiled a grin of bright-white teeth. His eyes lingered over her chest, and she felt the flush of recognition of his interest in her.

"What was it you said you were looking for?" he asked.

"I didn't tell you yet." Caroline leaned in. "But I'll tell you now," she breathed. "Yvonne Heller thinks her husband might have hidden something," she said, keeping her voice low so he had to lean forward to hear her. "An article he wrote."

"Where do you think it is?" the attendant asked, matching her sotto voce tone.

"That's what I'm hoping you can help me with. It could be anywhere. Maybe in a safe . . ." Caroline let the silence stretch out. If she got lucky, he'd do her work for her.

But the attendant sat back in his chair and shrugged. "Sorry, ma'am, but the only safe around here's the one in the locker room. But it gets emptied each night except for petty cash."

Caroline's face flushed. Not only had she hit a dead end, but the cute surfer guy had called her *ma'am*. She couldn't be more than five years older than him. Okay, maybe eight. Either way, she didn't deserve a *ma'am*. She was about to dismiss the dumb-ass desk attendant as dead to her when he said something unexpected.

"Have you checked with Trina?" he asked.

At the mention of Yvonne's best friend, Caroline's instincts sparked. Trina's casual arrival in Yvonne's sitting room had stuck with her. There had been something about the way Yvonne's eyes had tracked Trina around the Hellers' sitting room . . .

"No, I haven't talked to Trina. Should I?" Caroline asked.

"I dunno. But Trina and Yvonne are always together, so I just figured if it was something about the Hellers, Trina might know what's what," the desk attendant said.

"Is Trina around the club today?"

"No. She usually doesn't come in on Wednesdays until her two thirty tennis game."

Caroline glanced at the clock hanging over the locker room desk. It read 9:18.

She didn't have time to wait for Trina's arrival. Nor did she have the luxury of another fruitless detour. She had only six hours to find and file the missing article. She needed to focus. Franklin had sent his final text message to Yvonne, not Trina.

Caroline put her nose back down to the only trail she'd scented: The *babc* in the text message had to mean the Bon Air Beach Club. The question remained: Where could Franklin have secreted something away, knowing that he might die?

All at once, something occurred to Caroline.

"What about down at the beach? Are there any lockers down there?" she asked.

"Sure. The beach lockers. They're down below the terrace level." He pointed toward a flight of stairs.

"Thanks," Caroline shouted over her shoulder as she ran for the stairwell.

• • •

Caroline shifted impatiently from foot to foot while the female staffer fumbled with the master keys to the beach lockers. It had taken almost twenty minutes to explain to the staffer why she needed to search the locker, then another half hour for the staffer to reach Yvonne to get her permission to open the locker. A half hour Caroline didn't have.

"Here it is," said the attendant, holding up one of a dozen identical bronze keys. She inserted it into the center of the lock.

At the telltale click of the lock, Caroline's hands prickled with anticipation. This beach locker was the only space in the club where the Hellers exercised dominion, where Franklin could have hidden something and known it could be found even if he died.

This had to be it.

When the metal door swung open, Caroline stepped toward the locker, ready to plumb its depths. She found sandy beach chairs. Umbrellas. A pile of towels. Undaunted, she began removing the contents of the locker, leaning them up against the neighboring lockers, their long-dried sand flaking off in chunks when she touched them.

Soon, the locker stood empty except for a rubberized mat cut to fit the bottom of the space. Caroline squatted down to lift the edge of the mat, hoping to find a safe embedded in the floor. But when she pulled up the edge of the sticky mat, she found only solid metal.

Drawing out her phone and turning on the flashlight function, she craned her head into the metal space. Rust edged the jagged rivets that held the box together. Careful not to cut herself, she ran her fingers along the walls, tapping gently as she went, listening for a hollow spot that might indicate a hidden chamber.

But she found nothing. It was just an empty box.

Stepping back, Caroline ran a hand through her dark hair. It was just a plain, metal beach locker, filled with the residual sand of a thousand long-ago beach days.

No. This had to be it.

Leaning back into the locker, she pressed her palms against the sides, then the ceiling and floor. Nothing but metal, cool and sandy, met her touch.

Nothing. There was nothing.

With heaviness, she began replacing the contents of the Hellers' beach locker. There was no need to rush. No reason for haste. Arranging their old towels and beach chairs was just the depressing denouement to her quest. She'd come so far to accomplish nothing except dusting off the Hellers' beach gear.

"Did you find what you need?" asked the staffer, her voice cheerful. Her ponytail bobbed as she offered her the last of the beach chairs to load back into the locker.

"No, but it's okay," Caroline said, even though it wasn't okay. Even though they were going to lose the case now. Even though Jasper's brother, Tom, would die, along with a whole host of other Toms, leaving thousands of devastated Jaspers to grieve her failure.

Sighing, she grasped the corner of the locker door, preparing to swing it shut.

That's when she saw something. A handwritten note taped to the inside of the metal door.

She pushed the locker open to get a better look at it.

The four-by-six-inch note card had been affixed to the locker door with clear packing tape. On it there was a list of workout goals: "Franklin's AIM, upper body: lat pulldown 15x22; overhead press 5x18;

triceps extension 12x15; bicep curl 18x4. Lower body: adduction 3x8; abduction 5x3; lunges 11x13; running 1 mile; squats 20x5." At the bottom of the note card someone had scrawled a name with a bright-blue Sharpie: FERMAT.

The first thing that struck Caroline was the name. Wasn't Pierre de Fermat a French mathematician? Why had Franklin written Fermat's name at the bottom of his workout targets?

Then Caroline focused on Heller's workout. The numbers of repetitions were strange. Why would anyone do thirteen repetitions of eleven lunges? And fifteen lat pulldowns twenty-two times? None of it made any sense.

Caroline eyed the silent breezeway. Though unused in the winter months, she could imagine the bustle in the sandy-bottomed walkway on hot summer days as club members flocked to the coast. But now, in October, there was no one there. Dr. Heller wouldn't have used this locker for months at a time. And yet, he'd taped his gymnasium workout targets in an unused summer beach locker.

Maybe he was trying to avoid working out? Or maybe—

Caroline yanked her legal pad from her bag. She flipped through the pages until she found her notes from her conversation with Yvonne. Franklin's final text message.

Caroline looked down at the message, then back up at the workout targets.

She pulled out her camera and shot a picture of the workout targets.

Then she turned and ran back to her car as fast as she could.

• • •

Caroline sat in the Mustang, oblivious to the handful of other cars in the club's self-park lot. The car's ancient cigarette lighter powered the laptop balanced on her thigh. Her phone leaned against the windshield, the picture of Franklin Heller's workout goals displayed on the screen. On the passenger seat, she had angled the yellow legal pad with Franklin's final text message toward her—the one he had sent to his wife before he'd died on the beach.

She ignored the view out the window. The waves breaking along the deserted beach. The low hills dotted with chaparral. The sunlight glittering on the surface of the ocean. She had eyes only for the clues laid out in front of her.

She studied Dr. Heller's workout goals. The key was the first word: *AIM*. If she was right, *AIM* wasn't a reference to Franklin's fitness aims or aspirations. It was an acronym for Access Identity Management. Somewhere in the numbers and letters, there was an encryption key. But where?

Cryptology was as ancient as the Egyptians, but it always followed the same basic rules: the security of the encrypted data depended on the strength of the cipher and the secrecy of the encryption key. Caroline believed she possessed both the cipher and the key in the two strings of letters and numbers that Dr. Heller had written—the workout goals and the text message. But which was the cipher and which was the key?

Whatever the answers were, she needed them fast. The clock next to the odometer said it was 11:03 a.m. That meant she had two hours to file the article. Two hours before the doors of the court closed forever on every SuperSoy victim in the country.

With no easy answer presenting itself, Caroline turned her attention to the only piece of plaintext information she possessed: FERMAT. In bright-blue ink, the mathematician's name stood out against the typed black workout targets, as if Franklin had wanted Yvonne to focus on it first. But why?

Caroline knew Fermat had been a mathematician. But Dr. Heller was a research scientist, not a mathematician. So then, what was the significance of Fermat to him?

Caroline typed the name "Fermat" into the search pane on her laptop.

Search results spilled onto the page. Pierre de Fermat had been a lawyer and amateur mathematician. As an inventor of integral geometry, he'd invented a technique for finding the centers of gravity of various plane and solid figures.

Was the text message a mathematical equation Yvonne was supposed to solve?

Caroline shook her head. She was overthinking it. There had to be some more obvious answer here. Franklin wouldn't have made things so hard for his wife to decipher. He'd intended for her to find the article.

Running another search for the mathematician's name yielded another wave of Google results. Down at the bottom of the second page, something caught Caroline's eye. Among his many achievements, Fermat had been an amateur cryptographer.

With blood pulsing in her ears, Caroline ran a search for "Fermat's code."

The results were exhilarating. Fermat had invented an encryption method where each number corresponded to the position of the letter in the alphabet.

Caroline's heart pounded.

She scribbled Franklin's final text message vertically along one margin of the legal pad. Then she counted which letter each number corresponded to and wrote the letter on the pad: 620-16.5-14-9-7-13-1 became FTP.ENIGMA.

Caroline almost shouted with joy. The text message was an FTP address! That meant Franklin had an FTP site—a secret repository of document files.

To confirm her hypothesis, Caroline typed the words "FTP. ENIGMA" into the URL pane of her web browser. The page instantly changed, revealing that she had, indeed, found an FTP site. A site that now asked for a username and password. Caroline had neither. Yet.

Grabbing her phone, Caroline pulled up the picture of Franklin's workout targets again. She knew what to do now. She needed to apply

Fermat's code to what she now knew were not aspirational gymnasium targets.

Caroline's eyes grazed the clock on the dashboard—11:55.

Forcing her hands to stop shaking, she turned back to the workout goals. Fermat had designed a code that only worked on numbers. That meant that the words in the list of Franklin's workout targets were irrelevant noise. The letters were there just to hide the code.

Just as she had done with the text message, Caroline wrote the string of numbers corresponding to the upper-body workout targets vertically on the legal pad. Using Fermat's code, the string of numbers in the upper-body workout targets became *OVERLORD*.

Encouraged by the resolution of the numbers into coherent plaintext, she moved on with confidence to the lower-body targets. The numbers became *CHECKMATE*.

Caroline typed the words *OVERLORD* and *CHECKMATE* into the password and username fields on the FTP server's log-in page. Then she waited an eternity of seconds to find out if she'd gotten it right.

"Come on," she muttered at her laptop as the password page processed.

Finally, the screen changed. She was in!

Franklin's FTP site appeared on the screen. There she found three documents.

The first was Heller, F. and Wong, A., "A Comprehensive Analysis of the Damaging Effects of SuperSoy on Human Kidneys."

"Yes!" she shouted so loudly that anyone within ten feet of her car would have heard her.

As the information unfurled on the screen, Caroline almost cheered again. Dr. Heller's findings were stronger than she'd hoped. In meticulous detail, he'd described the precise mechanism whereby SuperSoy caused kidney cells to perish. The evidence was irrefutable. Dr. Heller's studies were larger than those in any of the other articles Caroline had reviewed. His supporting footnotes on methodology were clearly designed to permit others to verify his work.

Dr. Heller's article was gold. If only she could get it filed on time, it would radically improve their chances of winning.

Moving on to the next file on the FTP site, Caroline discovered the backup data supporting Dr. Heller's conclusions—159 pages of hospital records, questionnaires, assay results, reports, and other notes.

As she propelled herself down through the data, she recognized its significance. Dr. Heller's article might not have been peer reviewed, but she had no doubt it would pass muster with even the most stringent publication standards.

Caroline allowed herself a brief moment of joy. She'd found the key that would let thousands of plaintiffs all across the country have their day in court.

In her excitement, she almost didn't notice the final document in Franklin's FTP site.

Named "For Yvonne," the document took up only three kilobytes. Caroline narrowed her eyes at the file. Had Franklin written a final message to his wife? Had he known he was going to die?

Caroline pushed the questions from her mind. She had no time to probe the dead man's final missive to his wife. The message would have to wait. Right now she needed to get the article and supporting data filed.

The clock on the dashboard ticked down toward the end of the court day in New York. All evidence had to be filed by 1:00 p.m. Los Angeles time. The glowing red digital numbers read 12:02. That meant she had less than an hour to make everything happen.

She needed help.

Grabbing her phone, Caroline dialed her firm's number.

"I need to talk to Louis," she said when the receptionist answered.

"He's not here. Would you like his voice mail?"

"No. How about Eddie Diaz? Is he there?"

"Yes. Hold on." The receptionist clicked off.

Eddie's voice came on the line. "Hello?"

"I've got the missing article," Caroline said.

"Tell me what to do," he said.

"Find the editor of the *Fielding Journal*. Tell him we need him to sign a declaration explaining that he'd arranged to publish Dr. Heller's article on SuperSoy, that Heller's disappearance precluded it, but that he believes this is the article he and Heller discussed. We need to do whatever we can to establish that this is a true and correct copy of an article that was on the cusp of peer review and publication."

"Got it," Eddie said. "Hold on a sec."

Caroline could hear the clicks of his fingers on the keys of his desktop.

"The editor's name is Darren Halsgreth," Eddie said. "I'll call him now. I'll draft the declaration, too."

"Great. I'm going to get going on the motion to submit the article. If I can log on to the firm system from my car, I can do it from here—"

A tap at the car window jolted Caroline, setting her heart to hammering.

She looked over to find the Filipino valet.

"Are you okay, miss?" the valet asked through the closed window.

"I'm fine," Caroline mouthed. She pointed at her phone. "I'm on a call."

The valet gestured for her to unroll her window. When Caroline had done so, he said, "Sorry to bug you, but I had a thought about maybe where you could look for that thing you said you were trying to find."

"I got what I needed," Caroline said, turning her body away from the overeager valet, hoping he'd catch a clue. She didn't want to be rude, but she didn't have time to chat.

"Are you sure?" he asked.

Annoyance flared in Caroline's chest. Why was he still talking to her? It was like he was trying to stall her or something.

Sudden movement at the far end of the parking lot caught her eye. A van bearing the logo of Ajax Plumbing came rolling through the front gates. Fast.

All at once, Caroline recalled the locker room attendant's words about the plumbing: the pipes had been perfect ever since the club had fixed them.

Something was wrong now, and it wasn't the plumbing.

Caroline dropped the phone and threw the Mustang into gear, peeling out of the parking spot, her car fishtailing as the wheels sought traction. Adrenaline coursed through her bloodstream.

The plumbing truck angled toward her, cutting across the empty parking spaces.

Caroline looked for an access road or service entrance. She saw nothing. Instead, she spotted a golf road, narrow and cramped, threading through the trees. It would have to do.

She drove for it, fast, gunning the engine hard. In her rearview mirror, the plumbing truck gained, chewing up the distance between it and her, the lack of open road neutralizing the advantage of the Mustang's big engine. With a bump and a hiss, the wheels of the Mustang hopped up onto the smooth golf road.

Gripping the steering wheel with both hands, Caroline fought to keep the tires on the thin strip of concrete.

Ahead, she saw a tunnel. It wasn't much wider than her car.

She hit the gas, aiming toward the opening. She plunged into darkness and scraped through the tunnel with a screech of tearing metal and a spray of sparks.

She flew from the tunnel, back onto the golf road, weaving through a grove of fragrant eucalyptus trees. Seconds later, she popped out onto the main road, surprising a group of golfers.

She swerved onto the road and raced for the firm.

No plumbing truck behind her now. But the clock was ticking down.

CHAPTER 8

Caroline found Eddie waiting for her in the office lobby.

"What happened?" he asked as she entered the reception area. "I heard tires squealing—"

"No time," Caroline said, rushing past him. "How are we looking on the filing?"

"We've got a problem," Eddie said, keeping pace with her. "I can't find the editor of the *Fielding Journal*. I found his number, but the automated phone system just keeps kicking me to voice mail."

"I'll find him," Caroline said. She pointed a finger down the hall toward Eddie's office. "You get going on the motion to submit the article. It can be short. Just 'We respectfully ask the court to consider this critical piece of scientific evidence, blah, blah, blah.' I started a template for it last week. It's on the system in my *SuperSoy* file."

"Got it," Eddie said, turning on his heel to disappear into his office.

When Caroline reached her desk, Eddie had already e-mailed her the phone number for the editor of the *Fielding Journal*. She dialed it. Just as Eddie had warned, she was diverted to voice mail. She hit zero and a computerized voice came on the line, offering a company directory. Beginning with *A*, she began working her way through the staff, trying to find someone who would answer the phone and then answer her questions. When she got to *R*, a woman answered the phone with the easy cadence of a helpful assistant.

"I'm trying to find Darren," Caroline started right in. "He'll know what this is about. He'll appreciate the urgency." She wasn't sure it was true, but she needed the assistant's cooperation.

"I'm afraid he's out at lunch," said the assistant's voice.

Caroline's stomach torqued at the unexpected roadblock.

"Do you expect him back soon?" she asked.

"Hard to say. Darren's usually pretty fast, but today he's out with his wife at that nice Italian place for their anniversary."

"Italian place? Which one?" Caroline asked.

"I'm not authorized to say," the assistant said, a note of suspicion entering her voice. "You can try back in an hour. I'm sure he'll be back by then."

"That'll be too late—"

"I'm sorry. Please call back later," the assistant said. The line clicked off.

Caroline grabbed the komboloi beads from her pocket while her mind filtered and organized what she knew about the editor's whereabouts. Darren Halsgreth was at lunch at "that nice Italian place." The assistant's phrasing suggested the restaurant was somewhere the staff frequented. Somewhere for special occasions. Somewhere fancy, but local.

Reaching for her laptop, Caroline typed in the address of the *Fielding Journal*.

The search result came up fast: 15700 Von Karman Way, San Diego, California 92107.

With her fingers flying across the keyboard, Caroline typed the *Fielding Journal*'s address into the search pane of Yelp, hunting for listings of Italian restaurants within a two-mile radius.

She found only one: a Tuscan restaurant called Piccolo Ristorante.

She stabbed the phone on her desk for an outside line.

Forty-five seconds later she had the hostess on the line.

"I have to speak to Mr. Halsgreth," Caroline said.

"Who?"

"Darren Halsgreth. He's there with his wife. It's an emergency."

"Just a moment, please," said the hostess.

Caroline counted off the seconds. At seventy-two a man's voice came on the phone.

"This is Darren. Who is this? What's the emergency?"

"I'm Caroline Auden from Hale Stern. We spoke the other day about the *SuperSoy* case." When the editor grunted his recognition, she continued, "I found a copy of that article by Dr. Heller that you planned to publish. I just need you to authenticate it for me. It'll only take a minute, and it'll save thousands of lives. I'm not exaggerating."

"That's great you found it, but why can't this wait?" Darren said in her ear. His voice held the same annoyance he'd undoubtedly expressed to the hostess of Piccolo Ristorante upon being pulled to the house telephone during his anniversary lunch.

"Court's about to close." Caroline glanced at the clock. They had twenty-six minutes to make the filing deadline.

"Please," she begged. She wanted to jump through the phone to compel the editor of the *Fielding Journal* to cooperate.

"I'm sorry, I just can't—"

"Didn't you tell me that you were the little journal that made a big impact?" Caroline pushed. "You publish the articles that make a difference, right? Well, here's your chance."

At the editor's silence, Caroline pushed harder. "Or maybe it's just a niche for you? The renegade naysayer . . ."

"That's not fair," the editor said. "We've shown courage many times—"

"Great, then show some now. Please. All I need is your cell number and I can text you everything. This will only take a minute, I promise." Caroline waited in the painful silence that followed. All of her efforts.

All of her work. All of it would come to nothing if Darren Halsgreth refused her now.

Finally, the editor exhaled.

"Fine," he said, rattling off his cell phone number.

"Thank you," Caroline said, punching the number into her own cell phone. "Okay, I've now texted the article to you. I'll represent to you that we found it on an FTP site that we have every reason to believe belonged to Dr. Heller. I just need you to look at it and confirm it's the one you discussed with Dr. Heller."

There was silence on the line while Darren did as Caroline asked.

"The topic and author appear to be correct," Darren said finally.

"Good. Are you comfortable confirming in writing that this is, to your knowledge, the same article you discussed publishing for Dr. Heller?"

"I am," Darren said, "but I don't have time to write anything. I'm at lunch—"

"You don't have to write anything," Caroline interrupted. "You just have to sign the short declaration that I'm going to send to you right now. It will identify the article, describe what you discussed with Dr. Heller regarding its publication, and state that the *Fielding Journal* intends to publish it, assuming peer review approval, of course. All I need is your signature."

"Fine. I'll sign it as soon as I get back to my desk after I finish lunch with my wife." Darren emphasized the word *wife* in a way that made Caroline think that the wife was looking pointedly at Darren now from a red vinyl booth.

"But court will close—"

"Did I mention it's my anniversary? I'd really like to help you out, but compared to the fate of the world, my wife wins out."

Caroline stopped pacing. The editor was backing out. She needed to stop him.

Eddie poked his head into her office. "Motion's done," he said.

Caroline held up a hand to quiet Eddie.

"You don't have to go back to your office, Mr. Halsgreth," she said into the phone. "Just read the declaration I've texted to you. If it's accurate, sign your name on a napkin. Take a photo of your signature with your phone and e-mail it back to me at cauden@halestern.com."

Across from Caroline, Eddie raised a curious eyebrow, but she ignored him.

The editor huffed on the line but didn't hang up.

"All right, I've read the declaration and signed the napkin," the editor said. "I'm sending you the picture of my signature now."

Caroline watched the corner of her screen, waiting. After a half dozen interminably long seconds, the editor's e-mail appeared.

"Got it," she said. "Do I have your authorization to attach this signature to this declaration?"

"Yes, yes," Darren said, impatience creeping back in his voice.

"Thank you. Please enjoy your lunch. Sorry for the interruption. Happy anniversary."

Caroline hung up and opened the editor's e-mail. A photograph of a black signature on a white napkin filled her screen. Little smudges of tomato sauce marred the edges of the fabric, but the signature was clean. Good.

Blocking out the tomato sauce stains and shadows, Caroline pulled a tight square around the black ink, cropping the image. Then she captured the signature and saved it as a JPEG.

"What are you doing?" Eddie asked.

She waved him away. "I need to concentrate."

Her fingers flew across the keys as she loaded the declaration into a template, then grabbed the signature JPEG and merged the documents.

"Almost there," she murmured, looking at the now-complete declaration glowing on the screen.

"Wow," Eddie said behind her.

Caroline glanced back at him. Seeing the appreciation in his eyes, she warmed.

"We've got fifteen minutes to upload the article, the declaration, and the motion onto the court's system," she said. "This is going to be tight. Let's hope the courts have fast servers."

"I'll load the court's e-filing page so we can start the upload," Eddie said, hurrying from Caroline's office.

Suddenly, something horrible occurred to Caroline.

She leaped up from her desk and gripped the frame of her office door, catapulting herself down the hall after Eddie.

"Don't file anything yet!" she called after him as she ran the direction he'd gone.

She burst into his office to find him with his fingers poised over the keyboard.

"What's wrong?" he asked.

"We need a pro hac vice application. I can't submit the article to the New York court without one, and Louis is out of the office."

Grabbing Eddie's phone, she dialed Deena's extension. Maybe the New York associate could just file the article herself. Or maybe she could sign a pro hac vice application.

No one answered.

Time for plan B.

Pulling up the caption page of the *Daubert* brief, Caroline found Anton Callisto's phone number and dialed it as fast as her fingers could move.

Fortunately, Anton answered her call.

"Yeah, sure, send it over," he said curtly once she'd explained what she needed from him.

Hitting "Hold," Caroline turned to Eddie, who moved off his chair, making room for her to take over.

"I'm going to work up the pro hac application here. Go on the state bar website and download a Certificate of Good Standing for me," she said. "Use my desktop."

"I'm on it," Eddie said and jogged down the hall to Caroline's office.

With a couple dozen keystrokes, Caroline opened the document she needed and made the necessary modifications. Then she took the phone line off "Hold."

"Mr. Callisto, I've duplicated the pro hac vice application that I prepared for Louis and put my name into it." She hit "Send." "Substantively, it's identical to the one you signed for Louis so that we could file our *Daubert* brief." She paused. "You should have it now."

"Signed," Anton said so quickly that it was clear he hadn't even looked at it. "PDF version of my signature page coming your way now. Good luck."

"Thanks," Caroline said, hanging up just as the signed application appeared in her in-box.

At the same moment, Eddie appeared back at the doorway of the office.

"Your Certificate of Good Standing is on the system now. You just have to upload it with the pro hac application," he said.

"Good," Caroline said. "I've got the signed application ready to go, too."

With her fingers flying across the keyboard, Caroline brought up the district court's e-filing page. While she waited for it to load, she met Eddie's dark eyes.

"Once we file the pro hac vice application and Certificate of Good Standing, we can file the declaration and then the article," she said. "We've got to do it in that order . . ."

Caroline stopped talking as the court's e-filing page appeared.

A long list of detailed instructions disappeared down to the bottom of the screen. The Southern District of New York had imposed dozens of rules about how to perform an e-filing. The document had to be properly paginated and properly named. Exhibits had to be loaded separately, also named appropriately, and then linked in yet another field to the documents filed concurrently with them. And then everything had to be uploaded to one site, then disseminated to the service list, which also had to be uploaded separately.

Caroline froze. She had hacked the servers of major corporations yet couldn't even begin to decipher the court's e-filing protocol.

Before she could give voice to her distress, Eddie turned and ran from the office.

Caroline stared dumbfounded at the door. What a moment for him to bail.

Seconds later, he returned. Behind him, the bright-red hair of Silvia followed.

Without speaking, Caroline got out of Silvia's way.

The assistant sat down, and, chewing gum in time to her finger strokes on the keyboard, she began uploading the pro hac vice application and Certificate of Good Standing. She named the document, placed it in the queue, and hit "Load."

The e-filing server began to slowly absorb the first batch of materials. A white bar on the computer's monitor showed the speed of the upload. It was slow. Possibly too slow.

Caroline checked the time. They had seven minutes to upload the pro hac vice application, the editor's declaration, the seventeen-page article, and all 159 pages of backup data.

FILED, the screen read.

Even though the words were flat, unemotional text hovering on a page, Caroline thrilled at the sight of them. They were one step closer.

Without pause, Silvia moved on to the declaration. Named, formatted, and lined up in the queue, it too began the slow journey from Hale Stern's computers to the server of the Southern District of New York.

Again, the bar on the screen inched along as the document uploaded, and Caroline's awareness distilled down to the tiny movements of the pixels, willing them to move just a little bit faster.

She glanced at the clock. Five minutes left.

FILED, the court's website confirmed.

"I'm going to get the data file set up first," Silvia said. "It's going to take time to upload. I'll prep the article separately at the same time."

"Whatever you think is best," Caroline said. She wasn't going to micromanage how her assistant did her job. Silvia seemed quite capable. No surprise that she'd survived as Louis's assistant for so many years, even with grooming habits that the senior partner no doubt disapproved of. The woman was plenty competent.

Watching the upload of the backup data caused Caroline almost physical pain. She squirmed with impatience as the white bar crept at glacial speed. She glanced at the clock. They had two minutes. Two minutes before all of their efforts were for nothing. Two minutes before the gates came crashing down on Dr. Heller's life's work. Before the doors of the court slammed shut to litigants across the country.

As soon as the court's website confirmed acceptance of the backup data, Silvia began the upload of the Heller article. The single object of Caroline's quest. The singular achievement of her short legal career. And they had one minute, thirty-two seconds to load it.

The white bar began its slow progress across the screen. Caroline's eyes kept moving back and forth between the bar and the time on Eddie's clock. They'd come so far. And now they sat on the launch pad, ready to blast off into space or ready to explode.

Fifty-nine seconds left.

Forty-three seconds left.

Unable to watch, Caroline stepped outside Eddie's office. The graceful hallways and the light- wood credenzas were discordant with the gnawing desperation coursing through Caroline's gut. They had to be down to fifteen seconds by now. Maybe less.

She walked back into Eddie's office just as the notice came onto the screen.

"Filed," Silvia said.

"We did it!" Caroline shouted, throwing her arms around Silvia's neck.

"You're welcome." Silvia smiled, gently extricating herself from Caroline's embrace.

She finally knew what assistants did. They saved your hide.

• • •

"That was too close." Caroline's hands curled around a cup of tea. Decaffeinated because she was sure her nerves couldn't handle any more stimulation without her head exploding. "I definitely need to get Silvia something for Christmas."

"She earned a fruit basket for sure," Eddie said. He sat across from Caroline in her guest chair, one foot propped up on the edge of her desk.

"Or a new car," Caroline said. She was only half joking. "I think Louis is going to get her one if I don't." With a swell of warmth, Caroline recalled her boss's gratitude and joy upon learning that they'd managed to file the missing article in time. He'd promised her a celebratory lunch once the *Daubert* hearing was behind them. A hearing he now insisted she attend with him.

"Your mad skills came in handy, too. You said your dad taught you how to do that stuff? That's a very cool dad you've got there," Eddie drawled.

Caroline stayed silent. But with Eddie's warm eyes looking back at her, she found she wanted to tell the story. It was a story she'd told almost no one.

"My dad and I didn't hang out a lot when I was a kid," she began. "He was at work pretty much all the time. The one thing we shared, though, was a love of technology. We liked to do stuff together. We used to like to get into places where we . . . weren't supposed to be."

She paused to gauge Eddie's reaction. He looked steadily back at her, with no judgment in his eyes. So she took a breath and went on. "We had fun hacking together . . . until the day the police showed up."

She remembered the knock at the door. They hadn't been expecting anyone that night, so she'd opened the door expecting to find Jehovah's Witnesses. Instead, she found two officers with grim faces and handcuffs.

"What happened?" Eddie asked.

"We'd been hacking a hospital. Just for fun. We weren't going to steal any information or anything. We just wanted to see if we could get in. Hospital firewalls are especially hard to hack, because they have to protect all of that personal information for their patients."

"So it was a worthy challenge," Eddie surmised. His voice still held no judgment.

Caroline nodded. "We hadn't gotten past the firewall when my dad had to go to work. But I kept at it. I wanted to impress him. I found a weakness in the hospital's firewall and opened a port. I was going to show my dad later . . . when he got home. The problem was, later that day, cyberthieves used that port to breach the hospital's security."

"Did they get patient information?" Eddie asked.

Caroline swallowed, a sense of shame washing over her.

"No, but they grabbed information about everyone on the staff of the hospital. They also got the personal information of every juvenile dependent of every staff member. Social Security numbers and everything." Caroline stopped talking. For the rest of their lives, those children were going to have to worry about identity theft, about fraudsters setting up fake bank accounts or terrorists using their identities to get passports. And there was nothing she could do to fix it.

"Did you get arrested?" Eddie asked.

"My dad did. The police traced the hack back to our computer. It was my fault, too, of course. But my dad didn't want to get his little girl in trouble. So he said it was all him." Caroline looked down. Her guilt was still fresh, easily touched. That she'd breached the firewall to impress her dad just made the whole thing so much more desperate.

"It was a nightmare," she continued. "This thing we'd been doing together that seemed so harmless . . . it almost cost him his life, really. Even after he got probation instead of jail, I was scared. We never hacked again."

Caroline remembered the invisible barrier that had seemed to spring up around the study. As if by silent agreement, they never entered the room again. And they never spoke of it.

"And yet, you became a software engineer," Eddie said.

"It was the natural thing for me to do," she said. "But I didn't like software engineering."

"Really?" Eddie's tone held disbelief.

"I found it boring yet stressful."

Eddie raised a curious eyebrow.

"It's hard to explain. After my dad got busted, tech became like . . . kryptonite to me. But then, once I'd pushed past the fear and gotten back into the game, the stuff I was doing as a software engineer wasn't interesting. Coding someone else's designs wasn't all that challenging or creative. But when I'd think about what *was* exciting and creative, it was the stuff that got me into trouble, and the whole thing would start again . . ."

Caroline trailed off.

"But it all turned out okay for your dad, right?" Eddie prodded.

"It could have been worse," Caroline allowed. "He was able to prove he wasn't working with the cyberthieves—that it was just a fluke that we'd ended up helping them."

"That was lucky that the police believed him."

"It wasn't luck. It was a good lawyer." Caroline sent a spark of gratitude toward her father's criminal defense attorney. With his patchy beard and ill-fitting suit, he hadn't looked like he'd be able to do anything to prevent the weight of the law from crushing Caroline's family. But he had. He'd known exactly which levers to pull to save William Auden from jail. Watching the attorney work, Caroline had realized that law wasn't so different from tech. Both followed a set of rules that, once mastered, opened infinite possibilities, depending on the user.

"When my dad finished his probation, he became a cybersecurity consultant," Caroline continued. "He's still one, except now he lives back east with his new wife."

"Why'd you stay with software engineering for so long if you didn't like it?" Eddie asked.

"My dad left my mom a couple years after the hacking incident. His departure didn't have anything to do with it—their marriage had its . . . issues. But he pretty much vanished from my life when he moved out. He started dating Lily, the woman he eventually married. When they got together, he got wrapped up with her . . . you know how that goes."

Eddie nodded his understanding.

"In a way, software engineering was my way of trying to connect with him." Caroline paused, remembering the distant conversations she'd shared with her dad about her work at the start-up. Those stilted interactions were better than nothing, she'd told herself at the time. Looking back, she wasn't sure. Working in technology had done nothing to dissipate the awkwardness that had settled between them.

"When my dad moved back east with Lily, I was done trying to connect with him. I felt like I could finally—"

"—do whatever you wanted," Eddie finished for her. "It was also a way of giving your dad the middle finger for bailing on you, right?"

There was truth in his words, Caroline admitted silently to herself.

"I understand why my parents split up," she said, "but my dad didn't have to bail on me, too. When he moved back east, I gave up. I stopped trying to connect."

"What about now?" Eddie asked. "Are you close with your dad?"

"No, and I don't think we'll ever be again. He calls me sometimes, but I just can't talk to him. Not about anything real, anyway. It's like he wants forgiveness for leaving. Absolution."

Eddie studied Caroline's face quietly for a long moment.

"I'm sure he misses you," Eddie said finally. "And if you don't mind me being honest, it sounds to me like you miss him, too."

"Maybe," Caroline allowed.

Shaking off the heaviness in the room, Caroline smiled.

"What about you? What's your story?" She glanced at his expensive watch and gold cuff links. "Charmed career? Biggest struggle was deciding between the BMW and the Porsche?"

Caroline meant it as a joke, but Eddie's eyes sparked with sudden emotion.

"You have no idea," he said, his voice dropping to a lower register.

"I'm sorry," Caroline said, alarmed by the abrupt change in mood.

"No, I'm sorry," Eddie said. "My family's from a piss-poor town outside Oaxaca."

"But you were born here?"

"Yeah, my mama came across the border when she was pregnant with me. Don't ask me how. She cleaned hotel rooms for pennies until she had me. Then she left me with her older brother and went back home. Uncle Antonio gave me a place to live, but he made it clear he had enough kids of his own to take care of." Eddie shook his head. "No one's ever given me a thing. I've had to make my own breaks—which wasn't too easy when you're the smarty-pants kid with glasses in a rough border town."

Caroline's gaze traveled to the scar at Eddie's neck. Perhaps it was a remnant of an old scrape in his old life.

"I wish my mom had taken me with her," he said.

Caroline nodded in quiet understanding. Eddie's life, despite its successes, boiled down to one irreducible fact: he missed his mother.

"I'm sure she'd be proud of you." Caroline knew it wasn't enough. But it was all she had to offer him.

Eddie let out a long breath, the tension leaving his shoulders, the taut expression leaving his brow.

"I'm sorry I jumped down your throat like that. It's just when you suggested I hadn't struggled, it hit a nerve. My sister's disabled. My mom takes care of her. I've been trying to get papers for them to come over. But it seems like it's never gonna happen. Got this big ole house waiting for years for a family that never comes."

Caroline grimaced in sympathy.

"Oh, it isn't as pathetic as it sounds," Eddie said. "I have some fun, too, from time to time in that big ole house." He smiled wolfishly, the vulnerability leaving his eyes so quickly that Caroline wondered if she'd imagined it.

"Well, thanks again for helping me get the filing done," Caroline said, recognizing the need for a change of subject.

Eddie waved away the gratitude. "We both know you'd have filed it just fine even if I hadn't been here."

"I'm not so sure about that. And anyway, it was better with you here."

"Yes, it was," Eddie said, his eyes holding hers.

Caroline cocked her head at him. Was he flirting? Seeing the embers in his too-long-for-platonic-friends gaze, she concluded that yes, he was definitely flirting. She had a hard time believing he meant it. She knew she had nice eyes, a passable figure, and a mop of dark wavy hair that was best approached by hairdressers as topiary. But Eddie was in another category of good looks. He could have anyone.

"You have no idea how appealing you are, do you?" Eddie asked.

It was a pickup line. And yet, Caroline found herself wanting to fall for it. But then she recalled the platinum blonde in Las Vegas who might or might not have been a hooker. With her heavily processed hair and flagrantly revealing dress, she couldn't have been more different from Caroline.

As if sensing her thoughts, Eddie said, "I should warn you. I've got a thing for smart-as-a-whip women. Especially ones who know their way 'round a computer."

Rising, he placed his palms on Caroline's desk and moved slowly toward her.

Caroline was mesmerized by the fullness of his mouth. The way his lips parted as he closed the distance. She considered asking about the woman in Las Vegas, but she found she didn't care. She wanted this.

The contact was soft at first, then insistent.

She moved toward him, seeking more when he pulled back.

"Come to my hotel?" Eddie half asked, half stated.

Caroline heard the need in his voice.

She told herself to stop. She'd been chased. She'd raced to meet an impossible deadline. She needed to board a flight to New York in less than twelve hours.

Nodding at Eddie, she went in for another kiss.

• • •

Moonlight slipped into the hotel room through a gap in the drapes, painting pale lines on Eddie's arm, which was tossed casually over Caroline's waist. His body curved around her, his chest rising and falling in sleep.

Caroline commanded herself to get up. She had a flight to catch to New York in a few hours, and she still needed to pack. But her body refused to oblige. She didn't want to leave the warm tangle of limbs and sheets. She did not want to end this moment, suspended in time, when everything, for once, seemed perfect.

Even the room was perfect. In the dim light, Caroline's eyes traced the opulent furnishings. She'd expected something modest. Maybe a residence hotel. Something functional and basic. She hadn't expected a hand-tooled leather headboard. Lilies in a vase. Thick bathrobes embroidered with the hotel's logo . . . though their night had seen little use for bathrobes.

A smile crossed Caroline's face at the recollection of the last six hours they'd spent together in the Egyptian cotton sheets. But her smile faded at the recollection of the platinum blonde.

She scolded herself. What Eddie did wasn't her business. He lived in Atlanta and would return there soon.

So what if he had caramel skin that felt like satin under her touch? What did it matter that his lips were even softer than she had imagined? And who cared if he had strong hands coupled with a feline grace? And if those gentle butterfly fingers felt so fine on her breasts, her waist, between her legs?

As if sensing her gaze, Eddie opened his dark eyes.

In silence, his black eyes traced along Caroline's face. He reached out a hand and brushed it lightly along the curve of her hip.

Caroline's body responded, her skin flushing hot at his touch.

She told herself she needed to get up. She needed to leave.

But again, her body refused to oblige.

In fact, it did the exact opposite.

CHAPTER 9

Caroline floated through the airport. In her mind's eye, she could still see Eddie's appreciative gaze as he'd leaned against the headboard, one arm behind his head, watching her move around his dimly lit hotel room as she'd dressed. His eyes had tracked her until she leaned forward to kiss him one last time. It had felt good.

Now she walked down the Jetway, pulling her rolling briefcase behind her. Before she'd closed the three-ring binder and shoved it into the briefcase, she'd added the one final, key piece of the puzzle: the Heller article. That had felt good, too.

As she entered the plane, some part of Caroline's mind whispered that air travel usually triggered anxiety. But another part of her mind told her to stuff it. This flight was different. She was on her way to New York, where they were going to defeat Med-Gen's *Daubert* motion. The plaintiffs would get their settlement. The danger to her would dissipate. She could stop thinking about getting a gun and learning how to fire it.

Caroline spotted Louis and Dale in first class. Beside Dale sat a portly man with a beard that failed to make him look any older than the twentysomething he probably was.

"How's everyone doing this morning?" Caroline asked the group. In her ears, her voice sounded almost jarringly chipper. It couldn't be helped. Nothing could sink her buoyant mood.

From his seat by the window, Louis smiled. "The dogs let me sleep in, so I'm grand this morning, Ms. Auden. Just grand." Caroline knew the reason for his joy was more than his dogs. "I know I've thanked you already," Louis continued, "but I want to thank you again in person. Finding the Heller article was nothing short of brilliant."

"Yeah, great job," said Dale from across the aisle. "I read it this morning, and boy, oh, boy, is that good stuff." He gestured with his chin toward the man who overflowed the seat behind him. "This is my assistant, Harold. He's my tech wizard. He's the one I credit for getting me to step into the twenty-first century."

Behind Dale, Harold met Caroline's eyes and shook his head no.

Caroline allowed a flicker of a smile to cross her face in silent kinship with Harold. A fellow digital native trying to lead another digital immigrant into the future.

"Hello, Harold . . . I'm just glad we got it filed," Caroline said, lifting her rolling briefcase into the overhead bin before sitting down in the aisle seat beside Louis and across from Dale. "Once we add Ambrose's findings on mitochondrial degradation to Heller's findings about how SuperSoy affects mitochondria, I don't know how we can lose."

Caroline knew she was supposed to hedge. Lawyers hedge. Always. They operate in the gray areas, battling to convince judges to buy their version of events, to believe their narrative over the other guy's narrative. There's no such thing as a sure thing in the law. Ever. And yet, Caroline felt bullish about their chances. SuperSoy damaged kidneys. The conclusion wasn't debatable anymore. It was a fact.

She searched Dale's face to gauge his reaction to her assessment of Ambrose.

Dale shrugged. "I confess I haven't spent a ton of time with the articles. The way I see it, the meat of our argument is exactly what prompted us to file suit against Med-Gen in the first place—the proximity in time between the plaintiffs' ingestion of SuperSoy and their kidney failure. That's the best thing we've got. That a doctor would put SuperSoy on his differential diagnosis if he had a patient who came into his office with renal failure is going to be enough science for this judge."

"You might be right," Caroline allowed, "but the scientific literature helps us, too. You read those summaries of the main studies, right? Those short paragraphs I prepared?"

"I skimmed them. They were helpful and I appreciate you putting those together for me."

With a cold bolt of worry in her chest, Caroline nodded.

"Don't y'all worry," Dale said. "We've got a solid six hours. Plenty of time for you to get me all up to speed on whatever you think I need to know."

Sitting down in her seat, Caroline withdrew her laptop from her bag. "I've got everything here. We can just start going through the key studies and I'll—"

Dale frowned at the laptop.

Deciding to take his sour expression as a reaction to technology rather than as a reaction to studying, Caroline retrieved the three-ring binder of articles from the overhead bin. She opened the heavy binder on her lap and flipped to the page of summaries.

"We can talk the science through now," she said. "Just in case the judge has questions about some of the secondary articles . . ."

But before Caroline could begin, another passenger boarded the plane. A flash of geranium-orange Saint John jacket. Cashmere paisley scarf. The scent of Chanel No. 5.

Even before she saw her face, Caroline knew who it was. Deena. The New York associate's sheath skirt forced her to mince step her way down the aisle.

Dale's eyes traveled from Caroline's binder to Deena's figure.

Caroline resisted the urge to groan.

Deena stopped one row ahead of Dale and slipped into her seat in front of him just as the doors of the plane closed.

Pivoting around, Deena graced Dale with a large smile.

"You ready to go?" she asked.

"Just about," he said. "Caroline here's gonna help me out with my final preparations." Dale leaned toward his associate. "Open a template, Harold. Let's make a PowerPoint."

Then Dale turned back to Caroline, clapped his hands together once, and said, "So, what are we gonna argue tomorrow?"

• • •

Despite hours of work, things were looking grim, Caroline admitted to herself.

She sat beside Dale with her binder open in her lap. Across the aisle, in her old seat beside Louis, Harold worked on finalizing the slapdash PowerPoint presentation Dale had prepared with all the attentiveness of a husband being asked to choose between china patterns.

A row of small plastic bottles stood like soldiers along the far edge of Dale's tray table. The first three were empty. The last two were not.

"After I finish my proximity-in-time-to-injury argument, I'll give the judge the high points of each of the articles we've discussed, then I'll circle back to Heller one last time, then I'm done," Dale said. As if to punctuate his sentence, he twisted the top off the next whiskey bottle and emptied the contents into the well-used cup of ice.

"But what exactly are you going to say about each article?" Caroline said. She felt like a broken record. For hours Louis and now she had been trying to get Dale to focus. But Dale's response had been the same every time. He'd discuss the "high points." No details. No further elaboration as to what he meant. No chance of persuading the judge, Caroline finished to herself.

Beside her, she could feel the consternation rolling off Louis in waves. She didn't need to see her boss's face to know the vertical furrow beside his eyebrow was at least a foot deep by now. She knew that Dale had hired Hale Stern to help make himself look good, but he was making it awfully hard for them to help do that.

"Don't worry," Dale said. "I'm a game-day guy. I've done this hundreds of times—I get in front of the judge and the magic happens. I've got plenty to work with here. Trust me."

Caroline wasn't so sure. Even though she'd watched Dale spellbind the Plaintiffs' Steering Committee at the Las Vegas luncheon, she wasn't consoled. Neither was Louis. He'd taken Dale to the back of the plane to talk. While Caroline couldn't hear what he'd said to Dale, she'd easily read his expression. He was concerned. When he'd returned, Louis had told her to do her best to break through Dale's inebriation. As for himself, he needed to prepare for the next set of depositions in the *Telemetry Systems* matter. Unsaid was that Louis had turned his attention to the less hopeless task on the flight.

"Why don't you just spend a little time with the chart I made?" she began again, forcing patience into her voice. "Then we can talk about how the other articles all support Heller's conclusions. The flowchart I prepared for you shows how the articles interrelate. The chart is super helpful. I color coded it to make it easy for you."

"Sure, right, the flowchart," Dale said absently.

Caroline resisted the urge to smash her head into the seat in front of her. But that would wake up Deena, which would be worse.

"I'll be right back," Caroline said, standing up. She needed to regroup. She needed to calm down. She had to find a way to get through to Dale. They were running out of time.

Walking toward the back of the plane, she shot a look at Louis, whose white head was bent over a pile of deposition notes. He glanced up and met her eyes. She considered lamenting her woes to him, but she knew he already knew them. She knew he shared them.

Five minutes later, Caroline walked back toward her seat. She'd come up with a plan. She'd just tell Dale the highlights of each article. She'd read the summaries to him out loud if she had to. Even in his drunken state, he might absorb some pertinent information.

When she arrived at her seat, Caroline found Deena sitting in it.

"I decided to help out," Deena said, bumping Dale's shoulder with her own, eliciting a hearty guffaw from the Texan.

"I'll gladly take your help any time, little lady," Dale said, bumping Deena back.

"But I need to get Dale ready—"

"Remember, I read those articles, too," Deena cut Caroline off. "I can take over from here. Just take my seat. There's a *Vogue* magazine there you can read, if you'd like." She looked Caroline over with an expression that suggested Caroline could do with a little help from the magazine's fashion gurus.

Deena handed Caroline's laptop up to her, then turned back to Dale.

Sitting down in Deena's seat, Caroline felt tears of frustration welling in her eyes.

• • •

Calm. Balance. Equanimity.

These things were difficult for Caroline to find the morning of the *Daubert* hearing. She'd spent the night lying awake with dread in her gut. They were in trouble. Dale might not be ready, and there was nothing she could do about it.

Standing at the bathroom sink of her hotel room, Caroline noted her dark-ringed eyes.

She dashed off a quick text to Louis: I'll meet you at court.

Her boss didn't need to see her like this, before she'd found a way to cover her doubts. Before she'd donned enough armor to convey an impression of calm confidence. Before she'd wiped the exhaustion and despondency from her countenance.

Three coffees later, Caroline was awake. In fact, she was practically vibrating with the caffeine coursing through her veins. Not good for someone with a hair-trigger nervous system and a gut like a colicky child.

Dragging her rolling briefcase behind her with one hand and carrying her laptop bag over her shoulder, Caroline stepped out to the curb to hail a cab.

A gust of wind blew hard down the concrete canyon of buildings, blasting through her suit jacket. All around her, people wore long woolen coats. She'd apparently missed the Appropriate Fall Clothing Memorandum.

Shivering, she lifted a hand.

A cab pulled up immediately and Caroline rejoiced at her luck . . . until she noted the deep gash on the passenger-side door. At least someone else had rammed into the taxi, not the other way around. Right? Right.

She squeezed her rolling briefcase into the backseat, then climbed in after it.

"Where ya going, missus?" asked the driver. The streetlights reflected off his bald black head.

"District court. It's down on Pearl Street."

In the rearview mirror, Caroline saw the cabbie scowl.

"I know it's just a few blocks away, but I just didn't want to carry all this stuff. I tip well," she added. "I promise."

In answer, the cabbie jerked away from the curb with a quick swing of the steering wheel and a flash of erratic acceleration. Caroline reached for the door to steady herself. She hoped the day would go smoothly. Sometimes a day clicked together, each puzzle piece fitting effortlessly into the next. She closed her eyes and sent a wish, a prayer to anyone listening out there that today would be such a day.

A honk and a jolt broke her reverie. Even before she opened her eyes, she noted the disturbing absence of forward momentum. Traffic. Great.

She looked at her watch. The hearing would begin in a half hour. She thought she'd left herself enough time, but at zero miles per hour, she'd never arrive.

"How close are we to the courthouse?" she asked the driver.

"Still three blocks, missus," the cabbie answered in an accent from some indeterminate African country.

"Really?" The distance hadn't looked so great on the map. She didn't have time to sit in traffic. The whole point of traveling alone to court had been to keep herself relaxed, but now she felt the anxiety begin, nagging, pulling, tugging at her mind.

Suddenly, she couldn't get enough air.

"I'll walk." She pulled a ten-dollar bill from her purse and dangled it over the divider.

The driver didn't notice. He was too busy texting.

"Excuse me," Caroline said, a little more desperately. "I'm just going to get out here."

This time the driver looked up long enough to recognize that his fare was fleeing. He made a halfhearted effort to find a safe place to stop before letting Caroline exit in the middle of the street.

"Keep the change," Caroline called as she climbed from the cab and tried not to get run down by a bike messenger threading his way through the gridlock.

When she reached the relative safety of the sidewalk, she put her hands on her knees and drank in the cool air, trying to stop the dizziness that fragmented the street scene in front of her. The streets of New York were the worst possible spot for an anxiety attack. She imagined her frozen remains and bones picked over by scavengers. At least she had a driver's license. Someone could identify the body if she passed out.

Reaching into her pocket, she felt for the worry beads, letting the sensation ground her.

Gradually, her breathing calmed.

But her calm was short-lived. With a sudden bolt of awfulness, she realized she'd forgotten to grab her rolling briefcase.

She spun around, casting around for the cab, but it was gone.

Panic threatened to rise again in her chest, constricted and crushing.

Caroline forced herself into equanimity. The briefcase contained only hard copies of the articles. She still had her laptop containing the downloaded articles, all bookmarked and organized. She'd be fine, she told herself. She just had to be.

She had to stay calm. She just had to get to court.

Facing the rising sun, she began to walk.

• • •

Three long New York blocks later, Caroline's feet screamed in protest at her heels. Business attire sucked, she decided. Fortunately, her destination was ahead—a hulking gray structure with overwrought gray pillars and a statue of Lady Justice mounted before it.

Tourists clogged the sidewalk, all wearing matching shirts or caps, clustered around docents carrying flags bearing the names of different tour companies. Apparently, the historic courthouse was on an architectural walking tour. Weaving through the throngs of people, Caroline scanned the exterior of the building for an entrance.

Finally, she saw it glowing in the pale-yellow sunlight of early morning.

She jogged toward it and stopped at the security checkpoint. A line of litigants and lawyers stretched out onto the sidewalk, all waiting to pass through a single metal detector manned by a bored-looking marshal whose bloodshot eyes scanned a small screen.

She glanced at her watch. She had only ten minutes before the hearing. Louis would be wondering where she was. Forcing herself not to panic, she waited for the marshal to wave her through.

When she'd passed the checkpoint, Caroline entered the green marble rotunda.

She found the list of courtrooms posted on a dog-eared piece of paper on a pillar. Judge Todd Jacobsen's courtroom was on the second floor.

But while Caroline saw the down escalator located across from the exit to the courthouse, she didn't see an up escalator anywhere. She huffed in frustration, contemplating writing a sternly worded letter to the architect. While she appreciated the efforts of those who'd tried to locate the escalators in a manner that retained the building's original decorative details, it would have been nice to have up and down in the same general location.

Resisting the urge to check her watch again, she began to methodically check each hallway and corridor, hunting for the up escalator. She found it on the far side of the building, over a quarter mile away from the down escalator.

Finally, she stood at the doors to the courtroom.

She reminded herself this would all be over soon. She remembered her guided meditation from one of her favorite tapes. She imagined roots forming from her feet, traveling down into the loamy soil, gripping, grounding.

Then she entered.

• • •

The moment Caroline stepped into the courtroom, Deena approached. The New York associate's gold-link necklace turned a plain black dress into a backdrop for a bolt of fabulousness. It hadn't occurred to Caroline that an attorney could wear something other than a suit to court, but seeing Deena, it now seemed obvious.

"Dale's all ready to go," Deena said. "I worked with him all night." Caroline raised a mental eyebrow.

"The PowerPoint looks good," Deena continued. "He's good to go."

The sound of Deena's razor-edged voice was a buzz saw, its blade shredding the imaginary roots Caroline had just sent down to the ground. Something about the woman set her nerves on edge.

Beside Caroline, the door of the courtroom swung open. A familiar face appeared. Jasper, the gruff retiree who had elicited a promise from her to win the case. An absurd promise that she still irrationally hoped to keep. With his neatly pressed trousers and collared shirt, he looked like he'd donned his Sunday best for the occasion of the *Daubert* hearing.

Caroline wasn't sure which was worse: talking to Deena or talking to this poor soul whose brother's life depended on Dale's performance.

Excusing herself from Deena, she made her way toward Jasper.

He extended a hand.

She took it and found it rough and strong, callused from a lifetime of physical labor.

"Did you fly all the way out for this?" she asked.

"Nah. Too expensive. I drove. Can't do nothing about the result. But I can watch the hearing. And pray." Jasper squinted at Caroline. "You gonna be doin' the arguing today?"

"No," Caroline said. "I'm going to be doing my best to make sure the guy that's handling the argument does the very best he can." She patted the laptop bag slung over her shoulder.

"Good," Jasper said.

Caroline wished she could offer this man some help. Real help. As a child, she'd saved birds when they'd crashed into the dining room window. Befuddled and stunned, they'd lie in a shoe box until they got their bearings again, then they'd fly off. The same urge descended on her now as she looked at Jasper's hangdog face. But she had nothing to offer him except an encouraging smile and some false enthusiasm.

Caroline looked around the courtroom. "Where's Tom?"

"He couldn't come," Jasper said, looking down. "The kids at the school started a fund for him to cover the cost of his medication for another few months. Just to give us a little more time. After that . . . we're all out of options."

"I'm sorry," Caroline offered. The words felt inadequate to capture the enormity of the personal stakes this case had for this man.

"Everyone's sorry," said Jasper, his voice holding bitterness. "I don't need sympathy. I need you to win this thing so my brother can get his settlement."

Caroline inclined her head in sympathy.

"If we don't win here today, I don't know what's going to happen . . ." Jasper trailed off.

Caroline knew. Tom would die. The look in Jasper's eyes said he knew it, too.

The stern man cleared his throat. "I know you're going to do fine. You're our lucky charm, we've decided."

"Why?" Caroline blurted, appalled. She was just an associate. A lowly first-year.

"Because you care," said Jasper. "It's in your eyes every time you ask about my brother. That's how I know you're gonna save him," he said, his gruff facade cracking, showing the scared younger brother who desperately wanted his older brother not to die.

Caroline didn't know what to say.

"I'll see you afterward. After you've won," Jasper said before turning away and ushering himself to the back of the gallery to stand with the other family members of victims.

Turning away from Jasper, Caroline scanned the courtroom for a familiar face. Someone to help shoulder the load of the expectations that shone from the faces of the victims' families. But she didn't see Louis anywhere. Nor did she see Eddie.

Eddie had promised he'd make it in time for the hearing. With a kiss on the forehead, he'd vowed he'd see her just as soon as he arrived. But there was no Eddie. Just two teams preparing to do battle. Attorneys, paralegals, and support staff scurried around the clerk and audiovisual stations, testing the Elmo projector and arranging documents. Court staff took business cards and filled-out appearance forms. Marshals shifted from foot to foot, practiced movements honed by long hours of standing.

Caroline watched the proceedings with a deepening sense of doom. All of these lawyers, all of these preparations would amount to nothing if Dale couldn't pull off the argument. And she remained unconvinced that he could. She'd drilled him on the plane. She'd tried to stick her finger in the cracks of the dam . . . but would it be enough?

Her eyes settled on the door.

There was still time to flee the impending debacle.

• • •

Caroline sat in the bathroom stall with her head bent down, with the stench of race-day poop all around her. The smell of fear. The putrid odor that clung to the athletes' bathrooms and airport bathrooms and anywhere else where people's lower limbic nervous systems kicked in and told the body that death was imminent.

Ignoring the smell, she forced herself to breathe deeply. In, out, in, out. She willed her mind to find some distraction from the worry that contorted her gut, ping-ponging across her nerves. She begged some other thought to enter her head. Something soothing and grounding.

An image came. But instead of clouds or rainbows or puppies, she saw . . . monkey poop. She recalled traveling to the Amazon with her family in third grade. Paddling in a dugout canoe on a piranha-infested lake, they'd caught sight of a group of howler monkeys in the trees. The monkeys' response to the Audens' appearance had been instant. Showers of feces had cascaded down through the mangroves, a lower limbic system response to imagined danger. Unable to master their minds, the primates had been slaves to their visceral fears.

"I am not a monkey," she whispered to herself.

• • •

Water dripped down Caroline's chin as she leaned over the fountain outside the courtroom. She kept her face tipped over the basin so she wouldn't drench her suit. She cast a sideways look around for something with which to wipe her chin. Other than her sleeve.

A hand reached into Caroline's view, offering a clean, white handkerchief that smelled faintly of a men's cologne she didn't recognize.

She glanced up to see Ian Kennedy towering over her.

"Thanks," she said, taking the handkerchief.

She wiped her chin, then handed the damp fabric back to the tall defense attorney, who gazed at her with an innocuous, friendly expression.

"I thought I saw you head this way," Kennedy said, smiling his gap-toothed smile.

Caroline didn't smile back. Had he followed her when she fled the courtroom? Had he waited outside the women's bathroom? Creepy.

"Remarkable job filing that article," he said. "I saw the file stamp on it, just seconds before the virtual file window closed. That had to have been stressful."

"It was." She wouldn't give him anything more than that.

"Did you actually find the assistant scientist who wrote it?" Kennedy asked. "Or was the article someplace else?"

Caroline didn't answer. She knew he didn't expect her to.

"It is quite an article," Kennedy continued. "I read it and the supporting data as soon as they showed up on my desk. Dr. Heller's research was meticulous, I'll admit."

"That's true," Caroline said. "His sample sizes were impressive, too."

"Agreed," Kennedy said. "I'll do my best to debunk that article, but it has made this a far closer fight."

Caroline resisted the urge to respond, to continue talking about the article she'd worked so hard to find. Here, in her adversary, she'd found what she'd wished Dale had provided: a curious mind. That this curious mind also happened to lack all morality or scruples prevented her from speaking further. She shut her mouth and kept it closed.

"I knew you were something special." Kennedy smiled, the gap between his two front teeth more evident up close. "Louis is lucky to have you on his team. He really doesn't deserve someone of your quality. You really could do so much better."

Caroline remained silent. She prepared to defend herself. From what, she didn't know. Some threat. Even though she knew Kennedy wouldn't do anything in a courthouse. Even though she knew he didn't act directly. Even though she knew there were marshals around. Still, she feared him and his disarmingly benign demeanor. Benign like a sleeping cobra, she reminded herself.

"We offer attractive packages to our young associates," Kennedy said. "We also offer a stipend for a car lease. Plus, our firm banker offers very reasonable interest rates on home loans. The golden handcuffs, if you will." He paused. "We also offer generous medical benefits. Dental. Vision. Even . . . mental health."

Caroline blanched. Outside of a single notation in a student health record at UCLA, she'd never had a formal diagnosis of anxiety. Had Kennedy mined those records? She let none of her discomfiture show on her face.

"I've got to get back in there," Caroline said, nodding with her chin toward the courtroom.

"Of course you do," Kennedy said, inclining his head and stepping back to let her pass. "Just promise me you'll think about it. If ever things don't work out for you where you are . . ." He trailed off, raising an eyebrow to complete the sentence.

"I'm fine where I am for now, but I appreciate the offer," Caroline said. Perhaps if Kennedy thought she was vaguely interested, he'd be less inclined to kill her. Or something.

She turned to walk toward the courtroom.

The sound of her heels clicking against the marble floors echoed, obscuring her ability to sense if Kennedy was following.

She refused to look back.

But as she walked away, she shivered. Kennedy had only asked about the assistant scientist—as if he already knew the lead scientist was dead. While the newspapers had covered Heller's death, the scientist's demise wasn't something Kennedy had any reason to know about. Heller hadn't published, after all. They had no reason to know the article's history. Or the sad history of its author.

Had Kennedy just tipped his hand? Had he just revealed that he indeed had something to do with Dr. Heller's demise?

Preoccupied by the ominous possibilities, Caroline stepped back into the courtroom.

CHAPTER 10

The courtroom had filled to capacity. The room hummed with an undercurrent of anticipation. Everyone knew what was coming: showdown at high noon.

Caroline's heart began to pound in time to the ambient stress in the room.

"Hey," said a voice from behind her.

She recognized it immediately. Eddie.

She longed for an oasis of optimism. A friendly face. But there was no guarantee Eddie would provide it. Perhaps their night together had been born of euphoria after the breakneck-speed filing of the Heller article. Perhaps their connection had evaporated with the rising sun. Perhaps he was the sort of man who disavowed his sexual conquests with the cold shoulder of selective amnesia.

Caroline turned to face him.

In a pin-striped suit and wing-tip shoes, he cut a confident figure.

When Caroline met his eyes, he looked down.

Shyness, Caroline realized. She found it endearing. And encouraging.

"You made it," she said.

"My flight got delayed. But I'm on the one ahead of you back to LA, so I might beat you back." He met her eyes and held them.

Warmth blossomed in Caroline's chest.

"Though after we win this thing today," Eddie continued, "I'll have to clean out my borrowed office and go back to Atlanta." His dark eyes held genuine regret.

Caroline knew the expression in her own eyes matched his. She had known their fling would be short-lived. But she hated the reminder.

A light touch on her wrist brought her attention back to him.

"That's nice," Eddie said, his gaze traveling to her wrist where a bracelet formed of silver and gold Celtic knots hung.

She knew he was trying to change the topic. She decided to let him.

"It's called a Donegal," she said. "It's supposed to symbolize the harmonious weaving together of two paths. My dad gave it to me when I graduated law school."

"He must've been proud of you," Eddie said.

"He was, though I think he was also a little bit . . . conflicted." She shook her head. "It's a long story." She hadn't told her father the date of her graduation. They'd drifted so far apart that she didn't see the point. But a week after graduation, the bracelet had arrived in the mail, wrapped in raffia and accompanied by a handwritten note from the artist describing the meaning of the Donegal. Caroline knew her father saw symbolism in the gift. But she didn't call him to ask. And yet, she was wearing it.

"I'd like to hear the story." Eddie's eyes held hers. His fingers remained on her wrist. Intimate. Soft. Warm.

The heat in Caroline's chest spread upward to her face.

She felt a sudden wave of self-consciousness at the intimacy of their interaction in a crowded courtroom. A prickle of awareness caused her to turn.

She found Louis watching her from across the courtroom. Frowning.

Her heart sank. She could almost hear his thoughts—I told you not to trust the loaned associates, and now you've gone off and slept with one of them? She had no explanation. Except—passion isn't easily confined? We didn't pick this, it picked us? It all sounded cheesy and lame.

So she broke contact with Eddie's hand.

"I better go see about Louis," she said and withdrew.

Weaving through the sea of men in suits, toward the plaintiffs' side of the courtroom, she couldn't help but notice she was a foot shorter than everyone. The conversations going on around her were happening over her head. Literally. She was also at least a decade younger, and one of only a handful of women on either side, all of them junior associates.

Taking the last few steps toward Louis, Caroline easily read his mood in the compressed line of his mouth and the tightening of his jaw. He wasn't happy.

"Eddie helped me file the article—" she began.

"Yes, Silvia informed me. I'm grateful for his efforts," he said. His words were neutral, but there was no warmth in his voice.

Caroline didn't know what to say. She just knew with sudden urgency that she had to repair the damage her connection with Eddie had done to Louis's opinion of her. To his trust. She needed to figure out how to recover both.

But before she could speak again, Dale trotted up, his face flushed. His too-big mouth grinned widely like a golden retriever in the heat of a game of catch.

"We're almost ready to go," Dale said. "Herb's got the PowerPoint all set up."

Dale gestured with his chin toward the audiovisual vendor, who sat hunched over a laptop at a small desk behind the plaintiffs' counsel table.

"Plus, I wore my lucky tie." Dale fondled the lime-green tie with aqua dots, tilting it forward for Louis and Caroline to see. "My wife got it for me for Christmas."

Caroline kept her face neutral. What was Dale's wife like? Did she know about her husband's philandering? People were often blind to what they didn't want to see.

"I haven't lost a single case yet with this baby," Dale said brightly. "This is the longest run I've ever had for a lucky tie."

Caroline studied the talismanic piece of fabric. It didn't seem to have any unearthly glow or other special properties she could divine.

"I retired my last lucky tie after that loss in the Wrangler rollover case," Dale said, wincing. "But we've got a great presentation for the judge ready to go today. I just know he's gonna love it."

Caroline smiled gamely and made the noncommittal *mmm* sound people use to fill gaps in conversation.

The door to the judge's chambers clicked open, and the bailiff emerged.

"The judge will take the bench in five minutes," he announced.

In response, the attorneys scattered around the courtroom began to move toward the front, like goldfish rising to food. People began to take their seats. The show would begin soon.

"Hey, Dale," called a broad-shouldered man from the front of the gallery.

Caroline identified the man as Anton Callisto. Deena's boss. With his thick build and close-cropped silver hair, he was someone you'd want on your side if a fistfight broke out.

Anton waved Dale over to the counsel's table.

"Come on," Dale said to Louis and Caroline. "We need to decide who's sitting where."

Falling into step behind Dale and Louis, Caroline followed them to the front of the courtroom. She noted the strange layout. The podiums where the attorneys for each side would be arguing were positioned directly behind the long counsel tables, where another five lawyers for each side would sit. As a result, Dale would be looking over the heads of his seated colleagues when he stood up at the podium.

Other than the half-dozen lawyers who would sit up front at coun-sel's table, the attorneys would be relegated to the seats in the gallery. There weren't enough seats at the table for all of the attorneys on the Plaintiffs' Steering Committee.

Dale regarded the seating situation and rubbed his hand across his chin. Then he looked at Louis. "I'd like you up here, Louis," Dale said. "That leaves two seats for Anton and Paul."

Caroline watched the proceedings with dismay. After failing to induce Dale to study on the plane, this effort to relegate her to the back of the courtroom seemed . . . unwise.

"Excuse me," Caroline said. "Don't you think I should sit at coun-sel's table?"

Dale looked at her with a curious expression etched on his face.

"I wrote the section of our brief about the scientific literature," Caroline said. "You might have questions for me during the argument."

Dale shrugged. "Okay. Sure."

He grabbed a passing paralegal and said something into her ear. She disappeared then returned a few seconds later with a folding chair, which Dale wedged between Louis's seat and Anton's seat.

Squeezing herself between two large men beside her, Caroline felt small and invisible.

She opened her laptop and pulled up the index of articles. Just in case Dale needed it.

"Wish me luck," Dale said, sitting down on Louis's other side.

"Good luck," Caroline muttered.

The bailiff stood poised, waiting for the telltale click of the door and the soft shuffle and stir that would announce the arrival of the judge. The moment came with an electric jolt and a sigh. A door behind the curtain opened to reveal a man with copper hair and a dark goatee. His black robe swished as he walked over to the bench and sat down.

"Court for the Southern District of New York is now in session," the bailiff announced. "The Honorable Todd R. Jacobsen presiding."

The judge spread his binders and tablet on the table in front of him, neatly arranging his materials for the hearing. Caroline studied his face. He didn't look as young as she'd expected. She knew he'd been appointed to the bench only five years ago, but he already looked like a seasoned veteran.

Judge Jacobsen looked up with bright-blue eyes that held a twinkle of amusement.

"Welcome to the *Keep-Every-Lawyer-in-the-Country-Employed* case. What do you think the taxi meter is on all of your billable hours here today?" he asked.

The attorneys laughed as one. A bonding moment, scripted by the judge to relieve the tension in the room. Caroline appreciated the effort. From the taut expression on Ian Kennedy's face to Jasper's anguished squint, the courtroom was a soup of intense emotion.

"Thank you all for coming," the judge continued. "I know we're all going to learn something today. Lawyers are here to educate the judges, and we judges hope to be good students for you." Judge Jacobsen looked around as he spoke, making eye contact with each of the lawyers at each of the respective counsels' tables. "By way of full disclosure, I was a molecular cell biology graduate student before I went into the law. So I'd like to think I'm a slightly more sophisticated student. That said, I'm still here to learn. Let's get to it."

The judge turned toward the counsel table on the plaintiffs' side.

"Any time you're ready, Counsel."

"Thank you," Dale said, stepping up to the podium. "Your Honor, we've put together a presentation to help the court sort its way through these complex issues." He nodded to Herb, the audiovisual guy, and the first page of the PowerPoint presentation flashed onto the screen.

The word *DIAGNOSIS* arched across the top with a list of bullet points underneath that read *clinical diagnosis, medical diagnosis,* and *differential diagnosis.*

"I'd like to begin today by talking about bedrock science: diagnosing illness," Dale began. "For as long as there have been doctors, we've made diagnoses based on signs, symptoms, and laboratory findings. When a patient shows up at a doctor's office, that doctor has to determine which one of several diseases may be producing the symptoms—"

Judge Jacobsen leaned forward toward the microphone on the bench. "I'm sorry to interrupt, but I understand what differential diagnosis is. We have limited time today, so I'd like to stay focused on the science."

"With all due respect, Your Honor, differential diagnosis is science. It's the most basic, well-accepted science in the world, I'd venture." Dale smiled in a way that encouraged agreement with his words. "And it fully supports a link between SuperSoy and kidney injury."

"Be that as it may, I'd like to hear what else you've got," the judge said, smiling back, just as affably.

Caroline shifted in her seat. Judge Jacobsen hadn't mentioned the *Scziewizcs* decision, but he apparently subscribed to that decision's conclusion that something more than proximity-in-time evidence was necessary to prove a correlation between a substance and an injury. She hoped Dale could provide the judge with that something more.

"Well, all righty then," Dale acquiesced, prompting his PowerPoint until he reached the slide he sought.

"Here we have a diagram of a cell," Dale narrated. "Up there in the upper right corner, you'll see the mitochondria. The studies we'll discuss today suggest that SuperSoy causes some damage to different parts of the cell, especially the mitochondria."

"Excuse me again, Counsel," Judge Jacobsen interrupted. "I've read your papers. I understand your basic arguments. What I'd like to do today is drill down a bit. I'd like to know your thoughts on whether the Ambrose study's findings on mitochondrial degradation in rats can be extrapolated to humans. Yes, I know we'll get to the Heller study. But just as a starting point, I'd like to hear your views on Ambrose."

Dale blinked at the judge.

"The Ambrose study," Judge Jacobsen prompted. "It was performed on rats, right?"

Caroline turned around to face Dale and mouthed the word *yes*.

"Yes, Your Honor. It was done on rats," Dale said confidently.

"And the assay he used for his results was an end-point assay, correct?" the judge asked.

When Dale didn't respond, Caroline began to squirm. The answer was yes. Ambrose had used an end-point assay. The information was basic. But she'd already turned around once. If she fed Dale another answer, she'd begin to look like his ventriloquist. With great effort, she kept herself facing forward, her face an impassive mask.

"Ambrose is an important study," Dale began slowly, "because it teaches us that if enough cells die, a kidney will fail."

"Yes. Agreed," said the judge, "but I'd like to talk about the details of that study."

Dale shifted from foot to foot.

"Let's try this a different way, Counsel," the judge said, exhaling. "Let's talk about Heller. Perhaps we can explore the parameters of that study, then work our way back to the other science and evaluate whether that other science is consistent with Heller or whether Heller is an outlier."

"Sounds good, Your Honor," Dale said. Caroline could almost hear his relief.

"The Heller article is, of course, the centerpiece of the scientific literature," Dale said. "Although it wasn't published, it conclusively establishes a link between SuperSoy and kidney damage."

"I know that's your conclusion," the judge said, "but especially since the Heller article wasn't peer reviewed or published, I'd like to kick the tires on Heller's methodology. Let's begin with the basics. How large was Heller's sample size?"

"Sample size? I think I've got that right here," Dale said, prompting his PowerPoint again.

Images of cells and highlighted passages from articles flashed by on the screen.

Finally, a slide appeared that read in large red letters:

HELLER/WONG SHOWS DIRECT LINK.

HUMAN KIDNEY FAILURE CAUSED BY SUPERSOY!

There was no other information about the Heller article on the slide.

Caroline knew Dale was in trouble. She had to do something. Even if it looked bad, she had to try to help him.

Pivoting around in her chair, she handed Dale her laptop, opened to the relevant page of the Heller article describing the study's sample size. Now all he had to do was read it.

"Sample size. Sample size," Dale muttered.

Caroline resisted the urge to shout at Dale. She'd given him the correct page. He just needed to read what was on the screen.

"Please bear with me another moment," Dale said.

"Take your time, Counsel," Judge Jacobsen said, his voice flat.

"You'll have to excuse me, Your Honor. I just didn't realize we'd be gettin' into all these details today." Dale chuckled to himself.

The judge eyed Dale unblinkingly, unaffected by the Texas lawyer's avuncular charm.

As the silence stretched out, Caroline imagined Jasper at the back of the courtroom, scowling so deeply that the lines in his face looked like the Grand Canyon.

"I'm sorry, Judge, but I'm just not seeing it here," Dale said.

Caroline heard a murmur of whispers as the Plaintiffs' Steering Committee began to panic. They were going to lose. Not because they didn't have the science to beat Med-Gen's motion, but because Dale couldn't answer the judge's questions.

"I'll tell you what," Dale said finally. "What I'd like to do is start my presentation over. I think you'll find that the sample size in the Heller study won't matter when you see our whole presentation."

Cringing in her chair, Caroline suddenly understood the problem: Dale's superpower was telling a story. He knew how to charm a room, a luncheon table, or even the entire Steering Committee. But he had little patience for the intense schoolwork necessary to master complex science—complex science that this rare judge with a molecular cell biology degree wanted to discuss.

Desperate to express her distress, Caroline grabbed her legal pad.

"He's messing up," she wrote in a jagged scrawl.

She pushed the note in front of Louis, who tipped his white head down to read it.

The senior partner lifted his pen.

"Can you do better?" he wrote, tilting the legal pad toward Caroline.

"Yes," she wrote back.

Louis's response was only two words long: "Stand up."

Caroline rose to her feet so she stood in front of Dale.

She met the judge's eyes squarely. "I think what my colleague is trying to say is that the sample size was quite large. Dr. Heller conducted three separate longitudinal studies based on the records of over fifteen thousand SuperSoy patients across the country. His sample size is unimpeachable. As for the Ambrose study, while it was indeed an end-point assay instead of a kinetic assay, it still shows convincing evidence that SuperSoy thins cell walls because—"

"Excuse me, Counsel, but are you pro hac in this court?" Judge Jacobsen asked, his blue eyes narrowing.

"Yes, Your Honor," Caroline said. "I applied to appear pro hac vice when I submitted the Heller article yesterday. In accepting the article for filing, the court granted my application."

Judge Jacobsen turned to his clerk, who consulted her computer then whispered something to the judge. The judge nodded to his clerk then looked back at Caroline.

"You're correct. Please continue, Counsel."

Caroline stepped around the podium as Dale took her seat at counsel's table.

"As I was saying, the results of the Ambrose study are remarkable because that study mimicked conditions in human kidneys much better than any of the other rat studies. In addition to the Ambrose line of studies, the Wilson study and its progeny establish that degradation of mitochondrial DNA can be a precursor to apoptosis—that's spontaneous cell death. And as the Tercero study shows, that cell death is a harbinger of kidney death . . ."

Judge Jacobsen sat forward, his intelligent eyes taking in everything Caroline had to say, and when she stopped, he asked her a barrage of questions about each of the studies. Answering those questions, Caroline felt her words flowing out like a stream of clear water. The pieces of the argument fit together in her mind, one after the next, easy and logical. All of her restless energy laser focused down to a fine point. Article by article, point by point, she stated the plaintiffs' arguments. The sensation was like flight. Like a land-bound animal that suddenly realized it had wings.

When Caroline had answered the last of the judge's questions, she stepped back from the podium, yielding the floor to her opponent. She knew she'd done her best. Whatever happened, she'd explained the science as well as she was able.

Judge Jacobsen turned to the defense to invite refutations on behalf of Med-Gen, which Ian Kennedy provided in concise, well-spoken detail. As Kennedy spoke, his audiovisual vendor displayed demonstrative exhibits that underscored the key points in the scientific articles. Unlike Dale's superficial PowerPoint presentation, Kennedy's detailed slides acted as a wrecking ball, exploiting the weaknesses in the science supporting a link between SuperSoy and kidney damage.

Finally, Kennedy presented a giant table summarizing all of the science that had been presented in the course of the *Daubert* proceedings. In one column, the demonstrative exhibit listed the two dozen articles that plaintiffs' counsel had submitted that failed to draw any direct link between SuperSoy and kidney injury.

"After all of these hours of argument. All of these reams of articles. And what do we have?" Kennedy asked, using a laser pointer to trace a circle around the body of science in the first column.

"Nothing," Kennedy said. "We have absolutely nothing. Feinberg, Ambrose, Tercero, Wilson, et cetera, et cetera—not one of these studies ties SuperSoy to the degradation of kidney cells in humans. Not a single one."

Kennedy paused to allow his words to sink in.

"So then, what about the late-produced Heller article?" Kennedy asked, nodding toward his audiovisual vendor. On his cue, the Heller article appeared on the screen in the other, otherwise empty, column. The name of the article floated by itself in a field of white. Stacked against the dozens of articles in the other column, it looked immaterial and small.

Kennedy held up his right hand.

"Never published," he said, ticking off the article's deficits with his long fingers. "Never peer reviewed. Never subject to the same scrutiny that the rest of the scientific evidence underlying this case has withstood. No scientist has ever reviewed it. No studies have ever supported its results."

Kennedy paused again, giving everyone a chance to study the screen.

Watching Kennedy, Caroline had to concede that her adversary was more than worthy. He was good. Damn good. Everyone in the courtroom hung on his words. Even Caroline, who knew that the Heller article was a game changer, found herself carried along by the force of Kennedy's dismissal of Heller's careful, comprehensive masterpiece as a trivial piece of fluff.

"Your Honor," Kennedy began again, his voice affable, his tone matter-of-fact, "the whole purpose of a *Daubert* hearing is for our courts to protect juries from hearing cases that are premised on no evidence at all. We don't want to waste people's time. *Daubert* motions are powerful tools to allow judges like yourself to decide once and for all whether a given plaintiff's theory of liability withstands the test of plausibility."

Caroline resisted the urge to nod at his irrefutable logic.

"The reason we are here today for this particular *Daubert* hearing is so this court can discharge that solemn duty of ensuring that we don't waste the time, resources, or patience of thousands of juries across the country. And here's the bottom line: no published science links SuperSoy to kidney injury." Again Kennedy paused.

"SuperSoy is a highly beneficial product used by thousands, if not millions across the country," he finished. "It provides benefits to consumers, improving their quality of life. I urge the court to grant our *Daubert* motion and end this meritless case now, before it can further tax the system."

When Kennedy finished, the room quieted.

Everyone's eyes turned to the judge.

Judge Jacobsen sat back in his chair. He rested his elbows on the armrests and tapped his fingertips together. His eyebrows knit together in thought.

Caroline held her breath until her pulse throbbed in her ears.

"First, let me thank you for an excellent presentation today," the judge began. "It was quite informative. I admit, I came here inclined to rule against the plaintiffs. As defense counsel has correctly and eloquently explained, the science described in the plaintiffs' *Daubert* brief does not draw a direct link between SuperSoy and kidney damage."

Caroline resisted the urge to blurt, "What about Heller?" In a series of methodical studies, the Heller article illustrated the connection between SuperSoy and kidney failure. Surely, the judge had seen that.

Judge Jacobsen held up a ream of stapled pages. "I had actually prepared a tentative decision barring all claims on the grounds that the science didn't establish a link to kidney injury. While plaintiffs have showed that an inferential link may exist, I did not find that inferential link sufficiently compelling for the *SuperSoy* cases to go forward. I recognize that the Heller article is persuasive authority that there may, in fact, be such a direct link. The problem I'm having, however, is that the article was late produced and was not peer reviewed."

The judge paused. He gently placed his tentative decision down beside his tablet.

Caroline's stomach twisted. Her temples throbbed with tension. This was it.

"The arguments today have persuaded me that I should not be hasty in dismissing the Heller article. As plaintiffs' counsel has correctly noted, that article is remarkable in several respects, including its sample size and consistency of results." Judge Jacobsen paused again, and Caroline worried her heart might stop beating before he reached his ruling.

Finally, the judge exhaled like a man who had thought he'd reached the peak of a mountain only to find there were miles left to climb.

"Before I can determine whether and how to weigh Heller in my consideration, I need an understanding of why it wasn't submitted for peer review or published. I also need to understand where Heller fits into the other published science. I'm deferring ruling on the *Daubert* motion. I'd like to talk directly to all of the scientists of the articles you've cited. Subpoena them. Get them out here. I'll see you in one week. You'll have my ruling at that time."

With a sharp crack, Judge Jacobsen hit his gavel, and the hearing ended.

• • •

"That was amazing," Anton Callisto crowed. His usually taciturn face creased into a grin of underused smile lines. Behind him, the rest of the plaintiffs' attorneys agreed in a chorus of approving sounds. They clustered around Caroline, seeing her with new eyes. Or maybe seeing her at all for the first time.

"Thanks," Caroline said. In the wake of the argument, her teeth chattered, an electric humming coursing through her nervous system. It felt good. So did the attention of the Steering Committee. She felt like a lightning rod instead of a lawn gnome.

Even Dale looked relieved.

"We lived to fight another day, y'all," he said to everyone and no one. Another murmur of agreement coursed through the pack of plaintiffs' attorneys.

From the corner of her eye, Caroline spotted Jasper. He stood at the back of the courtroom, by the door. When he saw her notice him, he held up one thumb. Despite the approving gesture, his face still held the same pinched and worried expression it always seemed to hold. She knew the reason. He knew as well as she did that they hadn't won this thing yet.

"Can you come back here in a week to examine the scientists?" Paul Tiller asked, his cherubic face cracking into a likable smile.

Behind him, the rest of the Steering Committee nodded emphatically in agreement. All was forgiven of Dale, but they wouldn't soon let him argue again.

"Sure," Caroline said, despite the fact that she'd only conducted a cross-examination within the safe confines of law school. After seeing Dale flub the argument, she no longer believed she was unqualified to step in. At least she knew she'd study. She wasn't so sure about the next guy anymore. Especially if that next guy was Dale.

Louis wove his way toward Caroline until he stood beside her.

"If you don't mind," he said to the assembled lawyers, "I'm going to take my star associate here out for lunch."

As the members of the Steering Committee stepped aside, Caroline couldn't suppress the grin that spread on her face. Whatever disappointment Louis had felt in her for befriending Eddie had been obliterated by her strong performance in court. She knew he wouldn't mention Eddie again. Neither would she.

She followed Louis's tall frame through the throngs of lawyers, who parted like a Red Sea to his Moses.

"Are you really going to let me examine the scientists?" she asked Louis's back. Even with the buzz of the hearing still thrilling her senses, she knew it was unlikely her boss would entrust the witness examinations to a first-year lawyer.

"Absolutely," Louis answered over his shoulder. "You know the science better than anyone. I have full confidence in your ability to handle this."

"I promise I'll run all of my witness examination notes by you first," she said.

"Good. We'll make sure you're ready to go before the first scientist takes the stand," he called back to her. "We can set up some mock examinations with Eddie to help prepare you, if you'd like."

Caroline grinned at his unexpected mention of Eddie and his tacit permission for Eddie to help out. Louis was nothing if not socially graceful.

Louis led Caroline through the doors of the courtroom into the hall.

Once they were out of the earshot of the other attorneys, Louis stopped walking and turned to meet Caroline's eyes.

His face grew serious.

"Where are we on finding Dr. Wong?" he asked.

"We've subpoenaed her," Caroline said, jarred by the sudden change in her boss's mood. "There's a bench warrant out for her arrest."

"That's not good enough," Louis said, frowning. "There's no way to enforce bench warrants. Unless Dr. Wong gets pulled over for speeding or something, that warrant won't help us."

Caroline repressed her surprise. For some reason, she'd expected things like bench warrants to matter.

"We were very lucky to survive today's hearing," Louis said, still scowling. "Many judges would have simply dismissed an unpublished, non-peer-reviewed article out of hand. That Judge Jacobsen decided he wanted to talk to the scientists first is a result of your good work. You should be justly proud of what you achieved here today . . ."

"But we need Dr. Wong," Caroline finished, the last remaining shards of joy from the argument leaving her.

The door to the courtroom swung open, and Ian Kennedy emerged with two junior associates trailing behind him like black-suited ducklings.

As if by unspoken agreement, Louis and Caroline fell silent, waiting for him to pass.

But Kennedy slowed his step as he approached. He quirked a grin at Caroline.

"Like I said before the hearing, you're worth a raise," Kennedy said, holding Caroline's eyes a moment before continuing down the hall and out of sight.

As soon as Kennedy was gone, Louis rounded on Caroline.

"When did he talk to you? What did you say to him? Why didn't you tell me about this?" Louis's eyes narrowed.

Caroline reeled under the barrage of questions. "It was just a two-second conversation at the water fountain. I said nothing to him, don't worry—nothing."

Louis held her eyes, his jaw working.

"What's the big deal?" she asked.

"What's the big deal?" Louis repeated her words slowly, his pale eyes filling with fire. "The big deal is, Kennedy corrupts people. He can corrupt you."

Louis took a breath, as if consciously caging his passion. The fury in his eyes dissipated until the senior partner's face held an expression of pensive remorse.

"I'm afraid I wasn't completely candid when I said I'd only had one run-in with Kennedy," Louis said in a quiet voice. "The truth is, I know him rather well. In fact, I used to work with him."

Caroline opened her mouth to speak, but nothing came out. Louis's revelation was an awfully big omission.

"Ian and I began at the same firm out of law school," Louis said. "A white-shoe firm in Boston. Those old boys knew how to practice law, and they had no patience for Ian's shenanigans. Shredding documents and whatnot. He left the firm in disgrace."

He shook his head in disgust.

"I had hoped never to see him again," he continued, "but life is long, and mercenaries like Ian are attractive to clients that find themselves in dire straits. The scent of money and desperation is like chum in the water to him. I suppose I shouldn't have been surprised to see him on this case. Nor should I be surprised that he's courting you."

Caroline flushed at her boss's verbalization of what Kennedy's overtures meant. She moved quickly to disabuse him of the notion that those overtures had any chance of success.

"You don't have to worry," she said. "I'd never work for a fixer. I don't care what he offers me. It would never be enough to work for someone like him."

Louis's gaze thawed slightly. "That's welcome news. There are many people out there for whom morality is a convenience to be placed aside for the right price."

"I'm not one of those people," Caroline said, surprised by the vehemence in her voice.

Louis must have heard it, too, because his face calmed and his posture relaxed.

"Now that Kennedy knows we need Dr. Wong to win, he'll be mobilizing all of his resources to find her, too. Heaven help Dr. Wong if he gets to her before we do."

Caroline stayed silent. She waited for Louis to outline his plan. He was a chess player. A master litigator. He'd have a strategy. He always did.

But his next words left her worried.

"I'm going to be stuck here in New York for the *Telemetry Systems* depositions for the rest of the week, so you're going to have to take the lead in trying to locate Dr. Wong," he said. "Please keep me apprised of your progress."

Caroline's face fell.

"I'm sorry I can't help," he said, "but there's no way I can reschedule these depos."

He reached into his pocket and withdrew his wallet.

"But I can give you this." Louis removed a black credit card embossed with the golden logo of Hale Stern, LLP. He extended it to Caroline.

"This is the firm card," he said. "We usually only give these to our partners, but this is an exceptional circumstance. Please charge whatever you need to on it."

Warmed by her boss's trust, Caroline took the card from his hand and tucked it carefully into her wallet. But even that small patch of sunshine couldn't dispel the building maelstrom of worry coursing through her gut. If Dr. Heller had been murdered, those who'd killed him would now be gunning for Dr. Wong.

"I'm a little . . . nervous about going after Dr. Wong." Caroline cringed at her words.

"I understand," Louis said. "You'll have to excuse me. Sometimes I become so wrapped up with winning that I forget the human stakes involved in our cases." He released a long breath, then added, "You shouldn't do anything you feel uncomfortable doing."

Caroline considered his words. He was allowing her an out. A chicken exit.

"I'm okay," she said. "I'll keep going." At least for now, she added silently.

"Good," said Louis, looking at his watch. "Then you better get going. You don't want to miss your flight home."

CHAPTER 11

When Caroline exited the sliding doors of the airport terminal, she was greeted by the stinging odors of car exhaust and jet fumes. Vehicles of all sizes jammed the narrow road fronting the Arrivals curb. Some had trunks open, their occupants standing on the sidewalk hugging welcomes to their loved ones back from faraway places. Others sat waiting for passengers to appear from the black hole of baggage claim.

Caroline knew there was no one for her. Eddie was in transit. Her mom was in Oregon. Her dad was in Connecticut. Her best friend was traveling God knew where. And Uncle Hitch was likely curled up with a bottle of Grey Goose somewhere.

Making her way toward the outer ring of the arrivals area, Caroline scanned the signs until she found the one she sought: PARKING LOT SHUTTLES. A bus sat beneath the yellow sign, its engine idling, its bifold doors standing open.

Lucky break, thought Caroline, dragging her suitcase toward it.

After slotting her suitcase onto the luggage rack, Caroline sat down in one of the concave plastic seats. Almost immediately, the tiredness hit her. The last week had been a sprint. And the race wasn't over. She still needed to find Dr. Wong. More than that, she still needed to get Dr. Wong to come to New York for the hearing in six days. Just six days.

There would be no rest for her. She needed to get her car. Get back to the firm. Find Dr. Wong. In that order, and right away. Then she could rest. Easy.

The bus rocked as another passenger boarded. A blond man wearing a knit cap and an army surplus jacket made his way down the narrow aisle toward Caroline. Over one shoulder, he wore a black nylon messenger bag with gunmetal-gray buckles that clinked as he walked.

He sat down beside Caroline just as the doors at the front of the bus squeaked shut. With a rumble and a cloud of exhaust, the bus pulled away from the curb to begin its slow circumnavigation around the airport terminal, picking up more passengers before finally it would head to the off-site parking lot where Caroline had left her Mustang.

"How's it going?" the man said, jutting his chin toward her in greeting.

"Fine, thanks." Caroline hoped that would be the extent of the conversation. She wasn't in the mood to make small talk. During her long flight alone, the weight of her decision to look for Dr. Wong had settled over her like a shroud of worry. She was going to go head-to-head with Kennedy. No possible reassurance by Louis could convince her it wasn't dangerous.

"Where are you coming from?" the stranger on the bus asked.

"New York," Caroline answered. No such luck on the no-small-talk thing.

"Business?" he asked.

"Yes."

"Finance?" he asked, his eyes lighting up with interest.

"No, law," she answered.

"I work in finance," the stranger said. "My company just launched a new digital currency service. Payments work peer to peer."

"I know all about cryptocurrency," Caroline said. Though not yet mainstream, digital currency was a hot topic in tech circles. "Not everyone accepts it, though. People still prefer using money they can see."

"Some industries are painfully old-school," the man agreed, holding up a hand. He began counting off fingers. "Trust companies don't like digital currency. Neither do real estate investment traders. Or banks. Or car dealerships. But most individuals will accept it once they know what it is. Once they realize it's as good as cash. They just need to be educated."

Caroline shrugged. "Money's money. The world will come around. Eventually."

"Exactly," said the man. "Let me show you how our ledger works. I know I'm bragging, but it is superior to bitcoin or any of the other cryptocurrencies."

He pulled out his phone.

"Check this out," he said, opening an app displaying a payment ledger. "You can send money anywhere in the world. Payments can't ever be tracked or traced since there's no central administrator or country that runs it."

"I know how it works. But no cryptocurrency is uncrackable," she said, instantly regretting her challenge. She didn't want to start a debate with this stranger. She really didn't want to talk.

Glancing at the screen of the stranger's phone, Caroline saw her name.

Her fingers prickled with alarm.

"How did you know my name?" Caroline asked.

The man jutted his chin toward the luggage tag dangling off the side of her suitcase.

"Oh." Caroline relaxed.

But then, with a few more taps of his thumb, the stranger pulled up her bank and account information.

"Wait, how did you do that?" Caroline's heart began to pound. "This isn't right. You can't get a bank account just from a name."

The man didn't answer. Instead, he typed numbers into the ledger page, initiating a transaction that would transfer funds to her bank account.

"You see, it's super easy. I can just type in any amount here," he said, floating his index finger over the field to write a dollar amount. "For instance, what does it cost for a vacation these days? Ten thousand dollars? Twenty thousand?" He kept his eyes trained on his phone.

Caroline said nothing.

"Just for six days," the man continued. "A little vacation for a hard-working lawyer."

Caroline froze. The hairs on the back of her neck stood on end.

This wasn't an innocent conversation with a stranger. This man knew who she was. This man was trying to bribe her. Her mind understood what was happening, even as it tried to reject the reality. This man was Kennedy's agent.

She was in danger.

"I don't need a vacation," she said, noticing the birthmark on the man's cheek, near his mouth. Pigmented red, it looked like a dead bug with its legs in the air. "I appreciate the education in cryptocurrency." Caroline watched the airport terminal passing in the bus window. There was one more stop before the bus made its trip to the off-site parking lots.

"Everyone needs a vacation," the man said. "You could take a break or maybe even help out a struggling relative without worrying about work."

Caroline shivered at what might or might not have been a reference to her uncle.

When the shuttle stopped at the international terminal, Caroline leaped up. In one fluid motion, she grabbed her suitcase and charged off the shuttle. Hitting the last step of the bus, she pushed off hard, hurtling herself toward the waiting crowd. Then she ran down the terminal sidewalk, looking for a police officer. Someone. Anyone.

Behind her, the revving of an engine startled her.

When she spun around, the shuttle was gone. She was alone.

• • •

The first thing Caroline saw when she got back to her office was the package. Four inches tall and twenty inches long, it sat atop the legal pads and books strewn all over her desk. Cardboard and white, the package bore no markings except for her name, which had been scrawled in thick black ink across the center of the top.

Caroline's first thought was to call for a bomb squad. After her experience on the shuttle, her nerves prickled, filling her with edgy agitation. The appearance of the strange package seemed another ominous portent in a day filled with threats gathering like storm clouds.

She stood frozen in the doorway of her office for another few seconds before forcing herself to exhale. She ordered herself to chill out.

It was just a package. It wasn't ticking. Audibly, anyway.

Sitting down at her desk, Caroline lifted up the box. Someone, probably her assistant, had already created a long slit along one side so she could easily open it.

She eased the contents of the package onto her desk. Pictures and letters. Loosely shoved into the package, they looked as if someone had printed them out then hastily sent them to her.

A short cover letter from the Plaintiffs' Steering Committee's webmaster informed her that these materials had been sent to the Committee's public e-mail address in the last eight hours in response to a posting on the victims' Listserv and Facebook page. Seeing Caroline's name at the top of each letter, the webmaster had printed out and messengered the materials to her so she could "learn a little bit about the real people this case affects." The webmaster reported that many of the letters followed a similar script. They urged her "to spend some time getting to know the victims and their families."

Caroline's eyes widened. Strangers were writing to her? About SuperSoy?

She picked up the top photograph. A picture of a child wearing a reindeer hat smiled back at her. The little boy's feet were tucked into red-and-green socks with little antlers sticking up from the tops.

Reflexively, Caroline smiled at the sweet image. Clipped to it was a short letter.

> *Ms. Auden,*
> *Jasper Wilkens says you're helping us. I just wanted to thank you and tell you who I am. This is my son, Henry. He's three. This picture was from last Christmas. He doesn't look like this anymore. He's currently at Children's Hospital. He's stable at the moment, thank God, but his right kidney had been failing, so we went to the hospital. The medication seems to be helping him for now. I just wanted you to know how much it means to me that you're out there fighting for us.*
> *God bless you.*
> *Aubrey O'Malley*

Fascinated and appalled, she flipped to the next picture. This time, twin infants lay in matching hospital gowns, awaiting treatment. The accompanying letter told Caroline to "nail the bastards to the wall." Filled with vitriol and fury masking what Caroline knew had to be abject terror for the health of his children, this father had poured his desperation into the letter.

Caroline put the letter aside. It was too hard to read.

Especially since the incident on the airport shuttle had made her rethink her mission to find Dr. Wong. She shivered. One of Kennedy's agents had approached her, had tried to bribe her. Now that she'd rebuffed that attempt, what would Kennedy do next?

She needed to stop looking for Dr. Wong. Even if it meant losing, she couldn't risk her safety. No one could expect her to. Not even the victims. She felt bad for them, but she couldn't help them. Not without putting herself at great risk.

Caroline's hands traveled back to the pile of letters and pictures. She thumbed through the faces of the victims. Babies. Children. Sometimes adults. All of them depended on the *SuperSoy* litigation to ensure their treatment. To vindicate their injuries. To avenge loved ones who'd been ripped from the embraces of their now-bereaved families.

Caroline tried to distance herself from the onslaught. This was a blatant manipulation. Same as Jasper's brother's students showing up in court to try to influence the judge, this was a craven ploy intended to curry favor or sympathy from someone involved in the case. They wanted her to feel the weight of their sorrows, the heft of their nightly terrors, the full measure of their suffering. They wanted her to save them.

But she couldn't save these people. Heck, she couldn't even save herself.

Suddenly, her hands stopped at a familiar image.

The mother holding the child looked older, more worry worn and exhausted, but Caroline recognized the face of Amy Garber, the younger sister of her college roommate. During freshman year, Amy had visited often, sleeping on a futon in their dorm room.

Even after graduating, Caroline had followed Amy's blog. She'd read Amy's accounts of her time in Japan teaching English. More recently, Amy had chronicled her journey toward motherhood.

Caroline recalled the baby shower. Amy had already picked out a name for the baby. Liam. Named for her grandfather. Amy had beamed as she'd opened little towels and burp cloths and even the diaper disposal unit. And Amy had posted pictures of Liam after he'd been born.

Scrunched up and pink, he'd looked like a stricken chicken. But Amy had thought him to be the most beautiful creature in the world . . .

Now the image of Liam hit Caroline like a swift punch to the solar plexus, leaving her dizzy and reeling. The baby she remembered had been so healthy, so full of the promise of a whole life ahead of him. Now Liam's four-year-old visage stared wanly up at his mother, his arm hooked into a dialysis line.

Caroline could barely bring herself to read the letter clipped to the tragic image.

> *Caro—*
> *I couldn't believe it when I saw you were working on this case. I'm so glad it's you. You won't let Liam die. I know you and I know you're going to make sure Med-Gen pays for him to get the treatment he needs. I left my job to take care of him. Things are getting pretty desperate. We really need this, Caro.*
> *Love, Amy*

Tears welled in Caroline's eyes. The idea that Amy's son was sick was almost too much to bear. She knew she should feel the same way about all of the pictures now strewn across her desk, but this child wasn't a statistic. He was Liam.

The phone on her desk rang.

The number glowing on the phone's blue screen revealed who it was.

"Hi, Louis," she answered, wiping the moisture from her eyes and standing up, trying to get away from the pleading voices shouting at her from the pile of letters on her desk.

"I just picked up your voice mail. This is most disturbing," Louis said. "How are you doing?"

Caroline struggled for half a second to recall what he was talking about. She'd called Louis on her drive into the office, after she'd fled the man on the bus. Now she hoped her voice mail hadn't too obviously held the blinding fear she'd felt as she'd described what had happened to her.

"I'm okay," she said, even though it wasn't really true. She donned the headset and set out to wander the firm's halls. She needed to walk. She needed to settle her nerves.

At the late hour, only a handful of other lawyers occupied the offices ringing the windows of the firm. The rest of the offices were dark except for the ambient light from the neighboring buildings, seen like dark shadows up against the night sky.

"Much as it pains me to say it, I'm afraid we cannot hunt for Dr. Wong," Louis said in her ear. "It's too dangerous. I won't jeopardize your safety. Not for this case. Not for any case." His voice held a note of finality.

Caroline said nothing. He was right. Things had gotten too hot. Way too hot.

But what about the case? Some part of her mind still protested. They'd be forfeiting any chance of winning if they relinquished the search for the missing scientist. What about all those people? What about Amy and Liam?

As if anticipating her worries, Louis said, "I know I said we couldn't prevail without Dr. Wong, but that isn't true. We can have the other scientists testify about the Heller article. We'll make sure they read it before the next hearing. We'll fashion questions to elicit the answers we need to win this thing."

Caroline stayed silent. Her life was an exercise in forcing herself to live boldly despite her fears. She knew she worried. Sometimes excessively. Maybe almost always excessively, she amended. But this time her fears were well-founded.

"Besides," Louis continued, "Dr. Wong may yet show up of her own accord. She has subpoenas waiting for her at every known location she's ever frequented. You've left messages and sent e-mails to her last contacts."

"I could also see if she has a personal e-mail account," Caroline said, slowing her steps.

"Good idea. In the meanwhile, keep working on those witness notes," Louis said, taking it as a given that she'd given up the hunt. "Without Dr. Wong, we're going to need to push Dr. Ambrose to extrapolate from his studies on rats. We must get him focused on the similarities between rat and human mitochondria."

"I'm on it," Caroline said. Louis's directions made sense. Drafting witness notes. Conducting mock examinations. These activities were well within the purview of what she'd expected to be doing when she'd stepped into this office two weeks ago. She'd come to Hale Stern to practice law, not become a bounty hunter.

"Good," said Louis. Then he cleared his throat. "I want to extend my deepest apologies that your first case has turned out to be so harrowing," he said.

Caroline didn't know what to say. He was consoling her?

"No, I'm sorry," she said. "I wanted to impress you—"

"I am impressed," Louis said. "Finding that article, handling that argument . . . those were remarkable feats. Please rest assured that I am duly impressed with you. I look forward to our next—hopefully far more mundane—case together."

Caroline stopped before Louis's newest acquisition. Picasso's portrait of his girlfriend Dora Maar. Abstracted and shattered, the face read more like a mask. Caroline knew that as Picasso had soured on his girlfriends, he'd pulled apart their faces. No less violent than *Guernica*, Dora Maar's features were splayed across a canvas. Poor Dora had no podium from which to answer her ex-lover's ridicule, his almost comical dissection of her face. She was lost to history while the artist was and would always be . . . Picasso.

At Caroline's silence, Louis continued. "I'm stuck in New York. The time difference will make conversation difficult. But please, feel free to call me. Any time."

Caroline thanked her boss and hung up.

In the silence, the shattered face of Dora Maar looked back at her suspiciously.

"What are you looking at?" Caroline muttered at the image.

"I heard all that," came a voice from behind her.

Caroline turned to find Eddie leaning up against the door frame. He wore a cornflower-blue shirt rolled up to his elbows. His dark skin looked like satin.

"Eavesdropping?" she asked, quirking a smile at him to soften the accusation.

"You've been pacing right outside my office," Eddie said. "I was just working late on those witness examination notes you asked me to start when I got back."

"So, what do you think?" Caroline asked him. She turned back to the portrait on the wall, her eyes unseeing now as she became preoccupied with the question before her.

Eddie came to stand next to her. Together, they stood silently, facing the portrait.

When Eddie's triceps brushed against her shoulder, Caroline could feel the warmth of his skin even through his shirt. She knew he could feel her back, and that they were both enjoying the quiet proximity of each other. In the island peace conjured by the two of them standing side by side, she told Eddie all about Kennedy, about what had happened on the airport shuttle, and about the crossroads she now faced.

"Is it insane to keep looking for Dr. Wong?" Caroline asked, almost to herself. "These people . . . they probably killed Dr. Heller. They're seriously dangerous. I'd have to be crazy to keep looking for Dr. Wong, right?"

She wasn't sure whether she wanted him to agree.

"I don't know," Eddie said. "I can imagine someone going after a key witness like Dr. Wong, but lawyers are replaceable—we're like cockroaches, kill one of us and another will turn up to take his place." He smiled in an obvious effort to lighten the dour mood.

Caroline didn't answer. It sounded reasonable. It even echoed what Louis had said. But the churning in her gut said she still wasn't buying it.

"Do you think we can win without Dr. Wong?" she asked.

Eddie crossed his arms. "I'm a betting man. I'm always willing to take an across-the-board at the races. Big gambles mean big wins. But I don't like our odds without Dr. Wong."

Caroline considered her options. Louis would accept whatever decision she made. He'd given her permission to be prudent. To opt out of the hunt. But could she do so, knowing that they'd likely lose? That Amy might lose Liam? That Jasper might be left with nothing but memories of his brother? And that Louis, despite his professed understanding, would view her as the associate who'd lost the case?

"I think we need Dr. Wong, too," Caroline said finally.

Eddie turned to face her. His pitch-black eyes held a defiant twinkle.

"So then, are we going to keep looking for Dr. Anne Wong?" he asked.

The word *yes* leaped to Caroline's mouth, but she didn't give it voice. She examined her motives for continuing what had to be a fool-hardy—if not downright dangerous—endeavor. Was she so desperate for Louis's approval? No, that wasn't it. The need to keep going had become something else. A chance to do some good. An opportunity to right the scales, maybe a little, away from the things she'd done that had caused so much harm. If she could help Amy and Jasper and Liam, she couldn't be that bad a person. Right? The question hung in her mind.

"Let's see if we can figure out where Dr. Wong went," Caroline said, her voice full of sudden resolve. The complex mess of reasons why didn't matter. Boiled down, those reasons amounted to a simple imperative: she just had to keep going.

"Good," Eddie said. "What clues do we have? What do we know about Dr. Wong?"

"Come on, I'll show you," Caroline said, leading Eddie toward her office.

• • •

"What is that?" Eddie asked from over Caroline's shoulder. His attention was trained on the screen of her laptop.

"Franklin Heller's secret FTP site," Caroline said. "It's where I found the article. In addition to the article and the backup data, there was also a letter to Yvonne. I've been meaning to look at it."

She pulled up the document and read the one line hovering in the middle of the white screen:

I'm sorry. I never meant to hurt you. Love always, F.

"Weird," Eddie said. "It's like he knew he was gonna kick the bucket."

"He probably did," Caroline said. Although Dr. Heller had known what might happen, he'd been powerless to stop it. How horrific, she reflected. How horrible his last moments must have been, knowing all of his fears had been realized. Caroline studied the words of the scientist's final missive to his wife another moment before closing the document.

"But this isn't helping us figure out where Dr. Wong ran off to," she said.

"How do you know she ran?" Eddie asked. "How do you know she's not dead?"

"She definitely ran. She told her boyfriend she was leaving town and didn't know if or when she'd be back. As for whether she's dead, I guess we don't know for sure that she's alive. But I think she'd try really hard not to die. She's got a kid . . ." Caroline trailed off.

"What is it?" Eddie asked.

"She has a five-year-old son with asthma. He's on this experimental drug protocol to control it. It's called Telexo."

Caroline pivoted around until she faced Eddie.

"The drug manufacturer," Eddie said, his eyes widening.

"Exactly. Maybe they've got a genetic engineering division? Or the same parent company as Med-Gen?" Caroline turned back toward the laptop and entered a search for the name of the company that made Telexo. Annie's son, Nolan, needed Telexo to prevent his asthma attacks. A threat to his Telexo supply could have prompted Dr. Wong to run from the article she'd helped to author. That had to be it. That's why Dr. Heller's office was so orderly. No need for ransacking. Just a scientist with access who'd purged the computer of all information before she bailed.

Caroline tapped her foot with impatience while the page loaded on the screen.

When it finally appeared, she breathed out with disappointment. The Swiss pharmaceutical giant Gruezet owned the drug company that manufactured Telexo. There was no link to Med-Gen.

"Damn," Eddie breathed from behind her.

Not ready to give up, Caroline hunted for some other connection between Telexo and Med-Gen. She navigated to Med-Gen's website and began sifting through the corporate governance documents and quarterly reports and press releases. When those yielded nothing interesting, she tried Wikipedia.

She found a short summary of the long, sad history of Med-Gen. Founded in Atlanta, Georgia, in 1967, Med-Gen's predecessor had a good run making plastic bags for bread companies until 1973, when the oil crisis had choked off its petroleum supply. After standing at the precipice of bankruptcy, the company had received an infusion of venture capital and reinvented itself as a biotech company. Unfortunately, its early products experienced little success. Its asthma medication failed in clinical trials. Its diabetes treatments caused unpleasant heart palpitations and were soon supplanted by better products from other companies. Med-Gen's recent transition to creating genetically modified seeds had provided much-needed hope for Med-Gen's management. And its investors.

Caroline ran a search of investment advisors' evaluations of Med-Gen.

Almost immediately, she found an article bearing the headline "Med-Gen's One-Trick Pony."

"Check this out," Caroline said. "Med-Gen's stock got downgraded last year in light of the company's lack of diversified product offerings." She pivoted around to face Eddie again. "Translation—they're too dependent on SuperSoy for their revenues."

"Fine, so they have a motive to suppress the science that could sink SuperSoy." Eddie scanned the screen. "But there's still no link to Annie Wong."

"We've got one more clue." Caroline's fingers danced across the keyboard until she'd pulled up the video message. "Dr. Wong sent this to her boyfriend about a week after she left town. It's possible she shot the video wherever she's hiding out. But don't get your hopes up. There's not much to see. I've already watched it about a hundred times."

To prove her point, Caroline played the message.

Annie Wong stood in the half light between dusk and darkness. A wind stirred her jet-black hair. Even in the dim light, her face looked tired.

"I'm sorry, Henrik," she began, her voice tinny on Caroline's speakers, "but you've got to stop calling me. I don't blame you for not understanding. I barely do myself." The words were spoken quickly, as if she were afraid to stop her momentum. But then she paused. "Even if it doesn't seem like it right now, please know that I really do love you. I hope you can move on."

"Wait." Eddie pointed at the screen. "Right before the message ends, there's a flash."

"I know. I saw it. I think she was standing near a highway," Caroline said.

"Maybe so. Play it again," Eddie said.

Caroline obliged. Yes, there it was. A flash right before Dr. Wong had hit "Stop."

"That doesn't look like headlights to me," Eddie said. "It's too fast."

"I'll slow it down." Caroline configured the video feed to respond to the speed at which she tapped the space key. "I'm going to play it frame by frame," she said, tapping the bar. Dr. Wong's face moved in exaggerated slowness, the sound of her voice dragging and distorted. Six frames from the end, the light appeared. Right over Dr. Wong's left shoulder.

Caroline froze the image. Eddie was right. The flash didn't look like a car's headlights. It was too high in the frame.

"There's a sound in the background. Right at the end there," Eddie said.

Caroline turned up the volume and hit "Play" again, advancing the visual and audio feeds together, frame by frame, split second by split second. And this time, when she reached the end of the message, she heard it. A low sound, right when the flash occurred. A horn. A flash.

The conjunction of light and sound, linked in a memory of seashores.

"It's a lighthouse!" Caroline said.

She searched online for lighthouses with operational lenses and horns.

She found three in California. One in Mendocino. One near San Diego. One near Eureka.

"Guess it makes sense," Caroline said.

"Huh?" Eddie asked.

"Nolan has asthma. The coastal air is good for him." She pivoted around to meet Eddie's black eyes again. "Okay, so assuming Annie didn't keep moving after she recorded the message, we know she's near the coast."

"Yeah, but which coast? We've got three different lighthouses at three different locations." Eddie shook his head. "I don't know how we're gonna figure out this one. I'm a lawyer, not a private investigator . . ."

Caroline leaned back in her chair and ran her hand through her unruly hair.

Suddenly, she sat straight up.

"I know how to figure it out. There's someone I need to talk to," she said.

CHAPTER 12

Caroline spotted the artist talking to a group of patrons in the center of the cavernous warehouse art gallery. Henrik's shaggy mane of blond hair stood out above the group of men in suits interrogating him about one of his canvases. The artist had dressed up for the occasion. Instead of the paint-splattered jeans and loose tank top he'd worn the last time Caroline saw him, he wore khaki pants and a collared shirt. Only his wild hair hinted at the temperamental passion simmering beneath his now affable demeanor.

Upon seeing Caroline, Henrik's light-blue eyes ignited with interest. He excused himself and strode over to her.

"Did you find Annie?" he asked, his voice pitched low so no one around could hear.

"No. Not yet, but I've got some ideas where she might have gone," Caroline answered.

Henrik exhaled, his disappointment written across his face.

"I'm getting close," Caroline said. "I'm pretty sure she's either in Mendocino, Eureka, or San Diego. Do you know if she had any connection to any of those places?"

"I have no idea why she'd be in any of those places." His eyes narrowed. "Are you fucking with me?"

"No, I am not fucking with you. But I do need some more information."

"What do you want to know?"

"What's the name of the pharmacy where Nolan got his asthma medicine—his Telexo?"

"Nelson's Pharmacy in Santa Monica," Henrik answered. "Those guys are awesome. The big pharmacies were all a bunch of assholes."

"Why?" Caroline asked.

"The big pharmacies wouldn't stock Telexo. They told Annie they couldn't get a drug for a single customer. Too much hassle. But Nelson's rocked. Independently owned and totally legit." Henrik cocked his head. "Why does it matter?"

"Nolan needs his Telexo, right?"

When Henrik nodded, Caroline continued, "So, if Annie's living in a new place for any length of time, she's going to need somewhere to fill Nolan's prescriptions. Wherever that pharmacy is, Annie is."

"Smart," Henrik said, nodding to himself.

"I figure it would be easier for Annie to arrange for her old pharmacy to just forward the prescription to a new pharmacy rather than for her to try to get the drug company to coordinate with a doctor to write that prescription and send it to the new place. So, I just need to figure out where Nelson's forwarded the prescription."

Across the gallery space, a new group of patrons entered. A woman in a well-cut suit, escorting a young couple. Perhaps an art dealer or consultant bringing her clients to consider new acquisitions.

"Looks like you have more customers," Caroline said, withdrawing. She didn't want to explain to Henrik how she planned to find out from Nelson's Pharmacy where it had sent Nolan's prescription. To discover that information, she knew she might need to visit a place she hadn't visited in years. A place that both terrified and exhilarated her.

She'd almost made it out the door when Henrik called out, his deep voice booming across the gallery.

"Hey, Caroline."

Caroline froze. She turned to meet the artist's sky-blue gaze.

"I never cared what the deal was with that kid's dad." He held her eyes. "I would have adopted him. In fact, I still would, if they came back."

With much on her mind, Caroline ducked out into the alley.

• • •

Caroline stood at the threshold of the dark study. Nothing had changed since her father's departure. The same pictures still hung on the walls, the faces frozen in time. Younger. Faded. Long ago. The same plaid blanket draped over the armchair, still smelling faintly of mildew. The same books still stood neatly arranged on the long shelves.

The only thing missing was the computer. Three LCD monitors and a state-of-the-art IBM had once sat upon the metal desk that stretched below the bookshelves on one end of the room. Confiscated by the FBI, neither the monitors nor the computer had ever been replaced. Not by her father, while he'd still lived there. Not by her mother in the years since he'd gone.

In fact, Joanne had not touched the room. It was a memorial to a relationship.

But Caroline hadn't come to the study to pay homage to her parents' defunct marriage. She'd come to invoke her father's presence.

William Auden had always been so distant. So preoccupied and distracted.

Except in the study.

Here, father and daughter had found common ground, thrilling when they cracked another security code. Giggling like schoolchildren playing a prank when they erased the event logs and hid their tracks.

Together, they'd found information no one was supposed to see. They'd gone places no one was supposed to go.

Just like Caroline needed to do now.

She wished her father were with her. But he lived far away. With his new family. In his new life. And she needed to deal. Now.

Placing her laptop on the desk, Caroline rubbed her hands to bring blood to her fingertips. If all went as she hoped, she wouldn't need to do any real hacking. She'd avoid crossing the line she'd drawn for herself . . . though she might get a little chalk on her toes.

Like all hackers, Caroline adhered to a basic rule: always try the most vulnerable avenue of attack first. And like all hackers, she knew that the weakest part of any security system wasn't a firewall or a password. It was the human inclination to trust. The desire to be helpful was a bug in the human machine that allowed people to be manipulated into giving out information they knew better than to share.

Caroline found the phone number for Nelson's Pharmacy, and as soon as a technician answered, she set her trap: "I'm calling from Dr. Thompson's office. We have a new patient. Nolan Wong. We're writing him for Telexo, and I just wanted to check the dosage to make sure we've got it right. Do you mind letting me know what he takes?"

Caroline paused to let the innocuous question do its work. Once she got the pharmacy technician to give up this first useless piece of information, she knew she could get him to reveal the location of Nolan's new pharmacy. It was a trick, to be sure, but not a terrible one. A necessary manipulation, she assured herself. For a good cause.

"Sure," the technician said. "Nolan Wong, you said?"

"Yes," Caroline confirmed.

"Excuse me a second," the technician said.

In the background, Caroline heard the muffled murmuring of a conversation between the technician and someone else.

"The pharmacist is here," the technician said to Caroline when he returned. "She wants to know which doctor's office you're calling from."

"Dr. Thompson's office," Caroline repeated the false name.

In the silence that followed, her heart began hammering against the inside of her chest.

Something wasn't right. It was taking too long.

A woman's voice came onto the line. "This is Gerry Nelson, the pharmacist. I apologize, but like I said earlier, we just can't give any information about patients."

"I didn't call earlier," Caroline said.

Suddenly, she realized what must have happened: Henrik had called the pharmacy. Tantalized by the prospect of finding Annie, he'd tried to get Nelson's Pharmacy to tell him where it had sent Nolan's prescription.

"Oh, I see here that we've just received an e-mail confirmation of the dosage from the patient's mother," Caroline said, quickly hanging up. Social engineering depended on bringing down the target's defenses by garnering trust. Henrik's misstep had made Nelson's Pharmacy too suspicious. They'd never help her now.

She turned to the screen of her laptop.

In the darkened study, the glow of the web page obliterated her awareness of anything else in the room.

Caroline's stomach sank.

She hadn't hacked since the police had come to the door. She'd promised never to do it again. If the gods of justice were merciful and her dad didn't go to jail, she had vowed to turn away from the fun but dangerous world of hacking. Burned once, she'd avoid the stove.

Now she was going to have to break that promise. If she wanted to find out where Annie Wong had gone, she had to. She needed to take a step across the line. Not a giant one, but a step nonetheless. The thought gave her pause. Her father had almost gone to jail because of hacking. Because of her. Shame constricted her throat.

Through a crack in the drapes, Caroline saw a hint of late-afternoon sunshine. But she didn't open the blinds. This next task was best suited for the darkness.

She told herself she was hacking for the greater good. But her conscience wouldn't be caged. Letting the ends justify the means was the Machiavellian deal that devils of all stripes had used to justify their dark deeds through time immemorial.

But if she didn't find Annie, she'd be consigning people to death. To lifetimes of disability. Dialysis. Especially after reading Dr. Heller's article, she had no doubt that SuperSoy killed. So surely, this situation was different. Surely, this hacking was justified. It wasn't like she was hurting anyone . . .

Closing her eyes to the moral quandary, she brought her attention to the screen.

She knew the pharmacy's patient files would be encrypted. Another layer of protection for the most personal information. But she didn't need to access the patient files to find out where Annie had gone. All she needed was a communication between Nelson's Pharmacy and whatever new pharmacy Annie had asked Nelson's to forward the Telexo prescription to.

An e-mail would do.

The website provided her with the domain name for Nelson's Pharmacy. Now she just needed an e-mail address. She didn't see any e-mail addresses on the website, but she knew how to find one.

At the bottom of Nelson's Pharmacy's website, a list of hypertext links blinked.

IMMUNIZATIONS

HORMONE REPLACEMENT THERAPY

VITAMINS

SEND A MESSAGE TO A PHARMACIST

Caroline chose the last option.

"I've got a question for the pharmacist," Caroline typed into the "What's Your Question" field on the website. "I've got terrible psoriasis," she wrote, slightly concerned that the lie would cause her to actually develop psoriasis. "Can it be treated with over-the-counter medication?" She filled out her own e-mail address in the "About Me" field, then waited.

Moments later, she received an e-mail response from gnelson@nelsonspharmacy.com: "Over-the-counter medication can treat psoriasis," answered Gerry Nelson. "Specifically, fish oil and vitamin D will help. I just checked and both items are in stock now. Please let us know if you'd like to order some."

"Not now, but thanks for the info. I appreciate it," Caroline responded. She really had appreciated it. In far more ways than the unwitting pharmacy would ever know.

Now that she had an e-mail address and domain name, she just needed to hack into the e-mail account. Because the suffix on the e-mail address wasn't Gmail, Caroline figured Nelson's Pharmacy probably used the next most popular e-mail service: Exchange. That meant she could trigger Outlook's autoconfiguration protocol. All she needed was the password and username.

A brute force attack—systematically trying all possible username-password combinations—on the pharmacy's password and username might work. The problem was that Outlook's timeout interval would limit her number of tries. Caroline knew if she didn't get the right password-username combination in five or six attempts, the program would bar further tries for at least an hour. An hour she didn't have.

No, what she needed was a more sophisticated way to guess Gerry Nelson's username and password. She knew what to do.

She called on a trick she sometimes played at parties, where she'd guess her friends' usernames and passwords based on just a few pieces of information. A pet's name. A home address. If she knew just those things, she could usually guess both password and username in seven or eight tries.

Recognizing that she didn't have time to guess every combination, Caroline wrote a simple algorithm. She typed in Gerry Nelson's name, the pharmacy's name, the pharmacy's physical address, and several pharmacy-related terms. Dosage. Medication. Compounding. Pharmaceutical. Then she set the algorithm loose to do its work.

Moments later, she had her answers.

Username: Gerry

Password: Nelsonspharm

Caroline was in.

Now the final step.

She ran searches of Gerry Nelson's e-mails, hunting for any that contained the name *Nolan Wong*. She retrieved several dozen hits.

Opening the most recent e-mails containing Nolan's name, Caroline found what she sought: Nelson's Pharmacy had forwarded Nolan's Telexo prescription to the Arborville Pharmacy one month earlier.

Caroline considered the information. The first thing Anne had done after fleeing Los Angeles had been to arrange for the prescription to be forwarded to her new location. A careful, good mother. Even as she'd been running for her life, perhaps.

Caroline searched for "Arborville Pharmacy." Her first hit for the name appeared on a list of pharmacies in Northern California: Arborville Compounding Pharmacy, 2385 Linden Street, Mendocino, California.

"Gotcha," Caroline said aloud, a bolt of joy lancing her chest. Mendocino was one of the towns near a lighthouse!

Still, she restrained her celebration. She had one last step: finding Annie's address.

Surely the Mendocino pharmacy kept Annie's address on file. As Caroline searched for the pharmacy's website, she considered how hacking a second pharmacy didn't seem like much of a sin after hacking the first one. Funny how the conscience dulled with repeated transgression.

But her search for Arborville Pharmacy in Mendocino retrieved general hits on third-party websites. Yellow pages. Trade associations. Consumer reviews. There was no website for Arborville Pharmacy itself.

Caroline huffed in frustration. Arborville Pharmacy was probably a small-town mom-and-pop shop, where all of the customer information was kept in a file cabinet. Or on the owner's private laptop. Either way, Caroline recognized she'd reached the limit of what she could discover via the Internet.

With no obvious solution presenting itself, Caroline shut down her laptop and slouched low in the chair. She'd planned to end the day with an address. A destination. Now she had a thousand-person town to search. In two days.

The laptop's screen blinked off, and soon darkness reigned again in the study. The ambient warmth of the computer dissipated under Caroline's hands, which still hovered over the now-sleeping keyboard.

Without the hum of the laptop, she could hear her uncle moving around downstairs.

Perhaps Uncle Hitch would have some advice. He was an ex-cop. He had to know something about staking out people and approaching witnesses.

Then again, he was also an alcoholic. The difference between the Uncle Hitch she'd known growing up and the Uncle Hitch clanging around in the kitchen, looking for booze, was stark. He'd once been a fulsome, real person to her. She'd shared her stories. She'd listened to his. Now he'd become his pathology. His life's purpose had shrunk down to scoring his next bottle. And to his niece, he'd become someone to manage. Someone to humor. Not someone to trust.

And yet, pathologies were not immutable. Her mom had made the round trip, returning from illness to form healthy, current relationships.

Maybe Uncle Hitch would, too, someday. Meanwhile, maybe he could help Caroline figure out how to hunt down a reluctant witness.

Or maybe he could convince her not to try.

• • •

Uncle Hitch stood at the kitchen counter. The highball glass in his hand rested on his hip. His gray hair stood out in a halo of frizz around his balding head. He wore drawstring pajama pants and a stained undershirt.

If Caroline squinted, she could still see the build of a very strong, very thick cop, but if she didn't, he just looked fat and disheveled. His glassy eyes and slight sway told Caroline he'd already had too much to drink.

"Just me down here," he said, catching sight of his niece. "Your mom's still camping somewhere in the wilds of Oregon. Dunno when she's planning on getting back. Maybe next week."

"Actually, I wanted to talk to you," Caroline said, sitting down on a stool at the kitchen counter. "I need some advice. Police advice."

Raising an eyebrow, Uncle Hitch planted himself on the stool beside her and rested his elbows on the counter.

"What do you need to know?"

"I'm trying to locate a witness. She's somewhere up in Mendocino."

"Mendocino?" Uncle Hitch swiveled his stool around to face Caroline.

"Yeah, and I'm not sure she even wants to talk to me."

"Ah, she's hiding out," Uncle Hitch said.

Caroline nodded.

"You sure you need her?" Uncle Hitch asked.

"She's our key witness. I need to find her. After I find her, I've got to figure out how to talk to her without spooking her into running again.

And then after that, I need to get her to fly cross-country to New York with me and testify. Easy, right?"

Uncle Hitch took a slow sip. The highball seemed dainty in his large hand. When he went to place his glass down, a sudden jerk sent a splash of vodka onto the counter.

"There's an art to approaching skittish witnesses," Uncle Hitch said, ignoring the puddle. "You need to find a place that's public, so they feel safe, yet invisible so they'll talk freely. For instance, I once had this potential informant I needed to interview. I found out he was a baseball fan. So I ambushed him at the stadium's urinals during the seventh-inning stretch. Told him to stick around a little so we could chat after he finished up doing his thing."

He chuckled to himself at the recollection. But then his expression grew serious.

"Are there other people, um, interested in this potential witness?" he asked.

"If you mean, did this witness skip town because she maybe got bribed to bail or maybe she thought people were trying to kill her, the answer is yes."

Caroline watched a full harvest of worry blossom on her uncle's face.

"What's going on, Caro?" Uncle Hitch asked. Even despite his inebriated state, his words were clear and his worry was evident. The line of his mouth pressed together, grim and tight.

In broad brushstrokes, Caroline painted a picture of all that had happened in the last weeks. When she finished, Uncle Hitch stood up. He swayed and almost fell over. Gripping the stool, he caught his balance and carefully perched himself back in front of the counter.

"Christ, Caro. This is serious," he said.

"I know."

"We need to leave this house. We can't stay here. If they come for you, they'll come here. I've got this buddy downtown we could—"

"No," Caroline said. "I'm not staying with one of your drinking buddies."

"Fine, get a hotel room. Whatever. Just lie low for three days and this will end. Come home after that hearing's over and this whole thing has blown over. Promise me." He stared her down, his mahogany eyes holding hers, the frizz of his unruly hair making him look like a deranged guardian angel.

At Caroline's silence, her uncle jutted out his jaw.

"Then I'm going with you," he said.

"No. You're not healthy enough to go," Caroline said. And he wasn't. In addition to his tremor, Uncle Hitch's body showed signs of buckling under the strain of his alcohol addiction. His skin hung pallid and loose on the sharp angles of his face.

"You should see a doctor," she said.

"No doctors." Uncle Hitch's nostrils flared, his expression defiant and ready to push back against whatever harsh dose of reality his niece tried to force feed him.

But then his shoulders slumped, the fight going out of him. He looked down at his glass.

"I'm doing the best I can here," he said. "Things just haven't been . . . good . . . lately."

"I know," Caroline said softly. She watched him wrap his thick hand around the glass and tip his head back, taking another drink. Obliterating awareness. She couldn't stop him. She couldn't make him go to the doctor. She couldn't change any aspect of her uncle's trajectory in even the smallest way. But she could find Annie Wong.

"If I leave tonight, I can be in Mendocino before dawn," she said. "I know where the pharmacy up in Mendocino is—the one where this woman gets asthma meds for her kid . . ."

"What are you going to do?" Uncle Hitch slurred. "March in there and ask them to give you her home address?"

Caroline dug at the oak countertop with the tip of her nail. Hearing her uncle say it, her plan sounded even lamer than it did in her mind.

"I don't know yet." She shook her head and answered without looking up. "Mendocino isn't that big of a place. Maybe someone up there knows Annie Wong or her son."

She met her uncle's eyes. "All I know is, I've got to try. I need to talk to her."

"What happens if you don't find her?"

"I still go to New York for the hearing, but it'll be a trip across the country for nothing . . . We'll lose."

"If you're going out east, you should stop off in Connecticut," Uncle Hitch said. "Your dad would be glad to see you."

Caroline's face flushed. "No way."

"Suit yourself," Uncle Hitch muttered, taking another sip while Caroline returned to the splinter she'd been prying from the edge of the countertop.

Uncle Hitch coughed, clearing phlegm from his throat. "If this witness is so important to your case, you can bet your opponent's looking for her, too. In fact, you should assume they've beat you to her."

Caroline's finger froze on the countertop.

"You've got to be careful," he said. "Watch out for people following you. Be aware of any anomalies. Things out of place. That's the cardinal rule of policing. When something seems out of place, it probably is."

Caroline nodded her understanding.

"Do you want a gun?" Uncle Hitch asked.

Caroline considered the offer. She'd never fired a gun in her life.

"I don't need one," she said.

She hoped it was true.

Caroline looked up from the splinter and studied her uncle's face. His tremor. His balance.

"Are you going to be okay if I go?" she asked. She'd promised her mom she'd look after him.

"I'll be fine. I'm going down to the Ivy Lounge to see some friends."

Caroline shook her head. Uncle Hitch's friends were a group of veterans who hid out in the Ivy Lounge's dark recesses, sipping hard liquor and reminiscing about their misadventures. He always drank more when he was with them. If that was even possible. And if his friends weren't there, he always seemed to find someone else to buy his drinks. A world full of enablers . . .

She exhaled her consternation.

"Or I may stay home tonight," Uncle Hitch said quickly. "I was thinking of maybe staying in."

Caroline met his watery eyes, searching for truth in his words. She wanted to believe.

"Please text me to let me know, okay? Let me know where you are so I don't assume the worst. I'll be back home in just a few days."

She hoped that was true, too.

• • •

Caroline pressed down on the accelerator. The engine of the Mustang responded, the deep bass rumble vibrating up through the car's frame, more felt than heard. The sensation soothed her nerves. She had nine hours of driving ahead, capped by a frantic and dangerous search for a woman who didn't want to be found.

The car traversed the early-evening freeways, roads filled with taillights and headlights. Soon, the Mustang broke free of the gray landscape of human habitation. Tawny hills rolled out into the dusk, the first tinge of night settling onto their eastern slopes.

Caroline relaxed at the sight of something grander than the world of human things. The view was a rarity. Though mountains ringed the Los Angeles basin, she rarely saw them. Most of the time smog obscured the view, reducing the aperture on her world down to the near view.

She'd heard it said that Los Angelenos didn't trust air they couldn't see. Personally, she preferred taking air on faith.

She eyed the moon hovering over the hills. Not yet full, it competed with the sun's waning light and lost. In three days, it would be full. On the same day as the *Daubert* hearing.

An omen, Caroline decided. She was a logical person. She prized reasoning. Cause and effect made manifest in the empirical world. And yet, she still looked for signs. For the innate poetry of the universe. Connections, ephemeral yet real, beyond the ability of feeble human senses to detect. And this rising moon felt like a potent portent, there to shepherd in the ending. Caroline hoped this moon would favor her, bringing at its zenith a harvest of justice.

When she hit the long, straight shot of road that would carry her through the Central Valley, Caroline's mind turned to her uncle. Hopefully he'd be okay. She couldn't shake off the heavy shroud of guilt she wore for leaving him. It was difficult to keep her eyes trained forward when she knew things were falling apart somewhere behind her.

She'd seen them fall apart before.

Two years after her dad left, her mom had hit bottom. Depression. Alcohol. And the meds the doctor had given to Joanne hadn't helped.

In fact, they'd made things worse . . .

Caroline's mom's voice sounded all wrong on the phone. Hard edged and husky, the voice tortured its way out of her mother's throat like a piece of metal caught in a circular saw. The words hadn't made any sense, either. Babbling and paranoid, Joanne's demands that Caroline come home immediately sent Caroline into a panic.

Driving home from law school with a sick feeling in her stomach, Caroline wondered what she would find . . .

Chipped cinder blocks demarked the edge of the carport as Caroline parked. She climbed out of the car. Even outside, she could feel the demon energy swirling around the tract home. A restless, edgy, dangerous sensation that tingled her mental antennae and warned her to go anywhere other than inside the front door.

When she opened the door, she found Lola, the family dog, looking up at her with soulful, apprehensive brown eyes, as if the dog was considering taking her chances on the street rather than in this house full of crazy. Caroline put a hand on Lola's head.

"It'll be okay," she said, half to herself.

The dog sniffed in disagreement but leaned into the caress.

"Is that you, Caro?" Joanne's voice called from the bedroom. A manic edge rang rip razor through the ordinary low tones of her voice.

Caroline walked into her mother's bedroom, treading softly from long-time habit. She found her mother wearing a red bra and a faux Persian rug wrapped around her shoulders. A mound of clothing sat in the middle of the bed.

"Why are you wearing that?" Caroline eyed the unconventional accessory, the absurdity of the situation keeping her horror at bay.

"We must be practical!" her mother shot back, rearranging her grip on the rug that kept threatening to slip off her shoulders.

"Yes, we should," Caroline muttered. "Why don't you lie down, Mom?"

"We need to go!" Joanne said.

"Where are we going?" Caroline asked, putting calm into her voice to combat her mother's hysteria. People often said comedy and tragedy were close cousins, and now she understood why.

"We're going to Saskatchewan!" Joanne glared at her daughter like the destination was obvious, then she turned to her dresser and threw open the drawer. With her free hand, she began taking handfuls of underwear and socks and bras out and tossing them onto the pile on the bed.

Caroline watched in silence as her mother built a towering pile of fabric. Her mother had always tended toward the mystical, toward floating off the planet without the firm cord of her dad's pragmatism anchoring her. But this was something new. Something terrifying. This wasn't a flight into the mystic. This was a break from reality.

Unsure what to do, Caroline texted her dad then waited for a response. When her dad didn't respond, the fear descended on her. She needed to deal. Alone, apparently.

"We need to see a doctor, Mom," Caroline said. That much was obvious.

Instead of answering, Joanne speed walked to her closet and began tossing jackets onto her bed. She gave up on the Persian rug, letting it fall to the floor. With two hands now free, she could unload her clothing from the closets at an even more frantic pace.

"Come on, Mom, let's go get some help. Let's go to the hospital," Caroline said. If her mother wouldn't come willingly, would she have to call an ambulance? What would happen? Men with needles and a gurney?

"Hospital?" Joanne's brow furrowed. "No, I don't think I'm going there."

"Please, Mom," Caroline pleaded. "Just for a quick checkup. So we can see whether you're healthy enough for Saskatchewan," Caroline said, joining her mother on whatever plane of insanity she presently resided.

"Saskatchewan? Okay, I'll go if I can bring my eyeliner." Joanne began digging through the pile.

"We can get you some new eyeliner at the hospital," Caroline said, grabbing a sweatshirt from the pile of clothing and pulling it over her mother's head.

The orderlies at the hospital's sliding doors had struggled to sedate Joanne. And the drama hadn't ended that afternoon. For the next weeks, Caroline had made daily trips to the hospital, waiting for her mother to emerge from her psychosis.

Her dad had offered support on the phone, but it wasn't enough. Watching her mother lying on the hospital bed, her eyes blank and unseeing, Caroline hadn't known if her mother would return. She hadn't known if what she saw was a harbinger of the end . . . or the end itself.

But Joanne had returned. And she'd stopped drinking. And she'd gotten better. Too late to save the marriage, but she'd gotten better.

Now Uncle Hitch was the one on a downward slide. A slide that Caroline could watch but do nothing to stop. She'd been there before. She had a front-row seat to a train wreck.

Caroline knew what she needed to do. She needed to keep moving. She needed to keep functioning. Even after she'd spent a night in a hospital looking at her mom's vacant face, she'd had to get up in the morning and go to school. Even when she was racked with worry about what the next day would bring for people she loved, she needed to put on her game face and deal.

She had a pharmacist to interrogate. She had possible killers to avoid. She had no time to waste energy worrying about what she could not fix.

She drove on into the night.

CHAPTER 13

"How many nights are you staying?" the motel desk clerk asked. With his watering eyes and drooping mustache, he looked like he'd been sound asleep until moments ago. Which he probably had, Caroline reflected. A thin curl of smoke rose from a freshly lit cigarette in the ashtray beside the clerk's left hand.

"Two," Caroline said, noting a gamy odor beneath the smell of cigarette smoke. With an embarrassed shock of recognition, she realized she was smelling herself. She needed a shower. She needed a nap. She needed a meal and probably also a hug. With little hope of the latter, she turned to taking care of the former two as fast as possible.

She pulled the firm's credit card from her wallet and placed it in front of the desk clerk. Two nights at a seedy motel on the outskirts of Mendocino would be her first charge to Hale Stern. And an ignoble one at that.

The desk clerk shook his head. "Cash only. Up front." He took a slow drag from his cigarette while he waited for Caroline to replace her credit card and find the correct denominations of currency.

Once she'd paid, he placed a key on the stained oak counter beside a plastic case holding brochures for the Nightaway Motel chain. Caroline couldn't recall ever having seen another Nightaway Motel. Perhaps it was a chain more in aspiration than in reality.

"Thanks," said Caroline, glad to be on a fast trajectory toward bed. She had only a few hours before the pharmacy opened. She needed to hurry to get some rest before then.

And yet, when she stepped through the lobby door, she paused to admire the night sky. The sun would rise in an hour or two; darkness reigned supreme except for the bright, almost-full moon. A wind blew from the north, stirring the clouds casting a ring around the moon, splaying white around the clouds like the iris of an eye surrounded by a glowing cornea. If old seafarers' lore were true, it would rain tonight.

As if in answer, the first pattering of drops made dark marks on the pavement, barely visible in the parking lot's floodlights.

Ducking her head against the moisture, Caroline jogged to the Mustang to pull her suitcase and laptop bag from the trunk.

She paused at the door to the hotel and checked her phone. She had one text.

Uncle Hitch had written two hours earlier: Went to Ivy Lounge.

"Damn it," Caroline said to no one.

• • •

Three quick hours, one long nap, and a drought-inducing shower later, Caroline stood at the counter of the Arborville Pharmacy, telling her most recent lie.

"Annie Wong asked me to pick up her son Nolan's prescription," she said.

The bespectacled man behind the counter squinted at Caroline as if trying to identify her.

"She's a friend," Caroline explained. "I told her I'd be in the neighborhood, so it would be no trouble for me to come by to grab it for her."

In answer, the man shuffled over to a long plastic shelf of white-bagged prescriptions. With all the speed of a snail on sedatives, he thumbed through them.

He returned to the counter, shaking his head. "There's nothing here. Are you sure she didn't pick it up herself?"

"Guess she did," Caroline said, turning away. She felt the pharmacist's eyes on her back as she pushed through the screen door.

Outside, Caroline spotted a wooden bench. Lodged in the corner of the porch of the Victorian building housing the pharmacy, its white-washed comfort beckoned. It was as good a place as any to try to figure out what to do next.

Caroline pondered her options. The pharmacy had been a dead end, as had been the Internet, since Annie's name didn't appear in any of the local Mendocino directories. Whatever she'd been doing since she'd left Los Angeles, she hadn't participated in any civic events that had recorded her attendance.

And yet, Annie was close. Somewhere. But where?

Caroline studied the view across the parking lot. The rain that had pounded the roof of the motel had stopped just after dawn. In the storm's aftermath, the air tasted like a drink of cool water. In the sky, tall, white clouds piled high in confectioners' heaps, glowing against a deep-blue sky.

A minivan pulled up in front of the pharmacy. Matte blue and covered with small dents, the vehicle looked like a class full of kindergarteners had surrounded it and kicked the crap out of it. A woman climbed out of the driver's seat, her used-to-be-blonde hair tied back in a hasty ponytail. Then the door of the minivan slid open to reveal a boy holding a ratty blanket. White blond, with a head too large for his body, he ran to keep up with his mother's stride as the two of them approached the door of the pharmacy.

The mother slowed as she passed, meeting Caroline's eyes.

"Good morning," she said with small-town friendliness before opening the screen door for her son to pass.

"Wait a second," Caroline said, rising from the bench. "Can I ask you a quick question?"

"Yes?" said the mother, still holding the screen door.

"How many elementary schools are there in Mendocino?" Caroline asked.

"Just one. Mendo K through eight."

"Thanks," Caroline said, already in motion to her car.

• • •

Caroline pretended to look at her phone while she surreptitiously scanned the faces of the parents leaving the elementary school. She hoped she looked enough like a parent to blend in. Plus, she had the advantage of being a stranger to Dr. Anne Wong. The scientist shouldn't startle if she saw her.

The stream of departing parents flowed through the doors, some wearing jeans, others wearing scrubs or suits or other uniforms of other trades.

Caroline saw no one that resembled Dr. Wong.

She was just about to give up when she saw her. Birdlike and petite, with coal-black hair and crescent-shaped eyes, Dr. Wong looked like her picture on Dr. Heller's desk. In person, she had a brittle, breakable quality to her, as if she were made of toothpicks, not flesh. She wore a black fleece jacket zipped up against the cold.

At the top of the steps, Dr. Wong paused, scanning the landscape. Although the scientist didn't pause long, Caroline instantly knew what she was doing. She was looking for signs of danger. When the scientist reached the bottom of the steps, she put her head down and hurried toward the parking lot, looking neither right nor left.

Caroline left the sanctuary of the tree and trailed this stranger that she felt like she knew, having so thoroughly stalked, investigated, and pondered her. She shadowed Dr. Wong down the walkway until she reached the edge of the parking lot.

"Annie?" Caroline called. She hoped the use of the scientist's nickname would induce instinctive trust.

"Yes?" Annie stopped walking. She stood perfectly still.

"My name's Caroline Auden. I'm on the *SuperSoy* legal team—" Annie's eyes widened.

"I represent the plaintiffs," Caroline continued, and she thought she saw Annie relax slightly at the news she didn't represent the defense.

"I don't know anything about that," Annie said. "I've got to go." The scientist went from repose to jogging so quickly that Caroline almost staggered to keep up with her.

"Wait," said Caroline, jogging after her. "I just want to talk to you. SuperSoy is on trial. We're trying to show it causes kidney damage. Your article shows it does, but the judge wants to talk to you about it—"

"I can't help you," Annie said, approaching the side of a silver Toyota. Reaching into her purse with a shaking hand, Annie hastily withdrew her keys and climbed into her car.

"But we're going to lose this case if you don't come to New York with me to testify. The judge is trying the science—"

Without a backward look, Annie slammed the door and drove away, leaving Caroline standing alone in the parking lot.

● ● ●

Information is power. That's what Louis always said.

Caroline knew he was right. When the police had come to the Audens' door that dark day, eager to bust the hottest new cybercriminal in town, William had sat down and explained to his daughter that the reason cybercrime was so serious was that people needed to protect their information. Their Social Security numbers. Their tax identification numbers. But even more than that, their secret aspirations. Their kinks. Their quirks. Their private lives.

Information was indeed power.

And now Caroline needed power over Dr. Wong. She needed enough information to deliver a reluctant witness three thousand miles across the country to testify at court. To do that, she needed to get to Annie Wong. She needed Annie's secrets.

Sitting down on the motel-room bed, Caroline pulled her laptop to her. The mattress sagged under her weight, the springs weak from years of guests sleeping in approximately the same spot where Caroline now sat. Ignoring her discomfort, Caroline looked up at the cracked acoustic tiles gracing the motel room's ceiling, seeking inspiration in the yellowing patches left by the cigarettes the room's occupants had smoked over the years.

What did she know about Annie?

She knew Annie had run. She knew Annie might have tried to destroy the article she'd invested years of her life researching and writing. Annie must've been scared when Franklin died, but why didn't she talk to the police? Why did she just . . . run?

So then someone got to Annie. Someone bribed her. Or, more likely, threatened her. A threat to the scientist and her son would explain just about any deal with the Devil. But if Annie had repudiated her life's work to save herself and her son, how could Caroline get Annie to rethink that deal?

The answer lay in the intertwined lives of Franklin Heller and Annie Wong. The two scientists had known each other for over a decade. Together, they had turned down funding from the biotech companies. Together, they had run a lean but successful laboratory, turning out important papers on cutting-edge topics. Together, they had stood strong against financial pressures and even threats by powerful interests. Together, they had been brave.

Had they been brave together to the end? Or had Annie repudiated Franklin, too? Had Annie known about the escalating frequency of the phone calls to Franklin's house? Had she told her research partner to give up on the article? Perhaps he'd courted dangers she hadn't wanted to court? Or had something between Annie and Franklin changed before he'd died?

Look for anomalies. That's what Uncle Hitch had said. Fine, then. What were the patterns of Annie's life, of Franklin's life? Had they changed in any way before he died?

The answer struck Caroline quickly. There had been a change. But it had been Yvonne's change, not Franklin's. Six months before Franklin's death, Yvonne had finally accepted that her husband wasn't going back to his lucrative surgical practice. She'd started winding up the medical group, liquidating assets and closing its books.

Bringing her fingers to her laptop, Caroline ran a search for "Heller Medical Group."

The query retrieved old news articles about the plastic surgeon who'd shuttered his gold-plated practice to pursue a life of scientific research. The query also retrieved a real estate report on the value of the properties held by the Heller Medical Group. The oldest reference was to the sale of the medical group's office building.

Yes, Yvonne had mentioned that when Franklin had started his research laboratory, he'd sold his medical group's office space to fund his first project.

Caroline kept on scrolling down the page of property purchases and sales.

She stopped on the most recent entry. Five months ago, the Heller Medical Group had sold a single-family residence in Santa Monica.

What was Franklin's medical group doing owning a single-family residence?

Yvonne and Franklin's home wasn't in Santa Monica . . . but Annie Wong's was.

Grabbing her bag, Caroline pulled out her legal pad. She flipped through it until she found the notes she'd taken in her car after her first conversation with Henrik. Yes, there it was. Dr. Wong had lived in Santa Monica until recently, when she'd sold her place and moved in with her boyfriend before later disappearing.

Caroline turned back to her laptop. She ran a search in the property database for "Anne Wong." She found no property sales. Nothing in Santa Monica. Nothing anywhere.

She tried "Stengaard." Still nothing.

Putting her laptop aside, Caroline stood up and ran a hand through her hair. Had Franklin's medical group owned Annie Wong's house? And if so, what did that say about the nature of Annie's relationship with her research partner?

The buzz of a text message startled Caroline out of her reverie.

She lifted the phone from the stained quilted comforter and checked the sender: Silvia. Caroline had texted her assistant when she'd returned from the elementary school, knowing that Silvia would relay her text to Louis. With the time change and the distance, she hadn't expected such an immediate response. Silvia must have pulled Louis out of a meeting.

You found her? Silvia wrote.

I did, Caroline answered.

Seconds later, Caroline's cell phone rang. As soon as she answered it, Louis's blue-blood accent came onto the line.

"You really found her?" he asked, his voice giddy with excitement. "I need to hear it directly from you, Ms. Auden. Please. Tell me again."

"I found her." Caroline grinned. "Up in Mendocino."

"Superb. Just superb. And here I thought you'd given up the hunt. Have you arranged for Dr. Wong to come to New York with you?"

Caroline stopped smiling. "I'm still working on that part."

"You've already performed miracles. I am confident you'll perform another one."

"It could be . . . hard," Caroline said.

"Handle Dr. Wong gently, Ms. Auden, but handle her." Louis's tone brooked no disagreement. "Do whatever you need to do. Charge whatever you need to charge on the firm card. Just make sure she's sitting in court in New York in two days."

"I'll do my best," Caroline said, not entirely confident she could achieve it.

"Good. And stay safe, Ms. Auden."

"I'll do my best at that, too," Caroline said, not so confident about that, either.

When she hung up, Caroline sat back down on the bed. Her laptop shone with information: the property report for the Heller Medical Group.

Grabbing her coat, Caroline headed for the door.

• • •

Caroline hid behind the tree near the entrance of the school. She hoped Annie Wong would show up. She feared she'd spooked the scientist into grabbing her son early and leaving town. Banking on a mother's unwillingness to act precipitously, Caroline settled in to wait.

The scent of the fresh-cut grass reminded Caroline of her first day at school. The time folded back until the past seemed separated from the present by only the thinnest of gossamer veils. She'd been small for her age and shy. "Don't let anyone tell you that you can't do it," her father had told her as she'd clung to his hand. She hadn't asked what he meant. She'd been too busy planning what to do if the school caught on fire or if her parents forgot to pick her up. Or aliens landed.

The sound of a bell ringing jarred her back to the present.

A stream of parents flowed into the doors to pick up their children. From her vantage, Caroline couldn't tell whether Annie was among them. But she knew that in the wake of fears of school shootings, all schools now allowed only one public entrance. If the scientist had entered, she'd need to exit here.

Five minutes later, the doors pushed open and Annie emerged. Just as she had before, the scientist paused at the top of the steps. Parents and children flowed around her as she swept the landscape with her eyes.

Annie's paranoia was justified, Caroline knew. If Med-Gen had murdered Franklin Heller, they were playing the most dangerous kind of hardball imaginable. Annie had to know that the peace of her day could be shattered in a heartbeat. Anytime. Anywhere.

Apparently sensing no danger, Annie began moving down the steps.

From her angle, Caroline couldn't see Nolan, but she could tell from the way Annie walked that her son walked beside her. The scientist glanced down to her right, a soft smile on her face. In the presence of her son, she seemed less brittle. Less cold.

When Annie reached the bottom of the stairs, she squatted, then lifted up her son for a hug. With his kinky black hair and caramel-toned skin, his almond-shaped eyes, and his uncommon height among the other kindergarteners, he looked like a beautiful combination of Asian and African American.

Caroline stepped out from behind the tree, preparing to approach the scientist she'd been chasing for weeks.

But then she froze.

A plumbing truck sat parked across the street from the school. Through the windshield, Caroline could make out the shape of two men. Just sitting. Watching. Caroline's fingers tingled with adrenaline as her nervous system keyed up for a fight. Or flight.

Ducking back behind the safety of the tree's reassuring bulk, Caroline took a deep breath, trying to calm her nerves.

She risked a glance toward Annie, whom she could see in the parking lot, entering her silver Toyota with her son. In the other direction, the plumbing truck remained stationary. Good. Even so, plumbing trucks in Caroline's recent experience had a nasty habit of becoming dangerous.

Perhaps she should call the police? Caroline thought. And tell them what? That a suspicious plumbing truck might be stalking the same scientist she was stalking?

Rejecting the plan, Caroline focused on the task at hand. What she needed was a safe place to talk to Annie. She needed somewhere public yet invisible. Just as Uncle Hitch had said, she needed a perfect place to approach a skittish witness.

She hoped one presented itself soon. She was running out of time.

CHAPTER 14

Caroline stayed three car lengths behind Annie's silver Toyota. She couldn't lose her. Not now. Not when she had only forty-eight hours to approach the scientist again, convince her to come to New York, and get her there.

Caroline glanced at the clock glowing on her dashboard. There'd be no chance of catching a flight to New York today if she didn't talk to Annie soon.

She commanded herself to be patient. She couldn't blow her chance by acting precipitously. She needed to wait for the right time. A time when Annie would listen. A time when she might be convinced to leave the sanctuary she'd found in Mendocino. Caroline hoped when that time presented itself, she'd find the right words to persuade her.

Annie drove south on Kasten Street. At the end of the road, the blue sheen of the sea glittered in the midday sun. Grassy hills dotted with cypress trees rose up in the distance.

Caroline had already tailed the car from one end of Mendocino to another. She'd watched Annie and Nolan disappear into the library, then emerge with a cluster of other children and parents. While Nolan had spoken animatedly to the children, Annie had kept her face turned away from the well-meaning eyes of the parents.

Caroline felt a kinship with the beleaguered scientist, her nerves frayed by constant worry that there were killers nearby, just out of view. A cap gun fired by a kid on the street had made Caroline jump so high, she'd jammed her shoulder into the seat belt. It had taken a full twenty minutes for her pulse to return to a reasonable rate.

When Annie's car reached Main Street, traffic slowed. On the sidewalks, tourists clustered around artisanal food shops. A clapboard sign advertised goat cheese from a dairy where "all the goats have names!" Another promised the best baked goods in the county. Priuses and old trucks lined the curb on one side of the commercial district. A pasture of tall grass dipping down toward the bluffs bordered the other.

Annie turned north on Howard Street. A quiet, residential street.

Suddenly, the silver Toyota pulled over.

Caroline froze. Had Annie spotted her?

She cruised past Annie's parked car, then watched in her rearview mirror as the scientist grabbed Nolan's hand and tugged him quickly toward the steps of a white clapboard house with a sun-faded play structure in the front yard.

With stomach-sinking certainty, Caroline decided that yes, she'd been seen. This had to be Annie's home, and she was going to call the police—or, even worse, she was about to run.

Caroline scrambled to readjust her plans. If Annie bolted, she'd have to follow her. And then what? Wave her down on a country road? Cut her off? Follow her until she stopped somewhere for the night? None of the prospects were encouraging.

Reaching the corner at the end of the block, Caroline turned, then gunned the engine, driving fast to get back to the white house before Annie had time to grab her stuff and flee.

But when Caroline turned back onto Howard Street, Annie's car sat unoccupied. Whatever Annie was doing in the house, she hadn't finished doing it yet.

Unsure what else to do, Caroline overshot the house a second time. She drove another hundred yards, then pulled over and cut her engine.

With her eyes glued to the rearview mirror, she waited for Annie to emerge.

Ten minutes later, the door of the house swung open and Annie exited. Alone.

Caroline's brow knit. Where was Nolan?

Then the door of the white house opened again. A red-haired woman wearing a Mendocino Cardinals T-shirt waved Annie down and handed her a backpack. Nolan's, presumably.

Squinting at the open door of the house, Caroline thought she could see the shape of three small heads craning outside, two red haired, one dark and curly.

Nolan was at a playdate.

The knot in Caroline's stomach loosened. Annie wasn't running. Yet.

Caroline slid down in her seat, trying to make herself invisible.

After Annie's silver Toyota glided past her, Caroline started the engine and followed.

Annie turned east on Little Lake Street, then turned north on Highway 1, heading out of town. Sweat sprang to Caroline's forehead. Was Annie running?

No. Her son wasn't with her. Wherever the scientist was going now, it had to be a round trip. And that was just as well, since now Caroline could hope for a chance to talk to the scientist alone. Whenever she stopped.

Driving up Highway 1, Annie led Caroline away from human habitation toward a road bordered by pine trees.

Ahead, a road sign advertised the Point Cabrillo Light Station.

Caroline's fingers prickled at the name. That was the lighthouse where Annie had recorded her video message to Henrik weeks earlier. Annie must have had Nolan with her at the time, Caroline realized. Maybe she'd promised Nolan some sightseeing, the son excited, the mother struggling to maintain a sense of normalcy, fighting a losing battle to ward off the reality that they were fugitives. Had Annie picked up Henrik's last desperate voice mail, begging her to let him come to her? Had she then sent Nolan away so she could record her message? Or had Nolan been there, watching his mother's shattered face, unsure what it all portended?

Now Caroline wondered why Annie was on this same stretch of road again. Perhaps she'd turn off toward the lighthouse? Perhaps she'd hidden something there? Or maybe she was meeting someone there?

But the silver Toyota passed the exit for the lighthouse and continued up Highway 1.

Soon, Annie turned east onto Route 20, a long stretch of windy road, curving through the increasingly pastoral landscape. Caroline hung back, allowing Annie's car to all but disappear up ahead of her. She needed to be careful. Having approached the scientist once already, she had to assume that Annie would be on guard and watching her rearview mirror closely . . . almost as closely as Caroline herself was watching her own mirror, she thought ruefully, glancing into it again just to be sure no one was following her.

Twenty minutes later, Annie turned south onto the 101 freeway.

The adrenaline of the chase had worn off, leaving Caroline worried about the time—4:38 p.m. They'd already missed so many flights. Dozens left the Bay Area daily, heading east, their frequency tapering off toward night. Caroline had hoped to get to Annie early enough to convince her to catch one of the daytime flights. Now they'd be forced to travel late, or worse, to travel the next day. With no margin for bad weather. Or delays. Or bad guys. And with little time to prepare for the hearing.

The last part worried her almost as much as the rest. Going into court with an unprepared witness was dangerous. Even now, Eddie and Louis would be working with the other scientists to prepare them. Not scripting them, but giving them time to formulate answers. "Don't ever ask a witness a question you don't know the answer to," Louis always said. And yet the longer it took for her to reach Annie, the closer she got to doing exactly that . . . assuming Annie agreed to come with her at all.

After another few minutes, Annie piloted her car down an off-ramp. Up ahead, Caroline saw a gray stucco shopping mall complex, vast and surrounded by parking lots, the whole footprint far out of scale with the environment.

Watching Annie park her car, Caroline considered Annie's choice of places to do errands. Rather than patronizing the mom-and-pop stores in Mendocino, Annie preferred the stucco monstrosities that had risen like boils on the scenic landscape. Strange choice.

But as Annie walked toward a discount shoe store, a different explanation occurred to Caroline: Annie was saving money. The scientist didn't know how long she'd be hiding, so she was making sure her money didn't run out. The behavior struck Caroline for another reason: Annie's frugality meant no one had given the scientist a pile of money to skip town. Whatever her reasons were for running, they weren't pecuniary.

Fear, then. That had always been the most likely reason for Annie's behavior. And having a kid in tow must have affected Annie's calculus, too. Without Nolan, would Annie have stayed in Los Angeles and risked her life to publish the article she had written with Dr. Heller? Or would she have run anyway? What kind of person was Annie Wong?

As Caroline sat musing about the target of her stalking, Annie emerged from the shoe store holding a red plastic bag in her right hand. The scientist clicked the lock of her trunk, which sprang open far enough for her to deposit her purchase. But rather than climbing into the car, she grabbed a canvas bag from the trunk, then turned toward the grocery store at the edge of the mall.

Annie swung her canvas bag into a shopping cart, then steered it toward the grocery store's entrance.

When the doors of the store slid shut, Caroline exited her car and followed.

● ● ●

Caroline stood by the magazine rack, waiting for Annie to wend her way deeper into the grocery store. In the middle of a weekday, there were few other shoppers. As a result, Caroline could reckon Annie's location from the sound of the shopping cart's wheels.

When the sound had receded, Caroline put the magazine down and went to find a place to ambush Annie. Resolving that the freezer aisle was too cold and the bread zone at the front of the store was too public, Caroline settled on the vegetable section. She positioned herself beside the broccoli to wait. Cruciferous vegetables had always been her favorites. She hoped they'd be a good omen for her now. She sent a silent prayer to the other vegetable gods, just to cover her bases.

Soon, she heard the clatter of Annie's shopping cart approaching.

Her heart rate accelerated, and her stomach fluttered like a family of frogs had taken up residence in it.

This was it. The moment when she needed to set in motion the events necessary to win the case. She could not fail.

When Annie rounded the corner, Caroline stepped in front of her.

Annie froze. Her eyes widened.

"I'm not going to hurt you," Caroline said, holding up her hands in the age-old sign for harmlessness. "I just want to talk."

Annie didn't move. She watched Caroline with unblinking eyes, poised on the balls of her feet, as if ready to bolt.

"I know you're scared," Caroline said, pitching her voice slow and soothing and sympathetic. "I know what happened. Please just listen to me. Just for a minute."

When Annie didn't run, Caroline continued, "You already know about the *SuperSoy* case. You know about the people who got hurt. You know about the many people who are going to get hurt in the future if we don't win this case. You know how important this is."

Caroline took Annie's silence as agreement.

"The problem is," Caroline said, "the judge doesn't believe that SuperSoy can cause kidney damage."

"But it can," Annie said. Her voice was soft but sure.

"I know. That's what your article said."

"You found it?" Annie's eyes widened again.

"Yes. We found it, and the judge read it. But it wasn't published. It wasn't peer reviewed. He isn't going to believe what it says until he talks to one of the scientists that wrote it." Caroline paused. "That's you, Annie. He wants to talk to you."

"But if you found the article, then there's no reason to . . ." Annie looked around the grocery store, her gaze suddenly frantic. "I need to go." She took a step forward, her shopping cart forgotten.

"Wait." Caroline stepped into Annie's path.

At Caroline's quick movement, Annie's eyes flashed with panic.

"Please, just another second. Please," Caroline said, desperation creeping into her voice. "Without you, people will die. People will be injured. It won't stop. Ever. You've got to help. You're the only one who can do this."

"I'm sorry, but I've got to go. Now," Annie said, stepping the other direction to get around Caroline.

The panic in Annie's eyes told Caroline that if she lost Annie now, she'd never see her again. She needed to find a way to get her to listen.

"He's Franklin's, isn't he?" Caroline said, remembering Nolan's coloring and height. So different from Annie. So much like Franklin.

Annie froze again, the stillness of a prey animal descending on her again.

She met Caroline's eyes, as if trying to divine the lawyer's intentions.

"Yes." Annie finally nodded, looking down.

"And the house in Santa Monica. Franklin bought that for you, didn't he?"

Annie nodded again.

"But something happened, didn't it? Even before Franklin died, something happened to you," Caroline said. "And to him. I promise I'm not the enemy here. I just want to understand. So I can help."

Annie's eyes darted away, toward the zucchini display. For a long time, she didn't answer.

"What happened, Annie?" Caroline asked the question softly.

When Annie didn't answer, Caroline feared she'd overplayed her hand. She worried she'd probed too deeply, too personally, and the scientist was shutting down. But then Annie took a breath and let it out slowly, her shoulders slumping forward, the tautness leaving them.

"Franklin and I got together ten years ago," she began. "We were at a conference, and we just—" She stopped and shook her head. "We got together."

Caroline looked at the scientist with compassion. "And you got pregnant."

"Yes. Around the time I found out, I'd been thinking about doing a research project in Ghana. The pregnancy clinched it. I went to West Africa for three weeks. When I came back, I talked about the wild fling I'd had with a local Red Cross volunteer. Then, a month later, I announced I was pregnant. Franklin knew it was his, of course, but Yvonne accepted my story. They celebrated Nolan's birth, came to his birthdays—all that kind of stuff."

"But he ended it," Caroline said.

"No. I did. Two years ago, I told him I wanted to stop hiding. I wanted to live with him. Out in the open. No shame. No secrets. I wanted Nolan to know him as his father. But Franklin said he couldn't." Her voice held a touch of bitterness. "The reasons were all very sensible. He was too committed to Yvonne. Or to his marriage vows . . . or whatever."

"So you ended it."

Annie nodded. "I told him we needed to stop. I said I needed to move on. After that, things were awkward between us for a while. But then we kind of settled back into a rhythm. We just pretended we hadn't . . . didn't . . . love each other."

Caroline watched Annie's face shift at the admission. Instead of bitterness and anger, the scientist's eyes held infinite sadness.

"Even after I broke it off, he let me keep the house." Annie sighed. "I loved that house."

"But you sold it last year."

"Franklin asked me to," Annie said, the bitterness reentering her tone. "Six months ago, he told me he was thinking about leaving his wife. When he called me, though . . . it was like my whole world just . . . shifted. I'm embarrassed to admit I was ready to go back to him. I was going to break things off with Henrik. Just like that."

Caroline recalled the confusion and frustration on the artist's face at Annie's behavior. Henrik must have suspected it had something to do with Franklin.

"Franklin told me after I sold the house, we'd move in together," Annie said. "He said he was done running from love, from the life he wanted. He wanted to live for the moment."

"But it didn't happen," Caroline said.

"No. It didn't. After escrow closed, he invited me out to dinner. I thought he was going to say he'd told Yvonne about me. But instead, he told me he'd decided to stay with her. He said he just couldn't end the marriage. He told me he hoped he'd see me on Monday at work." Annie's face flushed at the remembered humiliation and disappointment.

"Actually, Franklin's medical group owned your house," Caroline said. "Yvonne was winding up the group and liquidating its assets. Franklin might have worried that she was going to find out the medical group owned a house in Santa Monica . . ."

Annie laughed a mirthless laugh. "That would have been hard to explain. I guess after the sale, he could make up some lame excuse about why his medical group used to own a house in Santa Monica. He could tell Yvonne some bullshit story about how he'd let celebrity clients convalesce there or something."

The expression on Annie's face hardened into downward angles. "For such a good person, he was always so full of lies . . ."

"And you got mad," Caroline finished for her. "Mad enough that when the agents of Med-Gen showed up, you talked to them."

Annie stayed silent.

"You wiped the computer and ran," Caroline said, careful to keep any judgment out of her voice.

"I didn't wipe the computer," Annie said. "I'd never destroy that article. In fact, I'd still like to see it published . . . someday. If we could submit it to the *Fielding Journal*, I'm sure they'd still want it."

Caroline considered the new information.

"I admit I got angry with Franklin when he told me he wasn't going to leave Yvonne," Annie continued. "After the shock and embarrassment wore off a bit, I was just so fed up with him. It made me stop . . . protecting him."

"What do you mean?"

"I'd always shielded Franklin from Med-Gen's annoying phone calls. They called us all the time. Offering to take us to lunch. Asking to hear about our other research projects that they might fund. I always got stuck dealing with those calls. Old habit, I guess. Franklin was the senior scientist, and shit flows downhill. Or maybe I just liked taking care of him . . ." Annie shook her head. "Whatever the reason, after the whole thing with my house and Yvonne and the rest of it, I was done protecting his peace."

A haunted expression crossed Annie's fine features. "The day he died, I'd answered yet another of those calls from Med-Gen. They wanted to talk to both of us. I told them they should just talk to Franklin when he got back from his jog . . ."

Annie paused. "I keep thinking that's how they found him that day . . . They said they just wanted to talk to him. I didn't know they'd . . . they'd . . . kill him." She choked out the last words in a whisper. Her face screwed up into a mask of grief, her dark eyes quietly stricken.

"Oh my God, I killed him," Annie whispered.

"You didn't kill him," Caroline said, resisting the urge to hug this brittle stranger grieving in the vegetable aisle. "You couldn't have known. No one could blame you for not knowing."

Annie gathered her composure. "After Franklin died, they came for me. I might have been braver on my own . . . maybe. But I couldn't risk Nolan. I promised them I'd just disappear. I told them I'd hidden a copy of the article and that if I died, it would be released . . . I think that was what ultimately convinced them to leave us alone."

Annie looked furtively around the empty market, the motion so practiced and instinctual that Caroline felt a sudden wave of compassion. The scientist had been on the run so long. Grieving and shell-shocked, she'd done what almost anyone would have done. To protect herself. To protect her son.

But what about Franklin? What machinations had he set into motion before he died? What plans had he made? Caroline had once believed that Franklin's note to Yvonne was an apology for getting killed—for doing what he loved, at the ultimate price. But that wasn't it. Franklin had snubbed Annie at the same time he was about to publish an article that would end Med-Gen's profits. He hadn't planned the timing. It had been thrust upon him. It was a perfect storm of danger for him.

But Franklin, like Louis, was a chess player. He knew that checkmate was coming. If Med-Gen got desperate and sent its minions to contact Annie, he was vulnerable. He knew if he died, the truth would come out—Yvonne would find out about the Santa Monica house and the affair and Nolan. He was apologizing for that, as much as for everything else. But Franklin had one last chess move to make. A move that was dependent on the woman he'd snubbed. Annie was the final piece on the board. And now she needed to play.

"Come with me to New York," Caroline said. "Come testify. Stop hiding and end this."

"But they got Franklin." Annie shook her head, her eyes wild. "I don't care about myself, but I can't leave Nolan without a mother. That's all that matters. I have to focus on my son. I'm sorry, but that's just the way it is."

"You aren't safe here, Annie," Caroline said. "The way I tracked you down—someone else could find you like that, too. But you could come with me to New York and end this—"

"I can't. I've got to go." Annie's eyes filled with the same sudden panic Caroline had witnessed before. She knew the reason. Annie's insurance policy had been telling the fixers that she'd hidden a copy of the article. Now her insurance policy was gone.

"That article was the best thing you ever did with your career," Caroline said, trying to head off the scientist's flight instinct. "Publishing it to save lives is what you wanted. It's why you wrote it. It's the reason you couldn't destroy it."

When Annie didn't disagree, Caroline continued, "Everything comes down to this moment. That trial is happening right now. You can't sit on the sidelines. Only you can prevent the deaths of thousands of people."

Annie stayed silent.

"You've got to come with me," Caroline said. "Please, let me take you to New York."

Annie nodded, but the motion was so slight that Caroline almost missed it.

• • •

Caroline zipped up her suitcase then straightened up, mentally saying good-bye to the motel room. A room that was so much different than the last hotel room she'd occupied. With Eddie. Suddenly wishing for his presence, she consoled herself that she'd see him soon in New York. Once she got Annie Wong to New York . . .

Through the window, the sky glowed orange with the sunset. As soon as the sun finished with the business of disappearing beyond the far curve of the planet, Caroline would pick up Annie and her son, drive to San Francisco, and fly to New York. A daunting task, but doable. If all went well, she'd still make it to New York a full day before the hearing. The pessimistic part of her mind hoped that Annie hadn't sent her off to her motel just to give herself time to grab Nolan and drive for the Canadian border.

She'd find out soon enough.

She stepped forward to grab her suitcase. Time to go see if Annie Wong was really going to come with her.

But then Caroline's phone buzzed with an incoming text.

She dug the phone out of her bag.

The message had no sender. That meant it had come through a proxy server.

Caroline's stomach twisted in concern. This couldn't be good.

She opened it.

```
Your uncle is in Northridge Hospital in
a compromised state. He will be released
```

```
and dumped on the streets of Los Angeles
tomorrow morning. You might want to come
home.
```

An electric bolt of fear lanced through her chest.

With her heart pounding in her ears, Caroline dialed her uncle's phone number.

No one answered.

She tried her mother's number.

Joanne's voice mail message promised a prompt response . . . as soon as she returned from her camping trip.

Forcing herself to keep breathing, Caroline pulled up the phone number for Northridge Hospital. When the receptionist answered, she asked for the charge nurse of the emergency room. A woman's weary voice answered, and Caroline started straight in.

"I'm calling for a patient, Daniel Hitchings. I've been led to believe he's there. He's my uncle."

The line went silent while the charge nurse checked her computer. Then the weary voice came back. "Yes, he's in room 3217. They're readying him for discharge tomorrow morning."

"Can I talk to him?"

"I'm afraid not. Mr. Hitchings isn't fully lucid."

"What's wrong with him?"

"I'm sorry, but privacy regulations prevent me from giving you that information."

"Who's he being discharged to? That's not a medical question."

"He'll be going home with the gentleman with the affidavit stating that he's the home-care nurse your mother set up for him. The gentleman is here now, in the waiting room, actually. We told him that we couldn't discharge Mr. Hitchings until we finish processing the paperwork, but he said he'd wait."

"You can't release my uncle to him," Caroline said. "He isn't really a home-care nurse."

"He's got credentials showing he works for Hugo Home Care," the nurse said. "He brought written instructions from your mother. Perhaps you should discuss this with her."

"My mom's camping in Oregon. She isn't reachable. She didn't arrange this." Caroline heard her tone grow frantic. She took a breath. "What does the guy look like?" she asked, trying to keep the nurse on the line.

"Tall guy. Green scrubs," said the nurse. "He's got a big red birthmark next to his mouth. Kind of looks like a turtle on its back."

Caroline's blood froze in her veins. It sounded like the man from the airport shuttle.

"Do you hold your uncle's power of attorney?" the nurse asked.

"No," Caroline said.

"Then you can't stop the discharge."

"But they're going to dump him on the street!" Caroline shouted. She took another breath and ordered herself to calm. "What can I do to stop this discharge?"

"We'd need a doctor's order from someone on staff," said the nurse.

In the background, Caroline heard an alarm buzzing at the nursing station.

"I'm sorry, ma'am, but I've got to go," the nurse said.

The line clicked off, and suddenly Caroline sat alone in a Mendocino motel room.

Caroline paced from the chipped enamel dresser to the yellowing posters of Mendocino on the opposite end of the room. But she saw none of it. Her mind spiraled into a tornado of second guesses and doubts. How could she have left her uncle alone?

She grabbed her phone and dialed 911.

"Nine-one-one, what is the nature of your emergency?" the dispatcher's voice asked.

"There's a man down at the hospital trying to get them to release my gravely debilitated uncle to him so he can dump him," Caroline said. "I need someone to stop it from happening."

"Please start from the beginning, ma'am. Where are you calling from?"

"Mendocino, but my uncle's in Los Angeles and I—"

"You're in Mendocino, but you need to prevent a discharge of a patient in Los Angeles?" The dispatcher's voice held a note of disbelief.

"Yes," Caroline said, her eyes raking across the digital clock on the bedside table. She didn't have time to debate the dispatcher. She needed action. Now. "The hospital thinks my mom authorized the discharge, but she didn't."

"And you know this because . . ."

"Because she's camping in Oregon," Caroline said, trying to control her exasperation.

"And you know your uncle is disabled because . . ."

"I got a text from the people who are doing this." Caroline realized she was shouting at the same moment she realized the call was useless.

"Never mind," she said, hanging up.

She ran her hand through her hair.

She needed another way to stop the discharge. She needed a doctor's order. She scanned her mental roster for someone who could help. College friends. Law school classmates. Acquaintances from her days as a software engineer. Anyone with any link to Northridge Hospital.

Suddenly, she stopped.

Picking up her phone, she dialed the phone number for Hale Stern.

"Deena Pensky," Deena answered.

"This is Caroline. You know, from work." Caroline took a breath. She needed to make sense. "I need to ask a huge favor." She paused, hoping that Deena had a soul somewhere beneath her designer clothes.

"Yes?" Deena said, suspicion coloring her voice.

"Your mom's working at Northridge Hospital in neurology, right?"

"Yes," Deena said, her voice rising at the end in question.

"I need you to call her. Or give me her number." Caroline took another breath to settle her nerves. "My uncle is at Northridge. I don't even know why or how he landed there, but it sounds like he's in really bad shape. He's had some drinking issues, and . . . it's a long story. Anyway, I'm in Mendocino trying to find that missing scientist for the *SuperSoy* case and someone—I think someone connected to the biotech company—is trying to get the hospital to release my uncle to some creep who's going to dump him on the streets unless I come home—"

"I get the idea," Deena cut her off.

Caroline's heart sank. Deena wasn't going to help. Her last desperate hope was gone.

"Hold on a sec," Deena said.

Caroline waited for the rebuff, but instead of words from Deena, she heard rustling, then a muffled conversation. When Deena came back onto the line, her voice was kinder than Caroline had ever heard it.

"I told her what's happening. She's going to call you. She's going to help," Deena said.

"Thank you. Thank you so much," Caroline said.

"No problem." Deena paused, an uncharacteristic break in her usual staccato delivery. "My brother has had some problems," she added quietly. "I know how it goes."

With those few words, Caroline's image of the snobby New York associate shattered, making room for a more nuanced and empathic vision of Deena Pensky.

"Good luck up there. I'll see you when you get back," Deena said and hung up.

Seconds later, Caroline's cell phone rang. When she answered it, Dr. Pensky-Levine introduced herself and said, "Your uncle was brought in by someone who claimed to have seen him wandering the streets in a state of extreme confusion. Our preliminary diagnosis is alcohol poisoning."

"Will he be okay?" Caroline asked, wondering at the identity of this supposed Good Samaritan and the odds that he or she had something to do with her uncle's gravely compromised state.

"It should resolve in the next day or so if it's alcohol poisoning," Dr. Pensky-Levine said. "But I want to rule out other potential causes for his condition. I've ordered a dozen tests. I'm requiring results before your uncle is discharged to home care. Don't worry. He won't be leaving anytime soon."

"Thank you," Caroline said. The two words were too small to encompass her gratitude.

"You don't have to thank me. These tests are absolutely medically indicated."

Caroline could almost hear the doctor smiling on the other end of the line.

"By the way, if anyone ever asks, this HIPAA-violating conversation never happened," Dr. Pensky-Levine said. "Good luck getting that scientist to New York."

And then the line clicked off.

Caroline sank down to the floor. She wrapped her arms around her body and held herself while she shook, the tension of the last minutes leaving her in fits of electricity. Her nervous system, keyed up to fight-or-flight readiness, twitched, looking for the hazard that had resolved itself.

I got a lucky break, she told herself. Uncle Hitch is safe.

She repeated these two facts over and over until gradually, slowly, the shaking stopped and was replaced with focus. Laser focus.

Caroline stood up, exhaling slowly and deliberately, finding her center again.

Now it was time to do what she'd come to Mendocino to do: get Annie to New York.

Nothing was going to stop her.

CHAPTER 15

Caroline parked in front of Annie's building and stepped out of the Mustang. Overhead, the moon's silvery light reflected off the white-washed siding of the turn-of-the-century structure, making Caroline feel as if she were bathed in a spotlight. Exposed. Dangerously visible.

She paused, her ears straining to detect any out-of-place sounds. But she heard only crickets chirping in the pasture beyond the row of sleeping buildings.

Slipping around the back of the building, Caroline found a door tucked in an alcove with a mail slot. The apartment wasn't recognizably an apartment. It was obvious why Annie had found it attractive.

Caroline tapped on the door.

Annie opened it a crack, as if she'd been waiting by it.

Upon seeing Caroline, she opened the door and stepped aside.

Entering the apartment, Caroline was struck by how sparse it was. No furnishings filled the living room, except for a single threadbare couch and a small, serviceable television set. This dwelling was intended to be a temporary arrangement, Caroline concluded. Even Annie hadn't been able to convince herself she'd stay for long.

Whether that was a good or bad sign, Caroline couldn't yet tell.

She glanced over at Annie, who stood with her eyes downcast and her arms folded across her chest. The overhead lighting reflected off the scientist's black hair. Dark circles ringed her eyes. A testament to sleepless nights.

"Are you packed?" Caroline asked.

Annie nodded once without looking up.

"Good. Let's get going. We have a long trip ahead of us," Caroline said, looking around for Nolan. "Where's your son?"

"Sleeping."

Caroline raised an eyebrow.

"I'm not so sure about this," Annie said. "This is a huge risk."

"Once you testify, you'll be safe."

"I know. I understand all of that," Annie said. "I know I need to get out of here . . ."

Caroline's eyes traveled back to the packed suitcases by the door.

Suddenly, she realized that Annie planned to leave. But she hadn't decided where to go yet. Tamping down her alarm, Caroline reminded herself that if Annie had wanted to run, she would've already done it. The fact that Annie hadn't left yet meant she wanted to be convinced to go to New York.

"I know you're scared," Caroline said in a quiet voice. "Honestly, I am, too." It felt good to admit her fear. Especially to Annie, who she knew shared it.

"But this is the right thing to do," Caroline said. "We both know it." Again, she spoke for both of them.

"I could leave here for two days, and then this will all end," Annie said. "Like you said, once the hearing is over, they'll have no reason to come for me."

Caroline considered what arguments she could use to try to persuade Annie to join her. She considered what manipulations or subterfuge she might be willing to utilize to win the case. But then she exhaled.

"You're right," Caroline said. She was done trying to persuade. Trying to manipulate. "It's true that it would be safer for you in the short run just to run away instead of coming with me to New York. But I can promise you this: nowhere else will give you your life back. Only testifying in New York will let you come out of the shadows."

Annie's dark eyes watched Caroline.

"Think about it," Caroline continued. "If you reappear after the *SuperSoy* hearing is over, you'll have to answer for so much. You'll be the reason why the *SuperSoy* plaintiffs got their cases thrown out of court. You'll have to live with that. Plus, the police will have a thousand questions for you." She held up her hand. "I stand by what I said—you didn't kill Franklin. But the police will have hard questions."

"That's the least of my worries," Annie said quietly.

"I understand," Caroline said. "But this is your chance to stop running."

Instead of answering, Annie turned away. She walked to the bedroom where her son was sleeping.

Caroline stood frozen in the foyer, waiting.

Annie padded softly back into the room, her arms around herself again, hugging her body as if to stop it from shaking. She met Caroline's eyes and said two words:

"Let's go."

• • •

Caroline led Annie and Nolan from the apartment. When she reached the street, she stopped, stretching out her senses for signs of danger. Scenting the air for predators.

She found none. Instead, the last light of day streaked the western sky. Somewhere in the distance, Caroline could feel rather than hear the deep bass thump of waves crashing against the bluffs, their rolling power relentless even in the night. Endless vibrations rising up through solid rock, the sound was both subtle and constant.

A sudden crack in the woods made Caroline's breath catch.

She froze, listening. Watching the darkness for movement.

Beside her, she could sense Annie Wong holding her breath, too, hoping that the calm evening wasn't about to turn into a nightmare.

When there were no further sounds, Caroline decided it must have been a deer or other nighttime woodland creature. Even knowing the sound didn't connote actual danger, she couldn't relax. Standing on the street, she felt exposed.

Her father's old Mustang offered an illusion of safety, as if his arms were wrapped protectively around her. Still, she wanted to hurry Annie and Nolan along toward it.

"Come on," Caroline murmured, stepping toward the car. She ignored the nose-to-tail gouge in the paint, a souvenir from her escape at the golf course. She just wanted to get inside. To get moving.

But Nolan stopped. He tipped his face up toward his mother, his eyes open and curious in the moonlight.

"How long are we going away?" he asked.

"Just a few days, honey," Annie replied. "We're going to go on a long trip, but then we're going to come back here and pack up all of our stuff and go home."

"Home to Henrik's house?"

Annie paused and met Caroline's eyes before answering.

"Yes," Annie said.

"Good. I like Henrik," Nolan said. "But can we come back and visit here some time? They have good ice cream here. And good swings."

Instead of answering her son, Annie looked toward the hills and pastures. Even in the darkness, the air was fresh, a verdant green moistness overlaid with sea salt. But despite the pastoral beauty, Caroline knew what Annie was seeing: a prison. Nothing could ever erase the reason why Annie had come to this place.

"Maybe someday we can come back here," Annie allowed, glancing at Caroline.

On the silent cue, Caroline led Annie and her son toward her waiting car.

Behind her, she heard Annie's words, softly spoken to her son. "I need you to try to sleep in the car. We have a very long trip ahead of us."

• • •

Annie strapped her son into the car seat. Then she moved to close the passenger door, her movements hurried and efficient, as if she felt as vulnerable as Caroline did in the open.

"Don't forget Dino," said Nolan, his almond-shaped eyes big and concerned.

Annie reached into the large purse slung over her shoulder. She fished out a turquoise dinosaur and handed it to Nolan, then moved again to close the passenger door.

"And Teddy," Nolan said.

In answer, Annie opened her bag again, withdrawing a tattered stuffed bear, which her son took and tucked beside the dinosaur.

Nolan opened his mouth, but before he could speak, Annie handed him a gray fox.

Nolan smiled a large smile and hugged the fox as his mother shut the back passenger door and climbed into her seat.

When Annie had closed the door, all was quiet. The streets of Mendocino lay dormant and empty in the moonlight.

"Is it going to be a long drive?" Nolan asked, breaking the silence.

"We'll be in San Francisco in about three hours," Caroline answered, pulling away from the curb and swinging the Mustang onto the road.

"Is Dino short for dinosaur?" Caroline asked Nolan, her conversation an attempt to ward off the seriousness of their journey.

"No," Nolan answered from the backseat. "It's short for what kind of dinosaur he is. See if you can guess."

"Can you give me a hint?" she asked.

"He lived in the Cretaceous period and liked to eat Tenontosaurus for breakfast."

"Dimetrodon?" Caroline asked, though she knew it couldn't be right.

Nolan laughed like she'd cracked a joke. "Dimetrodon wasn't even a dinosaur. Plus, he lived in the Triassic. Tenontosaurus lived in the Cretaceous. So he couldn't have been eating him. Dino's a Deinonychus. Duh," he added.

"Duh," Caroline repeated, smiling. She chanced another glance at Annie Wong, whose eyes remained unreadable.

"I got us a flight out of Oakland to LaGuardia," Caroline said, checking her rearview mirror as they drove out of town. Still no one else on the road. Good.

When Annie didn't respond, Caroline left the subject of their travel plans. Annie probably didn't care. She just needed to get the hearing over and done. So she could go on with her life . . . if that was possible after what had happened to her.

"Can we stop for food soon?" Nolan asked.

"As soon as we hit the 101 freeway, we can stop at a Burger Boy or something," Caroline said, trying to think of the quickest meal she could find. They had a few hours before their flight. Even so, she wanted to get to the airport early.

"Maybe you could get a milk shake or something," Caroline added.

"Woo-hoo!" Nolan crowed.

"If it's okay with your mom, I mean," Caroline added, casting the scientist another sideways glance.

When Annie didn't respond, Caroline took it as agreement. Or catatonia.

"It'll be my treat," Caroline said. She'd charge dinner to the firm. It was the least Hale Stern, LLP, could do.

• • •

Prickles of bile clawed at Caroline's throat. The oily film in her mouth was unpleasant but didn't account for the morbid funk that always descended on her after eating a bad meal. She only got so many meals in a lifetime. She hated to waste any of them on inedible food.

Nolan, on the other hand, happily slurped a milk shake in the backseat, his stomach apparently impervious to the trials of fast food. Caroline envied him his hearty constitution.

Accelerating back onto the highway, she checked her rearview mirror. She saw only a handful of headlights scattered far behind her. Good. Perhaps their trip down to San Francisco would transpire without incident.

In the backseat, Nolan's slurping slowed, becoming intermittent, and then finally stopped. When Caroline checked her rearview mirror again, Nolan lay sleeping against the seat belt, his milk shake still gripped in his hand, his menagerie of animals tucked across his lap. The child looked peaceful and not the least bit nauseated. Caroline envied him his comfort, too.

"Do you have any siblings?" Annie asked.

Caroline startled at the sound of the scientist's voice. After Annie's virtual silence during the meal at Burger Boy, Caroline hadn't expected much conversation.

"No, I don't have any brothers or sisters," Caroline answered. "How about you?"

"I have a younger sister."

"Are you close?"

"No. We used to be," Annie answered.

Caroline could feel a story lurking behind the scientist's tone.

"What changed?" Caroline asked.

"Nolan."

"She didn't like that you'd had a kid out of wedlock?"

"No. Neither did my parents. They stopped speaking to me." The words were hard and cold. The brittleness was back.

"I don't understand how a parent could do that," Caroline said quietly.

"They're very traditional. I'm second-generation Chinese American. I grew up in Chinatown in San Francisco until I was ten. My grandparents barely speak English. They live a totally ghettoized existence. My parents moved to Berkeley when my dad got his position there, but they're still very old-world," Annie said.

In the darkness, Caroline could feel Annie's sideways look at her, weighing whether to continue, whether to share a story that she likely had not told many people. If any.

"I met Franklin during my postgraduate fellowship," Annie began. "He gave me . . . freedom. He supported my research. He gave me wings. My parents were always trying to set me up with nice Chinese boys. They sent me to Chinese school. But I'm American." She paused. "I'm also not that into Chinese guys."

Caroline nodded, her mental image of the scientist's psychology becoming clearer. Given Annie's natural reticence, Franklin must've worked hard to earn her trust. What a horrible betrayal it must have been then when Franklin rejected her.

"But Franklin wouldn't leave Yvonne," Caroline said.

"He said he couldn't do that to her. Sometimes he could be annoyingly noble."

"Did she love him?"

"No," Annie answered too quickly.

The speed of her answer told Caroline there was something unsaid.

"Yvonne's father is the pastor at a super conservative megachurch in the congressional district that Franklin's father represented for twenty years. They were political allies. Two peas in a conservative pod." Annie shook her head. "Anyway, Yvonne and Franklin were like an arranged marriage. They'd known each other since childhood. Franklin's father is retiring after his term ends. Yvonne's dad is running for his seat."

"Is he going to win?" Caroline asked.

"Hard to know. He's got a well-funded opponent. It's going to be a tight race. They're already slinging mud at each other."

Before Caroline could probe further, headlights appeared in her rearview mirror. High up. A truck. Closing fast.

Swinging the wheel to the right, Caroline moved over to let the truck pass. But the vehicle moved behind her, still closing fast.

Caroline's nerves screamed up to full alert. She gunned the engine, and the Mustang responded, leaping ahead.

"What's happening?" Annie asked.

"Someone's behind us," Caroline said, checking the rearview mirror again. The black truck kept pace with her, accelerating until it was only a car length behind.

Gripping the wheel with both hands, Caroline pulled to the right until she was clear of the vehicle behind her, then she hit the brakes, slowing so fast that the truck barreled past her. But the truck's driver had good reflexes. He hit his brakes, too, slowing to run parallel with Caroline again, coming up fast on her left side. She glanced over. She couldn't see the driver's face in the dark. She hoped he didn't hold a weapon.

Seeing a sign for an off-ramp up ahead, Caroline floored the accelerator as if to try to outrun the truck. Behind them, the truck accelerated, too, its greater weight taking longer to catch up.

Soon, the Mustang's speedometer topped one hundred miles per hour.

Just as she was passing the off-ramp, Caroline hit the brakes. She turned the wheel hard to the right. Bumping across the low median strip, she shot down the off-ramp. The truck sped by, its momentum carrying it past the exit.

Watching the truck's taillights continue down the freeway, Caroline blew out a long, slow breath. It would be miles before the truck could find an off-ramp and double back.

They were safe. For now.

With her heart pounding in her ears, Caroline piloted the Mustang to the shoulder of the road and shut off the engine. Despite the quiet, her head still rushed with adrenaline. Her vision swam with sudden dizziness.

She reached for her worry beads. Closing her eyes, she forced herself to concentrate on the smooth stones. She wondered at the soft clicking she heard until she realized it was her hand. Trembling. She forced herself to flip the beads over as the old man in the Western Cyclades had taught her. The first times were hard. Her hand wasn't steady enough for a smooth flip. But gradually, she got the rhythm.

With a conscious act of will, she pushed everything out of her mind except the motion. The rhythm. The repetition.

"What the hell just happened?" Annie asked, her eyes wide. Then she focused on the worry beads clicking in Caroline's hand. "What are those?"

"They're Greek. They help chill me out," Caroline muttered. She took a deep breath, letting it out slowly, trying to cage the panic that raced around the edges of her consciousness, looking for a breach. She needed her nerves to settle. Fast. She didn't have time for an anxiety attack. Not here. Not now.

"How'd they find us?" Annie asked.

"I don't know." Her hand stilling, Caroline's mind raced through the possibilities. Had they LoJacked her car? Had they hacked her credit card? Had someone spotted them at Burger Boy? Anything was possible.

She checked the rearview mirror. Nolan remained miraculously asleep. Even the swerving ride off the freeway hadn't woken him. His face remained a picture of angelic repose, his breathing long and even.

"What do we do now?" Annie asked.

"We need to ditch the car. We need another plane reservation. We can't leave from San Francisco or Oakland. They'll expect us to fly to New York from one of those major airports. We need a different route. Something they won't expect . . ."

Annie pulled out her phone. The glow from the screen lit her face from beneath, casting sharp shadows up her cheeks and forehead.

Caroline inclined her head in gratitude. Her own hands were still shaking too much to type.

"See what you can find on Kayak.com," Caroline instructed.

"Looking now . . . San Jose doesn't have any flights to New York," Annie said.

"That's okay, we don't want to fly into New York. We need secondary airports," Caroline said. "Think smaller regional ones."

Annie went back to work, her thumbs pecking at her phone.

Then she looked up. "How about New Haven?"

Caroline paused. New Haven, Connecticut. Near her dad.

"That works. But we still can't fly out of San Francisco or Oakland. Or even San Jose. Too dangerous."

"I'll try Santa Rosa," Annie said. After a few moments, she shook her head. "There's nothing tonight."

"What about a charter?" Caroline suggested. "There's got to be some website that sells extra seats on charters . . ."

"Give me a second," Annie said, typing furiously on her phone. "You're right. Here's one . . . It goes in three hours. We can get three open seats on it to Denver for ninety dollars per person."

"Good. What's the routing after Denver?"

"Red eye to New Haven. It'll get us in around six a.m.," Annie said. "That's another hundred per person."

"That'll work," Caroline said. "Don't book it, though. We can't use a credit card. We're going to have to pay in cash."

• • •

After stopping at an ATM to withdraw as much money as the bank would allow in a twenty-four-hour period, they'd ditched the Mustang in the parking lot of the Oakland airport Marriott. But instead of taking the shuttle to the Oakland airport, they'd hired a driver to take them sixty minutes north to the airport in Santa Rosa. They'd moved quickly and without further incident.

Now Caroline walked with Nolan and Annie through the Charles M. Schulz Airport in Santa Rosa. She consoled herself that they seemed to have lost their pursuers. Soon, they'd fly to Denver, then from Denver to New Haven. It would take all night, but they'd still arrive twenty-four hours before the hearing. Exhausting, but doable.

In her mind, she repeated the mantra that kept the anxiety at bay: once Annie testified, they'd be free. Free of stress. Free of the danger that hounded them. She just needed to get the scientist safely to court in New York.

Passing through the final security checkpoint, Caroline found a uniformed flight attendant, who guided them down the deserted halls of the airport to a small door that opened onto the tarmac. The cool night air tasted good to Caroline after their long confinement in a car. She closed her eyes to savor the scent.

"Wow! Cool," said Nolan from behind her.

Caroline opened her eyes and froze. A turboprop plane sat in front of her.

The plane was so small . . .

By the time she reached the top of the stairs up to the tiny door in the side of the plane's metal skin, Caroline's forehead had sprouted a light sheen of sweat, and her mouth had grown dry.

"Do you think they followed us here?" Annie asked from behind her.

"What?" Preoccupied with dying in a plane crash, Caroline had forgotten their pursuers. Now she scanned the airfield for signs of danger. Floodlights cast puddles of visibility on the taxiways and service areas. All appeared to be quiet.

"I think we're okay," Caroline said, except she didn't feel okay. She reminded herself that the pilot wanted to make it home, too. But her mind didn't buy it. So the pilot's a fool, too, her mind retorted.

She took one final look at the world, then she ducked her head and stepped into the narrow fuselage. A cluster of men in clerical collars sat at the back of the plane. At the front of the plane sat a gray-haired woman who might have been a nun. The woman clutched a rosary in her hand, her fingers worrying their way down the row of beads.

Caroline took a seat on the wing.

Annie and Nolan sat across the aisle from her.

Caroline let her eyes settle on the possible nun seated at the front of the fuselage. She knew the old woman's rosary was a distant cousin of the string of beads she held in her own pocket. For thousands of years, people had been using little strands of beads to bind anxiety and direct attention outward toward a benevolent deity, or inward to their own focused mindfulness. Whatever the origin and etiology, the reason was always the same: terror.

"Are you okay?" Annie asked.

Caroline turned to find the scientist gazing at her with concern in her dark eyes.

"You look a little pale," Annie said.

"Being thousands of feet up with no wings of my own always makes me feel a little vulnerable. Especially in a small plane like this."

"You're far more likely to die in a car accident," Annie said.

Caroline shook off the platitude. "At least I'm in control when I'm driving. I took a course called Physics of Flight in college. I figured it might help me get less nervous—like maybe if I knew more about flying, it wouldn't be so stressful."

"Did it work?" Annie asked.

"No. Every lesson ended up with the same message: 'If you don't follow these procedures, you'll end up in a flat spin, crash, and die.'"

Caroline fell silent as the plane began to roll down the runway.

CHAPTER 16

Caroline gripped the armrests as another wave of turbulence coursed down the fuselage. She clamped her jaw shut so hard her temples throbbed. Her pulse raced and her stomach remained clenched even after the turbulence subsided. The symptoms were familiar, but unlike her usual bouts with anxiety, this one seemed entirely based in reality.

Across the aisle, Nolan pressed his nose up against the window. In his right hand, he held his fox up so that the stuffed animal could see, too.

Caroline looked away. The child was blissfully oblivious to their impending death via plane crash. And Annie? She scribbled sudoku answers in the back of the in-flight magazine.

The plane jolted, dropping twenty feet before righting itself and nosing back up to its altitude.

"The captain said there was unstable air over the Rockies," Annie offered.

Caroline looked over at her and grimaced. Unstable air. She knew all about the sheer currents that came screaming up the jagged peaks of the Rocky Mountains, sending updrafts that felt like they could tear a small plane apart.

"Have you been a lawyer for long?" Annie asked. "Have you had many cases?"

Caroline appreciated the scientist's effort to distract her but wished her choice of topic had been better.

"I just got licensed. This is my first case," she answered.

"Oh." Annie paused, and Caroline got the feeling the scientist might be rethinking her decision to put her future in her hands.

"What did you do before lawyering?" Annie asked.

"Software engineering," Caroline said. "Mostly sitting in front of a laptop. Writing code." It had been peaceful. Calm. Uneventful. Nothing like her current nightmare.

Another tremor rippled through the fuselage.

A corresponding wave of nausea coursed through Caroline's esophagus.

She closed her eyes until the turbulence passed, but the nausea remained. After a moment, it occurred to her how she must look to Annie. Sweaty and pasty and grim. She needed to reconstitute. To gather the pieces of herself and pull them back together so she resembled someone worth trusting.

"We should get you prepared to testify," Caroline said, grasping at the practical task like a lifeline. If they didn't perish, they'd land in New Haven and be in court twenty-four hours after that. That was a far more inevitable boogeyman on the horizon than the plane crashing.

When Annie didn't answer, Caroline glanced across the aisle.

Annie's face had grown ashen. At first, Caroline thought perhaps the scientist had realized the peril of their flight. Or perhaps she'd grown nauseous, too.

But then Annie stood up, bracing her hands between the seats to stabilize herself in the choppy air, and made her way over to Caroline's row.

Caroline scooted toward the window seat so Annie could sit beside her.

"What do you mean? What do we have to do?" Annie asked softly.

"We need to anticipate the hard questions the judge will ask. And the other side." Caroline had heard Louis lecture to her law school class about the need to prep witnesses, but he hadn't gotten into specifics. She wistfully wished they'd spent a little more time on that particular lesson.

"Like what?" Annie asked.

"Like why didn't you submit the article? Why didn't you talk to the police? Why did you run?" Caroline knew those would be the first questions everyone would ask.

Instead of answering, Annie looked across the aisle. At her son.

"I got scared," she said, meeting Caroline's eyes. "Our lab started getting . . . calls. They were vague. Just phone calls from people asking to speak with Franklin and me about our new article about SuperSoy. Someone must have seen Franklin's teaser in Hawaii . . ."

"How'd you figure out it was Med-Gen?"

"I didn't. Not at first. But then the calls got more persistent, and I knew . . . they had to be from Med-Gen. The questions were too pointed. At first, they wanted to offer support for our research. When we turned them down, they wanted to know who had funded our research. I didn't say anything, of course. Neither did Franklin. We've been up against intimidation before. It's pretty awful, but it's all talk. The climate change scientists get the worst of it. You should see the e-mails those guys get sometimes."

"So you didn't take them seriously?"

"No. Not yet. At that point, I thought they were just leaning on us. Trying to pay us off. Trying to at least just get us to talk to them . . ."

"But then Franklin died," Caroline supplied. She didn't need Annie to relive telling Kennedy's agents where Franklin was jogging. That wouldn't come up at court, and she needed Annie to stay focused on the bigger picture.

"You mean got killed," Annie said, meeting Caroline's eyes squarely.

Caroline nodded.

"After that, I didn't feel like I had a choice . . ." Annie looked away, her eyes brimming with tears. "Do I really need to relive this?"

"You need to be prepared to say all of this in front of the judge and a courtroom full of people. You can't look unsure or uncertain. I'll be there to help you, but you're going to be the one up there. It's important that you're able to get through this."

Annie hugged her arms around herself.

"Okay, let's keep going," Caroline said. "What happened next?"

"Franklin was dead. The article had disappeared from his computer, and all the links to our research had been taken down. By someone. I don't know who. Or how. The only thing left was me. I knew they'd come for me. And they did . . ."

Before Caroline could ask for more details, the plane shuddered. The pocket of choppy air gave way to a gust that jolted the passengers hard to the right.

Grasping for the armrest, Caroline gasped. Her stomach lurched, and her esophagus clenched.

Caroline lunged for the barf bag in the seat-back pouch. She barely had time to open it before she vomited up the contents of her stomach.

"Let me help," Annie said, holding Caroline's hair off her face until the wave passed.

"Thanks." Caroline gasped. "Sorry."

"Why?" Annie asked.

"I'm supposed to be helping you," Caroline said, embarrassed by her performance. An anxious wreck, retching on a plane. Just the thing to inspire confidence in your attorney.

"You've done great so far. Now it's my turn." Annie glanced at her child across the aisle. "I'm kind of an expert at it."

"Thank you," Caroline said before diving back into the bag again.

• • •

Caroline led Annie and Nolan down the Jetway. After hopscotching across the country, she felt like roadkill. Her mouth tasted like a turtle had crawled underneath her tongue and died. Still, she forced herself to look around the New Haven airport, scanning the space for danger. Other than an early-morning cleaning crew, the terminal was quiet.

Behind her, Annie held Nolan in her arms, the boy's eyes half-closed, his menagerie of stuffed animals tucked safely in her duffel bag. Despite Annie's efforts to soothe him into sleep, the five-year-old hadn't dozed off until they'd begun their descent. Now Nolan's deadweight caused Annie's legs to buckle and her back to arch as she carried him into the empty terminal.

At the sight of the long walk ahead of them, Annie groaned and shifted her hold on her sleeping son. Her dark eyes were ringed with puffiness. Her steps were uneven and exhausted.

Caroline pointed toward a vacant row of seats in the waiting area. "Sit for a second. We need to get a room." The hearing wasn't until tomorrow. They had time to rest. For a few hours, anyway.

Pulling her laptop out of her bag, Caroline sat down on the seat beside Annie.

But then she stopped. She couldn't use her credit card. Or her phone. Either one or both could have been used to track her down in Mendocino.

"Do you have any cash left?" Caroline asked, turning to Annie.

Without even checking her purse, Annie shook her head. "We used the last of it in Denver."

Caroline opened her wallet. Her stomach sank. The small bills wouldn't cover a room at even the seediest hotel.

Beside her, Nolan roused, lifting up his curly head from Annie's lap. He looked around with a befuddled look on his face, blinking his long-lashed eyes. Annie leaned toward his ear, trying to shush him, but his curiosity at his new surroundings brought him to full wakefulness.

Annie met Caroline's eyes.

"We need somewhere to sleep," Annie said with quiet desperation.

Caroline stayed silent. She believed that everything happened for a reason, that everything in life occurred exactly as it should. She knew the line very well might be bullshit, since atrocities throughout human history defied the subscription of any grand belief. But sometimes the fatalistic mantra still gave her peace. If everything happened for a reason, her sole mission was to divine that meaning, to suck the nectar from the moment, hummingbird-like. Even if that nectar tasted horrible sometimes.

So then, this, too, was happening for a reason. This latest hiccup in her already convulsive travel plans was to be embraced, not fought. The path was obvious to her. And yet, her mind still jangled with nervous tingles of worry. A week ago, she'd left the map of the normal and now she was improvising madly, just trying to make it to the next sunrise.

She knew where she needed to go to do that.

"My dad lives outside New Haven," she said finally. "We can go stay with him."

• • •

It had taken two hours for Caroline to find a rental car company willing to let her drive a vehicle off the lot with only a hold on her debit card for security. Now she estimated it would take thirty minutes to reach Shelton. Thirty minutes until she'd see her father's new home. His new life. His new kids. She wasn't ready, some part of her heart protested. Not yet. Not now. It was too soon. And she hadn't even been able to call to prepare him. She'd be ambushing him. Unannounced with two strangers in tow.

And yet, she knew he'd be happy to see her. He'd take her visit as a thaw in their relationship. She just wasn't sure she was ready for that thaw. He'd left. He'd disappeared from her life. He'd made a new one, far away. She knew he had the right to his happiness, but his departure had caused her so much difficulty. So much sadness. So much loneliness.

Caroline checked the clock. Seven thirty a.m.

With luck, she'd catch her father before he left for work. Despite her trepidation about seeing him, she preferred to speak to her dad rather than just Lily.

Entering the historic district of Shelton, Caroline was struck by the differences between this neighborhood and the ones where she'd been raised. Built in the eighteenth century, these homes boasted gracious porches and filigreed gables. Their postcard perfection begged a comparison with the places where Caroline had grown up. Hoboken, New Jersey, and Chatsworth, California. Tract homes with identical doors and windows, indistinguishable from the other houses on the block. If you knew where the bathroom was in one house, you knew where it was located in every house.

Finally she saw it. A Federal-style mansion halfway up the block. With a brick facade and black shutters, it sat confidently on its lot with a big front yard for her father's young sons to enjoy.

Caroline checked the address on her phone. Yes, that was it.

A sleek black Porsche sat parked in the driveway. Cybersecurity consulting had been lucrative. Or maybe Lily had money. Caroline hadn't ever cared enough to ask.

She pulled over to wait for her dad to exit the house.

Shivering, she crossed her arms to ward off the chill. Yet again, she didn't have a warm enough coat for the eastern weather. That was okay. She wouldn't be staying long. And she wouldn't be coming back any time soon.

"Is this where you grew up?" Nolan's voice drifted over from the backseat.

"No," Caroline answered. "My dad moved here with his new wife."

"What happened to the old one?" Nolan's voice held a serious note. "Did she die?"

"Shush, honey," Annie said, half turning to make eye contact with her son.

"It's okay. She's not dead," Caroline answered. "My parents just didn't . . . get along."

"I've just got a mom," Nolan announced. "I don't have a dad."

"I've got a dad, but I don't see him too often," Caroline said.

"Do you miss him?" Nolan asked.

"Yes," Caroline said, her throat clenching with sudden emotion.

Silence reigned in the car again. Even Nolan seemed to sense the topic was closed.

After another ten minutes, the door of the house swung open. A man stepped out. With wavy mahogany hair and green eyes, his resemblance to Caroline was unmistakable. Three small boys followed him out the door. The two eldest were sandy blond. But the youngest, the three-year-old, had a mop of dark hair, just like their father's. Just like Caroline's.

Caroline swallowed at the recognition.

Instead of walking to the Porsche, Caroline's father walked to the minivan. Clicking the key, he opened the sliding door. Then he ushered the boys into the backseat.

Caroline glanced back at the front door. Where was Lily? Surely, she'd come out soon to drive the boys to school. When Lily had gone, Caroline figured she could approach her father for the long-awaited, much-dreaded meeting. With Annie and Nolan as spectators.

She winced at the thought of it.

Her dad opened the driver's door and climbed into the minivan.

Caroline's mouth opened in surprise. Her father was driving the boys to school? She couldn't recall him ever having driven her to school. Always early to rise and early to leave for the office, he'd been a ghostly presence in Caroline's mornings, grabbing coffee on his way to the garage, and work, and a day away from the family until late at night.

The door of the house opened. A woman with blonde hair emerged.

Lily, Caroline identified her. Ah, here she was. Ready to take the kids to school. Except she was wearing pajamas. She jogged down the brick walkway holding a backpack. When she reached the minivan, Lily opened the sliding door and held the backpack out to the smallest boy.

He leaned out to take it with a sheepish smile. Lily kissed the boy's cheek, then straightened up. Meanwhile, Caroline's father had climbed out of the driver's seat to talk to his wife. While Caroline watched, the two grown-ups talked, smiling and laughing. Reluctant to part.

Caroline's mouth hung open in disbelief. Who was this man who looked so much like her father? Lingering in conversation? Smiling with ease? Driving his kids to school? Choosing a minivan over a Porsche? The evidence was irrefutable. Her father had followed his affinities to greater prosperity. And greater happiness, Caroline realized as she watched him laughing.

Watching the scene, Caroline was suddenly struck with a revelation so profound she almost gasped. She'd always chalked up her father's distance and remoteness to personality. Now she was faced with evidence that it wasn't personality at all. It was circumstance. Maybe he hadn't ever known which Joanne he'd get when he walked in the door. Maybe he'd faced the same Russian roulette of moods that had unsettled Caroline, too, when she was growing up. Maybe his distance from her wasn't a result of personality at all. Maybe it was collateral damage.

The realization and the reshuffling of what Caroline thought she'd known about her father made way for yet more insight. Perhaps, she realized, her own recent distance from her father had something more to do with the lingering effects of his remoteness growing up or her disappointment at his departure. Perhaps the guilt that he'd almost gone to jail on her account had driven a wedge between them. Maybe she'd been looking for reasons to avoid reconciling so that he could be the bad guy and she wouldn't have to deal with the shame.

Maybe there weren't good guys or bad guys in her family's story. Maybe it was just like Eddie said—there were just people trying to get by as best they could.

At bottom, Caroline faced a simple emotional truth: she wanted a relationship with her father. Perhaps her short visit now, as unlikely and strange as it would be, would begin that new chapter.

A spark of hope lit in her chest.

She edged the car forward toward the Auden residence. Still nervous, but growing more confident in her choice, she floated toward her dad's new house.

But then she saw something. An awning repair truck sat parked up the block.

Caroline's neck prickled with electricity as her instincts flared to alert.

There was something wrong with the scene.

The reason for the wrongness hit her: there were no awnings in this historic neighborhood.

Squinting, Caroline made out the shape of two people sitting in the front seat. Waiting. She knew exactly who they were waiting for.

She drove slowly past the house, then turned the corner. As soon as she was out of sight of the awning truck, she jammed down the accelerator, racing back toward the expressway. When she hit Highway 8, she turned south, glancing in her rearview mirror. She didn't see the awning truck following, but she knew they were back there. Somewhere.

"Where are we going?" Annie asked.

"We've had a change of plans," Caroline answered.

CHAPTER 17

"I know I told you to drop by whenever you wanted to, but this is ridiculous," said a long-limbed young man at the door of the New Jersey row house. His dark-blue eyes twinkled.

"It's good to see you, too." Caroline smiled. She turned to introduce Annie. "This is Joey Calvuto, my best friend from junior high. We hung out until my family moved out west."

"And then we e-mailed every day," finished Joey.

Annie nodded a hello, her eyes narrowing at Joey's perfect hair and toned biceps.

Caroline watched with amusement as Annie tried to surmise how this Adonis had come to live in a frumpy neighborhood in Hoboken.

"Come in," Joey said. "My mom's going to be thrilled to see you, Caro."

He stepped aside to allow them to enter the foyer. Loud furniture and louder wallpaper greeted them. Lawn signs leaned up against the wall of the foyer, stating in big magenta letters:

LET JUDI SHOW YOU!

"Mom's real estate business is booming," Joey said, just as the Judi from the sign appeared coming down the hall.

"Oh my God! Is that Caroline Auden?" said a woman in a hot-pink dress and bangles of costume bracelets climbing up both of her arms. With her too-bold eyeliner drawn around her large brown eyes, Judi Calvuto gave off an overexcited air that worked better than coffee on those around her.

"Thanks so much for letting us stay here on short notice," Caroline said.

"Forget about it. I have no idea why you didn't plan on coming here in the first place." Judi looked hurt.

"We were going to stay with my dad, but we ran into some . . . complications."

Judi nodded sagely, as if she was used to complications.

"And what's your name?" Judi asked Nolan, who clung to his mother like a koala bear and rested his chin on Annie's shoulder.

"Nolan. I'm five. I haven't pooped since Denver."

Judi suppressed a grin.

"You look exhausted," she said, turning to Annie. "Joey, will you get them settled? Then we can see what's what."

Judi grabbed Caroline's hand and led her into the living room, while Joey showed Annie and Nolan to the guest room beside his own room.

"He'll be back soon, and then you can tell us what happened," Judi said, looking after her grown son with fondness. Judi and Joey had always been close. So close, in fact, that Joey had moved home to go to graduate school in special education. He didn't tell his friends that, though. No one knew his mom still made him baked ziti every Wednesday night.

"Come, sit awhile, have some tea or whatever." Judi gestured to an armchair.

Caroline sank into the old chair with a sigh. Her eyes traveled across the familiar surroundings. The walls were a floor-to-ceiling gallery of pictures of Joey and his brother, Freddie, in all stages of childhood and adolescence. The boys in the snow. The boys at camp. The boys at school. In each of the images, Joey stood tall and wiry, his clothing pressed and neat, even in the shots taken after backpacking trips. His brother, in contrast, was disheveled and messy even wearing a tuxedo.

"Have you heard about Freddie?" Judi asked.

"Joey told me he's running a small business," Caroline said as Joey reentered the room.

"Small business? Ha!" Judi said. "Freddie's gotta lunch truck. He named it My Greasy Balls. Can you friggin' believe it? My Greasy Balls. Christ, my mother's turning over in her grave with a name like that. Anyway, he's making arancini—you know, those little deep-fried risotto balls stuffed with meat sauce? Yeah, he's making a living on his grand-ma's recipe. Still, he's staying outta trouble, which is a good thing, since he was pretty bent outta shape when my wuzband Buddy finally left, the no-good bum."

Unlike Joey, who could get along with anyone, Freddie was quick to anger. But Caroline knew Freddie was also quick to help his friends. Before Caroline could ask anything more about Freddie, Judi's face grew serious.

"So, you gonna tell me what's going on?" she asked.

"Yes, but can I get some water?" Caroline said. "It's a long story."

• • •

The sound of laughter woke Caroline. She was surprised she'd fallen asleep.

The weak light filtering in through the curtains told her that night would be falling soon. But with her nerves already twisting her gut, she knew she wasn't likely to sleep again before the hearing tomorrow morning. And she needed to finish preparing Annie to take the witness stand.

She wished she could call Louis for advice. Or instruction. Maybe he could arrange for marshals to escort her to court while he was at it. But she couldn't call him any more than she could call her father. Not only might her phone be bugged, but so might Louis's. It was safer to prepare Annie on her own. And get her to court. On her own.

Following the sounds of mirth emanating from down the hall, Caroline made a plan. She'd run through the Heller article with Annie, preparing her for all of the possible questions someone might ask her about it. Then she'd get Annie's views on the secondary articles. Just in case. She hoped Annie already had some familiarity with those other articles . . .

Caroline found Joey crouched behind the coffee table in the sitting room, making a puppet show for Nolan using the boy's stuffed animals and some kitchen implements. Nolan's laughter welled out of him in coughing fits that made Caroline smile, too, despite her preoccupation.

Seeing Annie nowhere, Caroline padded over to the kitchen.

Judi stood beside the toaster. She wore a zebra-print nightgown that clashed with the floral wallpaper. She held a copy of the *National Enquirer* in one hand and a glass of chocolate milk in the other.

Her eyes flicked up when Caroline entered the room.

"You caught me having a little something," Judi said, gesturing toward the toaster, which steamed with the smell of something sweet. "Have a seat. I'll fix you up a little something, too."

"I can't," Caroline said. "Where's Annie?"

"Poor girl just went to sleep," Judi said. "I thought she'd tip over, she looked so tired, but she just sat there staring at Nolan like she was drinking up the sight. When she closed her eyes with her cheek all pressed up against her hand, I finally convinced her to go to the guest room to get some shut-eye. You've got a big day tomorrow."

Caroline considered waking Annie. They didn't have much time before the hearing.

"Let her sleep," Judi said. "Whatever it is can wait."

Caroline opened her mouth to protest, then closed it. Judi was right. They'd been through so much. Whatever prep she had in mind was less important than sleep.

She sat down heavily at the cushioned banquette. She knew better than to offer to help Judi prepare food. Judi had been feeding her "a little something" since elementary school. Judi was an expert at snacking. If there was an advanced degree in comfort food, Judi had it. And in Judi's view, part of doling out comfort food was keeping its recipient cozy. Hence, the banquette.

"I've got the perfect suit for your court thing tomorrow," Judi continued as she moved around the kitchen, grabbing dishes and silverware. "It's candy-apple red. You'd look great in it. It would make a real statement."

"Thanks for the offer, but it'll be best if I blend in. Getting inside the courthouse could be hard." Caroline's stomach knotted with faint nausea, an echo of her flight from Santa Rosa. She had no illusions of safety. The courthouse would be guarded by those who wanted to keep Annie away—at all costs. Even after her long nap, Caroline felt the weight of that knowledge torturing her already frayed nerves.

Judi studied Caroline's face. "You all right, honey?"

Caroline shook her head. "It's been a hell of a week for me. The things I've been through . . . the things that have happened . . ." She trailed off, her throat constricting at the recognition of the danger that had been her constant companion.

"Honey, everyone goes through some stuff," Judi said. "Hell, I've got a kid with ADD. Not Joey, of course. He's an angel. But Freddie was a nightmare. He'd smear shit on the walls, then I'd have to go off and show houses to clients like nothing was happening. You've got to say to yourself, 'Well, that sucked.' Then move on. You can't bog down.

Yell when you're alone in the car. Talk to a friend. Get it out. Then clean yourself up and go to the bank or to the nail salon or whatever."

As Caroline considered Judi's words, the timer went off for the toaster oven.

"Want a Pop-Tart?" Judi asked, pulling one of the treats out of the hot oven.

Caroline contemplated the offer.

"Come on, honey," Judi said. "It's a hug in a box. Sometimes that's all you need."

• • •

"Joey can take care of Nolan while we're at court," Caroline said to Annie, who sat across from her in the banquette. Beside them, the breakfast dishes were piled in the sink.

Annie didn't answer. Instead, she kept her eyes trained on the coffee she held in her hands. With each passing hour, the scientist seemed to be sinking deeper and deeper into herself.

Caroline knew the reason. Terror. Fear of dying. She shared those emotions.

"We can't bring him with us," Caroline said gently. From the living room, she heard the sound of Nolan laughing as Joey choreographed dance numbers for his stuffed animals.

Annie turned to watch Nolan, who giggled as Joey paraded the dinosaurs across the coffee table in a curtain call, bowing each in turn as its name was called.

After a long moment, Annie pivoted back around to the banquette.

She reached for the pen and pad of paper on the counter. She wrote down a phone number, then pushed the piece of paper toward Judi.

"If anything happens, please call this number," Annie said. "It's my sister's number in San Diego. She'll . . . look out for him."

Judi took the number, but shook her head. "Nothing's gonna happen, honey. You'll come back here tonight, and we're all gonna celebrate with some pizza."

Annie tried to smile, but the creases in her forehead gave testament to her continuing consternation. She looked like a woman who was sure she wouldn't see another sunrise.

"Excuse me." Caroline lurched from the breakfast nook. She needed to get away, but there was no way to escape the weight of what she'd set into motion. She'd asked Annie to risk more than her own life. She'd asked her to risk making Nolan an orphan.

Caroline stopped in the darkened hallway, staring sightlessly at the family photos. What would happen to Nolan if Annie died? Would Annie's estranged sister take care of him? What about her father?

"Are you okay?" came Joey's voice from behind her.

"I'm fine," Caroline said.

"No, you're not," Joey said, coming to stand in front of her. "You've got that look on your face. The one that says you're about to plotz."

"What am I doing?" Caroline looked up into his face. "I'm just winging it and hoping it all works out okay. It's totally irresponsible. It's totally insane."

"Of course you're winging it. That's all anyone does. Fake it till you make it."

Caroline stayed silent.

"You're good at winging it, Caro," he said. "You're going to figure this out. You always do."

"Not with someone else's life on the line," Caroline said. She was terrified for herself, but her feelings about jeopardizing Annie's life added an overlay of crushing guilt to her terror. Fear with a light dusting of horror, served with a side of dread.

"You aren't forcing her to do this," Joey said, drawing her eyes to his. "She needs to do this for her own reasons. You aren't making her do it. She's a grown woman, and she's decided she needs to do this. You're just helping her to."

"But what if I get us both killed . . ." Caroline could not believe the words had come from her own mouth. In her entire life, she'd never done anything that could get herself or anyone else killed. This was insane. "What if I can't figure this out? The stakes . . . they really couldn't be higher," Caroline said.

When Joey spoke again, he had an embarrassed look on his handsome features. "I know it isn't the same, but remember when I went to go stalk that cute guy at the Gay Men's Chorus in Flatbush? God, I was so obsessed with him. Gregory. That was his name. I really thought he'd give me a ride home after the show. I was so stupid. He was eighteen, and I was what? Thirteen? Of course, he just left after the show, and I was stuck out there in Flatbush with no money and no way to get home. My parents thought I was at Tommy Tan's house doing homework."

Caroline remembered. Joey had been petrified. He hadn't come out to his family yet. He wouldn't have been able to explain why he'd been in Flatbush. It had been dusk when she'd started her journey into the city. The wind had blown cold off the Hudson and the bus drivers had cocked a curious eyebrow at the young girl climbing onto the bus alone.

"You came and got me," Joey said. "You could've gotten in so much trouble, but you didn't think twice about helping me. It was brave and it was kind."

He paused. "It doesn't mean you have to do this, though. You could both just stay here."

Caroline knew what he was doing. He didn't want to force her to do something any more than she wanted to force Annie. Everyone had to choose for herself what to do.

"I've got to do it," she said. And she did. Thousands of people were depending on her to bring Annie safely to court. If she didn't, every *SuperSoy* case would end. Today.

"Then you'll do it," Joey said simply.

"But what if it doesn't work? You know how I . . . get," Caroline said. She'd once told Joey that she felt like her mind was a fancy Italian race car. It could be blisteringly fast, or it could end up on the side of the road with smoke pouring out from under its hood.

"Why'd you quit software engineering?" Joey asked.

Caroline heard his implicit question. Why'd she leave her staid, safe job in the tech world? It was a good question. She'd never experienced fear there. She'd never spiked the terrors she'd routinely endured in the past weeks. She'd also never really felt like she was doing anything with any real meaning.

"I wanted to help people," she said. To her ears, she sounded pathetically idealistic.

Joey cracked a smile. "How's that working out for you?"

"Let's see, I've trashed my car, barfed my way across the country, gotten chased, and now I'm hiding out with you because I think some people might want to kill me. So . . . it's going great." Caroline smiled back at her friend, but then the smile faded from her face. "You want to know why I became a lawyer? The answer is, I didn't want to be ruled by my fears."

She looked down. Her fears were kicking her ass at the moment.

"You and me both, honey," Joey said. "Being scared is a natural response to living. But you get out there, and you figure it out. Honey, you can do this."

Meeting his eyes, Caroline found conviction. Absolute belief in her. That certainty in her merit, in her abilities was the gift her best friend had been giving her for as long as she could remember. The question was whether she shared his certainty that she could see this nightmare journey through to the end.

"You'll take care of Nolan while we're gone, right?" Caroline finally said.

Joey smiled. "I promise."

• • •

"The police station's automated phone system is a complete nightmare, but I finally talked to a real, live person," Caroline said. "They said they'd send a couple of officers to escort us into the courthouse."

"Really? How'd you get them to agree to do that?" Judi asked. "I can't even get them to come out here when the neighbors are dumpster diving in my trash cans. Don't get me started . . ."

"I told them I had a subpoenaed witness who was worried about getting to a hearing safely. They said they'll meet us at the north entrance between nine and ten a.m. The hearing starts at ten fifteen, so that should give us plenty of time to get upstairs."

"That's great," Annie said, her dark eyes sparkling with relief.

"It's still not ideal," Caroline said. "An hour window is really big. The more time we spend out in the open, the greater our chance of detection. But if we aren't there when the police get there, I'm worried they'll leave."

Judi nodded, her face showing her skepticism about whether the NYPD would wait.

Caroline tilted her laptop so Annie and Judi could see the map of the courthouse.

"What we need is a safe place where we can watch the north entrance." Caroline met Judi's eyes. "Is there a café or restaurant across the street?"

"No." Judi shook her head. "Just some office buildings and a subway stop. There's a dirt lot where they took down a building, but that doesn't help us."

From the corner of her eye, Caroline saw Nolan approaching. Judi and Annie must have seen him, too, since they stopped talking and took sips of their coffee with pretend nonchalance.

"Whatcha talking about?" Nolan asked. He wore a T-rex shirt, striped pajama bottoms, and a 49ers hat. At his hip, he'd tucked one of the kitchen implements from the puppet show.

"Nothing much. Grown-up stuff, honey," Annie said. "Mommy just needs to do an errand today. You're going to stay here with Joey until I get back."

Caroline watched as Annie held her breath, waiting to see if Nolan would reject the proposed plan. Instead, Nolan looked down at his mismatched outfit.

"Everything I'm wearing is awesome," he announced. "Just not together."

"What's the spatula for?" Caroline gestured with her chin toward the silver-and-black implement tucked into the waistband of his pants.

"It's an ax. For fighting bad guys."

Caroline smiled. "Good thinking. You can never be too ready for the zombie apocalypse."

"No, not zombies," Nolan said. "It's for regular bad guys."

Caroline caught Annie's concerned look over her son's head. Maybe Nolan had heard them talking.

"I know it looks like a spatula, but that's just to fool the bad guys. They're only going to *think* it's a spatula," Nolan explained. "I'm going to surprise them with it being an ax."

"That's genius," Judi said, her face lighting up.

"It is?" Annie asked.

"I've got an idea," Judi said as Joey came to lead Nolan back out to the living room.

• • •

Caroline and Annie squatted together in the aisle of Freddie's lunch truck. The wheels bumped along the uneven pavement.

When the motion stopped, Caroline straightened to standing and craned her head forward toward the driver's cabin, where Freddie sat piloting the truck through the dirt lot. She was pleased with what she saw. Freddie had found a spot on the edge of the lot, facing the courthouse. All around them, other lunch trucks were setting up, preparing for a day of business. Tucked among them, My Greasy Balls looked like just another vendor.

Freddie set the brakes and cut the engine with a jolt. He hopped out of the driver's side and lifted the sides of the truck to reveal the service windows. When he climbed back into the truck, the floor swayed with his weight. Unlike his brother, Freddie's thick figure bore the marks of a distinct love of carbohydrates.

"You girls doin' okay?" Freddie asked.

"Super," Caroline said, trying not to breathe in the scent of old cooking oil. Her stomach was already in knots as it was.

She glanced over at Annie, whose face held the same inward look it had borne in the Calvutos' kitchen. Caroline wanted to reassure Annie, to tell her that they'd make it back, but the words died on her tongue.

"We need to stake things out," Freddie said. "I brought supplies."

Reaching into a plastic milk crate, he withdrew three sets of binoculars. He offered a pair each to Annie and Caroline. He hung the third pair around his own thick neck.

Taking the binoculars, Caroline looped the strap around her wrist.

"First thing we needs to do is figure out who our surveillance is," Freddie said.

He pointed a thick finger at the side of the gray structure.

"That's the north entrance over there," Freddie said. "At lunchtime, hundreds of people are gonna come pouring outta there like ants. I always do good business in this lot. In the meantime, we should be able to see when your police escort shows up . . . and we should be able to see who's out there that don't belong."

Caroline put her eyes to the binoculars and focused the lenses. She swept them across the front of the courthouse in a slow, deliberate arc. She wasn't sure what she was looking for. As far as she could tell, it was just another morning at the United States District Court, Southern District of New York. Lawyers in gray and blue and black suits holding briefcases. Litigants in everything from dresses to torn blue jeans. The occasional staffer or security guard hurrying up the stairs to work.

Beside her, Freddie made quiet grunting sounds as he examined the scene.

"Ah," he said to himself, then, "Hmm."

Finally, he put his binoculars down and turned to Annie and Caroline.

"I count three guys we gotta be watching out for," he announced.

Caroline put her binoculars down and raised an incredulous eyebrow at the balding man. With his belly sticking out from his too-short T-shirt, Freddie was an unlikely expert on surveillance. Then again, she was an unlikely tech geek–turned–lawyer.

"There are three guys," Freddie said. "They pretend like they're walking by, but then they loop back around. They're changing their clothes somewheres, but the shoes don't change."

At Caroline's expression, he added, "Hey, you can tell a lot from a guy's shoes."

"Shoes?" Caroline repeated.

"Yeah. See the guy in the black jacket?" Freddie pointed at a man strolling past the doors of the courthouse.

Caroline put her binoculars back up to her eyes. Soon, she saw the man Freddie indicated. Balding across his head, the man wore a black leather jacket and tan slacks.

"I see him," she said.

"He's the same guy who walked by wearing a gray hoodie ten minutes ago. He's wearing green Converse. He must've changed his jacket at his car or something, but he didn't bother to change his shoes," Freddie said.

"Good catch," Caroline said, her tone holding appreciation for Joey's brother's abilities.

Freddie shrugged. "I saw it once in a movie."

Caroline watched the front of the courthouse with new eyes, focusing on the shoes of the people on the sidewalk. Sure enough, over the course of fifteen minutes, she saw the same three men circle back along the sidewalk. Their clothes changed, but not their shoes. She realized there had to be a car parked somewhere around the corner where the men were changing. Or an alcove somewhere out of view.

She shivered involuntarily.

The obvious planning that had gone into Med-Gen's surveillance disturbed Caroline. If there were creeps waiting on the sidewalk for them, there were probably creeps waiting inside the courthouse, too. She reminded herself that the metal detectors and marshals inside ensured that no one was armed.

They just had to get past the doors.

Caroline scanned the streets again. Still no police escort.

Settling in to wait, she kept the binoculars up to her eyes.

• • •

"Where are they?" Annie asked. The concern in her voice mirrored Caroline's mood.

"Maybe they got another call?" Caroline mused aloud. She let the binoculars fall around her neck. She checked her watch—9:48. The hearing would begin in less than a half hour.

"Can I use your phone?" she asked, turning to Freddie.

"Sure thing," Freddie said, fishing his phone out of his pocket and handing it to her.

Dialing quickly, Caroline called the NYPD. When she heard the menu, she keyed in zero. An automated voice offered her a menu of options.

"Operator," Caroline said into the phone. She didn't have time for automated menus.

"I'm sorry, we did not understand your selection," the voice responded in Caroline's ear. "Please dial one if you are complaining about violation of a noise ordinance. Please dial two if you are calling about vehicle impoundment. Please dial three—"

After a few more minutes of trying to navigate to a live operator, Caroline hung up.

She turned to Annie and Freddie. "I think we're on our own."

"But how can we get in with those guys out there?" Annie asked, a tremor in her voice betraying her fear.

"I don't know yet," Caroline said, lifting the binoculars to her eyes.

The three creeps were on a tight rotation. With staggered, overlapping beats, they were keeping the doors within a half dozen strides at all times. Caroline saw no way that she and Annie could slip past them unnoticed. And running straight at the doors was suicide.

"Whatever you're going to do, you need to do it soon," Freddie said from beside her. "That hearing's gonna start soon."

Caroline looked down at her watch. Damn it. They were running out of time.

Turning her eyes back to the courthouse, she noticed a flock of new arrivals to the sidewalk. The first of the many tour groups she recalled from her last visit had appeared at the foot of the courthouse steps. Holding matching magenta satchels with their tour group's logo emblazoned on them, the cluster of people moved across the sidewalk like an amoeba, the edges blurring as tourists stepped out of the clump to shoot pictures of the austere building.

The tourists obscured Caroline's view of the doors and of the three men casing the doors. Exhaling in annoyance, Caroline waited for them to move out of the way so she could see if there was a line at the metal detector.

Suddenly, her annoyance was replaced by hope as an idea occurred to her.

"I know what to do," she said.

• • •

"Free arancini!" Freddie called, standing on the sidewalk in front of the courthouse, holding pieces of paper out to passersby.

The yellow sheets from the legal pad weren't professional fliers, but Caroline hoped they'd work well enough. She couldn't hear Freddie's voice from the lunch truck, but she knew he was trying hard to hustle business.

She glanced at her watch. The hearing would start in ten minutes. Not good. She hoped Freddie was as good at salesmanship as he was at surveillance.

As Caroline watched, Freddie accosted a tour group wearing neon-orange baseball hats. Waving his arms around, gesturing toward the truck, he finally coaxed some interest from them. En masse, they veered from their regularly scheduled architectural tour across the street toward the parking lot where the lunch trucks were parked.

"Here we go," Caroline said to Annie. "Get those arancini out of the oil."

Annie pulled the rice balls from the fryer and spread them on sheets of paper towel to dry. A long apron covered her tweed slacks and collared shirt. Meanwhile, Caroline prepared a row of paper dishes, waiting to be plated. Once everything was ready, she turned to the service window in time to see Freddie jogging ahead of the tour group like an overweight pied piper.

He climbed in the back door of the truck then stepped up to the window just as the first wave of neon-orange-hatted tourists reached it.

"Welcome to New York!" he said. "What you've got here is a real local delicacy, just like my nonna used to make!" He reached for the first batch of arancini. "Who wants some?"

Several hands reached for the plates.

Freddie held them away, toying with the crowd.

"These here are the best arancini this side of the Atlantic. I'm not parting with them lightly," he said. A grumble went up from the crowd. "Just kidding!" He handed them out to smiles and cheers, then reached back for some more.

Frying arancini and plating them as fast as she was able, Caroline mopped her brow of the sweat from the heat and the hot oil. She hoped her suit wasn't getting too trashed. She also hoped that Freddie would get on with the plan quickly. They didn't have time for grandstanding.

"Let's play a game," Freddie said to the delighted crowd. "Whoever can guess the combination of meat in my nonna's ragù gets a free tiramisu!"

The tourists clustered closer to the window. The ones in front shouted guesses, everything from lamb chops to dog food.

Freddie groaned with the joking suggestions and pretended to ponder the serious one. Finally, he pointed to the back of the crowd.

"The guy in the Hawaiian shirt wins!" He handed a plate of dessert to the tourist. Then he held up his hands to quiet the crowd again.

"You guys are great. I wish I could keep you here wit' me all day," Freddie said. "Or, hey, maybe I wish I was on your tour. I know, maybe you could let me have one of those hats? You know, like as a souvenir of our time here together wit' you all." He looked down and patted his chest like he was getting emotional. "I'll tell ya what, I'll give out a free batch of lasagna and a drink to anyone that'll give me their hat."

The tourists crowding the window pressed closer, some holding hats out. It reminded Caroline of the pictures she'd seen of the New York Stock Exchange.

Freddie grabbed the two closest to him and passed them over to Annie and Caroline. With his other hand, he handed the winning tourists plates of lasagna.

Donning the hat, Caroline made a mental note. If she survived the day, she promised to tell Judi that her younger son was, in fact, highly talented. A total rock star, in fact.

Soon, the fun ended, and the tour group departed.

With two new members.

CHAPTER 18

The courthouse doors were only feet away, but they were far out of reach. Tucked in the center of the tour group, Caroline watched in silent terror as the man in green Converse shoes approached from the opposite direction, scanning faces of everyone on the sidewalk.

Caroline turned toward the building, suddenly enthralled by the overwrought pillars. Beside her, Annie pulled her neon-orange baseball hat down low over her forehead.

Holding her breath, Caroline watched in her peripheral vision as Green Converse came parallel with her before continuing past. When he disappeared around the corner, she exhaled and resettled the bag slung over her shoulder. Freddie had conjured the bag from the tour group so she wouldn't stand out. She'd stuffed her suit jacket inside, but in her dress pants and pumps, she still felt as vulnerable as a roofer in a hurricane.

She chanced another look at the doors. A line of people stretched beyond the threshold out onto the sidewalk. A line attesting to the backup at the security checkpoint. A line standing between Caroline and the safety of the courthouse lobby.

Caroline commanded herself to patience. They'd be inside soon. They'd be surrounded by court staff. They'd be within earshot of marshals.

But if they got caught before they cleared the doors, it would be over.

She and Annie would get only one shot. They needed to get it right.

Still, her stomach knotted with repressed urgency. The hearing had started already. Louis would be wondering where she was. Eddie, too.

She knew Eddie could handle the examination of the first few scientists. He'd helped her to prepare the witness notes, after all. He knew what questions to ask.

But she was supposed to be in there . . . instead of out here, trapped in a gaggle of neon-clad tourists.

Scanning the sidewalk, she looked for some sign of the thugs she knew couldn't be far away. Even though she didn't see anyone suspicious, she knew they were near. Somewhere just around the corner. Or across the street. Maybe even watching the tour group.

The guide began walking again, and Caroline followed, vaguely aware of him describing late Empire architecture in painstaking, monotonous detail. Her mind screamed at her to get inside the courthouse. They were running out of time. The questioning of the witnesses wouldn't go on forever, and she had the only scientist that mattered with her.

When the group pulled abreast of the doors, she saw that the line at the metal detector had all but disappeared.

It was time to go.

"Come on," Caroline whispered to Annie.

She broke from the crowd and walked toward the doors as quickly as she could without drawing attention.

Up ahead, dimly seen through the doorway, the marshal ushered a teenage boy through the metal detector. They were almost there.

Stepping into the marble foyer, Caroline placed her tour bag on the metal detector's conveyor belt. Then she waited for the marshal to wave her through. The seconds ticked by in a slow trickle, in danger courted by immobility. Until she passed the security checkpoint, her progress could be stopped by the cool muzzle of a gun pressed up against her back.

At the front of the security line, a woman fumbled with the zipper of her purse, stalling the progress of everyone behind her.

Caroline resisted the urge to push forward. Her heart slammed in her chest, propelling blood past her ears in a thunderous whoosh that drowned out all sounds, turning the ambient conversations in the line to murmurs.

A crack behind her made her freeze. Every shred of her awareness bent back, seeking danger. The skin on her shoulders itched, stretching out for contact, seeking awareness of what was behind her.

Unable to resist, she glanced over her shoulder.

A lawyer wrestled a heavy document case from the white plastic table to the metal rollers in front of the conveyor belt. Behind him, bored faces looked back at her, each borne by another soul waiting to enter the courthouse.

Still, Caroline didn't relax.

In her pocket, she gripped her worry beads. She forced her attention to their cool roundness, the tactile sensation providing her with sensory input beyond the flood of cortisol that kept her brain locked in a spiral of terror.

Finally, the marshal waved a weary hand, and Caroline stepped under the archway, saying a silent prayer that nothing she wore would trigger the metal detector's sensors.

The light on the archway stayed green.

The marshal stepped aside so she could pass.

As soon as the conveyor belt coughed up her bag, Caroline yanked out her suit jacket. The navy blazer was wrinkled and smelled of cooking grease, but it would do. She shoved the tour bag into a trash can and stepped aside to make room for those behind her to pass.

Without fanfare or delay, Annie followed through the metal detector.

Watching the scientist pass the security checkpoint, Caroline allowed herself a moment of celebration. They'd made it past the doors. They were inside.

Now they had just one final leg of their long journey: the short trip to the courtroom.

With Annie behind her, Caroline hurried into the lobby to put as much space between the doors and herself as she could. The green marble rotunda echoed with voices. Wan light filtered down from the high windows, dingy and unwashed. Straight ahead, the down escalator carried people to ground level, allowing those whose business was done to exit the courthouse.

Malachite-toned pillars rose on both sides of the escalator, holding a stone arch upon which someone had chiseled, "He who seeks equity must do equity."

Caroline looked forward to traveling the down escalator after the hearing, but right now, she needed to go up.

"The *SuperSoy* courtroom is on the second floor," Caroline called over her shoulder, ducking down the corridor she knew would take them to the up escalator quickly.

"Where are we going?" Annie asked, speaking up to be heard over the cacophony of footfalls and voices.

"The up escalator's on the other side of the building." Caroline maneuvered down the hallway she knew led from one side of the court-house to the other. Unlike the bustling main lobby, the hallway was uncrowded, so they could travel faster.

Caroline increased her pace until she was jogging.

She heard Annie matching her pace behind her.

Suddenly, she spotted two men running toward them from the far end of the hallway.

For half a second, she believed they had nothing to do with her. Until she recognized the taller of the two. The pale man from the airport shuttle.

Her breath caught, and her fingers tingled with a rush of adrenaline. They'd been found.

She cast around for a marshal, but there was no one around.

She grabbed Annie's hand and spun around 180 degrees, back toward the direction they'd come.

Sprinting down the hall, her footfalls sounded frantic in her ears. Above the sound, reverberating all around her, was the louder sound of the two men tearing toward them at full speed.

She needed to do something. Anything.

Ahead, she saw the light of the green marble rotunda. If they could reach it, they could call for help.

With a stab of desperation, she realized they'd never make it. Though she couldn't see her pursuers, she could feel them bearing down, fast. They'd be upon her in seconds.

Suddenly, an image from a cartoon flashed through her mind. Lord knew if it would work, but she didn't have a better idea.

Caroline yanked the strand of beads out of her pocket. She tore the end that bound them and threw the ruined strand behind her. The beads clattered to the floor in a smattering of staccato taps, a sound followed by a yelp and a crash as one of the men giving chase fell to the ground.

Without breaking stride, Caroline pulled Annie toward the end of the hallway, where it opened onto the grand green-marbled lobby. Then she sprinted toward the down escalator carrying people from the second floor to the first.

When she hit the lowest step, she lunged onto the escalator, crashing into the descending people.

"Excuse me. Pardon me," she said, pushing her way up, like a salmon swimming upstream. Lawyers and judges and litigants grumbled and griped and shouldered her in complaint, but Caroline pressed ahead, forcing her small frame to act like the prow of a ship crashing through waves.

Behind her, Annie struggled to keep up, her even smaller body buffeted by the flow of people pressing down toward the lobby below.

As she fought her way to the top, Caroline hoped her recollection of the courthouse's layout was correct—that the *SuperSoy* courtroom would be located at the top of the down escalator. And she hoped that their arrival, coming up the down escalator, would surprise the thugs she knew had to be waiting for them on the second floor.

When she reached the top of the escalator, Caroline pushed off the railing and spun around, ready to face any assailants. At the far end of the hallway, near the top of the up escalator, she saw a man standing, his eyes focused with intensity on those disembarking.

He swung around to face her, and his mouth shaped into an O before he began running toward her.

But Caroline knew that she and Annie had a head start.

She sprinted toward the door of the courtroom and threw open the door.

• • •

The courtroom's door shut behind Caroline with a too-loud click and everyone turned to see the cause of the disruption. On the defense side, Kennedy's forehead furrowed like a wrinkled sheet. His eyes flicked back and forth from Caroline to Annie. The corners of his mouth stretched downward in a grimace resembling pain.

Checkmate, Caroline thought with glee. Kennedy had tried to stop her, but he'd failed. And now there was nothing he could do. As if to prove that to herself, she guided Annie up the aisle, away from the door, toward the greater safety of the front row of the gallery.

Along the back walls, onlookers lined the edges of the courtroom. The families of SuperSoy victims, alerted to the hearing date by the Plaintiffs' Steering Committee's Listserv and Facebook page. There to watch. To witness. To wait for justice.

Behind her, she heard the door of the courtroom click open again. Her pursuers had arrived. But they, too, could do nothing. Like their boss, Kennedy, they had become mere spectators to what would happen next. They'd lost control over their quarry.

On the plaintiffs' side of the courtroom, the Steering Committee's members were a tableau of barely restrained jubilation. Dale smiled with his too-big mouth. Anton Callisto's usually stony face held sublime joy. Next to him, Louis's white eyebrows arched in surprise, the senior partner stunned into an apparent uncharacteristic shock.

Caroline nodded back at him. Yes, this is Annie, she wanted to shout. I did it—I brought her to court in time.

Louis got the message. He smiled a small, knowing grin before turning back around to watch the proceedings.

At the front of the courtroom, Dr. Ambrose sat in the witness box, his ill-fitting suit wrinkled and stained, his thin hair combed from one ear over to the other.

Eddie Diaz stood before him in a navy-blue suit and orange silk tie.

Caroline exhaled with relief. Just as she'd hoped, Eddie was filling in for her. He knew the witness examination notes as well as she did. Perhaps even better, since he'd finished polishing them while she'd been out chasing Dr. Wong.

Caroline sat back to watch.

"Thanks for traveling so far to be here with us, Dr. Ambrose," Eddie said, smiling affably.

"My pleasure," Dr. Ambrose answered in a thin, wheezy voice. "I've enjoyed listening to my colleagues testify."

Glancing at the clock, Caroline noted the time. The first few witnesses hadn't taken long, apparently. She was glad she'd hear Ambrose's testimony, at least.

"As I understand the finding of your research, you've concluded that SuperSoy can cause mitochondrial degradation in rats, correct?" Eddie asked.

"Yes," the scientist confirmed.

"Is this degradation unique to rat mitochondria?" Eddie asked.

"I've only studied rats, so I can't speak to anything but rats," Dr. Ambrose answered before launching into an exegesis about the unique architecture of rat mitochondria.

As Dr. Ambrose droned on, Caroline waited for Eddie to steer the scientist back to the point. While rat anatomy was vaguely pertinent, it certainly wasn't the point of the examination.

But instead of interrupting, Eddie put his elbow on the wooden divider separating the witness box from the courtroom and listened attentively to Dr. Ambrose.

Caroline's brow wrinkled. What was Eddie doing?

The examination notes required Eddie to be pushing Dr. Ambrose to draw the conclusions that logically flowed from his research on rats. Rat mitochondria weren't so different from human mitochondria. Ambrose would concede that was so if asked about the relevant organelles. But Eddie wasn't asking the right questions. Heck, he wasn't asking *any* questions.

At the back of the courtroom, the clock on the wall ticked loudly, competing with the wheezing voice of the ancient scientist.

When Dr. Ambrose finally finished his lengthy answer, Eddie walked back to the podium. He shuffled through his notes. Then he cleared his throat.

"I think that's all I've got for Dr. Ambrose today," he said.

Caroline opened her mouth in dismay.

But then her skin crawled with electricity as a terrifying possibility dawned on her. Eddie was throwing the argument. Someone had gotten to him, and he'd turned.

Unwilling to accept the implications of what she was seeing, she considered other explanations. Maybe he just sucked at lawyering. Maybe that's why Paul Tiller had been willing to send him out to Los Angeles. Maybe Eddie was a good guy who just needed to find some other profession.

Caroline had almost convinced herself of an alternate explanation when she spotted the woman. She almost didn't recognize her. Wearing glasses and a light-gray business suit with her bright hair pulled back in a bun, the woman bore almost no resemblance to the sexy blonde from Las Vegas. But it was her. Sitting on the defense side, right next to Ian Kennedy.

And as soon as Caroline placed the woman, she had no doubt. And she knew exactly what she needed to do.

Caroline rose to her feet.

"Objection, Your Honor," she said, her voice loud enough to carry even without a microphone.

The entire courtroom rustled as every head in the room turned to face her.

"Mr. Diaz isn't pro hac vice in this court," Caroline continued.

The judge raised an eyebrow. "You're objecting to your own side?"

"Yes, Your Honor," said Caroline, walking toward the front of the courtroom. "Mr. Diaz cannot be heard in this court without submitting a Certificate of Good Standing from the state bar of the state of Georgia and applying for and obtaining pro hac vice status. Neither thing has happened. As a result, he cannot argue here today."

"This is highly unusual," said Judge Jacobsen. He leaned toward his clerk, who typed on her computer, peered at the screen, then whispered something in the judge's ear. The judge nodded to his clerk, then straightened, his eyes focused on Caroline.

"Ms. Auden appears to be correct," the judge said to a ripple of surprised murmurs across the courtroom. "I'm sorry, Mr. Diaz, you cannot appear in this court."

"I'll finish the scientist examinations," Caroline said, walking toward the podium. "And I'd like to call Dr. Annie Wong to the stand."

Ian Kennedy stood. "Objection, Your Honor. Dr. Wong isn't on the witness list."

"Yes, she is, Your Honor," Caroline said, taking her place behind the podium and tipping the microphone down to her level. "At the last hearing, you asked to speak with, quote, 'all of the scientists of the articles,' close quote. Dr. Wong is coauthor of one of the articles we submitted. So even if she wasn't listed by name on the witness list, the spirit of the witness designation is wide enough to encompass her."

The judge cocked his head, considering the argument.

"In addition, we provided a list of all scientists to whom we submitted subpoenas," Caroline continued. "Dr. Wong is on that list."

The judge looked at Caroline unblinkingly.

"The only reason for the witness list requirement is to give the other side notice of what witnesses will be testifying," Caroline said. "Between the article itself, the court's last hearing focusing on that article, and the list of subpoenas, Med-Gen was on notice that we would be calling Dr. Wong. There's no possible prejudice to defendant here."

"I agree," the judge said with a nod. "You may proceed."

Caroline turned back to the gallery, where Annie Wong sat stock-still, an expression of terror etched on her face.

"Please take the witness stand, Dr. Wong," Caroline said.

Annie rose and walked slowly toward the jury box like a soldier facing a firing squad.

When she reached the chair, she sat down in the witness box. Her eyes widened at the dozens of lawyers assembled in the courtroom, staring back at her, waiting to hear what she would say.

Caroline stepped around the podium.

"Permission to approach the witness?" she asked Judge Jacobsen.

"Granted," said the judge.

Caroline approached Annie until she was close enough to smile encouragingly at the terrified scientist.

Annie attempted to smile back, but it came out like a grimace.

"Shall we begin?" Caroline asked the scientist softly.

"Okay," Annie said, her voice quavering.

Once Annie had been sworn in, Caroline met the scientist's eyes. Her own held a question.

After several heartbeats, Annie nodded her readiness.

"Were you the author of this study that was previously authenticated by the editor of the *Fielding Journal of Molecular Cell Biology*?" Caroline asked.

"I was the coauthor along with Dr. Franklin Heller," Annie replied, the microphone in the witness box amplifying her tiny voice.

"And Dr. Heller died prior to the publication of this article."

Annie paused, her mouth pursed.

"He did," she answered quietly.

"This article was not submitted for publication prior to or after his death, correct?" Caroline asked.

Annie nodded and looked down.

"Please answer for the court reporter," Caroline instructed. She needed to tread lightly. The hard part was still coming up.

"No, it wasn't submitted," Annie answered, still looking down.

"And why wasn't it submitted for peer review and publication at any point?"

When Annie looked up, she had tears in her eyes.

"Because I didn't submit it. I was supposed to, but I . . . didn't."

"Why not? Did you have doubts about the veracity of the results or whether the experimental data or other science was sound?" Caroline asked.

"No. It is solid. Totally solid." Annie's voice increased in strength as she evaluated the strength of her scientific data.

"Then why didn't you submit it?" Caroline asked again.

"Because my life was threatened."

A murmur traveled through the courtroom like electricity.

"Who threatened you?" Caroline asked.

"I don't know the identities of the people who made the threats. The threats were made on the phone. At night. In the line at the grocery store. Everywhere. Different people, but always the same threat. I'd be hurt. My son would be hurt. I assume these people were connected to Med-Gen, but I don't really know. They made sure of that."

"Why didn't you go to the police?"

"These people, they said if I talked to the police, they'd know. They said they'd find out and they'd . . ."

"Did they pay you to leave town?" Caroline asked.

"They offered to, but I didn't want their blood money." Annie spat the words out like broken teeth.

"But you ran anyway."

Annie looked down again, as if finding the tip of her shoe fascinating.

"I did," she said. "I was scared."

When she looked back up again, her eyes held determination.

"But I'm here now," Annie said.

Caroline mentally exhaled. Annie had made it through the mea culpa part of her examination with her credibility intact.

"Let's talk a moment about your research," Caroline said, pivoting to the substantive part of the examination. "The bottom line appears to be that in a certain subset of patients, SuperSoy causes kidney failure. Is that a fair description of your conclusion?"

"Yes. Unequivocally yes. I don't say that lightly. I'm a scientist. We're taught to constantly question our results. But the size of the sample, the types of experiments, and the consistency of our results were all remarkable. SuperSoy can and does cause kidneys to shut down with disturbing frequency. Everyone deserved to know it. We should have shouted it from the rooftops when we found out. We tried to do that . . ." Annie drifted off, her eyes suddenly haunted.

"How can you be so sure your results were sound?" Caroline asked, steering Annie away from her recent horrors.

"We ran studies on hundreds of patients, including those who had suffered no prior incidence of kidney problems," Annie said, her voice growing stronger as she testified about the science. "Children. Athletes. Everything we did confirmed our initial results. SuperSoy compromises kidney cells."

"How can one little genetic modification to a soy plant do so much damage?" Caroline asked. She knew she needed to ask every question in the judge's mind. Running away from doubts would not win this motion. Only by addressing the judge's doubts head-on would they carry the day.

"Designer foods may be a good idea in concept, but we've never really seen what happens when the known risks play out. What we're seeing with SuperSoy are the unintended consequences of inserting an alien gene into soy DNA," Annie said.

"What do you mean?" Caroline asked.

"The jellyfish gene that Med-Gen introduced to give the soy plant higher protein content also interacts with the native genes in the plant in other ways. One result of that interaction is that the soy plant now creates a kidney toxin—a toxin that can be deadly to people with genetic predispositions to certain kidney diseases."

"But if that's true, how did SuperSoy ever get approved by the FDA? Are you suggesting that you found out something the FDA missed? Something Med-Gen missed?" Caroline asked.

"Med-Gen had to know about the problems. Any biotech company that ran the trials they were required to run to get FDA approval would have seen the disturbing results."

"So then, what happened?" Caroline asked.

"I can only conclude that Med-Gen didn't tell the FDA what it needed to know to evaluate the safety of this genetically engineered plant. As a result, the FDA approved it based on an incomplete data set."

A murmur traveled through the courtroom. Annie's testimony was a bombshell. Caroline waited before continuing. She wanted to give the scientist's words a chance to make their maximum impact.

"Would you have any hesitation about submitting your article for peer review?" Caroline asked.

"No hesitation at all." Annie met the judge's eyes squarely. "The science is unimpeachable. Dr. Heller and I were very thorough." Annie paused. "Dr. Heller was the finest scientist I have ever known. He was my mentor. And my . . . my friend. I regret not submitting the article for publication after he died. I owed that to him."

Caroline turned to the judge. "I'd like to represent to the court that the article will be submitted to the *Fielding Journal of Molecular Cell Biology* for peer review and publication. We will let the court know when there's a publication date set."

Turning back to Annie, Caroline smiled, beginning to relax for the first time in weeks.

"Dr. Wong, before we finish here, I have just one final question for you. Do you have any reservations, caveats, or qualifications about your conclusions?"

"None," Annie said. "Absolutely none." She looked at Caroline with gratitude.

Caroline smiled back at her. The scientist had done well. She had a long road ahead of her, filled with reckonings, but at least the beginning was done.

"Any further questions?" the judge asked.

"None, Your Honor," Caroline said.

The judge turned to the defense team.

"Does Med-Gen have any questions for this witness?" he asked.

Ian Kennedy leaned toward the other lawyers. After a whispered conference, he stood up.

"We'll submit, too," he said. "No questions for this witness. Med-Gen rests."

Caroline met Annie's eyes in surprise. The defense had concluded there was nothing they could ask that wouldn't do further damage to Med-Gen's case.

"The case stands submitted," the judge said.

Then he paused and regarded the faces of the many lawyers filling the courtroom.

The room quieted until the ticking clock sounded like a hammer.

"I appreciate your forbearance," the judge began. "Thank you to the attorneys and to the scientists who came here today. It was an interesting session. You'll receive a full explanation of my reasons in my written ruling, but I'm satisfied that these studies demonstrate a link between ingestion of SuperSoy and kidney injury. The Heller article, coupled with Dr. Wong's testimony today, confirms that such a mechanism of injury exists. You will still need to litigate the circumstances of your individual cases and individual plaintiffs, but I will allow the cases to go forward. It is so ordered."

Judge Jacobsen hammered his gavel, and voices rose all around.

• • •

"Well done," Louis said, standing with Caroline on the steps of the courthouse. "I expect you may be receiving offers of employment from all of these fellows." He hooked a thumb toward Dale and Paul and the rest of the Steering Committee, who stood in a knot on the steps of the courthouse, laughing with the giddy joy of people whose team has unexpectedly won the World Series.

"That's okay," Caroline said. "I'm happy where I am."

"You'd make more with them," Louis said, his face serious. "Or with Kennedy."

"It doesn't matter," Caroline said as a cab stopped in front of the courthouse for Louis. She walked with him to the door. "Like I said, I like where I am." She saw the relief in her boss's pale eyes.

"Good." Louis smiled. "Then I'll see you back at the office, Ms. Auden."

He climbed into the cab and closed the door.

Caroline waved as her boss drove away. She was grateful for the opportunities he'd given her. Unlike the lawyers on the Steering Committee, Louis had never pegged her as too short, too young, too female, or too anything else to handle herself in court. He'd encouraged her and supported her, giving her everything from the firm credit card to the lead role in a major case. There was no way she'd take another job.

A tap on her shoulder made her turn. She found Jasper standing beside her.

"I just wanted to say thanks," he said.

"Turned out all right, didn't it?" Caroline smiled.

"It sure did. Thank you." Jasper's face transformed, the stiff frown lines abandoned in favor of deep smile lines around his mouth and eyes. Caroline realized this was a man as capable of joy as he had been of sorrow. He just hadn't had cause to smile in far too long.

"I can't take the credit," Caroline said. A brave scientist died on a beach and another made a leap into the abyss to save people she'd never know from injury or death. They were the ones who deserved his thanks.

Jasper nodded, his eyes scanning the courthouse steps.

Caroline knew whom he sought.

"Dr. Wong left right after the hearing," Caroline said. "She wanted to get back to her son. I promise I'll let her know you said thanks."

"I'm much obliged." Jasper held out a hand to shake Caroline's. Then he trotted down the steps with a spring in his steps.

Watching him disappear down in the crowd of people on the sidewalk in front of the courthouse, Caroline hoped his burden would be a little lighter because of what had transpired. She hoped Tom would recover. She hoped the brothers would travel together like they'd planned.

Caroline's phone vibrated in her purse. She withdrew it and found a text message from Amy Garber with a picture attached to it.

Thank you. Thank you. Thank you! Amy had written. Here's a picture Liam drew for you. He wants to give you the real one when you're back in Los Angeles. We'd love to see you.

Caroline opened the picture. In it, a little figure held hands with a taller figure beneath a rainbow tree, above which floated rainbow clouds against a brilliant blue sky.

A second text message from Amy pinged.

P.S. Liam hasn't drawn a rainbow since he got sick.

Caroline found herself smiling at the message. It was the best thank-you she could ever hope to receive.

Behind her, the voices thinned and quieted as people on both sides of the case departed for their offices or their hotels or nearby bars.

Suddenly, Caroline's neck prickled with the sensation of someone watching her.

She turned around. Only one person still stood on the steps. Eddie.

Caroline's heart sank down through her knees. She cast around for an escape. She didn't want to talk to Eddie. She didn't ever want to see him again.

But he approached her, stopping a few feet in front of her.

He opened his mouth to speak.

Caroline held up a hand.

"Don't," she said.

Eddie closed his mouth and waited.

"What did Kennedy's people offer you? Money?" Caroline asked, her chest filling with anger at his betrayal. She wondered if he'd deny it.

"The first time they came to talk to me, they offered me money. But I turned them away," Eddie said.

Caroline stayed silent. She knew it wasn't the whole story.

"But then they called me again a couple days ago," he said, "and offered me my family." Eddie searched her eyes for understanding. "You know how long I've been trying to get papers for my mom and sister. I've been trying for years. That woman, she offered to do it overnight. She said her boss knew who to talk to. Something about how information is power and her boss had it. What was I supposed to do? Turn that down?"

A dozen responses rose to Caroline's lips. She wanted to castigate Eddie for his weakness. She wanted to tell him that he should have held on to his principles, to his integrity. She wanted to berate him for selling the safety and health of tens of thousands in exchange for that of his mother and sister. But she couldn't.

Even though she wanted to believe she'd have rejected the soul-corrupting choice that Eddie had made, she understood what it felt like to feel impotent to take care of her family. She wondered if she'd pay in her soul's weight for her mother to be okay. For her uncle to be okay. For her father to be okay. To help save those she loved, would she give up . . . everything?

At Caroline's long silence, Eddie nodded.

"Are you going to tell anyone?" he asked.

"No, though I suspect I'm not the only one watching who noticed what you were doing. But I won't be the one to say it. We won today, so there was no harm in what you did. Not to anyone but you, anyway."

Eddie winced at her words.

"I'm so sorry," he said, his voice anguished. "I didn't know what to do. I've been trying for so long."

Caroline had no answer for him. No solace. She knew the well-pressed, easygoing face he showed to the world hid a lonely kid from a poor town who missed his mom. He'd faced a morally ambiguous conundrum and had weighed it so that love came out on top. His own love, to be sure, but still love.

"I figured we couldn't win without Annie anyway, so I figured it wouldn't harm anything . . ." He trailed off. Caroline could see his words sounded weak even to him.

"I understand," she said, "but I've got to go now."

She needed to escape Eddie's need for an absolution she could not give.

"Can I call you?" he called after her retreating form.

Caroline turned around to meet his eyes one last time.

"No. Not yet," she said.

She turned away, tears springing to her eyes.

She walked quickly away from the courthouse steps. Away from Eddie. She'd watched him offer up her work in sacrifice to the enemy that had threatened her own family. She'd seen Eddie forget the stakes, the difference the case made for thousands of people like Jasper and his brother. In the end, Eddie had made a deal with those horrible people, just because they knew the right people at Immigration and Customs Enforcement.

Information was power indeed, she thought bitterly.

Suddenly, Caroline stopped walking. Her eyes ceased to see the people around her. Her ears ceased to hear any sounds. Everything she thought she knew shifted, as if she had only just figured out she'd been looking through the wrong end of a telescope.

"Oh my God," she said to no one.

CHAPTER 19

Caroline stood at the threshold of Louis's office. The early-morning light painted the office buildings in his windows pastel shades. A distant hum of cars on the street far below reverberated softly around the space.

When Louis looked up, his face broke into an uncharacteristically broad grin.

"Ah, the remarkable Ms. Auden darkens my doorstep. I was beginning to think you'd never come back." He chuckled. "I assume you took a couple days off to sort yourself out after a long and stressful week. Well deserved, indeed. I hope you're ready to come back to work hard. I've got another case ready to go, if you're up for it."

Instead of answering, Caroline held out an envelope.

Louis raised an eyebrow.

"My resignation," Caroline said.

Louis took off his glasses and rubbed his eyes. Then he replaced them and met her eyes, his own filled with sorrow.

"Why, may I ask, are you quitting?" he asked.

"I can't work for a fixer," she said.

Louis stayed silent.

"It was you, wasn't it?" Caroline held up a hand. "No, don't answer. You'll deny it. But I know it's true. You told me once that you can set a person up to succeed or to fail. Looking back, I can see you set me up to fail."

When Louis didn't say anything, she continued, "At the beginning, I wondered why you'd staffed just one lawyer, a first-year associate who knew nothing about anything, on a huge case. But then, my ego liked thinking you trusted me to handle it. Like I was so great or something . . ."

She shook her head at her hubris. "But that wasn't why you put me on the case. You put me on *SuperSoy* to fail. It was just another way to sabotage the case. In case the hole you'd made in the evidence didn't kill it."

She paused, her eyes settling on a photograph on Louis's wall of a building that looked like an overwrought birthday cake perched atop a hill overlooking the ocean. Beachgoers populated the foreground, their peaked caps and bloomers exotic in their old-fashioned formality. Though the image was black-and-white, the reflections on the wet sand suggested a sunny day . . . a sunny day of people long since grown and dead.

"You weren't surprised about that hole in the science," she said, meeting Louis's eyes again. "Heck, you made it."

The expression on Louis's face feigned annoyance.

Caroline admired his acting skills.

"But your true genius showed when you let Dale argue that *Daubert* motion," she said. "You knew he wasn't prepared. You knew he'd bomb. You could've stopped him. You could've argued it yourself. But you didn't say anything to anyone on the Steering Committee. And when he messed up, there was no harm in letting me take a shot at it. After all, I'm just a first-year associate with no actual court experience. I wasn't supposed to do that well, was I?"

Still, Louis said nothing.

"I'm going to forgive myself for not catching on so early in the game," Caroline said. "But what I can't forgive is that I didn't figure it out yesterday when Eddie was up there trying to throw the argument. That should have tipped me off. You knew the witness examination notes. You helped write them. You knew exactly what Eddie was supposed to be asking Dr. Ambrose. But again, you just sat there, watching our side go down in flames."

Caroline held Louis's eyes. In them she saw the wariness of a shark who knows he's the biggest thing in the ocean but still makes a habit of watching his back. Just in case.

"The rest is easy to figure out once you realize who's pulling the strings. You bought off or blackmailed Yvonne, didn't you? That's how you got access to Franklin's computer."

Caroline grew reflective. "I think Yvonne knew all about the affair between her husband and Annie. She'd seen Nolan. She couldn't have missed the resemblance. That affair was the worst-kept secret in the world. And she also had to know that her husband's medical group had bought a house for Annie. Yvonne did Franklin's books. That house would've shown up as an asset on his medical group's tax returns for years. But Yvonne didn't really care about the affair. She's a lesbian, isn't she? She has her own thing going on with Trina."

Caroline recalled the easy familiarity of the two women. The two glasses of wine, one intended for Trina, the other for Yvonne.

"I bet all you had to do was threaten to publicize her relationship. Even aside from not wanting to get thrown out of the club or whatever else might have happened to her, Yvonne wouldn't have wanted to risk jeopardizing her father's congressional run," Caroline surmised. "Goodbye, article."

C.E. TOBISMAN

Louis cleared his throat. "This is all rather interesting storytelling, Ms. Auden, but I have work to do. If you aren't interested in continuing on at Hale Stern, I suggest you gather your things. But these accusations are, quite frankly, offensive."

He turned to his mail. It was an obvious dismissal.

Caroline didn't move. Not this time.

"There were so many other clues that you were the one manipulating things," she said. "When I was in Mendocino, everything was so calm at first. You thought I'd give up the hunt for Dr. Wong. But then, after I called to tell you I'd found Annie, all hell broke loose. That threat to my uncle . . ." Caroline shook her head. "That was low."

Louis put his hands on his desk as if to stand up, but Caroline held up one finger. She wasn't done. Not yet.

"After I called you from Mendocino, it was all about the firm credit card, wasn't it? You kept track of my charges. You could see where I was." Caroline considered her good fortune at having driven up to Mendocino. No credit card charge for a plane trip had meant a quiet couple of days to hunt for Annie . . . until she'd charged a meal at a roadside diner.

"You lost us on the flight east. You didn't know which of the reservations I'd used. But you knew my dad lived near the city, so you made an educated guess about where I'd go . . ." Except that he hadn't guessed where she'd ended up. Good thing she'd stayed with Joey. If she'd gone to her dad's house, they'd have gotten to her. She had little doubt what they would have done to her if they'd found her. She shivered at the close call.

Louis sat back in his leather armchair and idly twisted the pig's head ring on his finger. He gazed unblinkingly at Caroline, waiting for her to finish.

"I do wonder about Kennedy," she mused aloud. "Is he a coconspirator? Or is he just another lawyer?" She considered what she knew about the defense attorney. "I think he knows what you are. I think he suspects how Dr. Heller died. But he couldn't prove anything. Plus, he had an ethical obligation to his client, so he couldn't say anything to me . . ."

She considered Kennedy's persistent offers of employment in a new light. Perhaps he'd been trying to save her, in his own way. "I think he was just a regular guy caught in a really horrible situation," she concluded.

Caroline walked to the antique chess set sitting on the small table by the window. Turning her back on the view, she continued to hold Louis's gaze. "You said long ago that a fixer leaves no fingerprints. That may be true most of the time, but it wasn't true this time."

Louis's eyes widened slightly.

"Did you know Sotheby's keeps excellent computer records?" she continued. "Well, they do. Like you said, pedigree is everything. Especially for the top-shelf pieces. Like that Picasso. Imagine my surprise when I learned you weren't the purchaser of that painting. A holding company for Med-Gen won the auction then donated the painting to your private collection. And the timing was fascinating. Med-Gen transferred ownership to you the same week you called Dale to offer your services on this case."

Louis's face drained of all color.

"That coincidence got me thinking. What stories did the other paintings in your collection have to tell? Your curator uses a program called Art-Track to track all purchases made on behalf of its clients. All that information. Up in the Cloud. So easily accessed." Caroline tapped her lip with a dangerous gleam in her eyes. Hacking into Art-Track had been ridiculously easy. Art curators had no reason to erect complex security walls, apparently.

Louis opened his mouth, but no sound came out.

"Guess what I found out?" she asked. "The dates when you got your paintings corresponded to pivotal developments in your cases. The disappearance of key witnesses. Impossible settlements. Data dumps of incriminating evidence. And the way those paintings were purchased is fascinating, too. Cayman Island trusts. The private accounts of drug lords and fraudsters. It's all an intriguing web, and I'm sure the police will have fun untangling it."

Caroline thought about the many pictures that hung on the walls of the firm. All trophies of other Franklin Hellers. Other innocent people whose lives Louis had destroyed.

"But the best part of all is the link to your home computer," Caroline said, knowing she still had one more ace to play. "I won't bore you with the details, since we both know you're not a tech guy, but getting inside wasn't hard. Your wife gave the firm's IT guy access to remotely troubleshoot your home computer. Getting into the IT system and then accessing your home computer was a cakewalk. Keeping all that info on the firm server probably wasn't for you. In retrospect."

"But that's illegal," Louis said.

Caroline ignored the weak protest. While her hacking was certainly illegal, she couldn't bring herself to care.

"Unlike you, I've covered my tracks," Caroline said. "When the data flows to the police, no one will know I sent it. It will show up at their doorstep wrapped up with a bow and a tag from 'ANONYMOUS.'"

Caroline monitored Louis's face for his reaction. For his devastation.

But instead, his expression calmed. He leaned back in his chair, a small smirk tugging at the corner of his mouth.

Caroline's stomach sank at the self-assurance in his eyes. He, too, had another card to play, it seemed.

"Before you continue on this course you seem to have set out for yourself," he began, "I'd like you to consider a proposal that I had hoped to wait to make to you until you were more seasoned." Louis paused and folded his hands on his ink blotter. "I know some of my techniques are a bit outdated. The rudiments of helping my clients never change, but I will readily concede that your knowledge of technology is useful. It's why I hired you, after all."

He held her eyes.

Caroline's throat clenched at the implications of his words. He knew about her hacking background. He'd been testing her. He didn't like relying on outsiders to do his work. He wanted someone in-house. And he'd picked her. It was a dark compliment indeed.

"You've shown yourself willing to bend the rules to win," Louis said. "In fact, you've proven far more talented in that regard than anyone I've ever seen. Hacking. False identities. Trickery. You're good at this, Caroline."

Caroline's cheeks burned at the truth in his words.

"I know that money doesn't drive you," he continued, "but think of all the good you could do. You could choose whichever side you liked and put your thumb on the scale however you pleased."

"And where do you fit into all of this?" Caroline asked, perversely fascinated.

"I'm good at what I do. The best, in fact. Those who need my services always find their way to me. I've never much cared about the winners or losers, but I can see that you do. I'm willing to change my business model to accommodate your moral streak." He shrugged.

"I'm not interested," Caroline said, louder than she intended.

"Then you're a hypocrite," Louis shot back. "I know what you are. Every bit as much as you know what I am, I know what you are."

"I'm not like you," Caroline insisted.

Louis smiled a mirthless grin. "You can keep telling yourself that, but you like the game. You impose limits on yourself as to how far you'll push the envelope—limits that will eventually fall away. The more you bend the rules, the more you thrill at the victories."

"You're wrong. I only leveled the playing field. I gave the victims a chance," Caroline said. "Whenever there's someone like you out there, I hope there's always someone like me who can play your game."

Louis shrugged in a way that told Caroline he didn't believe her.

"Suit yourself. But you're putting yourself in a rather difficult position, aren't you, Ms. Auden," he said, the confidence never leaving his eyes. "Leaving a firm after only a month? You're going to have a rather difficult time getting another job. How will you pay off all of those loans you took out to pay for law school? How will you manage to ever move out of that house with your uncle and your mother?"

Caroline said nothing. She hoped he was wrong, that the police would move quickly enough that her departure from Hale Stern wouldn't be seen by other firms as anything but a completely sensible flight of a smart rat from a badly listing ship. But she knew the risks. She knew the potential consequences of confronting Louis. She loathed the price she might have to pay for what she was doing. But she had no choice.

"You don't want to work here. Fine, don't." Louis's voice was mild. "We can come up with a mutually agreeable explanation for your departure. Perhaps you realized you'd rather work in government. Or maybe your true calling is at a nonprofit or a defense firm. I have many friends in this city." He paused. His lips tightened. "But leave things alone," he finished, an undercurrent of menace entering his voice.

Caroline's heart began to pound. She was playing a dangerous game.

"Oh, you can rest assured that I won't hurt you," Louis said, reading her expression. "I know you'll have things set up to explode if anything happens to you. Mutually assured destruction." He smiled slightly. "We need each other. I need your silence. You need my reputation. That's why you came here, isn't it? Get a job at a prestigious firm, and all doors suddenly open for you."

"No," Caroline said. She shook her head as though a spell had been broken. "I came because I thought you'd be my mentor. Maybe even my friend. But you're a complete and utter fraud, Louis. In every possible way, you're a fake."

She gestured with her chin toward his ring. "I found out you weren't even in the Porcellian Club. You're not old money. You're part of the Stern family of Rhode Island that made a go of it in the steel industry before your great-grandfather lost his shirt in the Depression. I never cared about any of that stupid stuff. I don't care where you came from or who you are or how much money you have. I only ever cared that you were something special. But you're not. You're a fraud. Not to mention a murderer."

"I've never killed anyone," Louis said.

"Maybe not with your own hands, but it's all the same," Caroline said, mentally noting all the things Louis hadn't denied doing.

"Even so, there is a distinction," Louis said.

Controlling her emotions, she met his eyes with an icy calm.

"You might not like technology, Louis, but those contractors who you hire to do your dirty work for you sure do. The things they've done leave trails. Every money transfer, every communication. It's all there, on the Internet, just waiting to be found. Even cryptocurrency isn't immune to a subpoena. Once the police finish sifting through the data I'm sending them, they'll know where else to look. And they'll look. They'll find everything. False fronts for assassins, mobsters, and Lord knows what else."

She looked down at Louis's chess set. In the morning light, the antique pieces cast shadows across the board. The game had progressed since she'd come to work three weeks earlier. Black had a king and a pawn left on the board. White had only its king remaining. Black would checkmate with the pawn. It would take time, but she could see the endgame.

Caroline picked up the black pawn. Its dark facets glittered in the sunshine.

"You might be a good chess player, Louis. But you're a really bad boss."

She tucked the black pawn into her pocket and put the envelope on his desk.

"I'm out," she said.

Then she turned and walked away.

• • •

Caroline sat at a table at Black Dog Café, staring unseeingly at the chess game on her laptop. She knew that by now, the data transfer had finished. Information tying Louis to Dr. Heller's death and a bevy of other crimes had flowed to the police and the district attorney at thousands of bits per second. Auction records. Financial records. Case records. All laid out in incriminating detail.

The long-due reckoning had come for Louis.

Still, Caroline felt no joy. She'd trusted Louis Stern. She had looked to him as a mentor, maybe even as a kind of father figure. And he had betrayed her. The beginning of her career had nearly taken a sharp left turn off a cliff . . .

Someone put a mug in front of Caroline.

The smell of hot chocolate wafted up to her nostrils.

She looked up to find the barista with the blue Mohawk smiling down at her.

"It's on the house," he said.

"Thanks," she said, wrapping her fingers around the warm cup.

"Any time," he said and withdrew. Something about the expression on her face must have warned him not to make small talk.

Caroline turned her attention back to her laptop.

It might take the police time to untangle all of Louis's evil dealings, but that was their problem, not hers.

For her, the long day was over.

EPILOGUE

Caroline stood at the kitchen counter, chopping zucchini. For the first time in a long time, she had the luxury of time. She intended to savor it. The slow-to-prepare, quick-to-eat meal was the perfect activity for the day. After that, she'd figure out the next activity, and then the next. Reentering the work force remained somewhere on the horizon, a glowing necessity on her to-do list. But she hadn't yet figured out the details.

Visiting her father was on the list, too. When she'd seen him standing on his front yard with his sons, she'd wanted to talk to him. Even despite all that had transpired over the years. Even despite the guilt. He might have made some mistakes, but Lord knew, she'd made so many of her own, too . . .

The sound of the doorbell broke Caroline's reverie.

"I've got it," she called to the back of the house.

She found Deena standing on the front porch. The New Yorker wore a short white jacket with a wide collar. An alarmingly pink mini-skirt hugged her hips.

Caroline glanced down at her own ripped jeans and tank top.

She mentally shrugged. She'd make no apologies for who she was.

"Sorry for the short notice, but I wanted to say good-bye before I left," Deena said in a rush. Behind her, a black town car sat on the curb with its engine running.

"Thanks for coming by," Caroline said. Since leaving Hale Stern, she'd been surprised when Deena had reached out to her, sending her texts, asking how she was, how her uncle was, why she'd left. Even as she'd dodged the questions, Caroline had come to realize Deena cared. The woman might have a voice like a chain saw and a cadence that left the listener feeling vaguely bludgeoned, but she was a good person.

"I just wanted to make sure you were doing all right," Deena said.

"I'm okay. I just had a family emergency that I needed to take care of," Caroline said. She wondered how the firm had explained her abrupt departure.

"Did you hear Louis got indicted?" Deena asked.

"I saw it in the news." Caroline had watched the media coverage with fascination. The police had arrested Louis the same day she'd left the firm. They must've decided he was a flight risk. Two weeks later, the indictments had been handed down, laying out thirty-five charges of bribery, extortion, jury tampering, and murder. All in incriminating and copious detail.

"You're lucky you left before things got crazy," Deena said.

Caroline didn't respond. No one could ever know she'd been the source of the information the police had received. She needed to protect their ability to obtain additional evidence through legal means so that the case against Louis wouldn't be thrown out of court. She was pretty sure a whistle-blower's anonymous data dump passed muster, but she had to be extra careful, just to be certain.

Before Deena could probe the coincidence of the timing of her departure and Louis's arrest, Caroline asked, "How's everyone at the firm doing?" She hated the toll that Louis's departure would inevitably take on the innocent people at Hale Stern.

"As you can imagine, Louis's arrest was a terrible shock," Deena said, tutting under her breath. "Silvia's had her hands full trying to keep all of Louis's clients calm until everyone figures out how the firm is going to move past this . . . if possible. Thompson Hale has come out of retirement. He isn't happy about missing his golf games . . . but that's not really important, is it?" Deena paused, studying Caroline's face. "How's your uncle?"

"Still a mess," Caroline answered. Deena had earned some honesty on this topic. "He's only been out of the hospital a couple of weeks, and he's already drinking again. I've been trying to get him to go to meetings . . ."

"I know how that goes," Deena said, the mask falling, revealing vulnerability in her brown eyes. "Having an alcoholic in the family makes you always want to fix people, doesn't it? You feel like if you just try a little harder, things will improve. But then they don't. And it makes you feel like you're failing. Until you realize, finally, you have to stop trying to fix people. Except it's so hard to make yourself stop. That's the final irony, isn't it? You become addicted to trying to be a superhero. That's your fix. It's sick."

"It sure is," Caroline agreed quietly.

"Who's there?" came a voice from behind Caroline.

Joanne came into view. Taller than Caroline, but with the same slim figure, she wore a peasant shirt and jeans.

"This is Deena," Caroline said. "She's the daughter of that doctor who helped Uncle Hitch." She met Deena's eyes. "She's also my friend." She watched Deena's face blossom into a smile at the appellation.

"Please thank your mother for taking care of my brother," Joanne said.

"I will, but Caroline's the real hero here," Deena said. "Did she tell you? She won that case for all of those people."

"I didn't win the case. Just one motion," Caroline said.

"Whatever. One motion," Deena said.

Joanne looked at her daughter, her eyes glittering with the kind of pride a parent keeps on tap all the time, regardless of how successful or unsuccessful her child might be.

"I knew you weren't a Wendy," Joanne said.

Somewhere in the house, a phone rang.

"That's Bob," Joanne said, lighting up. "I've got to take that."

She withdrew, leaving Deena and Caroline alone on the doorstep.

"What was that about?" Deena asked.

"Bob's the guy my mom went on a date with when she was visiting her best friend in Portland. They've been talking almost every day," Caroline said. Who could have guessed that the training-wheels date Elaine had set up for Joanne would have gone so well?

"No, I mean the thing about you not being a Wendy," Deena said.

"Oh, that." Caroline quirked a half smile. "Wendy was my almost name. My dad liked it. My mom hated it. She said, 'Wendy didn't do a thing but natter and complain. Peter Pan could fly and fight and outwit Captain Hook.' I think she would've named me Peter if she could've gotten away with it. Anyway, she liked Caroline because it was a name you could take with you into adulthood. A name that would hold up in a boardroom. 'You can become president with a name like Caroline,' my mom said. Back when I was in school, my friends tried to shorten it to Carrie, but my mom nipped that one in the bud. And so I've always been Caroline . . . even on the days when it would be easier to be Carrie."

"I think you make a great Caroline," Deena said, looking at her in a way that made her wonder if Deena suspected her connection to Louis's arrest. Not that she could ever confirm that suspicion.

"You really came through for me," Caroline said instead. She hoped her tone conveyed the depth of her gratitude.

"It was nothing." Deena waved one manicured hand around.

"It wasn't nothing," Caroline said, holding Deena's gaze.

Deena nodded slowly, then smiled. "I'd better get going. Can't miss my flight." She turned to go but stopped and opened her purse. "Oh, I almost forgot. Dr. Wong came by the firm last week. She didn't know that you'd left. She asked me to give this to you."

Deena withdrew a small white box wrapped with a red ribbon. There was no card.

Taking the box, Caroline raised an eyebrow.

Deena shook her head.

Caroline opened the box.

Cradled in the white cotton padding, she found a new strand of komboloi beads. Onyx black and smooth, they were slightly smaller than the strand she'd sacrificed at the courthouse. She lifted the beads from the box and looped them over her hand. She flipped them over. Then again. They worked as well as the old ones had.

"You really are an odd duck," Deena said.

Looking at Deena stuffed like a sausage into her fuchsia miniskirt, Caroline smirked.

"Do you think you'll go back to Hale Stern once you've sorted out your family stuff?" Deena asked.

"No. Without Louis, it just wouldn't be the same," Caroline answered, giving an explanation that she knew was both true and misleading in equal measures. "I still need to decide on my next move."

"Whatever you do, it'll be great," Deena said, smiling. "Did you hear Med-Gen set up a huge settlement fund? It's even bigger than the Steering Committee thought it would be. All of the victims will be compensated and then some."

"I hadn't heard that. Wow. That's great," Caroline said, her chest flushing with warmth.

"It sure is," Deena said. She stepped forward and hugged Caroline, then withdrew.

Even after the sound of the town car had receded into the neighborhood, Caroline remained on the porch. Soon the requirements of life and lunch would draw her back inside, but for now, she wanted to enjoy the quiet.

She knew she needed to find another job. She had student loans to pay off. She had her mother's house to escape. But she needed to get the job thing right this time.

Sitting down on the railing of the porch, she considered her errors.

She couldn't believe she'd craved Louis's approval. What a terrible miscalculation. What an obvious displacement of affection. If she needed a father figure, she could reconcile with her own father. She didn't need to worship some creepy, psychopathic, wannabe blue-blooded fixer.

Bitterness rose in her throat, dull and metallic. But she knew the tang of disappointment covered something deeper. Something more problematic.

Reaching into her pocket, she withdrew a small figurine. Cool and smooth in her hand, the black pawn reflected the afternoon light. She'd carried it with her every day since she'd left Hale Stern. Its weight in her pocket felt like an indictment. A reminder of what she'd been. Of what she'd done. Of what she'd almost become.

Caroline ran her fingers over the smooth ball at the top of the statuette.

Louis had been a strong mentor in one way: he'd exposed who she really was. He'd shown her that despite leaving tech, she hadn't escaped the more sinister aspects of her nature. The thorny truth was that he hadn't been wrong about her. She enjoyed the dark thrills. Of hacking. Of prying. Of manipulating. She liked discovering people's secrets. She found joy in outsmarting firewalls and security systems. And she was good at it.

And yet, her survival, both physically and morally, despite Louis's mentorship, was itself some kind of statement of strength, wasn't it? Plus, she'd helped win a case that mattered greatly to a great many people.

For the first time since she'd walked out of Hale Stern, Caroline let herself feel something other than consternation about her law career. Things hadn't gone as planned, but she'd still done some good, hadn't she? Taking part in the grand struggle of humanity had been one reason she'd left the world of tech. While she might have gotten banged up in her first foray, she'd made a difference.

But what now? Could she really go to another firm?

She knew she'd never be able to trust another mentor. She'd have to rely on herself.

So then, perhaps she should go out on her own? She could hang out a shingle and take whatever clients she could find . . . as a first-year lawyer . . . fresh out of law school. The idea was daunting. And yet, whatever happened couldn't be worse than what had already happened to her. Reams of practice guides existed to teach lawyers the rules, the levers to pull. She'd figure it out. And she'd do some more good. Wherever she could. However she could.

In the meanwhile, she'd have to be patient. She'd just have to tolerate living in her childhood house a little longer . . .

Caroline exhaled.

There were no perfect answers.

Gently, almost reverently, she placed the pawn on the porch's railing.

The dark souvenir looked back at her, faceless and small.

Caroline walked back inside the house.

The porch door closed behind her with a snap of finality.

ACKNOWLEDGMENTS

Thank you to my family: Nicole, Eli, Alex, and Ava. You make every day fun (except the ones that aren't). Your love and support are life-giving. Thank you for all of your patience, all of your ideas, and all of your hugs when I need them. I truly hit the jackpot with all of you.

Thank you to Stephanie Delman, my amazing agent, whose good humor, work ethic, and instincts have been gifts. You totally rock. Thank you also to Heide Lange and Samantha Isman at Greenburger Associates, for believing in this project and giving it your love and attention.

Thank you to everyone at Thomas & Mercer, and particularly to editors JoVon Sotak and Charlotte Herscher, who have been insightful, supportive, and brilliant. Thank you to copyeditor Sara Brady and proofreader Toisan Craigg, who caught all kinds of embarrassing mistakes that thankfully you'll now never see.

Thank you to everyone who gave comments on the manuscript. Writing is like accretion. You provided sediment that stuck: Nicole Pearl, Stuart Tobisman, Hal Heisler, Ricki Tobisman, Lauren Antonoff, Suzanne Gordon, Karen Blackfield, Robin Simons, Charlene Tobisman-Davis, Barry Davis, Hank Jacobs, Stefanianna Moore, Natalie Friedman,

Todd Jackson, Allison Delman, Sarah Cypher, Alan Rinzler, Daryl DePollo, Ken Gross, Susan Levison, Stephanie Levine, Kaitlin Olson, Barbara Zimmermann, and Kevin McKernan. Thank you to Joel Gotler for suggesting that I write this book.

Thank you to my colleagues at Greines, Martin, Stein & Richland LLP, the best appellate firm on the planet. The folks there are not only smart and good at what they do, but also great people with whom I'm proud to work.

And finally, thank you to my parents for raising me in a house full of books and ideas, and for giving me a lifetime of love.

ABOUT THE AUTHOR

For fifteen years, C.E. Tobisman has been an appellate attorney, handling cases in the California courts of appeal and Supreme Court. After graduating from UC Berkeley and attending law school there, she moved to Los Angeles, where she now lives with her wife and their three children. *Doubt* is the first novel in her new series featuring Caroline Auden. Tobisman is also the author of *Inside the Loop*, published by Emet Comics. Find her on Twitter at @CETobisman_, on Facebook at www.facebook.com/cetobisman, and at www.cetobisman.com.